LIBRIOHEXER

Wolfman Warlock Book Two

JAMES HUNTER

DAKOTA KROUT

This is a work of fiction. Names, characters, places, and incidents either are the products of the author's imagination or are used fictitiously. Any resemblance to actual persons, living or dead, businesses, companies, events, or locales is entirely coincidental.

CHAPTER ONE

A bird chirped off in the distance, its shrill cry cutting through the gentle rustle of grass and the whisper of the wind. That was the signal: Sam knew it wouldn't be long now. He reached up and swiped a hand across his forehead, obliterating the sweat trickling down his face. It was hot out here on the plains. Waist high stalks of grass fought against the party at every step—and the fact that he was in heavy, brown wool noob gear didn't help things at all. He couldn't wait to swap out this trash gear for his Arcana's Finery. True, when decked out in his regular gear, he looked like a sixteenth-century cosplayer, spoiling for a fight, but *boy*, was it comfortable.

"Do you really think they'll let us in if we clear out this pack of Wolfmen?" a nasally voice on his right cut right through his thoughts. "I mean, I've heard like... only ten percent of pledges ever make it in good with the Rabid Inquisitors. That's *if* Back-Attack is in a good mood. Man, I sure hope he's in a good mood."

<This guy never shuts his pie-hole, does he?> Bill the magical book's voice buzzed inside Sam's head. <I mean, he

seems like a good enough kid, but seriously, learn to read the room.>

Sam glanced at the gangly noob, named Easy_Mac_Evan. The kid was decked out in rough leather armor that had seen its best days *years* ago. Easy_Mac looked to be roughly sixteen, if his thin cheeks, scrawny arms, and coltish legs were anything to go by. He had a starter bow strapped to his back and a shoddy spear gripped in one hand. Splashed across his slapdash armor were three bloody slashes running diagonally across a crimson eye. The guild mark of the Rabid Inquisitors—Sam had the same mark adorning his own armor.

<He just wants to fit in,> Sam sent back. He and Bill could speak telepathically, thanks to the Soul-Bond they shared, which was good, because Sam currently had Bill tucked away inside his Unending Flask of the Drunkard. On the surface, the device was just a simple worn drinking flask. In reality, it was a spatial container that allowed him to store up to two hundred extra pounds of gear. <I get that. I was a lot like him when I was that age, and I would've jumped at the chance to get in with someone like BackAttack. He's the teen version of 'coolest guy ever'.>

<Yeah, well, just make sure you don't pull your punches,> Bill grumbled in reply. <Remember, Legs... this is a war. If BackAttack and his crew get their way, they'll wipe every Wolfman and sympathizer off the face of the map. That includes *us*. Don't suppose I need to remind you that these guys have actively been hunting for racial-traitors? I haven't survived for three hundred years for some gawky ranger to stick an arrow through me.>

Sam grinned at the thought of this kid being able to take them down. <I thought you knew me better than that, Bill. *I'm* the one that set up this ambush.>

"I'm sure it's all going to be fine," Sam nonchalantly reassured Easy_Mac. "What could go wrong? I've heard BackAttack and his crew are one of the fastest up-and-coming guilds in the realm."

Evan hesitated for a beat, worry flashing across his face. Dropping his voice low, he leaned closer to Sam. "You must not know about the rumors."

"Rumors?" Sam quirked an eyebrow. It was always good to get as much intel as possible, even if the source seemed rather unlikely. But then, that was something he'd learned early on: no matter how new someone seemed or how low-level they were, they could always teach you something.

"They," The teen hooked his thumb toward a gruff, armor-clad tank leading the group raid, "don't like us talking about it... but apparently there's some kind of Wolfmen saboteurs who've been waging a silent war against the Rabid Inquisitors. Doing some serious damage, too. They burned down part of the first guild house, wiped out half a dozen raid parties, and even managed to poison every guild officer except for BackAttack himself."

"You don't *say*." Sam forcibly hid a smirk.

They had done all that and more over the past two weeks. Aside from grinding levels and doing a few simple fetch quests for the Wolfmen, knocking the Rabid Inquisitors down a notch —specifically by sabotaging them at every possible turn—had been the Wolf Pack's primary mission. With good reason; some of the other guilds were killing Wolfmen, but none of them were focusing on eradicating the Wolfmen to quite the degree that the Inquisitors were. Plus, BackAttack seemed to have a particular zeal for ferreting out players like Sam.

Players who had sided with the Wolfmen faction.

Another shrill bird call rose, this one an eerie little song that lingered in the air. The sound sent a shiver running down Sam's back.

<Get ready, Legs.> Bill's voice was brimming with equal parts excitement and anticipation. <We're gonna have to move fast. Well, *you* are; that's mostly your department. Since you have the body, and all that.>

Sam glanced left, scanning the party. Twelve legitimate pledges—most of them new and under level five—one senior guild officer and one sergeant at arms. The pledges were dangerous because of their sheer numbers, but they were about as skilled as newborn chimps; also, there wasn't a single magic user among them. Sam caught sight of Dizzy, walking near the sergeant at arms, the heavy tank clad in silvered plate mail. Rory was his name, and he was working toward his first specialization. He wouldn't stand a chance against Dizzy and her monstrous war maul, though.

Especially not with Finn lingering nearby, ready to spring into action. Not many people could survive a concentrated Mage attack at this stage in the game; the single biggest reason they'd been successful so far.

The senior officer, a scrappy Rogue in dark leathers, would be tougher. She went by the tag JumboKiwi and was level nine, like Sam. From the intel they'd gathered, she'd been with the Inquisitors from the very beginning and was on the path to assassin-hood, following in the footsteps of BackAttack himself. Sphinx and Kai were in position to deal with her. In a two-on-one fight, they would hopefully be able to end her before she could Shadow Stalk away and deal any real damage. That just left Arrow and Sam, near the rear of the party. They were the support power, tasked with cutting down the low-ranked pledges like a scythe through wheat.

"We've got activity up ahead," Rory grunted, raising a fist and sending out the signal to 'slow down and be quiet'.

Milling near a series of rocky boulders jutting from the ground was a trio of Wolfmen. Velkan of the Redmane Tribe led the motley group. He was smaller than many of the other Wolfmen that Sam had met, with coarse gray fur, wicked claws, vicious fangs, and amber eyes that seemed to take in every detail all at once. He wore crude leather armor and carried a short-hafted axe with a yellow bone axe head. Despite his size, Velkan was a beast, fast, nimble, and ferocious. He acted as the team's scout more often than not and was an indomitable front-line fighter.

Rory glanced back at a group of enemy archers, waiting

near the rear of the formation, including poor Easy_Mac_E-van, who was about to have a very, very bad day. Rory signaled *make ready* without ever speaking a word, his fingers flashing in rapid fire. The archers obliged, nocking arrows in a clatter of wood and a hiss of bow strings.

That's when the birdcall came for a third time, this one long and haunting.

Sam moved in an instant, pulling free his Dagger of the Mystic Path from a simple leather sheath at his roughshod belt. He pivoted on his heel, dropped low, and lashed out just like Sphinx had taught him, driving the tip of the razor-sharp blade directly in between the gaps in Easy_Mac's armor, right into his kidney. The blade sliced cleanly through the cotton undershirt, then parted the skin with ease, stopping only when the hilt hit leather. Evan let out a startled gurgle and gasp, his eyes wide. All around, screams of surprise cut through the air, accompanied by the ringing of blades and the sizzle of magic.

"W-what?" Evan stammered, turning an accusatory gaze on Sam as his health dropped like a stone.

"Sorry, man." Sam pulled the dagger loose, then stashed it in the sheath. With his other hand, he pulled Bill free from the spatial flask.

The book exploded to life, tethered to Sam's hip by an ethereal silver chain that burned with a subtle blue power. Evan's eyes swiveled to the floating book and seemed to bulge to the size of tea saucers. Understandable, in Sam's estimation. Bill himself was a sight to behold—and an unsettling one. He was a thick burgundy book with golden runes sparkling along the weathered spine. A humanoid face jutted up from the book cover, crafted in a patchwork-fashion from various strips of hide. His emerald eyes were sharply intelligent, and rather menacing if you didn't know him.

"Orbital Tome of Casting!" Sam cried, conjuring a flurry of heavy leather volumes from the soul space inside Bill. The books, all six of them, took to the air with a life of their own, slowly circling around Sam like planets orbiting a sun.

Orbital Tome of Casting was the Bibliomancer's primary method for spell-slinging. Sam could bind and summon up to six books at any given time, each with its own spell assignment, which would revolve around him, just waiting to be activated. Basically, he had six floating, book-shaped machine guns. Some fired fast and held a ton of rounds, like his Paper Shuriken tomes, while others were more powerful but lower capacity, like his Rorschach Spell or Papier-Mache Mage.

With a brilliant shimmer of opalescent light, a wide-brimmed cavalier hat appeared in Sam's waiting hands. With its puffy feather and bright silk band, Bill's Foppish Hat was a pretty ridiculous item, which would've fit on the set of a Three Musketeers flick. It also happened to be ridiculously useful, boosting his Strength, Dexterity, and Charisma by five points each, while also adding a ten percent resistance against Fire and a plus two to his Bladed Weapons skills. He felt better the second it was on his head.

"You're *him*," poor Evan stammered, dying but not dead yet. "You're the traitor! The *Bibliomancer*."

"Word of warning... leave the Wolfmen alone." Sam swung a red-bound volume to the six o'clock position. The cover parted and unleashed a pair of folded paper stars that were bleeding a soft orange light. Sam had a variety of abilities, thanks to both his class and Bill's tutelage, but Paper Shuriken was definitely his go-to attack spell. Additionally, each page in this volume had been meticulously inscribed with a simple Fireball Spell, significantly amping up the damage potential. The projectiles slammed into the wobbly-legged new player, lodging deeply in his chest before exploding with a wave of heat and light. "Bye-bye, Easy_Mac."

Sam quickly toggled out the Fire Shuriken Tome, switching it to the nine-o'clock position, and brought forth a green volume that spewed out a whirlwind of sheets at a thought. The pages swirled around him for the briefest instant, latching onto his threadbare newbie gear. In mere seconds, he was encased in what appeared to be Spanish conquistador armor, with its rounded breastplate, flared pauldrons, tapered waistline, and bulbous, balloon-like pantaloons.

It looked ridiculous, but just like Bill's hat, it was some of the best armor a Mage like Sam could ever hope for. Papier-Mache Mage allowed him to cocoon himself in a layer of flexible yet versatile papier-mache. Every point of mana devoted to the spell negated two points of damage from primary physical sources, and half a point from magical sources. Its only real weaknesses were against fire and water, for rather obvious reasons.

<We've got incoming on the left, Legs,> Bill called. Having to share headspace and soul space with Bill all the time definitely had its drawbacks, but it was *awesome* in combat. It was like having a certain arachnid-sense—though a sassy, sentient arachnid-sense. Using his dual casting ability, Sam swapped Papier-Mache Mage for Fire Shuriken and a royal blue volume that contained Shuriken with an Ice Orb enchantment. Rushing toward him was a spearman in segmented, Roman-inspired plate armor, while JumboKiwi was nowhere to be seen—wait, no, *there* she was! Of *course* she'd managed to give Sphinx and Kai the slip and was flowing toward him like a river, blades clutched in both hands, a cloak as black as a raven's wing flowing behind her. This would be… less easy.

Fire Tome on his right, Ice Orb Tome on his left, Sam spammed a wave of Shuriken at the oncoming attackers in a hail of mini explosions and glimmering ice bursts. He triggered his Bookmark ability after the first star landed on each target. Bookmark wasn't a standalone attack, but a secondary spell script that caused a spell to auto-fix on a primary location or target—sending each subsequent attack to the same exact target. Even if that target happened to be on the move.

Exploding fire Shuriken bombarded the spearman, stopping him in his tracks and eating through his health at a ferocious rate. Being a Mage with the College was terrible, but being a freelance Rogue Mage? Yeah, that was awesome. The Ice-Orbs landed with less force and destructive power, but they had a more *insidious* ability.

Damage dealt: 75 (70 + 5 Ice Orb) Target slowed 12%!

A layer of crystalline blue hoarfrost snaked across JumboKiwi's armor and clawed at her skin, slowing her down, though not stopping her completely. Despite Sam's best efforts, she was getting awfully close, and the daggers in her hands looked like serious business. He spammed another three Ice Orb Shuriken at her, while simultaneously keeping the pressure on the spearman with Fire Shuriken. But the would-be assassin slipped and ducked his attacks with unnerving ease. She was fast and agile as all get out, plus Dual-Casting had the unfortunate effect of lowering Sam's accuracy rate.

<Sword up, kid! Do it now—I'll take over controlling the meathead with the spear.>

Sam backpedaled, opening up a little space between him and JumboKiwi. He extended his hand, and twenty-three mana vanished from his Core as the oversized ostrich feather jutting from his cavalier hat leapt into the air, transforming into a glimmering Quill Blade, a gleaming sword with ghostly blue runes running down the blade, the handle wrapped in leather and capped by a fine silver nib. Perfect for stabbing someone in the eye or endorsing one of those giant novelty checks. Very versatile.

Sam dropped into a high guard and quickly adjusted his stance—feet shoulder width apart, hips slightly cocked, weight evenly distributed on the balls of his feet. JumboKiwi darted left, toward his open side, and lunged in quick as a striking viper, the daggers twirling in her hands. She was faster than he was, a *lot* faster, but his blade had a longer reach. With a bit of fancy footwork and a couple of well-placed strikes, Sam managed to parry the flurry of blows. Still, his stamina was dropping at an alarming rate, and there was no way he'd be able to keep pace with her for long.

She was built for combat, while he was built for holding up magical jazzhands.

There was a way he could level the playing field, though it would cost him. Sam feinted left, then darted right, slashing downward with his blade. She slipped the attack, turning his sword with a flick of her wrist, then dealt a nasty slash that bit into his deceptively weak-looking paper armor. He didn't feel a thing, although the blow did chew through a hefty chunk of his Papier-Mache protection.

124 damage absorbed by Papier-Mache Mage!

The gambit had bought him the time he needed. Sam rotated a jet-black book into the dominant position. The cover snapped open, the pages rustling in a flurry, and he unloaded javelin after javelin of inky blackness toward the incoming assassin. His Ink Lance attacks landed with a successive series of wet slaps, followed by an audible **sizzle** as acid began to bite into JumboKiwi's armor. That wasn't all it did. *Oh*, no. The black goo wriggled to life, crawling across her arms and legs and latching onto her face like a blob of hot tar. She screamed, fighting to pull the living ink off her… but it was futile.

While she was distracted and slowed by the roving finger of ink, Sam rotated Paper Shuriken back to the front and unleashed the abyss. Whirling paper slammed into her like a hail of bullets, exploding one after another, until there was nothing left but a body converted into toothpaste. Slimy, yet satisfying.

<That was pretty good work, Legs. Although—and I mean this from the bottom of my heart—your sword form is utter trash. I mean, good on you for being a Mage who even learned to use a blade, but seriously… we need to work on your physical capabilities.>

"Later," Sam shot back, still breathing hard and blinking back the fresh sweat streaming down his face. "Maybe when we're not in the middle of battle?"

<Pfft. Look around. There's no battle left.> Bill wasn't wrong. Bodies lay scattered across the field, many of them littered with arrows or crisscrossed with claw marks—courtesy of the Wolfmen.

Of the Rabid Inquisitors, only the sergeant at arms, Rory, remained. Even he'd seen better days; currently his face was a sheet of blood, and one arm hung limply at his side. He was still fighting, but Dizzy had his number. She was coming at him hard, whipping her oversized maul around like it was made out of cardboard. It didn't hit like cardboard, though. The wooden maul smashed into Rory's armor, badly deforming the metal from the impact and dropping the man to his knees.

Alive, but only just.

"You know BackAttack is gonna find you, right?" Rory's voice was heavy and pained. "You can't keep this up forever, and once we *do* finally get ahold of you, he's going to make you *hurt.*"

"Well," Finn the Mage slid up beside Dizzy, "that's where I think you're wrong, friend. It seems to me we've been doing a fine job undermining your clan."

"We won't stop wrecking you guys until you back off," Dizzy raised her maul up high. "Give our regards to your boss."

She brought the maul down in a vicious arc, smashing through his head and sending him for respawn in an instant. Dizzy threw her head back and howled. Sam joined, letting loose a cry as experience rolled in like the tide. Since Sam and company were officially no longer part of humanity, not only did they not get penalized for PKing players, but they gained experience and skill gains for every single kill.

Skill increase: Orbital Tome Casting (Beginner II). Yeah, we get it, you have a bunch of magical books. Talk about picking the low-hanging fruit, since there is literally no way for you not to increase this if you are casting spells!

Skill increase: Paper Shuriken (Novice IX). You're really learning how to slice and dice with the best of 'em. Get those creases sharp!

Skill increase: Magical Origami (Novice VII). Hard for a derivative skill to outrank the skill it comes from, know what I mean?

Skill increase: Origami Activation (Novice VIII). Are you making progress? Sure. But how's about you learn some other spells, huh? In this case, repetition makes for slow progress. Variety is the spice of progress, or something like that.

As he read, Sam felt a surge of power. Golden light swirled around him in a cloud, lifting him into the air and filling his body with sheer euphoria. Raw energy ripped through his veins, sprinting along his nerve endings. He was figuratively floating: he'd just leveled up, and more than that—he'd finally hit level ten. That fact opened a *world* of new possibilities. Sam would finally be able to pick a second profession, and even specialize as a Bibliomancer. Despite the sassy comments from the system, he couldn't help but grin.

Being on Team Wolfman was the absolute best.

CHAPTER TWO

By the time Sam and his crew got back to the Wolfman outpost of *Narvik*, the sun was lingering just above the horizon, threatening to disappear at any moment. Not that Sam had to worry about the setting sun the way the rest of the human-aligned players did. Sure, the threats that roamed the land after sunset were serious business, but the biggest threat of all was the Wolfmen themselves. That, at least, was one enemy Sam and company didn't have to fret over. Still, it was nice to be back.

They'd been out since the crack of dawn, grinding through low-level bunnies and foxes along with the rest of the pledges, and Sam was feeling exhausted and ready for something hot to fill his belly. His team could've headed back to Ardania after TPKing the Inquisitor party, but it was far easier to operate out here on the edge of civilization, well away from the prying eyes of guards and bounty hunters looking to take down a couple of Rogue Mages like Sam and Finn.

More than just the convenience, Sam had honestly come to enjoy the Wolfman encampment and the creatures that called it home. Narvik was far more rustic than Ardania, that much was true, and it lacked the sprawling houses and winding cobblestone streets, but it had other charms. The outpost was about the size of a small town and was entirely encased in a tribal-style wooden palisade, twenty-five feet tall, with the poles strategically sharpened at the top.

For some reason, today the usually simple yet pristine walls were stained with blood.

There was no door or gateway, since the Wolfmen didn't need them. Sphinx had taught Sam and the rest of the party how to scale the walls using simple ropes. Having to climb in and out of the outpost certainly was quirky, but it was still better than getting grilled by city guards every time they wanted to go grind some mobs. Inside the intimidating walls, it felt like another world: a lush landscape flourished with ancient trees intact, reaching their stately branches skyward. The enclosure was filled with gardens and brooks, vegetable patches, and nooks filled with greenery and flowers.

Enormous tree boughs supported a variety of wooden huts, all connected by a series of narrow walkways and precarious-looking rope bridges. Just navigating the area had earned Sam more than a few points of dexterity—and also one dislocated shoulder, though a Wolfman Shaman had been *kind* enough to casually pop it back into place. More huts lined the ground, which contained shops or other communal spaces.

Clanging resounding in the early evening air as Wolfman blacksmiths worked steel recovered from guards they'd taken down, while others baked bread, fletched arrows, or mended armor. Packs of young wolves roamed about, play-fighting—though drawing very real blood in the process. In many respects, Sam and his friends were a lot like those pups, learning to navigate the complexities of Wolfman society. How tall to stand, when to genuflect, when to bare the throat or snarl in defiance.

In the two weeks they'd spent with the Redmane Tribe, Sam had leveled up his Wolfman Language ability to seven of ten proficiency, making him... well, not *fluent*, but close enough for government work. Even that wouldn't have been enough, if not for Velkan, who'd taken to them like flies to stink. Right now, the conversations floating around were muted, angry, and twice as hard for him to understand.

From the snippets he could catch, it seemed the outpost had been attacked, but no one was explaining what had happened. He looked to their guide, who seemed unconcerned with the strange tension and various blood splatters, but perhaps that was just what living at war for hundreds of years did to a person. Velkan had decided that he had a blood-debt to Sam and Bill for saving him from the Mages, and he had adopted them like wayward pups. The Wolfman was *determined* to teach them the ways of The People.

So, maybe Narvik was a little backward, but it was also usually peaceful. It felt far more like a community than the every-man-for-himself attitude that permeated the human capital. Sam grunted, barked, and nodded to a few of the friendly faces he knew on sight as they carved their way through the twisting dirt streets toward the south side of the encampment, where their Clan tent was pitched. Even as a Wolfman Noble—a title bestowed on Sam by The O'Baba herself—and the first human Clan with a charter, nothing was *given* in Wolfman society.

No one was just supplied a house or even food. Everyone contributed, everyone hunted, everyone gave to the pack. Among the Wolfmen, each member earned every honor through blood and sweat. This meant that they didn't have a proper HQ yet, just a rough tent and bed rolls, but it was still nicer than Sam's time at the College. Out here, he got to sleep under the stars and hang out with his friends. He would meditate in the morning, then grind through mobs or sabotage humanity whenever he had the chance. Not a bad life, all things considered.

It wasn't long before they were back at their modest encampment, which butted up against the palisade wall. The tent was less of a lean-to and more of an octagonal yurt made of rough leather, which they'd harvested from the countless rabbits and foxes they'd killed since entering Eternium. Sam had done the bulk of the stitch work, since binding books and sewing leather had a surprising amount of overlap. There was a little stone firepit with banked coals at the bottom, along with rough oak chairs that Finn had bartered off a Wolfman woodworker named Ravi Treesplitter.

Everyone made friendly chit-chat while Arrow got the fire roaring and Finn passed out wooden skewers lined with lean chunks of fresh rabbit meat. Sam eased himself into his customary seat, glad to have the weight off his tired feet, then opened a small pouch at his belt filled with a variety of seasonings he'd picked up either in town or out in the wilds. He rubbed down the leg and loin meat with some coarse salt and a splash of black pepper, then added a little crushed orkia root, a pale zixie berry paste, and a dash of dried moonseed… then he was ready to cook.

Sam had pilfered a basic Herbalism tome from the College before making his grand exit with Bill, and it had proven to be one of the most useful books he'd ever read. He couldn't blow anything up with those skills—at least, not *yet*—but since he had to cook ninety percent of his meals, knowing what was seasoning and what was poison was an invaluable tool. The delicious aroma of cooking meat quickly filled his nose, his belly rumbling and mouthwatering in anticipation.

"Anyone figure out what was going on?" Sam looked at the others, but only Velkan looked at him with a knowing expression. The others apparently hadn't noticed anything wrong, and the conversation soon swept the concerns from the Bibliomancer's head.

"Sorry to change the topic bro, but can I just say that I think this was our most epic hit yet. Like, for real. The look on that kid's face when Sam shanked him in the kidney?" Kai leaned back in his own chair, already munching on succulent rabbit. He grinned with grease decorating his clean-shaven face. "Totally priceless."

Sphinx snorted and shook her head. "Maybe it was the

biggest party we've taken out, but the best was when we burned down their headquarters."

"Well, you *would* say that," Arrow replied, swirling a ram's horn filled with a type of Wolfman mead called 'sima'.

Sam wasn't a big one for drinking, and it didn't mix well with magical classes, which was good, because that stuff tasted more or less like paint thinner. The Wolfmen said that even your drinks should cause at least a little bit of pain, *'in order to properly harden your in as well as out'*. Frankly, most of the Wolfman food was spicy enough to melt skin; just another reason Sam was forced to do so much of his own cooking. They were strange folk, the Wolfmen, but they were also strangely endearing. Certainly nothing like the *monsters* the humans had painted them to be.

"That's only because you and Sam were the ones to get all the experience from that little infiltration op," Arrow continued petulantly. "The explosion was neat and all, but we just stood around in those shoddy guard uniforms while you two got to have all the fun."

"Hey, woah now," Bill interjected, his eyes shifting to lock onto Arrow. "I was there too, ya know. I mean, Sam is basically my sidekick—not the other way around. Let's not forget it, either."

"Deepest apologies, Sir Book," Arrow replied with an exaggerated dip of his head.

"Naw. Today was the best." Kai refused to acknowledge Sphinx's statement. "That Rory guy hit like a sledgehammer, but our fearless leader Dizzy put him in his place. Sam. *Dude.* That was a wicked KO against the assassin. She never should've gotten past me and Sphinx, but she was faster than a riptide. But you *smashed*, bro. Your bladework is really paying off, my dude."

"Thanks." Sam pulled his rabbit from the fire. Golden brown and charred in all the right places, the seasonings had caramelized against the skin.

"Phft. *Please.*" Bill was fully indignant. "Once again, I feel the need to point out that I did most of the heavy lifting. If it weren't for *my* spectacular casting, those goons would've swarmed us in a second. Also—and I mean absolutely no offense—but I've seen drunk squirrels with better footwork than Sam. The Bravi in me is absolutely mortified. I'm thinking we'll have to add to the morning practice roster."

Dizzy snorted and rolled her eyes. "Bill, I have literally never heard you compliment *any* swordsmen. Ever. Not even when we went up against that level eight Sword Singer a week back. They're always 'clumsy cows' or 'half-witted walnuts' or 'all thumbs'."

Bill shouted with righteous anger, "Hey now, in my defense… that fighter *literally* had all thumbs. Musta been some sort of genetic condition."

"No, he didn't," Dizzy shot back around a mouthful of food. "The point is, no one is ever going to be as good as you *remember* yourself being."

"It's not my fault you all are so green that you've never actually seen a decent swordsman! Remember, I have three-hundred-years' worth of experience under my belt. But if I can get two-left-feet McGee here," the book flapped his pages at Sam, "to finally pick a specialization, I might be able to make some real progress!"

"Wait." Dizzy froze and looked at Sam expectantly. "Does that mean you finally did it? You hit level ten?"

Sam grinned and nodded. "Yep. Taking out that assassin put me over the edge. *Ding*."

The pronouncement was greeted by a raucous round of hoots and cheers. Kai and Arrow both raised their flagons of mead in salute.

"Level ten, and after only three weeks in this world? Well, that's absolutely brilliant, isn't it?" Finn clapped Sam on the shoulder and pulled a rabbit skewer from the flames. He shook his head, lips pursed into a thin line. "It's an impressive feat, Sam. One you should be proud of. Have you given any thought about your specialization? Or your secondary profession? You get to choose another one of those at tenth level, you know."

"Are you kidding me?" Bill broke in. "That's *all* we've been talking about. The kid's as wishy-washy as a wet mop. Gaining a specialization as a Bibliomancer ain't easy, but we definitely have options. Loads of 'em. If he wants to actually become formidable with a blade, I can incorporate my Bravi training, and we can walk the path of the Biblioblade and eventually ascend to Paper Samurai. Or, if he wants to stick to AoE and support casting, we can choose Bibliognost and eventually end up as a Curator Paragon. Or we can go the jack-of-all-trades route, and shoot for Libriohexer before advancing to Archivist Summoner. Like I said, we have *options* out the wazoo."

"That's the actual problem," Sam admitted with a shrug. "It feels so *permanent*, and I don't want to lock into a specialization that I'll be unhappy with in a month. My gut reaction is that Biblioblade sounds amazing, but that would really only make me a hybrid fighter. Long term, that doesn't seem like the best choice."

He sighed and bowed his head. "Honestly, it's more than just picking a specialization. All this stuff brought back the fact that my family is expecting me to pick a specialization of sorts in the real world as soon as my time in Eternium is over. My parents are pushing me toward a law degree, which I just don't want."

"I just want to focus on the *fun*. Choosing a secondary profession is the same deal," he continued after a moment, rubbing a boot toe through the dirt. "Thanks to Bill's encyclopedic knowledge of this class, I know about every possible secondary profession that might benefit me, but there are just so many options. Translator, Scholar, Inscriptionist, Duelist, Pagesmith, Navigator, Publisher—even a Chicken Keeper, for reasons I can't quite figure out. This feels like a huge choice, and I really don't want to mess it up."

"Yeah, but you have to make a choice sooner or later." Dizzy shrugged off his concerns. "The longer you put it off, the more damage you'll do in the end. You need to start focusing on your training."

"That's what I keep tellin' him," Bill sighed with overdramatized exasperation. "It's not like there's a *bad* pick. Being a Bibliomancer is amazing, and all of those specializations are gonna put us in the top one percent, no matter what we do. It's a no-lose situation."

"I'm not going to put it off forever." Sam defensively raised his hands in mock surrender. "I'm on a characteristic threshold."

There was a collective gasp, and conversation died around the firepit.

"Oh, gosh." Sphinx's normally easy-going demeanor slipped and her face grew strangely serious. "Which stat is it? I managed to get my dexterity up past the first threshold by level eight, and it was…"

She faltered and gulped. "It was terrible. *Painful.* Worth it, but holy cow, it was unpleasant."

"Yeah," Sam muttered while thinking back to his own experience. He'd started off the game with a subpar perception stat. When he pushed over the threshold for normalcy, he'd blacked out from the pain. When he'd finally awoken, he'd been covered in rancid black goo, and every sensation had amplified tenfold. That was the *normalcy* threshold. Sam was sure this one would be ten times worse.

"It's the Intelligence threshold," he offered uneasily. "I know it's going to be unpleasant, but I'm hoping I'll be able to understand what the best options are once I recover. I'm at forty-nine right now, and I saved one point after leveling to nine. I plan to advance before bed. Hope that it will give me a little clarity when I get up in the morning."

"It's not a bad plan," Finn agreed as he rubbed at his chin, "but maybe consider sleeping outside the tent tonight? Purification always smells so atrocious."

"Consider it d-" The words died on Sam's tongue as a pair

of Wolfmen materialized out of the darkness, stepping into the firelight like menacing specters.

The first was Velkan—no surprise there—but the second was a Shaman and their primary handler: Yurij. If he was here at this hour, it could only mean trouble.

CHAPTER THREE

"Greetings, whelps," Yurij snarled, opting to use the human tongue instead of speaking Wolfman. Although Sam spoke the language of The People almost fluently, the rest of his pack members weren't quite so far along, and while Bill knew every word, he couldn't properly speak it at all, since so much of the communication had to do with body language: a fact that Bill felt personally slighted by.

The fact that Yurij was one of the few Wolfmen in the encampment who spoke fluent Common was probably the reason why he'd been appointed as their handler. The fact that he still despised Sam and his friends was unfortunate, but it came with the territory. Nothing was given among the Wolfmen. *Everything* was earned. That included personal respect.

"Shaman BrightBlood brings dire news." Velkan's words were more guttural and less practiced. He was working to learn Common, but it was a slow process. "As Sam noticed. Outpost attacked. Much concern and..."

The Wolfman tried to find the correct word in Common, but just hunched his shoulders and stopped talking after a moment.

"Indeed," the Shaman stepped into the silence, baring his fangs to show the seriousness of the conversation. "The People are losing ground in our war against humans. Last night marked a mighty blow against The People; one of our great workings was subverted and turned against us, bringing the terror of the night to our walls. To The People, instead of against the humans and their allies. The magical sabotage killed… many. Hundreds, perhaps thousands. Many, *many* of The People were in the open when the shadows turned against us."

Yurij's lips twitched over his teeth, a motion that needed no translator. He was abjectly furious. "Your pack is doing well, but if the Wolfmen are to survive the conflict to come… we need more weapons. We need more allies. The greatest benefit of humans is numbers. We are the stronger race—of this there can be no doubt—but they are more plentiful. Even a mighty wolf may be felled by a pack of foxes. Although your skirmishes with the Rabid Inquisitors have been fruitful, imagine what you could accomplish with ten times your numbers. The O'Baba granted you a charter to form a guild, yet still there are but five of you."

"I count!" Bill grumbled. "Why does everyone forget about me?"

Yurij flicked his ears in annoyance but inclined his head a fraction of an inch in apology. The O'Baba was definitely on Team Bill—the book was older than dirt and that alone gave him some serious brownie points. The fact that he was also a rebel and nemesis to the Mage's College didn't hurt. "Seven."

"Eight," Velkan grunted, crossing his arms. "They are my pack by choice, even if not by blood."

"Eight. But *eight* is far from enough. It is time for your pack to recruit more *humans*." He emphasized the word while shooting a nasty look at Velkan; Yurij looked like he was about to climb up a wall. "Allies, as you promised The O'Baba you would. In my eyes, you are failing to uphold your end of the bargain. You must do more. Playing games with the Rabid Inquisitors is no way to win a war. You need to build an army. No one will flock to your banner without a proper guild headquarters."

The disdainful Shaman paused, sneering at their modest yurt. "A hastily pitched tent is hardly fitting for a guild. A *true* guild leader would know such things."

That was a shot at Dizzy, plain as the snout on Yurij's face.

"Well, you haven't exactly made that easy for us, you know." Dizzy was standing, her hands balling into fists, letting him know in no uncertain terms that she wouldn't be pushed around. "No one will rent us space, and we haven't been approved to build a treehouse like the rest of the Wolfmen."

"You are a *guild*," Yurij snarled at her, "not a family! Would a simple tree dwelling accommodate a group of fifty? It is ridiculous to think so. You have not learned enough of our ways. Guilds do not operate in settlements such as this. Velkan should have taught you this by now. If you want to be a proper guild that keeps the respect of The People, you must secure a den to operate out of."

"Den? Is that an acronym?" Arrow interjected, as if to remind the others he still existed.

"No, it is a *den*," the Shaman repeated coolly. "Human guilds often operate out of inns or taverns, but as they get bigger, they typically expand and take over whole towns. But The People are different. We are creatures of the wild, beasts of the field and forest. Our clans have no need to build permanent settlements. We are a monstrous race, and as such, we can clear and claim dungeons as our own. Convert them into dwelling places or guild strongholds."

"Wait..." Kai nearly bounced on his toes in excitement. "Like, *dude*! Are you saying we get to design our own dungeon?"

Velkan answered before the Shaman could respond. "In a way, yes. The dungeon will be hostile, but if we can capture the various dungeon junctions, the dungeon will then serve our pack. We will be able to fill it with traps and wards. Even minions, depending on the type of den we choose to establish."

"Velkan has the right of it. You must find such a den *soon.*" Yurij agreed shortly. He paused, lifting his snout to taste the air. "We break camp in the morning. All of Narvik will be gone by the setting sun tomorrow."

"Wait, what?" Sam stammered, feeling the world reel around him. "This is a city. Well, maybe not a city, but certainly a town. You can't just move it."

"It is the way of our People, especially when we are taken by surprise as we were last night." Yurij was clearly unconcerned with Sam's protest. "In our tongue, Narvik means *restless.* We are *Beasts*, not meant to sit and grow fat, as you humans do. We range. We move. Besides, we believe the location of Narvik has been compromised. These 'Rabid Inquisitors' have captured valuable information about the location of this site. After what we experienced with Octavius Igenitor, we cannot risk losing The O'Baba again. Better to migrate. We will move this location to a secluded area deep within our territory, in the very heart of the Forest of Chlorophyll Chaos—a place humans fear to tread."

"You, however, will not be welcome," he continued flatly, crossing his arms. "Already we have coddled you too much, and for this failing, you have my sincerest apology. You and your guild may freely visit New Narvik for trade or training, but you will be cast out after sunset. It is time you become a Wolf Pack in truth, not just in name. You have two choices: One, crawl back to your human dwellings, tails tucked between your legs. Or two, search out an occupied dungeon inside of the *ranging* territory of New Narvik and conquer it through claw and fang. Claim it as a den for the glory of your pack and the greater glory of The People. This is the way."

Quest alert! A Den To Call Your Own:

Your Wolfman handler, Yurij BrightBlood, has informed you in no uncertain terms that the Wolfman outpost of Narvik is moving, and that you're not welcome in New Narvik. You can go home, but you can't stay here! Instead, you need to find an occupied dungeon to crash and convert into a cozy little nook just for you and yours. It may seem a little harsh, but a growing pack does *need room to expand. Yurij has specified that the dungeon must be within ranging distance of New Narvik—which is classified as the maximum distance that a Wolfman can run from the boundary of the outpost and return before sunset.*

Accomplishing this task isn't going to be a walk in the park—more like a stroll through a dungeon. If you can do it, you'll finally earn the begrudging respect of the Wolfman Shaman Yurij BrightBlood. Capturing new territory will also increase your reputation with The People and will have the added benefit that your guild, the Wolf Pack, will be added to the official leader board. Reward: +1,000 Reputation with The People. Inclusion on the official leader board. Exp: 5,000. Accept / Decline

The quest was a no-brainer and Sam accepted without a second thought.

"Okay," Dizzy spoke slowly, "so we need to capture a dungeon. That seems doable—but do you have a particular dungeon in mind? Or can you point us in the right direction, maybe?"

Yurij grimaced, ears laying back flat against his head. "You are the Pack Leader now, DizzySparrow. I shouldn't need to weaken you further or lead you by the snout like some young whelp. If you do need such instruction, then perhaps you are no Pack Leader at all. Perhaps it would be best to step aside and let others guide the hunt. Here is the location The O'Baba has decided on for our new outpost. Remember it well, for by this time tomorrow, Narvik as you know it will be gone."

He eyed Sam, a weighing expression in his gaze. Evidently dissatisfied, he snorted and turned, swishing away from their campfire without another word.

"Man, that guy has a chip on his shoulder," Arrow muttered as he watched Yurij's silhouette disappear into the night. "If I were to guess, I'd say that he thinks that the calamity that hit here is somehow your fault."

"Yeah, like totally bad energy, you know?" Kai shook his

head seriously. "He needs to chill. Maybe meditate and get centered. Carrying around all that anger is no bueno."

"It is the way of our People," Velkan explained, not realizing the remark was rhetorical. "To be part of our Pack, it is no small thing, understand? To trust outsiders with our most treasured secrets, it takes a tremendous bond of faith. You have convinced The O'Baba, but Yurij is the second in command. The Wolf-Eye, we call such a leader. It is his job to be distrustful. To weed out the unworthy and cull dead weight."

"What if he's right?" Dizzy groaned, plopping down in her chair and deflating like a popped balloon. "What if I am dead weight?"

She ran a grease-stained hand through frizzy red hair. "I mean, sometimes even *I* think Sam should be in charge of the guild. He's the only one here with a Wolfman title. He's the one who gained The O'Baba's trust. He's the one that arranged the raid against the College. I mean, without him, the four of us-" Dizzy swept a hand toward Kai, Sphinx, and Arrow, "-would probably still be kicking around the Square Dog Inn, desperately trying to get picked up by a better guild. Yurij's right. We're in a *tent*. We should be doing more, and that's on me."

"Gosh, hon." Sphinx stepped in with her midwestern twang, scooting her chair closer and giving Dizzy's arm an appreciative squeeze. "Don't go thinking like that. We all know how hard you're working, and we *all* think you're doing a great job."

She pulled free a dagger, which she twirled with a deadly flourish behind her back, giving Bill a dirty look, in case he was feeling sassy. "Isn't that right?"

"Yes, you're doing a capital job. I grew up crushed under the weight of expectations. Expectations that I would be some great Mage. That I would lead my family back to riches and glory and honor. I'm just glad you're running the show and not me." Finn took a deep breath, savoring the crisp evening air before flashing her his most winsome grin. "I've never felt freer than I do now, and I owe it all to you."

"Look Diz," Sam chimed in, "I know this is hard. The truth is, I probably could run the guild right *now*... but like Yurij said, we only have eight members, counting Velkan - who isn't human - and Bill the *book*."

"That is the most upsetting thing you've ever said about me," Bill grumbled quietly, his eyes tracking the warning knife in Sphinx's hand.

Sam forged on, ignoring Bill's protests. "The question is, what about when the guild really starts picking up steam? What happens when we have twenty members? Or fifty? A *hundred*? Maybe I could run the show, but just managing that many people is going to be a full-time job. Then there's politics, maintenance, and supply management. Supplying teams for quests and dealing with all the egos. I don't want to do that stuff—not any of it. Plus, you're good at it. You've run fifty-member raid parties before, and you've crushed it every time. Believe in yourself, because I do. And so does everyone else here."

"Thank you." Dizzy pushed herself to her feet. "All of you. Sounds like tomorrow is going to be a rough one. I'm going to call it a night—start fresh in the morning with a clear head. I suggest you all do the same."

She waved goodnight, then vanished into the yurt, the tent flaps curling closed behind her. Sam finished eating while the fire flickered and danced, heat soaking into his bones. After another few minutes, he excused himself as well and headed into the tent to grab his bedroll and drag it outside, where he wouldn't disturb the others. After kicking off his boots, he crawled into his makeshift sleeping bag—just a padded leather mat with a fur-lined blanket above. Full dark had set, a crescent moon hanging high overhead, and sleep called out its alluring siren song, but Sam resisted the temptation to close his eyes.

It was going to be an early morning; Dizzy was right about that. But then, *every* morning was an early morning with Bill. The book didn't sleep, and as a result, he had a devilish penchant for waking Sam up before first light.

Still, Sam had no intention of going to sleep. Not yet. He

wasn't ready to choose a specialization or a secondary profession, but for better or worse, he *was* ready to cross the Intelligence threshold. He pulled up his character sheet, reading over his current stats:

Name: Sam_K 'Experimental Forger'
Class: Bibliomancer
Profession 1: Bookbinder
Profession 2: Unassigned
Level: 10 Exp: 55,146 Exp to next level: 10,854
Hit Points: 113/140
Mana: 526/526
Mana Regen: 13.68/sec
Stamina: 154/154

Characteristic: Raw score (Modifier)
Strength: 20 (15+5 gear bonus) (1.20)
Dexterity: 34 (29+5 gear bonus) (1.34)
Constitution: 19 (1.19)
Intelligence: 49 (1.49)
Wisdom: 48 (1.48)
Charisma: 21 (16+5 gear bonus) (1.21)
Perception: 20 (1.20)
Luck: 14 (1.4)
Karmic Luck: +1

<You ready to do this?> Bill sent inside his head. <Threshold changes are a big deal.>

<Nope. But I don't think I'm ever going to be ready. Now's as good a time as any.> Sam grimaced and added his one unspent characteristic point to Intelligence, pushing him over the threshold.

<That's the spirit. See you on the other side, Legs. Remember, you can do this.>

Warning! You have reached fifty points in intelligence! I would sit down if I were you, because we are about to upgrade your mind and it can get…

well, a little brutal. Because you have both Mana Manipulation and Coalescence, you will have a chance to increase these skills while unconscious! Hope you have nowhere to be or anything urgent going on, because this can take a little while. Body modification in process in three… two… one…

CHAPTER FOUR

Sam blinked his eyes open, which felt all wrong, since he knew without a shadow of a doubt that he was asleep and passed out on his bedroll in the Wolfman outpost. With a grunt, he gained his feet and took a long gander around. The yurt was gone; so was the dancing fire, as well as the wooden palisade walls that enclosed Narvik.

Instead, Sam found himself lying on a vast plain inside his own head, the space he'd come to think of as his Soul Chamber. He'd been here many times before, guided by Mage Akora during his time in the College, and countless times since while meditating under Bill's watchful gaze. Directly in front of him was his core, although something was wrong there.

Something big.

Typically, his core resembled a perfectly round ball of power that looked like a snow globe filled with a real snowstorm. Now, however, the snowstorm had morphed into an apocalyptic blizzard, and his core had swollen to a shocking size—almost as large as a compact car—and it was straining against his will with ferocious rage. This was all wrong. His core was supposed to condense, to *shrink*, as he leveled up and grew more powerful.

"This is a major threshold," a voice cut through the quietude filling the cavity in Sam's mind. Out of a corner of inky darkness, which refused to be illuminated by the flickering light of his core, stepped a figure, tall and whip-thin, with lean muscle and a neatly trimmed beard clinging to his jaw. His outfit was outdated, his leggings bulbous around the thighs, his shirt red velvet and trimmed in gold, with a frilled collar around his neck. A foppish oversized hat with an elegant feather poking up from the brim completed the ensemble. Although Sam had never seen the man before, the emerald eyes and ridiculous hat gave him away in an instant.

Bill.

"Lots of people think crossing the threshold is easy," Bill let one hand come to rest on his hip, "but believe you me, as a Mage, it can tear you apart if you aren't careful. Especially the Intelligence barrier, since it's directly tied to your mana reserve."

"Are you really here?" Sam momentarily ignored the swirling ball of power pulsing at his center. It wasn't easy to do, but seeing Bill in the flesh—so to speak, at least—was a gut punch.

"Eh. Real enough," Bill replied with a lopsided shrug. "I'll probably never have a body again, but as you get spiritually and mentally stronger, I remember more about myself. The Arch-Mage, he stripped me down when he 'bookified' me. There's a lot I don't remember from those days—my mind is still fragmented. But that's the thing about thresholds; they allow you to understand things you literally couldn't before—make connections that would otherwise be impossible without the additional neural pathways created by advancing. Enough about that for now. We've got work to do."

He cracked his knuckles, then popped his neck, first left, then right.

"What do we do?" Sam turned his attention back to his turbulent center.

"Don't play dumb, Legs," Bill replied with an exaggerated

eye roll. "The Mage's College is just about worthless, but if there's anything they taught you, it's Mana Manipulation and Coalescence."

He paused and stole a sidelong look at Sam's core. "Admittedly there are a few extra steps, but I'll walk you through those once we get there. First things first, though." He pointed a slender finger at Sam. "You gotta condense. Get this mess under control."

Sam licked his lips and swiped his sweaty palms along his trousers. Bill was right; he *did* know the fundamentals of mana Coalescence—that, at least, had been drilled into his head. Taking a deep, calming breath, he imposed his *will* upon the swirling, tumultuous ball of energy, smoothing out the rough edges and rolling that teeming mass of energy between the palms of mental hands, all the while compressing it, forcing it back in on itself, like kneading dough. The ball responded, slowly at first, but more quickly with every second of focus. Before long, it was spinning furiously and shrinking down to a far more manageable size.

Into a more compact and efficient form.

It was hard to tell how long the process lasted—a minute? An hour? Ten?—but Sam was so absorbed with the process that he hardly noticed time passing. What was more, his mana Pool was far more pliable than it had ever been before. Usually when performing this exercise, the ball of energy hit a certain size, then simply refused to compress any further. Not this time. This time, Sam kept working the energy, spinning it, pressing on it, shaping it. It compressed more and more and more, until it was only a little larger than a quarter. There seemed to be a barrier of sorts, a certain resistance he'd never experienced before, but it *didn't* feel impassable.

"Good," Bill's voice drifted in from far away. "That's the threshold you're feeling. This is where things get a little tricky. There's a lot of wrong ways to do this, and really only one right way. First step is to crack the egg."

"Crack the egg?" Sam managed to ask through gritted teeth.

"You heard me," Bill replied with a bob of his head.

That seemed like a bad idea, but Bill hadn't led him astray so far.

With a heave, Sam threw his will against the barrier, feeling the invisible force strain under the weight of his *intent.* A spike of pain radiated outward, but he pressed on, feeling the force surrounding his core begin to splinter. Then, in a heartbeat, something inside the tightly packed ball gave way with a sharp **pop*, and the gaseous ball lit up like a fireworks display. When the light show faded, there was a single drop of Mana, no larger than a penny, right at his center. The drop of mana was shifting quick-silver that looked for all the world like a dollop of mercury suspended in midair.

Circling around the drop of silver was a gaseous cloud of white, gold, and opal. Some part of Sam expected the gas to drift away now that it was no longer contained in his core, but the tiny ball of mercury at his center seemed to have a certain gravity that held everything together.

"Hey, not bad. Not bad at all. A lot of people can't push themselves to fracture the outer casing. Sometimes it takes years to do it. Takes guts, you know. Only one piece left of the puzzle, and that part, I can help with." Bill strutted forward, reached a hand outward, and grabbed a fistful of the gently ebbing gas as though it were cotton candy. With a tug, he began to walk away from the core, spooling the gas along behind him in a tether as he headed for one of the mana pathways leading deeper into Sam's mind. Those pathways were the key to utilizing Mana, cycling it through the body.

"Well, don't just stand there. Grab an end and get to work." The thin man turned on a heel and disappeared into one of the tunnels, hauling the cloudy energy behind.

Sam grabbed a handful and followed suit, though heading into one of the other pathways. There was a whole interconnected network of pathways, but most were still closed off—he figured that would change as he leveled up both his stats and his Mana Manipulation ability. Focusing, he stretched the cloudy energy thin and trudged onward. About halfway along, he saw Bill, who gave him a grin and a lighthearted salute before disappearing around the bend. Sam forged ahead, each step a little more difficult than the last, until eventually, he reemerged in the Soul Chamber containing his core.

Bill was already done and waiting for him. "Any day now, huh? We have more work to do yet."

Sam nodded, feeling worn out to the bone, and pressed forward, reconnecting his line of energy to the swirling ring of gas. A terrible weight vanished in an instant, and a message appeared.

Mental attributes upgraded successfully! Base modifier for Intelligence has reached '2'! Congrats—you are no longer the dullest knife in the drawer! It's a step in the right direction, though make sure to get your Wisdom up, or you'll find yourself making smart, but potentially unwise, decisions!

Calculating…

Skill increased: Coalescence (Apprentice II). You have reached the beginning stage of liquid Mana! Your mana has gained an attribute, and as you increase in rank, this attribute will grow based upon your areas of focus. No longer will your mana be swept aside by another, blown by the wind like a morning mist. You have unlocked a character trait: Dual Core Processing.

Dual Core Processing: Because you have the presence of a secondary core connected to your own, you are able to regenerate mana far quicker than mages of a comparable level and will have an opportunity to unlock additional mana pathways at earlier levels! mana regeneration speed increased by 50%!

Skill increased: Mana Manipulation (Beginner IX).

Sam started awake with a gasp, lurching upright in his sleeping roll, then propping himself up on his hands. The first thing he noticed was the barest crest of light peeking up over the horizon, the dark purple sky giving way to streaks of light gray. The world seemed sharper—clearer than it had ever seemed before—and Sam instantly knew that it was a quarter past five, given the position of the sun. Full daybreak was still an hour off, which is when the rest of the team would likely pull themselves from their beds. Well, everyone except Arrow. He was a habitually late sleeper.

The next thing Sam noticed was how bad he stank. Royally *reeked.*

There was a thin layer of slimy black substance coating his skin, and it reminded him of the inside of a sweaty tennis shoe. He lifted an arm, took a quick sniff, and promptly started gagging. *Probably not the wisest thing to do,* he grumped at himself. He stood with a groan; his body was achy, and every inch of him hurt—or maybe it was just the fact that his mind was more acutely aware of everything happening around him. Either way, he needed to get clean. The camp was quiet, and he didn't want to disturb his crew, so he silently stole across through the high grass, angling toward their bathing area, which consisted of a large wooden tub with a copper bottom suspended above a bank of hot coals.

Peeking around to make sure there were no unwanted eyes, he stripped down to his birthday suit and crawled into the warm, burbling water.

It felt like heaven against his grimy skin, and after scrubbing at his arms, chest, and legs with a thick cake of yellow soap, he felt mostly human again. <It didn't work, Bill.>

<What are you talking about?> Bill replied, floating in book form outside of the tub. Bill wasn't a big fan of water for obvious reasons. <I was there, remember? You crossed the threshold like a champ. Saw it with my own eyes. Abyss, you even managed to condense your core, which is a pretty impressive feat for a level ten.>

<Not that,> Sam replied, waving away the response with one hand. <I still don't have any answers. I feel smarter, sure. I mean, suddenly I know the viscosities of various inks, for reasons I can't even begin to fathom. I'm also making connections that I never would've before, but I still don't know what specialization to pick or what profession to choose. I thought

crossing the threshold would do the heavy lifting for me, but I feel just as lost as I was before.>

Sam stared down into the waters as though there might be answers waiting there. In a lot of ways, this felt like a reflection of his entire life. He'd always been pressured by his family, pushed toward higher education. Toward a role in the family business. Going into college hadn't been high on Sam's priority list, but he'd reasoned that by the time he had a degree in hand, he would finally know what he wanted to do with his life.

Except that hadn't been the case at all. Now here he was, stuck in the exact same place: he knew so much… except what he should do next. He slapped a hand against the waters, disturbing the accusing reflection staring back at him.

Bill was silent for a long moment. <Look, I know it's hard. Magic is cool, but it can't solve all of your problems. Not always. Sometimes, the only magic solution is to trust yourself, make a choice, and throw the dice. Come on; we have work to do before the rest of these knuckleheads wake up.>

When that didn't evoke a reply, Bill tried harder, knowing he was right, but that the fact wouldn't make this any easier for his human. <We used up a ton of resources during that last encounter. All that paper ain't gonna fold itself, you know? When you don't know what to do, *work* through it.>

The book was right about that, too. Reluctantly, Sam pulled himself from the warm waters, shivering as the crisp morning air washed over his skin, raising goosebumps along his arms and legs. He quickly toweled off, pulled a fresh set of undergarments and his armor from his spatial flask, then headed over and plopped down on his bedroll. Being a Bibliomancer was awesome, but it was also a ton of work behind the scenes. Although in the heat of a battle, it might seem like he had spells for *days*, it all depended on forethought, prior preparation, and tons of material resource management. He retrieved a fresh stack of blank pages, various inks, and specialty quills, and then set to work.

Every Shuriken had to be inscribed with the proper folding instructions.

Every Ice Orb and Fireball spell needed to be inked in exacting detail. Each sheet tagged by the Bookmark spell.

Then, all of those pages were added to the correct volume and carefully sewn into the interior.

It wasn't hard work, exactly—he'd done it a thousand times or more and had each movement committed to muscle memory—but it was time-consuming. He worked in silence, hands moving with a purpose all their own, while his mind cast about for answers. What was he destined to do? What specialization was he meant for? When the sun fully rose and the rest of his crew stirred in earnest, he still felt firmly in the dark. Fortunately, he'd had one revelation. He might not know what *he* was supposed to do, but he thought he might just have an answer to a different problem.

Where the team was supposed to find a dungeon to call their own.

CHAPTER FIVE

Sam wrapped up his work, bound the final set of pages into his Fire Shuriken Tome, then headed over to the campfire where the rest of the team was milling around in a rather leisurely fashion. Surprisingly, Arrow was up, though he looked more than half-asleep. Purple bags showed under his eyes, his hair ruffled and standing up at odd angles. He'd probably stayed up too late drinking, which was how he spent most nights. Kai, by contrast, sat a way off from the others, crossed-legged, with fists pressed together in meditation. No sign of Velkan yet, but that wasn't a big surprise; the elusive Wolfman liked to spend time with his clan whenever they were back in camp.

Sphinx lounged quietly, meticulously sharpening the edge of a dagger, while Finn — the self-proclaimed company chef— whipped up a breakfast of scrambled eggs and lean strips of rabbit left over from the night before. Growing up in a Noble house, Finn had always had his meals prepared, but ever since venturing out, he'd taken to the culinary arts like a duck to water. Finn had a pot of coffee burbling away along with another pot of hot water, which was perfect for Sam; he wasn't much of a coffee drinker. A strong cup of what passed for Earl Grey tea would set him straight in no time at all.

There was a sense of early morning relaxation hanging in the air… for everyone except Dizzy.

Their disheveled guild leader was furiously studying a book, writing down notes in her blocky script, underlining something, then promptly crossing something else out. She stuck her tongue out as she worked, smudging the charcoal across the page in a way that made Sam flinch. Her penmanship was just… just *terrible.* The way she was treating those poor pages was a crime against books and paper everywhere. If he tried to inscribe a spell like that, he would blow himself back into the Dark Ages, along with everything in a two-block radius.

"Well, now," Finn grinned at Sam as he tromped over, "don't *you* look bright eyed and bushy-tailed? I take that to mean you crossed the threshold?"

"He handled it like a champ," Bill offered his support, a rarity in fun group settings like this. "With a little guidance from yours truly, of course."

Sphinx immediately sat up and let out a little **squee** of excitement. "Oh gosh, don't leave us hanging now! Tell us what happened; what's it like? You're the first person I've ever met who crossed the Intelligence threshold. I know when I crossed the Dexterity threshold, everything changed, like I'd been moving through molasses my whole life and didn't realize it until suddenly… I wasn't. Took a while to get used to, now, didn't it? Everyone around me seemed to be moving at quarter-speed, out of sync with how fast my brain could process everything. I bet you feel sorta like Einstein now."

"Eh, I'm not sure I would go that far," Sam replied with a shrug. "I mean, it's definitely a big improvement. My mana pool grew, my mana regen went up, and I feel like I could cast all day, so… that's a plus. I definitely do feel smarter, like my brain is able to more easily retain info. It's not an eidetic memory, but it's an awful lot closer to that than it was before."

"I would've given my left arm to have this kind of recall

back in college. Still…" He trailed off, rubbing absently at the back of his neck as he smirked and shook his head. "Well, I was hoping crossing over would help clear some things up for me. Didn't really work out the way I thought it would."

"Dude." Kai looked up from his meditation to offer his thoughts. "Intelligence isn't *wisdom*. Even the smartest people need life experience, my guy. Give it time, and eventually the universe will supply the answers you need."

"Alright, everyone," Dizzy barked, clapping her charcoal-covered hands sharply. "Let's huddle up. It's going to be crazy-busy today, and we have a ton to do, especially if we want to avoid turning into wandering murderhobos without a place to sleep by day's end."

Velkan appeared as though summoned from thin air, while Kai unfolded himself and joined the others around the dancing fire. Finn quickly handed out breakfast, served on tin camp plates, then took a seat where he would have an unobstructed view of Dizzy. Finn tried to hide it, but he was carrying a torch for the tank that was big enough to light up the beacon at the Olympics; not that she seemed to notice. Everyone else did, even Yurij, who seemed to think it was the funniest thing he had ever seen.

"I've been thinking a lot about what Yurij told us, and he's right," Dizzy began as soon as everyone was paying attention. "I feel like I've been falling down on the job as Pack Leader. We've been spending so much time undercutting the Rabid Inquisitors over the past couple of weeks that we haven't really managed to do much of anything else."

She paused, lips pressing into a thin, judgmental line. "That's on me. I got so caught up on a few individual trees that I neglected the forest all around us. Not anymore. We're done taking out lowly pledges; we need to be hunting bigger game.

"If we want to have any shot at winning this war against humanity, we're going to have to *significantly* boost our numbers. Before we can do that, we're going to have to scale up our own infrastructure and lock down a legitimate base of operations.

The human guilds have everything going for them. Inns, taverns, access to merchants and skill trainers. All we have is this shabby tent," she gestured toward the yurt, "and that isn't exactly a selling point. We'll be lucky to even have *that* by the end of the day. Which brings us to today's real mission: we need to find a dungeon. Velkan?"

She pinned the Wolfman in place with her icy stare. "You must know more about the Forest of Chlorophyll Chaos than any of us. Think you could point us in the right direction?"

The Wolfman grunted, ears twitching in agitation and nostrils flared. Sam could tell from the gestures that the Wolfman was deeply uncomfortable with the questions.

"No," Velkan finally said. "As the name implies, the Forest of Chlorophyll Chaos is… it is *chaotic*. The forest *shifts*. Changes. It is like the wind. When you enter the wood, it will randomly send you deep into its embrace. Our Pack leaders are insightful; once the new outpost is set up, they will create totems that will allow us to easily find the camp. But until the wards and totem markers are set, we will be at the mercy of the forest, just like any other creature. There is no sure way to lead you to a dungeon."

Velkan snarled and dropped his gaze, as though the admission was a terrible failure on his part.

"That's unfortunate," Dizzy grumbled with a heavy sigh. She lifted her notebook and drew a sharp line across the paper. "Which means we're going to have to find one the old-fashioned way. Wandering around aimlessly, grinding every mob that comes at us until we find something that fits. Not going to be a quick or easy process, but there's nothing left but to do it."

"Or maybe you could ask the amazing levitating book and his bumbling sidekick," Bill offered easily. "Me and Legs here came up with a solution to our little dungeon problem. Show 'em."

"Crossing the intelligence threshold may not have given me a solution about my specialization…" Sam dipped a hand into Bill's Soul Space and pulled free a thick brown tome with a ruby the size of a robin's egg embedded in the center: the *Compendium on Protected and Dangerous Locations.* "But it did allow me to read and understand this bad boy."

Sam let it drop onto one of the makeshift benches with a *thud.* "I grabbed this on my first trip out of the College. That title screamed 'quest fodder' to me, but I wasn't smart enough at the time to understand the contents of the book. Not until this morning. None of you will be able to decipher what's inside, but Bill and I can. We took a read through it this morning. It's no wonder the Mages had it secreted away in the Sage's Section of the Infinity Athenaeum."

"I'll bite." Finn leaned forward, elbows resting on his skinny thighs. "What's in it?"

"Exactly what it sounds like," Sam informed him while flipping open the cover and turning toward a section with a detailed map etched across the pages. "The whole thing is a list of secret, dangerous, and valuable dungeons scattered across this realm and others. It details a dozen different dungeons. When I say 'details,' I'm talking about history, floor layout, info on minions, traps, and other dangers. It's a bit rough in places, and I'm not sure how reliable the info is, but it's definitely a heck of a lot better than going in blind."

He couldn't help but grin in triumph. "Even better, it turns out there's a dungeon that fits our needs like a glove, and it's less than ten miles from New Narvik. The Compendium calls it the *Irondown Burrows*."

Dizzy narrowed her eyes, forehead furrowing in suspicion. "Sounds too good to be true. What's the catch?"

"The catch," Bill interjected, so that Sam didn't get all the credit, "is that the Irondown Burrows are Dwarven ruins and are entirely out of our league. Like *way~y~y* out of our league. The Dwarves are tough sons of steel and stone. More than that, they are crafty like you wouldn't believe. So far as I know, the Dwarves have moved on to another realm, but I can *guarantee* you they've left behind a host of nasty surprises for us. Traps. Automatons and the like. Who knows what else? The book documents a few of the things we're probably gonna be going toe to toe with… and they're bad. Killing 'em is gonna be ugly."

"But there might be a way around that too," Sam broke in before Bill could scare everyone off for good. "With Octavius dead and gone, no one at the Mage's College knows about his research on the LAW. But *we* know. We have his notes, even if they are incomplete. We also know exactly how powerful a weapon like that is. He could've leveled this whole outpost with a single spell if we hadn't gotten in the way."

Former Peak Student and Sam's college-appointed tormentor, Octavius Igenitor, had pioneered a new type of weapon: a Long-range Amplification Weapon, or LAW. The system used an arcane principle called 'Sympathetic Magic and Twining' to cast and amplify spells, even at great distances. It was deadly, game changing, and everyone that knew about it was dead.

Everyone except the Wolf Pack and The O'Baba.

A lot of the principles behind the process were still fuzzy at best to Sam, but he was sure that between Bill, Finn, and his new-found Intelligence that they could get their own version of the LAW up and running. Probably wouldn't be easy, but worthwhile things rarely were.

"We'll have to assemble the tower," Sam blurted out in a rush, "and we'll likely have to manufacture the parts necessary to create the Twining system, but if we can get it up and operational, it might help us take out the dungeon guardian. Even if it *doesn't* do that, having a weapon like that in our back pocket could seriously help in the war effort against the human race. It's a win-win, as far as I'm concerned."

"Dude," Kai's mouth was slightly agape. "You, like, really *are* smarter."

"Totally agreed." Dizzy was giving Sam an appreciative sidelong glance. "We should've been doing more to assemble the LAW from the get-go. It's an edge that we can exploit, assuming we can figure out how to get it to work."

Finn's hand shot up into the air. "Leave that bit to me, yeah?

I worked closely with Octavius on the schematics and blueprints. Considering that he's gone, I probably know more about the system than anyone else in Ardania. Plus, I still have connections inside the city through my family line. Admittedly, I'm a wanted man."

He stated the last bit rather smugly, straightening his robes, "But Nobles *always* have a network of eyes, ears, and hands scattered throughout the city. Especially my family."

Finn came from House Laustsen, one of the oldest and most infamous Noble houses in Ardania. Although few talked about ancient history, King Henry and Queen Marie hadn't always been the monarchs they were today. Once upon a time, there had been a bloody and brutal civil war; would-be-lords and ladies all fought and killed to be king of the hill. House Laustsen had been a very vocal supporter of the losing faction, the Sect of Leader Charibert. Most of the opposing houses were scrubbed from existence, but not Finn's family. They were nearly driven into bankruptcy, but wiping them out root and branch would've devastated Ardania's economy.

So they'd been begrudgingly given a pardon after 'seeing the error of their ways'.

"We've always been rebels," Finn continued soberly, "though, truth be told, we always half-expected the tyrant King and his bloody Queen to come for us sooner or later. Although we weren't *actively* fomenting rebellion against the crown, we were prepared to do so if the tides ever changed. Chances are high that my family will shelter me despite the various warrants out for my head. They might even honor me as a hero. Better still, I suspect I can get everything we need from my covert suppliers."

"I could also help!" Sphinx was excited to be able to contribute. "I just don't think it's good to have Finn go it alone, especially since he can't respawn, dontcha know. Plus, I feel like I'm getting a little rusty. This'll give me a chance to work some of my Infiltrator skills and some time in the city would do some good. I need to get back in touch with a few of my contacts inside the Upright Men."

Dizzy frowned but nodded. "Yeah... better to have someone watching his back."

"Sounds airtight to me, too," Arrow added, rubbing at his chin thoughtfully. "But we still have one big problem. If the Irondown Burrows really are as tough as Bill seems to think, we're going to need all the help we can get. With Sphinx and Finn both gone, that only leaves six of us."

"*Thank* you for including me in the count!" Bill crowed, ruffling his pages like a peacock fanning out its feathers. "*Finally*, someone who realizes how important I am to this team."

"Always, Sir Book," Arrow replied with a devilish grin and a tip of his hat. Sam couldn't tell whether Arrow was mocking Bill or not. He was a hard one to read, easygoing, but relatively tightlipped. Still, a compliment was a compliment in Bill's book. "But even with your assistance, we're going to be badly disadvantaged at running a hardcore dungeon. Truth be told, I've never even heard rumors of Dwarven dungeons before, so I can't imagine how difficult they'll be to take down."

"Yeah, but dude, that also means we'll get another world first," Kai enthused. "Think about it, bro. Another title. Having access to our very own Dwarven dungeon is going to be wicked sick, and it'll make pulling new recruits so much easier. I mean, a tavern is cool, but not cooler than Dwarven-ruins-turned-stronghold."

Arrow seesawed his head before nodding. "Got a point there, I suppose."

"Also, there's no other way around it," Dizzy sternly informed them. "We aren't exactly spoiled for choices at the moment. Sure, having Finn and Sphinx along would be helpful, but I think we'll be more than capable of at least running a quick recon mission. I know you're a Ranger and not a Rogue, but you have Trap Sense, right?"

Arrow grunted, folded his arms across his chest, then nodded reluctantly.

"Well, there you go, then." Dizzy waved her hand emphatically. "You can run point for us, disarm any traps, or at least make sure we don't blunder headlong into 'em."

"Oh joy," Arrow sighed dramatically. "I get to be cannon fodder. *Yay*!"

"Don't be that way, Arrow." Dizzy's voice softened a hair. "We'll be alright. Sam and Bill are practically a force of nature at this point, and I'll play tank and pull aggro. Kai can tag-team point with you and keep you safe. We'll have Velkan shadow Sam and Bill; make sure they don't take a crit early on. That's about as well-rounded a party as we could hope for going in. It'll be tough, but we can handle it if we play smart."

Arrow folded in on himself a little, then threw up his hands. "Gah. *Fine*. I'm in. But everyone here owes me enough beer to drown a horse."

"For what it's worth," Bill unnecessarily cleared his voice, "I'm with you. Might be we're running a suicide mission. But I'm not the one with nerve endings, so what do I care, amiright?"

That was more than a little *unnerving*, but Bill was always a naysayer. Besides, grinding through a ridiculously tough dungeon might just help Sam get his mind off his specialization for a little while. Honestly, he couldn't wait to get into an ol' fashioned, mind-numbing *brawl*.

CHAPTER SIX

The sun was hanging high overhead and sweat was streaking down Sam's face when they finally pushed through a patch of bushy ferns and hanging moss. The trek through the Forest of Chlorophyll Chaos had been exactly as difficult as Sam had envisioned. The second they had crossed over some mystic barrier, they had disappeared in the span of an eyeblink, their whole party materializing deep in a boggy section of forest with sucking mud pits, a tangle of creeping vines, and swarms of biting mosquitoes.

Had Sam been alone, it almost certainly would've been the death of him. His family had taken camping trips nearly every summer, but his family's version of camping was decidedly different from the typical tent camping that most people did. Usually, they stayed in plush cabin retreats with all the amenities anyone could ever ask for. 'Roughing it' usually meant a trip out in their state-of-the-art RV, complete with air conditioning, composting toilet, and a stand-up shower. Sam would never be accused of being the woodsy sort; what he knew about wilderness survival could fill most of a thimble, with room to spare.

But, between Arrow's *Navigate* ability and Velkan's *Bushcraft* skill, they quickly found dry ground and managed to get oriented with a little help from the rising sun. Although they had been randomly dropped in the middle of the forest, the relative location of places within the forest remained constant. Since they had a rough idea of the dungeon's location - thanks to the Compendium - Arrow was able to scamper up a tree, find a prominent landmark, then shoot an azimuth that took them more or less in the direction they needed to go. From there, Velkan's keen senses kept them from blundering headfirst in pitfalls or hostile monster burrows.

They'd still had to battle through their collective body weight in bunnies, feral foxes, and onyx caiman, earning Sam a solid five hundred and thirty points of experience before they'd even reached their destination. Thankfully, they were finally here. On the other side of the foliage was a clearing, sixty feet wide and ringed by gnarled oaks and looming ash trees. The leafy canopy blocked out much of the oppressive heat, but errant sunbeams streaked through the leaves, illuminating the structure protruding from the underbrush like a cancerous growth.

Those sunbeams reflected off the golden minarets poking up from the Dwarven dungeon fortress. Arrow whistled softly through his teeth, hands planted on his hips and eyes squinted as he took in the building's façade. Kai let his own awe linger in his voice. "You can say that again. This place is *totally* epic, dude."

Sam had to agree. He wasn't sure exactly what he'd been expecting; maybe a cavern system or the shabby remains of some ancient temple? It certainly hadn't been the artfully carved building of stone and bronze before them. A set of immaculate gray steps led up to a pair of massive double doors covered in intricate patterns, pitted cogs, and long silent gears. The building itself was crafted from slabs of gray stone inset with ornate bronze panels, depicting an elaborate series of geometric designs, all interlocking in ways that seemed impossible at first glance. Flanking the doors were a pair of grim-faced bronze figures, squat and outrageously broad, holding out their hands, palms open and cupped together.

"Sacred Geometry." Bill's voice cut through the quiet reflection and heavy breathing. "I never spent any time with the Dwarves. They moved on before my day, but I was buddies with a Dwarven historian, Smelly Pete. His odor had absolutely nothing to do with his work. Great scholar, just terrible hygiene."

Bill paused to collect his thoughts. "Might've actually been some sort of skin condition, now that I think about it... anywhoo, Smelly Pete and I were thick as thieves during my tenure with the College, and he was *always* nattering on about Dwarves and their Sacred Geometry. Kinda makes sense for a bunch of guys that were obsessed with gears and cogs to be big into *shapes*."

"I don't like this." Velkan took a few tentative steps forward, then dropped into a low crouch, his clawed fingers tracing over the ground. "Observe. There are no signs of prey here. No tracks. There is no scent of game lingering in the air. Surely these ruins have been here since before the humans rose to power, yet no creature has made this into a lair."

"*Yeah.*" Bill gave the Wolfman an exaggerated eye roll. "Of course they didn't. Dwarves were dangerous, and their fortresses were even more so. People and animals alike left this place alone because they weren't stupid and didn't want to die horribly. According to our handy-dandy Compendium, the Irondown Burrows are infested with mechanical Dwarven nightmare fuel. No one in their right mind would go in there."

"What does that say about us?" Sam quipped, his joke going over like a lead balloon.

"It says that beggars can't be choosers, and desperate people make desperate choices," Dizzy replied with a clenched jaw, her face set as hard as the panels of bronze adorning the ruins. "Now come on. No sense cooling our feet out here. Let's see just how bad this place really is."

Tentatively, they made their way up the steps, the sound of

their footfalls unnaturally loud in the hush of the clearing. Sam mentally prepared himself for the bronze figurines flanking the doors to leap to life and clobber them where they stood, but they remained statue-still. Their metal eyes were vacant, their palms still stretched out in supplication. Dizzy nudged Arrow in the ribs with her elbow, spurring him into motion.

"Yeah, yeah," he grunted, examining the doors. He was a Ranger, not a Rogue, Lockpick, or proper Thief, but with Sphinx gone, he was the best they had. Using Trap Sense, he searched for any malicious mechanisms, but found nothing. Unfortunately, he also didn't find a way to open the doors. There was no handle, no lock to pick, no secret lever or hidden switch that jumped out. Not exactly the most auspicious start to their raid.

Once it was clear that the doors couldn't be bludgeoned open, Dizzy had them break into pairs and circle the building, looking for some alternate way in. That, or maybe some way to trigger the doors. Sam and Bill took a lap with Kai in tow - making sure they had a little muscle in case anything nasty jumped out - but found a whole lot of nothing. The exterior portion of the ruins, though impressive in design, was actually fairly small in scope. But that matched up with the info they'd read about this place. According to the Compendium, most of the compound was below ground, nestled in a twisted series of tunnels and rooms. Toward the rear of the building, they did find a sealed stone door.

The door was flush with the ruin's exterior, however, and looked like it could only be opened from the inside, which meant it was probably an exit from the primary Boss Room.

When the trio finally got back around to the front, Velkan had turned up a lead. He began tracing a nail along a line of script hidden within the palms of one of the guardians. "There is something inscribed within the palms of these figures. It reads '*Give the Smith his due.*'"

"Can't believe I forgot that," Bill chuckled ruefully. "Of course there's an entry price. The Dwarves are big into barter and reputation. There's always a price with them. Hmm... *Give the Smith his due.* Hey, Legs. Grab out some loose pocket change. Any coin should do it, but silver or gold is probably best."

Sam frowned but complied, pulling out a pair of silver marks from the coin pouch at his belt, then tossing them into the open hands. The second the metal **clinked** against the bronze hands, the figure's eyes erupted with electric blue light.

"Yep. Just like I thought. Go ahead and toss a Fire Shuriken into the other one," Bill instructed, sounding rather smug and self-satisfied. Sam hated that he was right so often; sure, it was great to have someone with his level of experience, but abyss *below,* could he be insufferable.

Sam quickly summoned his red leather tome, plucked out a page, and tossed it into the other statue's expectant hands. The scroll ignited on impact, a ball of yellow-orange flame jetting up. The second figure's eyes also illuminated with the same ghostly blue hue, and an audible **click** floated through the air as the gears and cogs decorating the doors rapidly spun and whirled to life. Once the frantic motion stopped, Arrow pushed on the doors, and they swung inward on silent, well-oiled hinges to reveal a circular entry room lit by watery blue wall-mounted crystals. It was the closest thing Sam had seen to electricity since coming to the game.

A moment later, a popup appeared in front of Sam. From a casual glance around, he realized the rest of the party had received the same notice.

Quest alert! A Den to Call your Own II. Hey, will you look at that! Your party has just accessed the Irondown Burrows, a lost dungeon located in the dark heart of the Forest of Chlorophyll Chaos. As a Wolfman-aligned guild without dedicated headquarters, you can lay claim to this abandoned dungeon... including its resources and any minions within. Assuming that you can subdue it. Would the Wolf Pack like to lay claim to the Irondown Burrows and attempt to convert it into a guild den? Note: This action must be approved by majority vote of the Wolf Pack guild officers! Accept / Decline

Sam didn't even have to think about it. This is what they'd

come for, and they would never get a better chance to carve out a place of their own. The screen disappeared, only for another to appear.

Okay, I know everyone accepted, but seriously, are you sure you want to lay claim to the Irondown Burrows? Once you officially lay claim to a dungeon, you cannot lay claim to another dungeon location until this one is subdued. There are consequences to choices! So, let me ask again: would the Wolf Pack like to lay claim to the Irondown Burrows and attempt to convert it into a guild den? Note: This item needs to be approved by majority vote of the Wolf Pack guild officers! Accept / Decline

Sam accepted once again, then read over the new prompt that appeared.

Congratulations, members of the Wolf Pack. You have just laid claim to the Irondown Burrows of the Forest of Chlorophyll Chaos. You can now begin the reclamation process! Claiming a dungeon is no easy task, nor is it a quick one. Located throughout the dungeon are key Junctions *that need to be captured. Some may even need to be refurbished to working order. Once a* Junction *is captured, you can access and even use that part of the dungeon... though be warned,* Junctions *are often ferociously guarded against interlopers by powerful Keepers.*

In order to reclaim the dungeon and transform it into a guild den, you'll need to capture all of the Junctions.

Good luck! I have a sneaking suspicion you're going to need it.

Irondown Burrow Junctions Capture: 0 / 8

Dizzy was staring blankly at the air in front of her, clearly still reading the game notice. After a beat, she blinked the message away and licked her lips. "Well, I guess we're in it now. I hope we made the right choice."

"We can't second guess ourselves." Kai dropped a friendly hand on her shoulder. "If my life has taught me anything, it's that our choices are cumulative. Just look at us: none of us would be where we are if we'd played things safe or followed the well-trodden path, but there's like no place I'd rather be than right here with you guys."

"You're only saying that because you aren't the one looking for traps," Arrow muttered morosely.

"Don't worry, bro," the Monk trumpeted. "I'll be right beside you to pull your bacon out of the fire. We got this."

Sam wasn't quite as confident, but he appreciated Kai's positive outlook.

"Hippies and their flippant..." Arrow drew a curved bow from his back, checking the quiver at his side. The leather sheath was chock full of black-feathered arrows. Sam summoned his tomes and cast Papier-Mache Mage in a swirl of pages, while the rest of the party stacked up, getting into position. Arrow and Kai were in the very front, with Dizzy close behind. Sam and Bill lined up behind her, tucked away from the bulk of the action, while Velkan took up a position just to Sam's left.

The doors opened into a circular chamber that looked like a steampunk wonderland plucked from a different age. The floor was polished stone, *immaculate*, which Sam found strange, but the walls themselves were covered with brass and iron as often as rock. Overhead hung an enormous chandelier that displayed a series of metal orbs rotating around one another in intricate patterns that reminded Sam of a model of the solar system. Planets and moons, orbiting the sun in a never-ending cosmic dance.

<Yeah, that's not at all a model of any solar system,> Bill sent, reading Sam's thoughts. <That's a model for core cultivation. Like I said before, those Dwarves are *super* into body cultivation. They are all about them gains, and their sacred geometry plays into that. *A lot.* That, and following the 'whey'. Not the 'dao', the 'whey'. I get the strange feeling that you're gonna like Elven society more than Dwarven, if you ever get a chance to interact with either.>

The entry room connected to a set of wide stone stairs that cut deeper into the earth. Arrow moved slowly, cautiously, examining each step before gingerly placing a foot with a grimace and a wince, and for good reason. On the fourth step down, a stone shifted, and a flashing buzzsaw as big as a truck tire erupted from the floor, screaming to life. Thanks to his high

Dexterity, Arrow narrowly danced out of the way just before the blade extended from the floor. Had he been half a second slower, he would've lost a foot in the best-case scenario. "Uh. Trap here. Maybe give that one a wide berth."

"Gee, thanks for the warning," Dizzy taunted, getting a rude hand gesture in reply. The stairs eventually dumped them into a long hallway, studded by metal pillars and surprisingly high arched ceilings. The pillars were inscribed with more sacred geometry and were studded by intermittent cloudy glass orbs protruding like bulbous eyes. They flickered with the same artificial blue light that Sam had noticed above.

This place hadn't been occupied in hundreds of years, so it must've been some sort of magically-generated power. Cogs, gears, and churning pistons dotted the walls. Those, in turn, connected to a series of gleaming brass pipes running up the walls and along the ceiling, where they wouldn't obstruct foot traffic.

The pipes groaned and rattled overhead, hissing out an occasional burst of steam from pressure release valves. Each section of flooring was as immaculately clean as the entry room had been; no sign of dust or wear at all. The pipes seemed brand new and meticulously maintained.

More red flags raised in Sam's head.

They padded forward on silent feet, winding through a short series of passageways that concealed a bevy of deadly surprises: a false floor with a spike-studded pit, hair-trigger pressure plates that would've released a barrage of poison-tipped darts, and another of the buzz-saw traps connected to a tripwire. Thankfully, after their narrow escape the first time around, Arrow had figured out what to look for, and they managed to avoid the deadly pitfalls without suffering any of the horrific side effects.

Eventually, the twisting hallway led to a small room with two branches jutting off, one cutting hard left and another continuing straight as an arrow. Dizzy gave a set of orders in a low whisper. "Kai, post up straight ahead, Velkan, guard the left-hand tunnel. Arrow, I want you scanning for traps. I know we haven't seen any unfriendlies yet, but we need to stay sharp."

She paused and searched the darkness up ahead. "They're out there somewhere. I can feel them. Sam, mind if we take a look at the compendium? We need to decide where to go from here."

"On it," he replied, pulling the thick tome out from his Flask while the others spread out, following Dizzy's orders.

The book itself was a monstrous thing of red leather, with gilt edges and delicate lettering on the spine. He balanced the thick volume on one hand and quickly rifled through the pages until he found the section detailing the Irondown Burrows. On the first page was a brief description of the dungeon itself, while the opposite page contained a crudely drawn map of the dungeon. The lines were smudged in places, and the map looked far from precise - almost as though it had been drawn while on the run - but it gave them a rough layout to go by.

"Not sure what you're waiting for, but I can't read any of the information in the book, so give me a rundown," Dizzy exasperatedly demanded after a few moments of silence.

Sam traced a finger along the path they had followed so far, through the main foyer, down the stairs into the entry hall, then along the snaking pathway to the first main fork. As a stream of consciousness, he explained that they had two options: If they headed left, it would bring them to their first major Junction, marked *Barracks*. Going straight would usher them deeper into the heart of the dungeon and toward a pair of Junctions, one marked *Library* and the other labeled *Control Room*.

The fact that this place had a Library at all made Sam salivate in anticipation. He couldn't help but wonder what secret knowledge was tucked away in a place like this. Abyss, even if the books were useless, having extra paper would be a steal all on its own.

"Well," Dizzy murmured as she tapped her chin, "we need to try to capture one of these Junctions, but the question is... which one?"

"Hold on one sec." Sam flipped through the pages until he found a reference section that detailed the various rooms contained within the dungeon. He tapped a finger on the page. "Look at this, there are eight rooms, each with a Keeper. Now, this book doesn't specifically list out the Junction points, but the quest prompt told us there are eight of them. Eight Junctions, eight rooms. I'm guessing that isn't a coincidence; these are the points we need to capture in order to convert the dungeon. Barracks, Library, Control Room, Kitchen, Alchemy Lab, Training Hall, Flame Forge Armory, and Husbandry Pen."

"Airtight logic," Bill announced brightly. "Unfortunately, whoever wrote this thing wasn't thoughtful enough to mention what kind of threats we'd be facing, but he did leave a few notes in the margins about each room."

Husbandry Pen – the foulest of fowl; very protective, but not terribly dangerous. Still, proceed with some caution.

Flame Forge Armory – The master of the Irondowns dwells within. Avoid this room ***at all costs****!*

"Okay." Dizzy considered the options seriously. "The question is, do we try for the most practical room, or the easiest? Also, for the last time, *stop* showing me the book. I only see gibberish, and it bothers me that this world can make it impossible to read stuff!"

"The most practical would have to be the Library," Sam commented instantly, trying and failing to keep the greed from his voice. "Listen to the description. 'Library–a cunning creature of paper and steel haunts the stacks. Step quietly, or perish'."

"For you and Bill, maybe," Dizzy replied with an eye roll, "but for the rest of us it would have to be either the training hall or the armory. Think about all the gear this place probably has. Besides, that description doesn't exactly make it sound like an easy fight. To be fair, the training hall or armory likely won't be any better."

"This is just my two coppers," Bill interjected, breaking up the debate, "but I'm thinking we should just work our way up from the bottom. Start with the easiest Keeper and grind our way to the top. That way, we can gauge exactly how tough these things are, and it'll allow us to collectively level up as we move on to the more difficult challenges. If I'm reading this book right - which I am, because if there's one thing I know, it's books - then the easiest Junction is the Barracks, which is only a stone's throw from our current location. 'Long abandoned by the Dwarves who called the Irondown home, only a lowly House Keeper remains, sweeping floors and folding linens that will never be used'."

"Sounds almost like a maintenance automation," Dizzy nodded slowly in acknowledgment, "which makes sense. This place has been abandoned for what? A hundred years? Two hundred? It's still meticulously clean and well maintained; that doesn't happen by accident."

"Plus, the quest prompt did say that once we capture a Junction, we can use it, even without capturing the rest of the dungeon." Sam shrugged off the fact that he'd need to wait for the library. "As of this morning, we're homeless. Capturing the barracks would give us a safe place to sleep."

"It's not as glamorous as storming the armory," Dizzy grumbled almost too softly to hear, "but I suppose in terms of practicality, this *is* the best choice. If the Keeper there really is a pushover, we can always try our luck with another room."

"Sounds like we have a plan," Sam replied, stashing the dungeon compendium. "Let's go check out the barracks, shall we?"

CHAPTER SEVEN

"Well, is it warded?" Dizzy was getting too impatient, which Sam expressed with a single annoyed glance. The team crouched at the top of a short descending staircase which ended at a set of impressively large bronze double doors, studded with rivets. A simple lever protruding from the wall on the left appeared to be the activation mechanism, but no one wanted to pull it until they were sure the door was the *only* thing it activated.

"Looks clean to me," Arrow swallowed nervously. He licked his lips, pressed his eyes shut for a long beat, then opened them and threw the switch down. "Guess we're gonna have to pull it to find out for sure."

The doors swung out on silent hinges, oiled and as meticulously maintained as everything else in the dungeon. Better still, there were no darts or saws or mechanical flame throwers to charbroil them. They inched forward, past the threshold and into the connecting room, which, if the map was correct, was the barracks. It certainly looked like a barracks at first glance.

The floors were rather plain and bare, while stone-wrought bed frames lined each side of the room at evenly spaced intervals, trailing off into the cavernous darkness on the far side of the space. Somehow, each bed still had a mattress covered with neatly folded linens, and a hulking mechanical footlocker remained perched by each foot board.

With a quick scan, Sam counted thirty beds, though there were likely more that he couldn't see, even with his Dark Vision ability—a little skill he'd picked up, thanks to his *Night Prowler* title. Although there was an ambient glow spilling in from the wall sconces in the hallway, the lighting here wasn't on. He glanced at the arched ceiling overhead and noticed a series of hanging crystalline lights, suspended from thick iron chains.

All were dead.

"Wedge formation," Dizzy whispered as they pushed forward into the room. She shouldn't have bothered to keep her voice down, since the sound of their footfalls was thunderous in the otherwise quiet chamber. They advanced slowly, clearing each set of beds in passing, making sure there weren't any nasty surprises waiting to spring out from behind bulky frames or hulking footlockers.

Velkan stopped suddenly, fur standing on edge, ears laid back, and teeth bared. He lifted a balled fist, *hold*, raised his nose, and took a long, deep whiff. A resounding **clang** cut through the silence. The scrape of metal over stone floated out from the darkness up ahead. "There is something foul in the air. Something is in here with us. It smells of oil and metal. Of *death*."

Sam instantly toggled forward his Fire and Ice Shuriken Tomes to active positions, ready to unleash a flurry of paper at whatever horror-show was coming toward them. Around him, the others dropped into fighting stances. The **clang** came again, closer this time, accompanied by a flash of movement in the pool of inky blackness ahead.

"It sounds enormous." Dizzy's fingers tightened around the haft of her war maul. "Divines, but I hope we didn't make a mistake by coming here."

Sam held his breath, his heart thundering as the

approaching creature stepped into the ambient light for the first time… and he had to refrain from laughing.

He'd been mentally preparing for some King-Kong-sized metal golem, studded with spikes and wielding rusty machetes and gatling guns. Instead, he found himself facing down a pint-sized mechanical minion that couldn't have stood more than four feet tall, whose middle was dominated by a metal potbelly with a sapphire pulsing at its center.

The creature was balanced on a pair of spindly legs shod with comically oversized metal boots. Its arms were likewise scrawny, ending in bulky forearms that would give Popeye a run for his money. The mechanical automaton had a humanoid face, with a pronounced nose, wide blue eyes, and—most unbelievably of all—a handlebar mustache crafted from bronze.

A hipster robot.

The mini automaton bore a hubcap-like shield on one arm, which ended in what looked like an arc welder. In the other hand, it wielded a wrench that was nearly as big as it was. Honestly, Sam thought the little guy looked cute. It could've passed as a card-carrying member of the Lollipop Guild.

The shadow of a smile slipped from Sam's face when he heard another **clang**, then another… and another still. Three more of the automatons stepped into view, one carrying a comically large mallet alongside a head as large as a cinderblock, another with a buzz saw affixed to the end of one wrist, and the last wielding what appeared to be a mechanical mop.

The wrench-wielding leader of the quartet regarded the interlopers for one long second more, canting its head to the side like an inquisitive puppy. It abruptly let out an odd, high-pitched chatter. Its fellows responded in the same nattering language, their eyes pulsing as they talked. Wrench finally straightened its head and squinted, mustache quivering in anger. It opened its mouth, let out a raucous, shrill squeal, and charged.

Naturally, the others followed in its wake, spidery legs eating up the distance in no time, their impromptu weapons raised and ready to kill. Dizzy's voice rang off the walls and brass pipes, "*Incoming*! Kai, Velkan, create a funnel. Basic arc formation, centered on me! Arrow, back! Sam, suppressive fire!"

Everyone moved with the practiced ease of muscle memory, effortlessly falling into the formation that Dizzy had drilled into them a hundred times over. Dizzy bolted forward, her war maul ready to swing, while Kai dropped back half a step on her left, forming one leg of a reverse V. Arrow planted a foot on one of the heavy footlockers and launched himself into the air. He landed behind Dizzy in a crouch, bow drawn with an arrow nocked and ready to fly. Meanwhile, Velkan bolted forward in a blur, forming the right leg of the V. Sam turned on a heel and vaulted up onto one of the beds, giving him a clear field of fire.

That was one of the worst parts about being a spell-caster.

Out in the open, he could sling magic without worrying about hitting a teammate, but in tight confines like these, it was almost impossible to safely spam spells without the risk of hitting a friendly.

Elevation fixed that nicely.

The first of the mechanical contraptions had rushed into the mouth of the V-shaped funnel, herded straight into Dizzy by a combination of swift punches from Kai and vicious claw slashes, courtesy of Velkan. The iron-sided munchkin lashed out at Dizzy with the oversized wrench, but she dropped low and batted the blow aside with her war maul. The automaton was fast, though, feinting left, then driving forward and smashing in the side of her knee with his impromptu weapon. She let out a grunt of pain but somehow managed to keep her feet. Honestly, Sam had no worries about Dizzy.

Although her raw damage output wasn't quite as high as Kai's, she was a tank with enough constitution to take on a wrecking ball in a head-to-head skirmish… but there were still three more of the mechanical automatons to deal with.

Buzz Saw and Mallet peeled off in a herringbone move like a pair of seasoned warriors, rather than desperate mechanical janitorial staff. Buzz zipped toward Kai, while Mallet took a ponderous swing at Velkan. The third minion launched himself onto one of the bulky bed frames, just as Sam had, then did something completely unexpected: it lifted into the air, propelled upward by telescoping mechanical legs. It leveled its mop, bringing it into place like a sniper rifle, and started firing off globs of water at the party. One of the watery blasts side-swiped Arrow like a battering ram, knocking him onto his back.

Arrow managed to gain his feet quickly enough, though, and started launching return fire at Mop. His aim was uncanny as ever, and one of his rounds careened directly into Mop's mustached face with almost no effect at all. The razor-tipped arrow ricocheted harmlessly off the tough metallic exterior.

Sam had to imagine that piercing weapons would be at a significant disadvantage to hit against the iron-skinned androids; but he was eager to see how they held up against *magic*.

"Let's rock and roll, Bill!" he shouted as Mop focused on Arrow, who was successfully dodging the watery bolts. Velkan and Kai, however, weren't handling things quite so well in the melee department.

With a shout, Sam sent a Fire Shuriken whirling toward Buzz and an Ice Orb Shuriken screaming toward Mallet. The Fire Shuriken hit with an explosion and a flash of orange light. The force of the blow pushed the mechanical construct back a step or two and left a darkened soot smear across the creature's breastplate, but that was it. The automaton looked annoyed, but it certainly didn't seem to be hurt by the attack, which made a certain sense to Sam. The shuriken itself primarily dealt slashing damage, which wouldn't be effective against the heavy-duty metal, and the fire, likewise, wouldn't do much against something created in a forge.

His Ice Orb Shuriken, on the other hand, was *extraordinarily* effective. The paper star shattered on impact and a coat of blue-white arctic power stole across the surface of the creature's metal skin. Fingers of freezing magic crept down its arms, forming into deep crystals in the joints.

"The metal is a perfect conductor," Bill shouted in excitement. "Plus, these things are powered by steam. All we gotta do is cool the water down enough, and we'll probably take 'em out of the fight for good."

"On it," Sam shouted in reply, triggering Bookmark, then unleashing a hail of Ice-Orb Shuriken at Mallet. Already, the automaton was moving at a snail's pace, its limbs flailing around at quarter speed. The gem in its belly had begun flickering wildly, and Sam knew that could only mean one thing: the water flowing through its coolant tubes was freezing. Velkan took advantage of its handicapped state and darted forward, lashing out with his razor-sharp claws. As with the arrows, Velkan's claws bounced along the surface, leaving shallow scratches in the metal but failing to penetrate the automaton's exterior.

But Velkan was smart.

The Wolfman quickly reevaluated his tactics and readjusted, targeting the limbs and the relatively vulnerable joints. He dropped onto all fours and darted in, his mouth closing around a knee and crunching down like a hound gnawing on a bone. The metal groaned and, when Velkan shook his head, the limb snapped and popped. The automaton teetered precariously, its arms pinwheeling to compensate for the missing leg. Velkan pulled the limb from his jaws and wound it back, smashing the clunky metal foot into the bot's head with a resounding **clang**. The creature landed flat on its back, the light in its belly and eyes guttering like a candle flame before dying altogether.

"Heads up, Sam!" Arrow yelled, though his warning was about half a second too late.

An orb of water the size of a bowling ball slammed into the Mage's chest, hurling him from the bed and knocking the wind from his lungs. Sam landed hard on his side, clutching at his ribs. Thank the celestial for his Papier-Mache *Mage spell*, though. His health was still abysmally low, compared to the rest of his party members, and the armor had almost certainly saved his life. He couldn't afford to take another blow like that, however, especially not from whatever water magic Mop was slinging around.

Since his armor was literal paper, both fire and water magic types dealt significantly more damage than normal melee damage. Bill thundered, "Legs! You gotta get up! We've got an angry janitor coming in to clean house!"

"Working on it." Sam pushed himself upright with a wince, just in time to see another orb of water flying straight toward his head. He dove to the side, falling back on his rusty Judo skills as he tucked into a tight roll, which brought him to his feet. He immediately thrust a hand straight out and launched an Ice Orb Shuriken in response. Mop batted it from the air with the head of its weapon and sprang forward across the mattress tops on its telescoping legs. In seconds, the automaton was behind their lines and descending on Sam with a twirling mop of doom.

Sam acted on instinct, channeling energy into his palm and summoning his Quill Blade.

Twenty-three mana vanished in a rush, and the oversized ostrich feather poking up from his hat darted into his hand, transforming into the gleaming silver weapon he'd become so familiar with over the past few weeks. He brought the sword up high, just in time to block an overhand blow from the mechanical mop. Shifting his stance, he sidestepped and turned away the improvised cleaning-tool-turned weapon with a flick of his wrist, then shot in, slicing at Mop's exposed neck. Unfortunately, the automaton was lightning-fast and wielded its mop like a bow staff.

The cleaning implement was a whirlwind in the droid's metal fingers, dancing and swooping, blocking every attack and quickly putting Sam on the defensive. The android countered a hasty thrust and lashed out with a kick that smashed into Sam's ribs with a furious **crack**. A lance of blinding pain shot through Sam's body, making it hard to think for a moment.

"What in the abyss are you even doing?" Bill thundered at him. "You're getting beat by a mop! A *mop*, Legs! Remember your footwork! Get inside its guard and work the body. Control the fight."

"Not helping, Bill," Sam shrieked as he fought to right himself. Sweat poured down his face, and his arms were already aching from the strain of the battle.

Bill wanted him to finish this fight up close, but Sam could already see he wasn't a good enough swordsman to end things with the blade. He wasn't built for a sustained melee assault; what he needed to do was open up some distance so he could sling some magic. Thankfully, Arrow provided him with an opportunity to do just that when he launched a feathered shaft into the automaton's face. This time, his arrows were tipped with small glass vials that exploded on contact, splattering a corrosive green goop across Mop's face. The concoction sizzled and burbled, leaving corroded metal in its wake.

It also bought Sam just enough time to reach into Bill's Soul Space, pulling free a non-magical book that he'd picked up in a second-hand shop. Scrawled across the back of the volume was a simple activation rune, which would transform the boring book on common garden pests into a lethal bomb, fueled by wildly unstable Mana. With *Book Maker's Book Bomb*, Sam could weaponize any book he could get his ink-smeared fingers on. He hurled the tome into Mop's chest at less than three feet out, shouting the activation word as the book thumped into the droid. "*Flash Bang!*"

The book erupted in a curtain of golden light, enveloping the robot in a furnace of flame and oppressive heat that slapped Sam away like an oversized hand, badly singeing the skin on his exposed face.

Mop stumbled back drunkenly from the momentary inferno, armor scorched in places and charbroiled in others. The bot looked dazed and confused, and Sam didn't give it a moment to get its bearings. He launched a fresh wave of Ice Orb Shuriken, then darted in while frosty streaks of magic slowed the automaton. With a shout, he dropped low and jammed his Quill Blade through a vulnerable shoulder joint and into the bot's torso. The creature sputtered and sparked, its head spasming as its eyes grew dim, the light fading to darkness.

Sam ripped his sword free and planted a foot in the automaton's chest, knocking it to the ground with a clatter. "One down."

CHAPTER EIGHT

Sam dismissed the sword with a thought and an effort of will, then took a quick moment to survey the battlefield.

Dizzy was busy bludgeoning Wrench, the unfortunate droid, into the ground with her war maul, though she looked decidedly the worse for wear. She was limping badly, and one arm hung mostly useless at her side, burned thanks to the arc welder attached to one of the automaton's hands. But the droid had also suffered its fair share of damage. Its body was littered with dings and dents, its head partially caved in on one side. Dizzy would prevail, Sam had no doubt, but Kai was in real trouble: he was busy fending off Buzz.

The warrior monk flowed and danced, narrowly avoiding the whirring saw blade, though his arms, legs, and chest were covered in shallow cuts and deeper gouges. Despite their relatively small stature, these things were *fast.* Kai's counter blows were as ineffectual as Velkan's claws had been against Mallet. Arrow was launching more of his acid-tipped arrows at the bot, but its buzz saw was still whirling madly. The automaton hacked at the air, preventing Kai from closing the distance. Velkan was circling around, trying to flank the creature, but the bot seemed to sense the Wolfman and constantly readjusted its position.

Though Sam felt exhausted, he knew he could help level the playing field.

Taking a deep gulp of delicious air, he rushed once more for a nearby bed, springing up onto the mattress. He locked onto the target and let loose with a fresh barrage of Ice Orb Shuriken. The paper stars riddled ol' Buzz like a meteor shower, spreading their icy fingers and drastically slowing its erratic movements. But even though the mechanical munchkin was slowing, the whirling blade was generating too much friction for the frost to do its work. With that blade still swinging freely, it was too risky for Kai or Velkan to get in close. Thinking fast, Sam brought Ink Lance spinning around to the front, launching a trio of sticky jet-black globs in rapid-fire succession.

The first went wide, splattering against the wall, while the second hit the automaton in the chest. The jet-black goo spread like an ink stain and set the metal to sizzling, thanks to the spell's corrosive properties.

Damage dealt: 4 acid damage per second for 15 seconds! Target slowed by fourteen percent!

The third lance hit precisely where Sam was aiming, exploding against the screaming buzz saw in a shower of black goo. Tar-like tendrils immediately clogged the blade's mechanism and the saw lurched to a stop, the motor sparking and smoking from the strain.

"That's a *heck* of a shot," Bill crowed wildly. Sensing vulnerability, Kai launched a blindingly fast assault of fists and feet, targeting the sections of metal pitted by Arrow's acid attacks. This time, his blows landed with enough force to at least dent the metal, leaving fist-shaped craters across its torso. The automaton still had some fight left in it, though. Buzz lunged in, sweeping its motionless saw blade left to right in an attempt to disembowel the maneuvering monk.

Kai leapt straight up, executed a flawless flip in the air, and landed behind the automaton in a low crouch. He drove forward and smashed his fist through the metallic backplate, pulling out a handful of metallic guts. “Quivering Starfall Palm!”

Tubes, pistons, and delicate clockwork gears dangled from his closed fist like war medals. The light went out of the automaton's eyes, and it toppled forward, a plume of smoke drifting up from its devastated back. Dizzy raised her maul a final time and brought it down with a roar, crushing the last android’s head like a soda can.

Just like that, the battle was over.

Still reeling from his own battle, Sam slipped from the mattress with his army of tomes circling around him as he prepared for more of the little mustached minions to come scampering out of the metaphorical woodwork. But the only sounds were the clanks from the steam pipes overhead and the labored breathing of his friends. A pop up appeared a moment later, indicating that combat had officially ended.

*Exp: 738 (Maintenance Automaton Keeper x 4) (123 per Automaton * 1.5 difficulty)*

“Good thing we listened to me and started out with the barracks, am I right?” Bill quipped amid the after-battle heaving and attempts to calm down raging adrenaline. “All things considered; I’d say this went surprisingly well.”

“Yeah, that’s because you’re not the one with bruised ribs and an aching skull.” Sam winced at the sound of his own voice.

Bill flapped his covers in his imitation of a shrug. “Not my fault your bodies are so squishy and fragile.”

“I have to go with Sam on this one, book bro.” Kai lifted a forearm to show one of the many gashes crisscrossing his flesh. “Those things were tougher than any of the other enemies we’ve fought so far. Besides Octavius or some of the other players, I guess?”

“No, Bill’s right.” Dizzy mopped her sweaty forehead with the back of one hand. “Kind of. Obviously, that wasn’t an easy fight, but we won without a single casualty. In the compendium, the Barracks is listed as the *easiest* Junction. The guy who wrote the book described these things as lowly *House Keepers*. Even so, they almost killed us all. I'm not even sure these things are even *technically* monsters. Did you see their description? 'Maintenance Automaton Keeper'. I mean, in the practical sense, they're mobs, but clearly combat isn't their main function."

"Yeah," Arrow agreed with a nod. "Wrench. Mallet. Arc welder. Mop. The only one that had anything that even remotely resembled a real weapon was ol' Buzz Saw, and that was probably for pipe cutting."

Velkan dropped down into a crouch and inspected the mechanical repairmen, his ears laid flat against his skull.

"I'm guessing these are the guys responsible for keeping everything up to code." Sam opened his book and started taking notes. "If these guys are the maintenance crew, just imagine how tough the other things in this place must be. We're definitely going to have our work cut out for us."

"My thoughts exactly," Dizzy said. "Everyone stay sharp. Who knows what else could be waiting for us here? I want this barracks locked down. Arrow, Velkan, you two secure the rest of the room; make sure there aren't any more of these guys hiding in a broom closet somewhere, waiting to get the drop on us. Kai, why don't you loot our half-pint steampunk friends here? See if there's anything we can use."

"Sam." The guild leader turned her steely gaze on him. "Let's split up and look for some way to claim this Junction. My guess is there must be a switch or control box."

Sam and Bill backtracked toward the front of the entryway doors, searching the floors, ceiling, and walls for anything that stood out. Mostly, it was clunky bed frames, old mattresses, and beefy metal chests, all of which were empty. Whoever had called this place home had done a thorough job of picking up after themselves before moving on. Despite the lack of loot, Sam was still ecstatic; this place was seriously amazing. Sure, there were deadly traps around every turn, and vicious monsters to clear out, but once they managed that, this place would be perfect for a guild headquarters.

He'd only see a fraction of what the Irondowns had to offer, but the barracks alone would probably allow them to sleep fifty people or more. Having a facility like this would make recruitment a thousand times easier, once they were finally ready to expand.

"Hey, kid." Bill pulled Sam from his musings. "Up there on the wall. My magical book sense is tingling."

Inscribed onto one of the stones was a runic symbol no larger than the size of Sam's palm. The etching was dull and lifeless; if he hadn't known what to look for, it would have been easy to pass right over without a second glance. Sam was quickly gaining a mastery of runic symbols and their meanings; he certainly used them enough in his scrolls and spells. This one was about as basic as they came.

It was a distinct activation ward, not so different from the rune he used to make his Book Bombs go **kablooey**.

"Think I've got something over here," Sam called out over his shoulder. Without waiting for a reply, he approached the rune and extended a hand, pressing his palm against the marking gouged into the stone. It thrummed beneath his skin, radiating an inviting warmth that pulled at his Core. A prompt appeared a moment later:

Holy guacamole, you actually did it! You claimed a Junction on your first try! Not bad. You've narrowly *managed to defeat the Keepers of Junction 1, the Barracks, and found its corresponding Activation Rune. Once the Junction is claimed, you will be able to utilize the space with all its corresponding perks, although both Traps and Keepers will remain defunct until functionality is restored through the Control Room. More good news: the other residents of the Irondown Burrows will generally avoid this area, since it will become hostile territory.*

Would you like to trigger the Activation Rune and claim this Junction on behalf of the Wolf Pack? Yes / No.

Sam hit 'yes' and felt mana rush out from his body, pulsing down along his arms, through his hand, and into the sigil. First a trickle, then in a great roaring rush, over *half* of his five-hundred and forty-five mana abandoned him like passengers jumping over the rails of a sinking ship. The surge of power left him feeling weak and hollow inside, his knees shaking from the strain. But then the pull on his core trickled and ebbed, dying off as the crystalline lights blinked on overhead and illuminated the room in warm yellow light.

That wasn't the only change, either.

The walls swiveled out, revealing a stone armor rack beside each bed, perfect for holding gear. Across the room from him, a secret door also opened with a **click*. The* huge slab of gray stone and metal slid away to reveal a darkened room, full of mystery and potential.

Congratulations! You have claimed Junction 1 of 8. Reward, Exp: 500. Not bad; keep going at this rate, and you just might be a team to watch out for.

"Dude, like... *whoa.*" Kai spun in a slow circle as he took in the area. "This place is totally epic."

"You guys are going to want to see what's in here!" Dizzy called exuberantly, peering into the darkened chamber.

"Some sort of secret weapon stash? Please?" Sam questioned aloud. What if it was a treasure vault, containing all the goodies that the heavy trunks didn't? He beelined across the room as fast as his legs would carry him, despite the weariness from activating the Rune. He had to know. Just *had* to. He was rubbing his hands in greedy expectation, but nothing could have ever prepared him for what he saw.

Dizzy stepped into the room, and the crystalline orbs set into the walls blinked on, revealing not a hidden vault full of gold and jewels, but something that was—in its own way—worth its weight in gold.

A bathhouse-sized tub sunk into the floor.

It was a wide pool, laid with silver tiles that reflected light from the orbs like diamonds. Wisps of inviting steam drifted up and swirled in the air, dancing like sirens of mist. Brass pipes ran down the walls and disappeared into the floor, presumably to heat the water in the pool. It was glorious: a hot tub big enough to seat twenty people.

No more cold showers. No more wooden tubs in the middle of Wolfman-controlled territory. It was more than Sam ever could've asked for or imagined.

Kai immediately began stripping down to his underclothes, then cannonballed into the water with a splash. His head disappeared under the surface, only to reappear a moment later as he let out a joyous hoot, "It's amazing! The water is totally perfect, brohams. Come on in."

Everyone looked at Dizzy, but she was already scrambling to get in after Kai; who could blame her? In less than a minute, everyone had removed bulky, stained armor and luxuriated in the pool of water, soaking up the soothing heat. Except Bill, who floated just outside the water, glaring at everyone for excluding him. Despite his protests, Sam found the book eyeing the water longingly. *Wistfully,* even. Bill hadn't always been a book, and there were few pleasures better in life than a good soak after a hard day of work.

"So," Dizzy breathed out as everyone finally settled in and the mood mellowed, "Kai, did you find anything useful on our feisty metal friends?"

"Tons of scrap metal," the monk offered, spreading his hands wide. "We might be able to smelt them down for resources or sell the parts directly to collectors, but for now, I say we just leave them here. Maybe we could store them in a few of the footlockers? Carrying all that iron and steel around is going to weigh us down. Those little dudes are small, but they have to weigh a couple of hundred pounds apiece. But I also found a couple of these."

He reached over into his gear and pulled out four glimmering sapphires, each the size of a silver dollar. "Trash-tier monster Cores. Worth three hundred experience points a pop. They'd probably fetch a wicked-good price on the market."

"It is true," Velkan agreed easily. "My kind values such cores highly. They are valuable components in many of our most potent spells. The Shaman Yurij Brightblood would pay well for them, if you had a mind to sell."

"No." Sam shook his head. "With my Coreless Spell Infusion, we basically have a license to print money. Between me and Bill, we can produce enough spell scrolls to keep the Wolf Pack in the black. They're worth more to us as experience; that, or we hang onto them for Finn. See if he could use them for anything. Let's pocket them for now?"

"So what's next?" Kai asked as he tucked away the four Cores in a leather pouch attached to his gear.

"It's late," Dizzy murmured as she rubbed at her eyes, "and I know everyone's beat, but I suppose we could push on. Maybe try to capture another Junction before we call it a day? I wouldn't mind taking the Kitchen."

Bill laughed, the sound rippling through the room. "Are you kidding me? Guys, I don't want to be the Debbie Downer here, but this room was the easiest of the bunch, and we barely made it out. Our party almost got wiped by something whose only weapon was a mop. A *mop*. Maybe if we had our party at full strength…? But with Finn and Sphinx gone? Yeah, no. Listen, I've been in the adventure game long enough to know when to hold 'em and when to fold 'em. Right now, we should fold."

"Yeah, but we have no idea how long it'll be before Finn or Sphinx get back," Arrow argued. "Could be *days*. As much as I like sitting around and soaking up the water, we can't afford to waste that kind of time."

"So we *don't* waste it," Sam slowly stated, even as the thought appeared in his head. "We use it to get better. That's always the answer, right? We train. I mean, the Forest of Chlorophyll Chaos is new to all of us, with the exception of Velkan. True, some of the areas in the Irondowns might be a little out of our league right now, but I bet there are a ton of things out there in the forest that we could grind for points. I'm just a single level away from surpassing my wisdom threshold, and Dizzy's on track to push past the strength threshold. I say we get some sleep, hit the forest as soon as the sun's up, and find some monsters to kill."

"Why wait?" Velkan grunted and waved at the exit. "If your goal is to 'get gud,' as I have heard many of you humans say, then there is no time better than the present. If you desire to increase specific traits, then the best place is the Totem Grounds."

"Totem Grounds?" Sam tested the new words while cocking an eyebrow.

"Wolfmen training grounds," Velkan replied, as though that said everything that needed saying.

"I'm on board," Arrow enthused, "but it seems like making a run in the morning would be better, when we aren't all exhausted, and hungry."

"No." Velkan flicked his ears. "Sleep deprivation, hunger, and physical exhaustion are good; they lower the walls of pride and help bring out the truth. This is a lesson all Wolfmen know. How you fight when you are tired is how you truly fight. Who you truly are. The Totem Grounds will push you to the very edge of yourself. If you are *already* at the very edge of yourself, the training will be even more effective. Such is the way of The People."

"I say we do it!" Bill chimed in.

"You *would;* you never need sleep." Sam snorted, then paused, tapping idly at the water with his fingers. "Still... I think Velkan has a good point. My dad always says that the greatest challenges give us the greatest opportunities to grow. Growing isn't always fun, but it is always good. I'm game if everyone else is."

"Sam's right." Dizzy seemed down that she hadn't been the one to come up with the concept.

Bill stage-coughed. "Uh, 'Sam' is a funny way to say my name."

Dizzy snorted and rolled her eyes. She stood with a splash, the ghost of a smile on her face, "Fine. Bill's *also* right. So what are we waiting for? Let's go do some growing."

CHAPTER NINE

It was full dark when they finished dressing and left the Irondown Burrows behind, trading heated water and comfy beds for biting mosquitoes and the gloomy shadows engulfing the Forest of Chlorophyll Chaos. Arrow was disgruntled, and Dizzy seemed to be on the *hangry* side, since Velkan insisted that they forgo eating. The Wolfman was as stoic as ever, but Kai and Bill both seemed to be in good moods, and Sam was actually feeling pretty happy with the choice to venture out right away. He was tired, and his muscles ached from the strain of the day, but he knew that nothing good in life came without putting in the work.

Even in the dark tangle of the forest, Velkan navigated the landscape like a homing pigeon, moving with the sure footsteps of someone who had walked this path a thousand times. Except he insisted he'd never come this way before. That was his Bushcraft skill at work. The Wolfman seemed to instinctively know when to duck hanging branches or sidestep snagging roots that tripped up others.

Though he had only the wan light of the stars and moon to navigate by, Velkan never missed a beat or a step. As for how he knew *where* to go, he said that was something all Wolfmen could do, and insisted that eventually they would be able to do the same as their connection to The People grew. The Wolfman outposts moved constantly, so the Shamans had devised a spell that allowed The People to sense the Totem Grounds, which were always located near the Den; a neat trick that demonstrated that the Wolfman were far more than the monstrous beasts the humans made them out to be.

It took the crew almost an hour of hard trekking before they emerged from a thick pocket of trees and encountered the looming palisade walls of *New Narvik*. The landscape had changed. The pine trees, maples, and firs were gone, replaced by bushy hemlock, towering ash, and gnarled, moss-covered oaks, but honestly, New Narvik looked nearly identical to Old Narvik. Warm firelights illuminated the night, silhouetting the Wolfman sentries peering down from the guard towers that dotted the perimeter. Seeing the different, yet somehow *same,* outpost, was oddly reassuring. Sam hadn't realized just how much he'd come to enjoy their time in the mobile Wolfmen village.

"This way." Velkan jerked his head away from the palisade walls and toward a wide clearing off in the distance.

"Can you tell us any more about the Totem Grounds?" Sam inquired as they walked, forging through the swaying grasses surrounding the newly constructed outpost. "Obviously it's used for training, but what kind of training? Is it like an obstacle course, or are we going to be fighting monsters?"

"You will fight monsters," Velkan replied, glancing back over his shoulder, his golden eyes gleaming with hidden delight. "But not the sort you are thinking of. They are the monsters inside yourself. The People value strength. Every interaction is designed to refine. To make us better than we are. Even a simple touch..."

He extended a claw and, with a flash, left a searing scratch across a surprised Sam's cheek. "...Can improve us. This fortifies our constitution and hardens our flesh. It is not only strength of body we value, but strength of character, will, and mind."

Velkan tapped on his temple. "It is within the mind of a wolf where true strength must be cultivated. Our greatest enemy is not others, but ourselves. Our own weakness and fear. The Seven Totems are empowered by the Sacred Shamans of Old. They allow us to train our seven individual attributes: Strength, Dexterity, Constitution, Intelligence, Wisdom, Charisma, and Perception. No two training sessions are the same. The Spirit Guides bound to the Totem give us what we need to push us or break us. Often, you will experience death within the Totem Grounds."

"Wait. *Death*?" Sam's eyebrows rose in surprise. "But Wolfmen can't respawn."

"This is the secret," Velkan replied cryptically, "because inside of the Totem Grounds, death is only a stepping stone toward rebirth. It is a special place. We are here."

He gestured to a mostly empty clearing that looked remarkably similar to the grassy sea they'd just trekked across. Mostly clear wasn't *entirely* clear; there were seven gateways arrayed in a circle, though they didn't seem to lead anywhere except to the center of the meadow. Each gateway consisted of two massive wooden poles, carved to resemble fearsome creatures, with a simple wooden beam running across the top.

"Walk with me. This is the Totem Ground, a place to master self. Each Totem Gateway represents a single characteristic." Velkan growled, setting off to lead them in a lap around the clearing. He waved toward a gateway, held up by a burly bear covered in tribal swirls. "Mother Bear represents the strength of the arm and body. Father Bison, constitution. The power of stamina and fortitude. On and on, it goes. Brother Peacock, charisma. Sister Rat, perception. Cousin Crow, intelligence. Great Auntie Owl, wisdom. Uncle Monkey, dexterity."

"I'm sorry," Bill interrupted with barely contained mirth. "Did I just hear there's a monkey's uncle? Just me? Fine."

"Our People use these Totems," Velkan continued, unperturbed by Bill's commentary, "to both increase our levels through experience gains, as well as to refine individual attributes. You may go in as a group, but for first time, is best you go alone."

"Dude, this is totally *Zen.*" Kai was grinning madly. "I'm all about this aesthetic. Like the spirit animals and stuff. So rad."

"Yeah, sure. It's cool," Arrow admitted, his tone far more cautious, "but you still haven't told us what actually happens once we go in. Is it a time trial? Or are there waves of monsters?"

Velkan just nodded his head. "Yes. It is all of those. As I said, the Totems decide what will grow you best, and they will set the trial accordingly."

"That sounds a lot like the trial I went through when I first entered Eternium," Sam stated, getting nods from the others. "I wonder if it works on the same principle?"

"No idea. Dibs on Father Bison!" Kai took off at a sprint for a gateway held up by a stylized buffalo rearing up, its great horned head raised toward the sky. Kai's legs were a blur as he ran. Everyone watched as he dashed through the gateway without even pausing… and disappeared.

There one second, gone the next.

Bill let out a low whistle. "Does that look familiar, Sam?"

"Yeah," Sam replied with a bob of his head. He had definitely seen power like that before… but only in one place. The Mage's College. "That looks an awful lot like spatial magic."

"Bingo-bongo," Bill chimed like a dinner bell. "Spatial magic is impressive enough on its own, but the fact that these Shamans can tear those things down and pop 'em back up in a day? That's some next level spell-craft, if you ask me. Usually, spatial magic is built around fixed temporal points, but they must be using the Totem Gateways themselves as artifact anchor points. I wonder how they're powering them, though? That kinda magic doesn't come cheap, and there's no way they can draw from the users, since most of the Wolfmen don't actively have a mana pool."

"Any idea how this works, Velkan?" Sam prodded hopefully.

The Wolfman just shook his shaggy head. "This is a thing of Shamans. It is not for us to know, only to accept that it works."

<Gotta be an uber-powerful monster Core,> Bill sent silently, not wanting to upset Velkan with his academic thoughts. <I bet these Totem Guardians are similar to dungeon bosses. Abyss, these might even be portable instances. Wild that these fur-faces are just sitting on some of the most powerful magic I've ever seen in my life, and I've been around a good, long time.>

"Alright." Arrow pulled his bow from his back, then checked his quiver. "I guess my interest is officially piqued. Looks like I'll be a Monkey's Uncle."

"*Thank* you!" Bill shouted. "Finally."

"No, *Uncle* Monkey," Velkan corrected, as though speaking to a daft child.

"Well, what are we waiting for?" Bill hurried Sam along before he had to choose last. "Come on; let's go explore already. I gotta know how this works. Since you're what, two points away from the wisdom threshold, I say we go see what ol' Auntie Owl has to throw at us."

"Guess that leaves me with the strength bear." Dizzy pulled free her war maul with an expression of grim determination. "Be safe in there, Sam. I'll see you back on the other side."

Sam moseyed along at a much slower pace, using the time to conjure his spell tomes. He was running low on pages in his Papier-Mache Mage volume. Each use cost twenty-five sheets, since it took proportionally more paper to cover a person than it did to fold a throwing star; by contrast, the Shuriken spells had a one-to-one ratio. He had enough remaining for one use, but he didn't want to waste it, so he left that tome tucked away inside Bill's Soul Space and opted instead for Ink Lance, Fire, Ice, and Paralysis Shuriken, as well as his ultimate AoE spell: Rorschach Test.

As ready as he was ever going to be, Sam stepped with Bill through the Owl-Totem gateway and right into the heart of a raging blizzard. He whirled around and found the Totem gateway behind him, looking out on the swaying, grassy meadow outside New Narvik. Everything else was different. He was somewhere high in mountains that reminded him of the white caps of the Rockies in the dead of winter: all jutting gray stone and snow-swept peaks as far as he could see. He caught a blur of movement in the corner of his vision and spun again. A person bundled in a mass of blankets trudged along a winding, snow-packed trail.

No, not a person, Sam realized after a second. Something else.

Nearly as big as a bear, the thing somehow had the head of a barn owl and a pair of curling deer antlers protruding from its feathery scalp. It wasn't alone. A trio of tiny creatures, two or three feet tall and covered in thick white fur, danced around the horned owl's feet, harassing the much larger creature with scratching claws and jagged, biting fangs. The owl was doing all it could to get away, slapping at the white-furred things with gangly simian-like arms and lashing out with taloned feet. Despite its best efforts, they were too fast, and their frantic attacks were becoming more persistent by the second.

<Don't just blunder in,> Bill sent silently into Sam's head. <Look at the situation. *Think* about it. What's the best play here, huh?>

Sam's gut reaction was to shoot first and ask questions later, but he didn't have all the answers. Not even close. Who would he even shoot? He squinted against the howling winds and considered the scene more carefully.

If he fired on whatever those white-furred creatures were, he risked bringing them down upon himself, which could spell disaster. What were they, and could he beat them in a brawl? Three on one wasn't especially good odds. Even if he did manage to hurt them or drive them off, what were the chances that he would then have to face down the owl monster? Was it better to just wait things out and let the monsters kill each other, then mop up whatever remained? That was his initial reaction, but after watching the owl for a moment, he tossed the idea right out the window.

Although the owl-thing wasn't human, it was wearing traveler's robes… and the fear in its golden eyes was very real and telling. Plus, this *was* the Totem of Great Auntie Owl. He couldn't just leave it to die, not if he could help. He *could* help.

Ice Orb probably wouldn't do much against the white puffballs of teeth and malice, but those little critters looked flammable enough. With a thought and a whisper of mana, Sam unleashed a wave of Shuriken, peppering the creatures in an onslaught of fire and folded paper. His stars sliced through thick, matted tangles of hair, leaving black char marks in their wake. The creatures howled and rounded on him, their beady red eyes like hot, angry coals. They squawked at each other, gibbering like monkeys, then dashed toward him as one, propelling themselves forward on all fours with gorilla-like gaits.

"Quick thinking," Bill scoffed condescendingly. "Glad we made the right choice there, by bringing them down on us like a plague. Cool. Cool, cool."

"These things look scary, but they *don't* look very smart," Sam shot back, bringing a brown volume with a gold spine to the active position. Rorschach Test was his only current AoE spell. Sam rarely deployed it because it cost a staggering one-hundred and fifty sheets per use. He could only cast that spell twice before needing to resupply, but it was a *great* ace in the hole when things got dicey. Like right now, for instance. Pages and ink burst forth in a whirlwind, spinning and distorting as they took to the sky, morphing into a single giant scroll.

Because of his position, Sam couldn't see what was inked on the front side of the floating sheet, but from the spell description, he knew the little horror shows would be seeing a giant Rorschach Test; one designed to induce absolute terror. The three white-furred critters skittered to a stop; their eyes wide in abject fear. Without missing a beat, they broke in every direction, each one wailing in hysteria as they disappeared, swallowed by the swirling blizzard. The fright Sam had seen on their faces was a firm reminder that you really were your own worst enemy.

"Hurry, child," the owl cawed. "They won't stay away long. Best we seek shelter. My cave is just here." It nodded toward a dark fissure, partially obscured by a snow drift. Without waiting for a reply, the owl creature ducked its antlered head and dipped into the crack.

"You sure about this?" Bill whispered against the wind. "This could be some sort of elaborate trap."

"Yeah," Sam replied with a shrug, "but I don't think it is. I know that thing looks like a monster, but so do *you*... and here we are."

"Hey, I resemble that remark!" Bill protested with a chuckle. "Though I suppose, to be fair, you have a point. I *hate* the snow. If that thing is going to murder us horribly and wear your skin like a coat, at least *I'll* be warm. I say throw caution to the ice-wind and do it."

"Always glad to have you in my corner, Bill." Sam tromped through the shin-deep powder and wriggled into the fissure in the rock face. He gulped, half expecting to be greeted by flashing claws. But that didn't happen. Instead, the narrow passage slowly shifted to the left, then opened out into a single-room cavern with a small fire already burning inside in a stone-ringed pit. The owl creature crouched on the far side of the pit; its clawed hands held up to the crackling flames.

"Well, come on in then." Its voice was distinctly feminine. matronly.

"Are you Great Auntie Owl?" Sam quizzed as he padded forward to feel the delightful warmth of the flames on his skin.

"Indeed I am. Indeed I am. Now come. Sit. Let me make you a cup of tea to thank you for your help."

"It was nothing," Sam waved away the remark.

"Oh, but that is where you are wrong, young one." She rustled her wings, pulled aside her thick robes, and revealed a silver teapot, which she slowly prepared and placed next to the fire to warm. "You see, young man, you could've done nothing. Yet you chose to act, at great personal cost to yourself, no less. That is the first lesson to learn: Both action and inaction are choices, and all choices matter. Our choices are cumulative, you see. Why, you wouldn't be here if that weren't so. A human Mage, where only wolf pups tread? I can only begin to fathom the choices that have brought you to my humble cave."

She fell silent as her little teapot vented a small column of white steam, producing a pair of porcelain teacups with an artful flourish before carefully pouring each of them a cup. Sam watched her drink first, making sure it wasn't poison, then tentatively took a sip. It tasted like old bathwater and mud. He suppressed a wince and held his tongue.

"There's wisdom in that, too; knowing when to hold your tongue, and when to speak," the old owl crooned, seeming to catch the gesture. She sipped slowly, evidently savoring the flavor of the awful concoction. "Tell me why you attacked the *Yorlings* and not me, hmmm?"

"Because he's a bleeding-heart softie," Bill scathingly replied on Sam's behalf. "I tried to advise him to ride it out, but no~o~o, not Sam. Kid's always got to *do* something."

"Perhaps this one could learn a little about holding his tongue." She blinked, the motion slow and ponderous. A weight seemed to settle over them. Magic, but like no spell that Sam had ever felt before. When he glanced at Bill, he saw with great astonishment that the book's eyes were closed. He was asleep. That was impossible. Bill never slept. He couldn't.

"Sometimes, you will find wisdom takes a quiet mind." The owl turned her attention back to Sam, ignoring the softly snoring book. "Now answer: Why spare me and not them, hmmm?"

Sam shrugged as he tried to regain his bearings. "I don't know. I guess the safer bet was to let you all duke it out? That way, whoever was left alive would've been weaker if it came down to a fight. But then I saw your eyes. There was something there that I connected with. The fear, maybe? Or the pain… hard to say. All I know is that I hate bullies, and those things looked like bullies to me. It was a risk, but I would rather take a risk in doing what I think is right than play it safe by doing what I feel is wrong."

"A *wise* choice, it was. Had you waited, I would've turned on you the very moment I dispatched the Yorlings." The great owl nodded sagely before hunching forward, peering at him with too-big eyes. Weighing him. Measuring and evaluating him. "Level ten Bibliomancer. Rare, but I would've destroyed you in seconds in my wrath."

Sam's blood ran cold under her withering stare. "What wisdom would that have taught me?"

"That not all things are as they seem. That a scorned foe is more dangerous than a hungry wolf." She leaned back and offered him what he took to be a smile, her beak cracking just a hair. "But that is not what happened. You took the risk. You trusted yourself and earned the wisdom of experience. Now, drink."

Sam suppressed a grimace but took another long pull to be polite. This time, though, the tea tasted sweeter on his tongue. It hit his belly with a pleasant warmth that spread through his limbs. He felt tired, but not anxious. He dreamily stated, "This isn't at all what I was expecting. I mean, the monsters. The fighting. *That* was what I was expecting. But not this."

He swept an arm around the cave.

"Wisdom comes in many forms." The wizened owl's voice seemed to reverberate in his brain. "There is the wisdom of the battlefield, an insight born through bloodshed and hurt. Such is the lesson you would've learned, had you failed to intervene. But there is also the wisdom of the kind soul. I can see that you are bold and decisive when confronted with an external enemy, but in your own mind, you are divided."

"Your path is clouded. However, since you have shown me a kindness, I will show you one in return, young one." She reached forward with her enormous, gangly arms and tapped his forehead, then took the cup and pressed it to Sam's lips, forcing the remaining tea into his mouth. Now it tasted of honey and wildflowers. "Wisdom is bitter at first, but sweeter the more you taste of it. You have walked a strange path to end up here. The unwalked path requires the greatest wisdom to navigate. Trust your instincts, and remember... all is not as it seems. Often the road scorned conceals the greatest treasures of all."

The owl blinked her eyes again, the weight returning and settling over him like a heavy blanket. "Follow your gut. Embrace the eccentric, for there lies true power."

Sam was so tired that he hardly saw the notice that popped up across his vision.

Wow. I can't believe she actually talked with you. She usually just eats people!

Wisdom +2.

By surpassing two thresholds, you have upgraded the title Soul-Bound Level 1 to Soul-Bound Level 2 (Upgradable)! Effect: Receive a one-time character bonus as a result of absorbing a portion of the Bibliomancer's Sacred Tome's Characteristic Points. +1 Strength, +3 Dexterity, +1 Constitution, +5 Intelligence, +4 Wisdom, +2 Charisma, +2 Perception, -5 Karmic Luck (Artificially Artifact bonus).

As you bind more closely with the Bibliomancer's Sacred Tome, you can upgrade this title to a maximum of Soul-Bound Level 4, unlocking a new, one-time character bonus with each successive upgrade! Until the maximum rank, this title cannot be combined with any other title, nor removed for any reason.

Warning! You have reached fifty points in wisdom! This one's going to hurt, but it's going to be worth it. As they say, wisdom is better than silver and more valuable than gold. Real power waits just on the other side. Body modification in process in three... two... one...

CHAPTER TEN

"I've got you." Two powerful arms reached down and pulled Sam into a princess carry, and his face was cradled against a warm feather bed that moved as whoever held him sprinted away. Sam tried to understand where he was, what had happened, but his senses weren't to be trusted, and his mind was spinning. Had he taken a blow to the head?

He pulled in a deep breath, the smell of blood, fire, and an animalistic scent that reminded him of thanksgiving meals with his family warred in his sinuses. Confusion and curiosity forced Sam to open his bleary eyes, and he looked up at the person holding him; but frankly, that didn't help his confusion at all.

A pair of arms that wouldn't look out of place on a body-building gorilla were cradling him against a feathery chest. There was armor above that, it had to be armor, a helmet that was shaped like a plague-mask… no, a vermillion bird from legends? Or… Sam flinched as the head tilted down, and he peered into a clearly avian eye. "Master, fear not. This humble servant will ensure your safety, no matter what. Don't worry, they'll love you. They'll have no choice."

They stopped suddenly on the edge of a cliff, and another of the bird-beasts rubbed something on his forehead, splashing it in his eyes so that Sam sputtered and wiped the fluid away.

At that moment, his protector lifted him into the air, its huge hands supporting him under his armpits, and he dangled over the cliff as thousands of humans, Wolfmen, and animals of all types trumpeted and screamed in excitement before bowing toward him.

The creature flipped him around so they were face-to-face, and opened its beak…

Bawkawwwwwk!

"What in the abyss-" Sam spasmed awake in fright, and the avian scream faded from his mind, replaced by the sound of gently lapping waves. A mixture of confusion and disorientation hit him in equal measures. For a lengthy moment, he couldn't remember what had happened, where he was, or how he gotten… well, wherever in the abyss *here* was.

It was dark, and he felt the gentle warmth of water surrounding him, which was strange. Had he fallen asleep in the bathtub? No, that didn't explain the sound of the water. Almost like surf…? For a brief moment, his mind flashed back to his summer days in high school.

His family would frequently head down from Orange County when the brutal inland heat rolled in around July, making for the cooler coastal air of San Diego, Pacific Beach, or La Jolla. They would rent a beachfront AirBnB for a week and spend the days and nights soaking up the sun and the waves during the day and congregating around beach bonfires at night, toasting s'mores while Sam's dad played the guitar and sang old classic rock tunes. He'd fallen asleep more than a few times around those bonfires, lulled into slumber by the sound of his dad's singing and the rhythmic splash of the inrushing evening tides.

This reminded him of those days, but the water was too warm.

"Are you finally awake?" came a familiar voice, though one that he couldn't quite place. "Hey, Eternium to Legs. You awake or what, huh?"

Bill. Right. Bill.

He wasn't sprawled out on the sandy shores of some

southern California beach; he was in Eternium. He blinked away the haze of sleep, his mind slowly clearing, and finally focused on his surroundings. He lay partially submerged in a pool of crystal-clear water with wisps of steam curling up from the surface. The light orbs set within the walls were off, leaving the bathing area shrouded in darkness, but suddenly he realized where he was: back in the Irondown Burrows, in the bathing facility attached to their newly claimed Barracks. The real question now was how in the world he'd *gotten* here.

The last thing he remembered was sitting around a flickering fire, drinking tea with a monstrous owl creature while a blizzard raged outside of a mountain cave. He'd been drinking tea… terrible at first, but better with every sip, and then… it was hard to say. He could only remember snatches, but one thing jumped right to the forefront of his mind. "Bill! You fell asleep!"

"Tell me about it. I haven't slept, *really* slept, since the College bookified me all those years ago. I mean sure, meditative coma, but that's not the same thing as sleeping. I *dreamed*." The tome choked up. "I saw my old life again. Saw my family. Saw things and remembered things I didn't think were possible. At least, not for me. If I ever see that old bird again, I'm gonna kiss her right on her ugly owl mug! Seriously, I haven't felt this good in *ages*."

"Yeah, me too." Sam was rather surprised about that fact himself. His muscles felt fresh and strong, and though he was still a little groggy, he was surprisingly clear-headed in other ways. It wasn't *quite* the same feeling as when he'd surpassed the intelligence threshold—his head suddenly crammed with knowledge he'd never known before—but it was definitely in the same ballpark. His thoughts were more *orderly*. It was almost as though his head had been a messy office before, full of books and papers all thrown together in a haphazard jumble without any real rhyme or reason. Now, however, it was like his family housekeeper had gone through and put everything in its place.

Papers neatly organized and filed into cabinets. Books all

alphabetically placed onto bookshelves. All the assorted nooks and crannies of his mind dusted and filled with memories, like baubles on display for visiting guests. He hadn't leveled up—he still needed almost ten thousand more experience points until he hit level eleven—but thanks to his time in the Totem Grounds, he'd managed to break through the wisdom threshold. That was the cause of this astonishing clarity. Someone *had* come through his mind and tidied up.

But he still didn't know what had happened to the others, or how in the world he'd gotten back here, and it was high time he figured that out. He stood with a splash of water and padded out of the pool, grabbing a neatly folded towel that lay waiting for him in the corner. He dried himself, spending a few minutes to get his luscious mane of hair under control, then headed back out into the barracks proper.

"Hey, look who's finally back to the land of the living!" Kai was bright-eyed and grinning from ear to ear. There was something different about him, a glow that burned with pent-up vitality.

"We were worried for you for a while." Arrow was sitting with his legs crossed on top of his mattress, fletching arrows by hand, nimble fingers attaching colorful feathers to wooden shafts quicker than thought.

"What happened?" Sam rubbed the back of his neck as he squinted against the light.

"We found you passed out face-down in the grass outside of the Owl Totem gateway," Dizzy announced as she strutted into the room. "Well, *they* found you, anyway. They found me face down outside the Bear Totem, covered in black goop and smelling like the inside of a clogged sewer pipe."

"Does that mean you passed a threshold?" Sam quirked an eyebrow.

"Strength. Finally hit fifty." She straightened, lifted an arm, and flexed. She looked visibly bigger than she had before, but it wasn't just the sheer size. There was more muscle definition. It was also deeper than that; it showed in the way she carried herself. She was like a sheathed blade. A coiled spring on the verge of bursting loose.

"I've never felt better," she released a happy sigh of contentment, "but divines above, was it an unpleasant experience. I got stuck in something called the Goldilocks scenario. Three bears challenged me to a series of strength tests. Like a Strongman contest, but with hungry bears. Actually passing through the threshold? It felt like having my whole body shoved into a wood chipper."

"Certainly sounds way less fun than our tea-time experience with Auntie Owl," Bill smugly informed her.

"Wait. You had *tea*... and broke through?" Kai sounded genuinely confused. For the next few minutes, they swapped stories, sharing about all the craziness they'd experienced on the other side of their respective totems. Sam and Bill detailed their quick and dirty battle against the white-furred Yorlings, then explained about their fireside chat with the monstrous owl creature.

Kai's trip through the Totem Grounds was far less peaceful, though the monk seemed thrilled with both the experience and the results. Apparently, he'd stepped through the gateway and into an unending stampede of enormous, angry bison. He'd had to sprint to stay ahead of wave after wave of charging buffalo, or risk being ground into the dust by razor sharp hooves or gored with ebony horns. Like the Running of the Bulls, but with certain doom on the line for a single slip-up. It sounded horrifying, but Kai insisted that there was no better training motivation on the planet than the threat of imminent and painful death. Although he hadn't passed the constitution threshold, he had gained two points and two hundred experience points.

Arrow was a bit more tight-lipped about his encounter, but from what he did share, Sam got the sense that it involved dodging and plucking rotten fruit from the air as it was hurled by a chipper, though oversized, chimp. Velkan had slipped into the Totem of Cousin Crow, but whatever he had undergone within, he kept to himself; the experience was a sacred ritual to The People, and he wasn't even remotely interested in discussing the details of his enlightenment. That said, he seemed delighted that the rest of his adopted packmates had so enjoyed their time within the training grounds.

Not that he said so, but there were subtle signs. The tilt of his head, the position of his ears, the slight flare at the edges of his mouth. For a Wolfman, he was practically bouncing on his toes in joy.

"Honestly, I can't wait to go back." Dizzy strapped freshly cleaned armor into place. "I could use a constitution boost, for sure. I'm thinking we head over as soon as you're ready to go, Sam."

"Same," Kai replied. "I'm crazy-stoked to see what Sister Rat has to offer. I could use a few extra points in perception."

"As excited as I am about the Totem Grounds," Sam countered their enthusiasm with logic, "I think we need to focus on the Irondown Burrows first. Things sort of came together for me last night. I think I know what specialization and secondary profession I want, but I need to check something out before I decide for sure."

Everyone offered him and Bill quizzical glances. Bill flapped his pages at them indignantly. "Hey, don't look at me. This is news to me, too. Care to share with the rest of the class what you're thinking?"

Sam shifted uncertainty from foot to foot under the weight of their expectant gazes. "I'd rather not. Something that Auntie Owl said to me just sorta stuck in my head. She told me to trust my instincts. She said that the road scorned conceals the greatest treasures of all, and that the path of the eccentric carries true power. It might be nothing, but I have a hunch I'd like to explore."

"Hey," Dizzy raised her hands in surrender. "If you want to play your cards close to your chest, that's fine with me. Just tell us what you're thinking."

"Well, we need to capture more Junctions." Sam put

forward his plan. "I mean, we're rested and fresh. Plus, I've crossed the wisdom threshold, and you just surpassed the strength threshold. Seems as good a time as any to challenge the next boss."

"Fair enough," Dizzy allowed, even as she pointed out the obvious. "We aren't ready for the more difficult Junctions like the Armory or the Control Room, but the Kitchen doesn't look too challenging. Or do you want us to push for the Library? You looking for some type of book, maybe?"

Sam cleared his throat sheepishly. "Actually, the boss I'm thinking about tackling is a little more… *unconventional.* I want to try to take the Husbandry Pen."

"The Husbandry Pen?" Dizzy gave him a flat stare as she crossed her arms. "Your grand hunch about obtaining power is for us to go capture the Husbandry Pen. Instead of the Library… or even the Kitchen?"

"Hey, he doesn't share everything with me, either," Bill offered apologetically, clearly as confused as everyone else.

"Please?" Sam turned on a thousand-watt smile. "I don't want to say more until I can confirm a few things, but I'm telling you, some of the answers I need lie in the Husbandry Pen."

"This wisdom is passed on from Great Auntie Owl?" Velkan inadvertently assisted Sam, who nodded. "It is decided, then. We will take the Husbandry Pen. Great Auntie Owl, like Wisdom itself, is a fickle creature. She rarely speaks with visitors directly, and it is doubtful she will speak with you again. If she has imparted such wisdom, we must heed it. To ignore her words would be to our detriment."

"Yeah, I totally agree with my fur bro," Kai concurred as he finished tying the cloth protective wraps around his wrists. "Sounds weird, but if this is, like, the will of the universe or whatever, who are we to stand in its way? Besides, we need to capture all of the Junctions anyway, and this one will probably be easier than most."

"Not only that," Sam pulled out the Compendium and

flipped to the section about the Irondown Burrows, "but there is an added bonus."

He tapped on a rough sketch of the dungeon layout. "There's an auxiliary entrance that connects to the Husbandry Pen. A secret backdoor. Might be nice to have a second way in and out of this place that only we know about. Besides, I think we have a decent chance against whatever the Junction Guardian is. 'Husbandry Pen, the foulest of fowl, very protective, but not terribly dangerous. Still, proceed with some caution'."

"Jeesh." Dizzy rolled her eyes. "Fine. *Fine*. You've sold me. Let's go tangle with whatever nasty surprise is waiting for us in the Husbandry Pen. If we get our butts handed to us, I'm blaming you, Sam."

They took another few minutes to gear up, then set off for the next Junction, located past the kitchen proper and down a winding tunnel. The traps in this section of the Burrows were just as brutal as those they'd faced on the way in, but now that Arrow knew what to look for, they had far fewer close encounters of the deadly kind. There was one new trap—a floor maze with a series of pressure-plated tiles that needed to be navigated in the correct order.

Better still, they didn't run into any mechanical minions looking to defend their territory. In next to no time, the party found the hallway gently rising, heading toward a room with sunlight streaming in. The passageway eventually leveled out, dead-ending at a gate reinforced with thick iron bars. On the other side was their destination.

The room itself was constructed of gray stone, all carefully parceled into gated stalls, perfect for housing animals. A crystalline dome overhead let in plentiful sunlight, and a heavy steel door, inset into the far wall, presumably led to the secondary entryway into the Burrows. Unfortunately, standing in their way was the Guardian, and the Compendium hadn't been lying… it truly was the *fowlest* of beasts.

Kai laughed and Arrow chuckled, but a ferocious scowl

from Dizzy quickly silenced both of them. She growled under her breath, "I don't care what it looks like. We don't want to draw its attention. Remember, a hipster mech with a mop nearly caved in our heads yesterday. Let's keep some perspective?"

It was great advice, but honestly, it wasn't hard to understand Kai and Arrow's amusement. In the center of the Pen waited a mechanical chicken the size of a Rottweiler. The oversized bird had been cobbled together from steel plates and bronze cogs; the scraps studded with thick iron rivets. It roosted in a nest of shredded paper and loose bits of metal; its eyes closed to the world. Sam would've thought it was dead, or at least out of commission, if not for the fact that it clucked gently every eight seconds.

"I'm sorry," Bill lightly sneered, "but how seriously can we take this? It's a chicken. *A chicken*, for those in the back of the classroom."

"People might say the same about you," Sam shot down further arguments. "I mean, you're *only* a book."

"Eh, touché." Bill drifted over to Sam's shoulder and lightly **whapped** him on the head. "I'm dangerous, though, and don't you forget it."

"Besides, I bet it has some wicked sharp claws." Sam ignored the book's antics. "That bronze beak looks sharp enough to punch through armor."

"Sam's right. Chickens can be mean." Dizzy shuddered at a memory. "My grandpa used to have a farm, and during the summer, we'd go to harvest the eggs from the coop. Some of those birds left scars that I still have. But since you're so sure of yourself, Bill, maybe you and Sam want to go in first?"

"*Phft*," Bill rolled his eyes. "The kid might have a point about not judging certain things by their covers, but it is *still* a chicken. I'll bet ten gold that Sam and I can take this thing out by ourselves."

"Hey, that's my money," Sam protested weakly.

"We share a soul," Bill replied matter-of-factly, "so I think that whole *mi casa es su casa* thing extends to our wallet. Now don't be a wuss. Let's go show these turkeys that we have nothing to be scared of from this overgrown turkey."

"As much as I'd *love* to take your money," Dizzy snapped at them, "we don't have time to be taking unnecessary risks. Besides, if you died, which you *would*, the AI would punish you ruthlessly for such an act of utter stupidity. We can't afford to have Sam—notice I said *Sam*—sidelined for a day or two. So, we're doing this together."

"There is much wisdom in this," Velkan grunted. "We Wolfmen respect all of our adversaries, but there is only one foe we truly fear: the might of the fearsome Cobra Chicken. She and her honking offspring are truly a force to be reckoned with. This creature is close kin and not to be underestimated. Best to take no chances."

Velkan seemed to be as serious as a heart attack, his delivery absolutely deadpan, which only set Arrow and Kai off into another roaring fit of giggles. Dizzy rolled her eyes and threw a brass lever protruding from the wall. The bars let out a clatter as they withdrew into the floor and, of course, the metal hen's eyes popped open, burning like red coals.

A Devil Chicken if ever there was one.

It stood slowly and spread great metal wings, light gleaming off of razor-edged feathers. It flexed its feet, each one as big as a yard rake and capped with glimmering claws. Suddenly, Sam recalled hearing about how the Australians had lost a war against emus. At the time, it had seemed funny ,but now that he was starting down a giant steel murder-chicken. it somehow seemed far less amusing.

The chicken opened its beaked mouth and let out an inhuman shriek that sent shivers racing up Sam's spine.

CHAPTER ELEVEN

"Everyone get to the stalls! *Now!*" Dizzy bellowed while barreling forward with her war maul raised high.

Sam didn't think twice. He bolted right, running as fast as his legs would carry him and vaulting over the wooden gate that led to one of the holding pens. He dropped, breathing hard, then cautiously peeked over the top of the stone retaining wall. His eyebrows climbed in shock as he watched the Junction Guardian lunge forward, its claws slicing through Dizzy's armor like the gear was made of tissue paper. Kai and Velkan charged in, flanking the creature on both sides, while Arrow took cover behind a stall on the opposite side of the room from Sam.

Despite being outnumbered, though, the full metal chicken was handily holding its own. Its wings flashed out, flapping madly at Kai and Velkan, keeping the two at bay with razor-tipped feathers.

"We could use some covering fire out here!" Dizzy narrowly turned a flashing foot with her maul, then side-stepped a beak thrust.

Arrow slipped from holding pen to holding pen until he had a clear shot at the chicken's unprotected back. He launched a barrage of caustic arrows. The feathered shafts exploded against the fowl's metallic plumage, splattering green acid against steel and brass, but doing a pitiful amount of damage overall. Time for Sam to roll up his sleeves and get busy. With a thought, he toggled his Ice Orb and Ink Lance Tomes to the active position, then stood and let loose the first, both hands outthrust. Faintly glowing Shuriken smashed into the chicken and spread icy tendrils along its metal feathers.

Sam triggered Bookmark, spamming the spell with laser precision before launching a flurry of Ink Lance from his secondary Tome. Blots of ink splattered against the raging fowl, eating small holes across metal skin, clogging up gears, and gumming up its deadly talons. Unfortunately, that only seemed to make the fowl's mood even fouler. The murder chicken threw its head back, raised its beak toward the crystalline ceiling, and let out an enraged caw that rippled through the air like a bomb blast, the sound of a thousand knives and forks screeching on a thousand plates all at once.

The noise rippled out in a force ring, blasting Dizzy back and hurling Velkan and Kai into adjacent stalls. Sam was safe from the blast itself, thanks to the stone retaining wall providing him with meager cover, but he still dropped to a knee, wincing and clutching his ears.

The chicken used the brief reprieve to change up its tactics.

It dropped its feathery head, hunched low, and began to spin like a top, its wings extended horizontally. It twirled, *faster, faster, faster,* until it was a blur of motion, a lawn mower of steel feathers whirling across the floor. Dizzy, Kai, and Velkan had regained their feet, but no one could get close enough to do anything; even the ranger's acid arrows ricocheted harmlessly away. That only left Sam. He rained Ice Orb down, but as with the incoming arrows, Sam's Shuriken bounced away, careening instead toward his teammates. One bowled into Dizzy's chest like a sledgehammer, knocking her from her feet.

<That doesn't seem to be doing the trick,> Bill sent inside his head.

<Well, we're not exactly spoiled for options,> Sam sent back as he cut off the flow of Shuriken. <I'm open to suggestions, though.>

<We need to interrupt the spin,> Bill said after a beat. <There has to be some sort of mechanism in the legs that allows it to move like that. We disable that, we end this attack. We'll still have to kill it, but at least the ground pounders will be able to get close enough to land a blow.>

Sam said the first thing that crossed his mind, <Book Maker's Book Bomb?>

<*Absolutely*,> Bill confirmed, <though this time, I think we hit 'em with the *Dictionary*.>

The way he said it should've been accompanied by dramatic music, and with good reason. The Dictionary in this case happened to be the dictionary of Royal Pedigrees, a bone-dry tome as thick as a phone book, which Finn had nicked from his family library. It was literally the largest book Sam had ever seen, and though it wasn't magical in the least, it was perfect fodder for a Book Bomb. Even with that, instead of leaving well enough alone… Sam and Bill had done a little *experimenting*.

Sam had sewn a variety of spell scrolls into the book: nearly half a dozen Fireball spells, three Ice Orb scrolls, and a pair of Weak Acid Spray attacks. This particular Book Bomb was *extremely* costly to produce, not to mention so incredibly unstable that jostling it the wrong way was liable to set the thing off and blow everyone up.

But there was never a better time to try it out than against a creature they absolutely needed dead.

Licking his lips, Sam reached into Bill's Soul Space and pulled the fat volume free, feeling the thrum of potent, conflicting magics the second his fingers ran across the binding. Sam bellowed over the pen wall, "Everyone take cover, *now*!"

He waited for a handful of seconds while his friends scrambled for safety. Dizzy bodily hurled herself over a gate as the others quickly ducked out of sight. Muttering a silent prayer,

Sam popped up and lobbed the book side-arm like a live grenade. He watched it arc and spin through the air, pages fluttering like mad, a nimbus of light building around it as the spell pages destabilized. It thudded into the whirling chicken a second later… and Sam couldn't help but watch the chaos unfold.

The book hit with a dull **thump*…* and then the Fourth of July light show began in earnest. A fireball of orange and gold ballooned up and out in a small mushroom cloud. Swirling within that fiery bubble were streaks of blue power and angry lines of green lightning. Terrible heat radiated outward, scorching Sam's eyebrows and leaving his skin red and raw, while his luscious locks billowed out behind him like a cape caught in a gust of magically charged wind. A second later, the **boom** followed, rattling the floor and the crystalline ceiling overhead.

<Get *down*, kid!> Bill squawked as a wall of flame crashed toward him. Finally, Sam dropped low and pressed his back against the stone, hoping he hadn't just killed everyone. Dust and debris rained down from above, sprinkling his shoulders. He held his breath until the rumbling from the explosion subsided. Tentatively, he turned and glanced over the lip of the wall. The room was still blessedly intact, and none of his teammates seemed to be dead, though there was an enormous scorch mark marring the stone floor. Most amazingly of all: the android chicken was still alive.

Bill whistled softly. "I retract my previous statement. Like your mother, that is one tough bird."

Sam slapped at the book halfheartedly. *Tough* was the correct descriptor. The metal fowl was missing its legs and one wing had been ripped clean from its body, but its murderous red eyes were still open, and it looked like it was spoiling for a fight. Dizzy, Kai, and Velkan emerged from their stalls, all looking battered and cut up, but they were all definitely alive and ready to finish the job. They pressed in on the chicken from all sides, closing tight like a noose.

But the chicken wasn't done. Not yet. Maybe it couldn't move, and perhaps its legs lay ten feet away—a smoldering pile of slag and steel—but this fowl still had some fight left. It opened its beak, and Sam braced himself for another screech. Instead, the overgrown fried family meal started launching soft-ball-sized eggs from its throat, peppering the room with shells that dealt blunt damage upon impact, followed by acid damage from the gooey yolks.

Arrow fired with practiced ease, targeting the eggs themselves and blasting them from the air like shooting skeet with a shotgun. Sam toggled Fire Shuriken to the active position and joined in, rupturing the incoming projectiles before they could land and do any real damage. Unfortunately, he wasn't nearly as accurate as Arrow, so his Shuriken missed as often as they hit. When one did land, Sam was rewarded with an explosion of fluffy scrambled eggs.

Now in range, the three melee fighters laid into the chicken, Velkan's claws slashing, Kai's fists pummeling, Dizzy's war maul bashing through metal armor. They hammered relentlessly at the downed creature until a cloud of acrid gray smoke wafted up and the angry red light vanished from the chicken's blood-thirsty eyes.

Exp gained: 651

Skill increased: Book Maker's Book Bomb (Beginner I). What's that you're reading? A question best not asked to someone with your uneven temperament, unruly disposition, and bizarre skillset. You are more than willing to throw the book at 'em with explosive and deadly results! Just make sure you know which books are which, or you're liable to crack a novel for some relaxation and blast yourself into the next century!

Skill gained: Spell Alchemy (Novice I). Combining magics and spells in such a spectacularly crazy and reckless way is a good way to die early and painfully. That said, the difference between crazy and genius is often a fine line, and honestly, this is also a great way to combine regular ol' spells in new and interesting ways. Some of the best magics were discovered by accident, you know! When combining spells, you have a 2% chance to add an additional spell effect, and a 1% chance to generate an entirely new spell! Intelligence +1.

Kai let out a whoop, pumping a fist in the air while the others crowded around the fallen beast, presumably to raid the creature and discover whatever goodies it might be hiding away. Sam ignored their celebration, only sparing a quick glance at his updates as he headed over to an angular sigil carved into the wall on the frame of the entryway door. This had to be the Junction activation rune. He pressed his hand against the etching and let the gentle heat from the symbol flow into his outstretched palm.

Two for two! Color me impressed! I honestly didn't think you'd capture another Junction—not this quickly. True, it was a giant chicken, *so maybe stay humble moving forward? Congratulations are in order! You've defeated the Keeper of the Husbandry Pen and found its corresponding Activation Rune. Once the Junction is claimed, you will be able to utilize the space with all its corresponding perks, although both Traps and Keepers will remain defunct until functionality is restored through the Control Room. More good news: the other residents of the Irondown Burrows will generally avoid this area, since it will become hostile territory.*

Would you like to trigger the Activation Rune and claim this Junction on behalf of the Wolf Pack? Yes/No

Sam braced himself, remembering what had happened last time, and gritted his teeth as he accepted. The familiar rush of mana leaving his body in a sudden deluge dropped him to his knees, the world reeling drunkenly around him.

His stomach clenched like a fist. Curiously, this Junction took less mana than the Barrack had—only a scant one-hundred and fifty, instead of two-hundred and seventy—but losing that much mana that quickly was still an unpleasant experience. The discomfort was gone in a flash, and the rough gemstone lights embedded in the stall walls flickered to life, filling the room with both an amber glow and an uncomfortable heat.

In seconds, it felt as humid as the inside of a greenhouse.

Congratulations! You have claimed Junction 2 of 8. Reward, Exp:

500. Claim one more, and I might actually have to sit up and start taking notes.

Note: The Husbandry Pen is unlike other structures within the Irondown Burrows. This area acts as its own self-regulating ecosystem, often called a Food Dungeon. *Deep magics built within the structure cause food sources, both plant and animal, to grow and reproduce at exceptionally fast rates. Moreover, successive generations raised within the Pen will evolve at accelerated rates based on a variety of different factors. Food Dungeons are perfect sources of nourishment for an army on the go, especially one in hiding.*

Sam paid far more attention to this notification. "This is it. It's all coming together!"

While the others continued to celebrate, Sam turned his attention to the overly large nest of metal and wood, miraculously intact despite the carnage from the devastating Book Bomb Blast… almost as though the mechanical chicken had been sheltering the nest from the explosion. If Sam's hunch was right, then what he needed would be tucked away inside that nest. His feet moved of their own accord, compelled forward by some gut instinct created through wisdom.

"Hey, uh..." Bill tried to break his trance. "You okay, or what?"

"Or what." Sam dropped onto a knee beside the edge of the oversized nest. There in the center, peeking out from beneath a layer of dust and rocky debris, was the shell of a golden egg. Sam brushed the dirt free and carefully, *ever* so gently, wiggled the egg loose. It was larger than any chicken egg he'd ever seen before, closer in size to an ostrich egg; the shell perfectly smooth and warm to the touch. This wasn't a relic, but a living thing locked away in this Husbandry Pen, and it had been watched over by an angry, giant mechanical nightmare until the right person showed up to claim the real reward.

"'Often the road scorned conceals the greatest treasures of all,'" Sam muttered under his breath, repeating the words that Auntie Owl had entrusted to him. "'Embrace the eccentric, for there lies true power.'"

"Dude, what'd you find?" Kai asked from the other side of the room.

"My calling," Sam replied with a grin. "Now I'm sure. I know what I want my specialization and my secondary profession to be."

There was a collective gasp, every teammate going stock-still as they stared at the golden egg clutched in his hands. Bill broke the tension with a squawk. "About *time*! So, what's it gonna be, huh? Wait, I know. Specialized as a Bravi with a secondary Duelist profession. That's it, right? Bravi Duelist. Or wait. No. Bibliognost with a focus as an Inscriptionist. *Nailed* it!"

Sam shook his head. Bill raised a leathery eyebrow and weakly offered, "Libriohexer?"

"Libriohexer," Sam stoically confirmed.

"That's the toughest of the three. You know that, right?" Bill argued with him. "I mean, powerful in the endgame, but resource management is a nightmare. The amount of work is crazy. Not a bad choice, just a hard road to walk... but you have the *Legs* for it, I suppose. If you're set on Libriohexer, then I guess you're gonna go with Contractualist? Or maybe... Publisher? You'll need a ton of content to fill a spatial summoning library, and Publisher seems like it could be a good fit for reasons that I can't fully seem to explain. Publishers are just cool."

"Not Publisher. The answer should be obvious." Sam shook his head again, his smile growing wider by the second. He lifted the golden egg high for everyone to see. "I'm going to be a *Chicken Keeper*!"

There was a moment of stunned silence. Bill snorted, the sound turning into a deep belly laugh, which spread like wildfire to the others. Kai, Arrow, and Dizzy all joined in. Velkan didn't laugh. No, the Wolfman looked grave and thoughtful, his lupine eyes staring at the egg, ears twitching in what Sam knew was an expression of mild confusion. But there was no chuffing, no mirth in his body posture. The Wolfman knew Sam was serious as a heart attack, even if no one else did, and he wasn't ready to dismiss the radical notion.

"Good one," Bill finally allowed once the chuckling died down. "Chicken Keeper. Can't I just see that? You meticulously jotting out scrolls, covered in ink and feathers, while a bunch of dirty chickens cluck all around you. Classic Legs, amiright?"

"I'm not joking," Sam cradled the egg fondly. "I'm picking Libriohexer with a secondary profession as a Chicken Keeper."

The room went dead silent.

CHAPTER TWELVE

"But that doesn't make any *sense*," Dizzy repeated her protest weakly, speaking slowly as though explaining a simple concept to someone with a serious head injury. "Chicken farming has nothing to do with books or paper or ink or magic."

"Then why is it an option for my specialization selection?" Sam shot back instantly. "All of those professions are supposed to help with my specialization, and Chicken Keeper is there for a reason."

"Yeah, as a *joke.*" The disbelief was strong in Bill's tone. "Not sure if you've noticed, but the resident quest giver has a wonky sense of humor. That's why it's an option; because it's *funny*, not because it's a good option. I mean... *seriously*. What *possible* reason could you have for wanting to be a Chicken Keeper? Am I just not seeing the connection? Before you speak, remember that I'm a three-hundred-year-old sentient book, so me being dumb isn't actually on the table."

"You already brought up the reason," Sam explained comfortably. He had thought this through, and he *knew* he was right. "Resources. Libriohexers need a lot of them."

"I'm sorry," Kai interrupted while raising his hand, "but,

like, what exactly is a Libriohexer? Also, does anyone know where I can get some popcorn? Because I totally just want to sit back and watch this meltdown happen."

"Maybe once I get my chicken farm up and going, I'll look at growing corn," Sam joked.

"*Har, har,*" Bill grunted as the others chuckled. "Real funny, guy, which is good because our life is about to become a giant joke. No one is going to respect us if we're running around in overalls, tending to a bunch of dirty *chickens.*"

Sam ignored Bill, answering Kai's question. "Libriohexer is the first stepping stone on the path toward the Archivist Summoner. Basically, as a Bibliomancer, Bill and I can bind ourselves to books, which we use for spell casting, but as a Libriohexer, I'll start constructing an Interspatial Library or a Portable Library, which will act as my new binding totem."

"Yeah, but it takes a ton of resources and time to build a proper Interspatial Library," Bill protested weakly.

"You're not wrong," Sam agreed as he gently tucked the egg in his pack and rubbed his hands gleefully, "but once it's done, I'll be a force of nature."

"Ahem. *We'll* be a force of nature," Bill corrected dryly.

"What's so special about an Interspatial Library?" Dizzy asked.

"What's so special-?" Bill choked out. "Are you *kidding* me? What do they *teach* kids these days? It's one of the most powerful weapons known to Mage-kind! For one, Sam will have instant access to any knowledge stored within the Library and, for *another*, it will act as an interdimensional base that he can physically escape into. A proper Interspatial Library will also drastically limit the amount of prep time we'll have to spend to cast our spells—though how that works is complicated.

"But that's only the *start*! We'll still have access to some formidable spells for personal protective use, but—as the title suggests—Archivist Summoners mostly focus on summoning abilities. The things we summon are made out of paper, ink, and whole *truckloads* of magic. Hence the resource requirements... but once we're ready, we'll be able to whip up an army of origami nightmares to do our bidding without a second thought. As we construct the Sacred Geometrical Tiers of the Library, we'll gain insight into the nature of reality itself! With that kind of awareness, we will be able to augment body and mind—even unlock the secrets of planar travel and time itself!"

"Dude," Kai sounded utterly wowed. "*Wicked.*"

"Yeah... that," Bill vigorously agreed. "Easily the most powerful of the Bibliomancer Specializations, but it's *hard* to do, with a capital H. Costly. We're talking a hundred-*thousand*-gold worth of resources to get properly started."

Arrow whistled through his teeth. "That's a million real dollars."

"Unless I'm wrong," Dizzy coughed and looked at Sam pointedly, "you're running low on funds at the moment."

Sam put his hand in his pack and stroked the egg. "Which is where this thing comes in. See, initially I was thinking about the Publisher profession. I thought I could use that as a way to amass content for the Interspatial Library, but it's too slow. As an Outlaw, I'll never have the connections to make it work. But after passing the wisdom threshold, it all came together in my head. As a Chicken Keeper, I'll be able to produce an almost endless amount of resources myself. Thanks to my Hair of the Dog Blessing, I have access to enchanted binding thread, and now I'll have quills, custom vellum—which holds mana seventy percent better than even high-quality parchment—and meat, which I can sell on the side. I'm telling you; this is a bonafide resource farm."

"But... but... I mean, yeah, *technically* that's correct, but fowl vellum isn't even a thing!" Bill exploded in exasperation. "Chickens are too small to produce usable sheets! The best quality vellum is calf, sheep, or goat. Even if you *could* make it work, the quantity we need would be impossible to produce-"

"*Without* a Husbandry Pen," Sam cut him off. "You're right, chickens are too small and not of good enough quality. We won't be *using* regular chickens. Look around. We have a base with a Husbandry Pen. We can use it to spawn chickens at an incredible rate, plus they'll be bigger, stronger, and faster than creatures produced outside of a Pen. As a Chicken Keeper, I'll be able to evolve them until they have magical properties. Eventually, they won't just produce meat; they'll also produce monster Cores, which we can sell or use for experience. Think about creating vellum out of a creature that is already imbued with mana! This might not be the *glamorous* choice, Bill, but trust me. It's the right one. I'm doing it."

Sam focused on the egg in his hands and a prompt appeared.

You have acquired a Prime Brood Egg, containing a Prime Brood Matriarch. This item can be sold, hatched, or turned into a yummy omelet. Would you like to hatch this egg and unlock the secondary profession of Chicken Keeper? Yes / No

Despite Bill's emphatic protests, Sam didn't have to think twice and accepted his new profession.

Profession Unlocked: Chicken Keeper (1/10)

Congratulations! You have bonded with the Prime Brood Egg and unlocked the secondary profession, Chicken Keeper. Honestly, I didn't see this coming, but you're a weird egg yourself, so maybe I should've guessed. Sometimes weird even pays off.

Title Unlocked: Chicken Whisperer Level 1 (Upgradeable). Effect: Chickens just positively egg-dore you, you have +10 Charisma Bonus with all chickens, and a +5 Charisma Bonus to fowls of all varieties. As you grow your brood, you can upgrade this title to a maximum of Chicken Whisperer Level 5. Then it will transform into the Title 'Chicken King', unlocking additional upgrades at each level.

Husbandry Pen Bonus: Good News! Having access to a coveted Husbandry Pen comes with some serious bonuses. Increase Egg Laying Rate by 25%; Increase Egg size by 37%; Increase Overall Chicken Size (type, variable) by 24%; Hatcheries Refill 12% faster; Incubation time is reduced by 17.5%; Increases Harvested Egg and Meat Quality by 19.5%.

Warning! You have reached ten total titles. The maximum number of titles you can have at any given time is ten. Upon unlocking your next title, you will need to select one title to remove.

Profession - Chicken Keeper: The humblest of paths, the noble Chicken Farmer tends to the lowly fowl of the land, raising a brood and keeping food on the dinner tables of the folk of Eternium. It's a dirty job, no doubt, and hard work to boot. Why anyone would choose such a path is a mystery, yet there are rewards in store for those who master this profession: lots of scratches. You'll be lucky to keep both your eyes—these chickens can get ornery if not properly cared for!

Profession benefits at first level: The Prime Brood Matriarch will imprint on you and will be unwaveringly loyal! The Prime Brood Matriarch will respawn four hours after death and will naturally spawn successive generations of finger-licking-good chicken. Over time, the Prime Matriarch Chicken will produce new Lesser Brood Matriarchs, who will also have the ability to respawn four hours after death. Chickens within your brood mature 25% more quickly than other chickens and each successive generation has a 7% chance of experiencing a naturally occurring beneficial mutation. Both overall egg size and egg laying rate is increased by 12%.

"Are you seeing this?" Bill sounded like he was holding back tears. "This sounds like a nightmare. What have you gotten us into?"

"I've just nabbed us the keys to an Interspatial Library," Sam promised him. "Trust me."

For the next hour, the crew cleaned up from the battle, set the Husbandry Pen into working order, and talked about what they should do with the rest of the day. It was still early morning, the sun was steadily working its way toward the noontime zenith, and no one wanted to burn extra daylight. They had too much to do, and too little time as it was. Taking on another Junction Keeper was probably a stretch, since they would only get increasingly harder; but another trip to the Totem Training Ground wasn't out of the question. Dizzy was jonesing for a shot at the Constitution Totem, Kai wanted to experience whatever Sister Rat was serving up in the Perception Totem, and Arrow insisted he needed a rematch with a disgruntled monkey's uncle.

Finn and Sphinx were due back at some point today, so Sam opted to stay behind and wait for them just in case they happened to show up early. He was dangerously low on resources, anyways—his three Shuriken Tomes were close to 'E', and his Papier-Mache Mage Tome was completely devoid of pages. Some long-overdue crafting was in order: being a Bibliomancer was a double-edged sword in that way.

Sure, he could spam spells like no one's business during combat, all without ever running the risk of draining his mana reserve, but the flip side was that he needed to constantly prep materials beforehand. In this case, it was a nice break in the action, since all he really wanted to do was hatch his egg.

Velkan also decided to remain behind.

The Wolfman said that he wanted to more closely explore the area surrounding the Irondown Burrows, but Sam suspected he had other motives. After rescuing Velkan from his captivity in the Mage's College, the Wolfman had formed an odd, unspoken bond with Sam. True or not, Velkan felt he had a blood debt to Sam and, as a result, the Wolfman seemed oddly protective where Sam and Bill were concerned. Velkan rarely spoke about the debt, because acknowledging it would be to lose respect—a grand sin in Wolfman Culture—but he was always near at hand and ready to help whenever Sam needed anything.

First, Sam took care of his new charge: the golden egg. Although he'd bonded with the prospective Prime Brood Matriarch, the egg wouldn't hatch without a little assistance. The Husbandry Pen was humid and warm, but still not quite warm enough for the egg to hatch on its own. He had a plan for that. Sam tasked Velkan with gathering wood and tall grass from the surrounding forest, while he set about making a few warming stones. He collected a variety of smooth-faced river rocks, each about the size of his fist, then rolled up his sleeves and got down to business.

As a Bibliomancer, Sam primarily cast spells through the use of spell scrolls and tomes, but thanks to his specialty inks, penmanship skills, and his Coreless Spell Infusion ability, he could inscribe a spell on just about anything. At least in theory.

He didn't have the skills to engrave permanent spells onto things like armor or weapons—at least not *yet*—but it was relatively simple to imbue the stones with mana in the same way that he prepared glass vials to hold infused ink. The next step was a little trickier. Under Bill's watchful eye, Sam carefully traced a simple version of the Fireball spell onto each stone, then activated the spell form using his Coreless Spell Infusion ability. In principle, Fireball spells were basically mana batteries that, when activated, released all the stored mana as a single burst of flame and heat. But, with a little delicate finagling, Sam managed to tweak the rate at which the stones released their stored heat energy.

Instead of emitting all at once, the energy would bleed mana in a steady stream, filling the rock with a gentle warmth. Perfect for incubation stones. By the time Sam was done with his impromptu crafting session, Velkan had returned with both arms full of smooth branches and piles of tall green grass. Sam quickly formed the materials into a rough nest, stacking the wood to form a ring, then placed his heating stones in the bottom. He piled the grasses on top of the rocks, creating a downy bed which gently cradled the weight of the golden egg. He piled more grass on top of the egg, obscuring it from view, and a timer popped up in the corner of his eye.

Incubation conditions met! Estimated time until Prime Brood Egg hatches: 23:21:15!

Note: Husbandry Pen has reduced the Incubation Period by 17.5%!

New Estimated time until Prime Brood Egg hatches: 19:21:15!

"I still think this is a terrible idea," Bill grumbled, "but since it seems like you're committed, I'll try to keep an open mind. I know we need to resupply, but since you've finally made up your mind about your specialization, I think it's time I taught you a few new spells."

"Wait, you've been holding out on me?" Sam looked up at the book incredulously.

"Yes and no," Bill replied without really admitting anything. "Crossing the intelligence threshold let me remember some of my more powerful spells from the olden days, but I still didn't have the wisdom I needed to either teach you how to cast them, or which ones I should teach you in the first place—especially since I didn't know which specialization you were leaning towards. Because of my background, I have access to a wide array of spells, but the types of spells you choose and the way you use them is what is going to push us toward one specialization over another."

"Why not just teach me all the spells?" Sam pressed, genuinely curious.

Bill snorted at that thought. "Because magic is fickle, and the way the spells interact with each other can be hard to predict. Plus, it takes a lot of time and effort to learn spells. Even if I taught you *everything* I could, it would take you ten natural lifetimes to master them. In my experience, being the master of a handful of powerful skills is far better than having access to a hundred options and sucking at all of them. Believe you me, we want to be masters of our craft. I couldn't even begin to nudge you in the right direction until you decided what you wanted to be when you grow up. So let me ask you one last time: Libriohexer. That's the way you want to go? Once we start down the road, there's no turning back."

Sam took a deep breath and nodded. This was a huge choice, and it would be the most difficult possible path to walk, but it would also be the one that would offer the best reward in the end. "Yes."

"Would it change your mind if I told you that I'm not one-hundred percent sure how to build an Interspatial Library? I know some of the theory, but it isn't going to be cut and dry like the other specializations will be. There's going to be trial and error; a *lot* of it is going to be as new for me as it is for you."

Bill's admission gave Sam a moment of genuine pause. Bill was a seemingly endless fount of knowledge and confidence—he wouldn't ever say he didn't know something unless he had some very real reservations. If Bill *wasn't* sure what they would have to do, it could slow the process down significantly. Did that change anything? Running a Biblioblade build would definitely be the easier option, and he'd still be extremely powerful within the context of the metagame. Spell Swords always were among Sam's favorite classes to play.

Yet… his gut told him this was the right thing to do.

"Even better," Sam finally broke the silence, "because that way, we really will be partners. I love how much you know, but this will let us forge a new path together. I don't care if it's hard. The things that are the hardest to accomplish are always the things that have the best payout in the end. I want to be a Librihexer and ultimately, an Arcane Summoner."

Quest alert! A Libriohexer Walks into an Interspatial Library…

Well, you've finally made up your mind and decided to embark on the Path of the Libriohexer—getting your specialization isn't gonna be a walk in the park, you know. In order to unlock your class specialization, you must discover the secrets of Interspatial Nodes and build one to call your own. Reward: Class Change: Libriohexer. Exp: 2,000. Accept / Decline

Mind made up; Sam accepted.

"No turning back now. Buckle up, Buttercup." Bill gravely regarded him. "We have some spells to learn."

"Nice," Sam replied with a wolfish grin, rubbing his hands together in greedy glee. He was already envisioning burying his enemies under a mountain of books or drowning them in rivers of ink. "I love my current spells, but it would be awesome to have something that hits a little harder. I hate having to spam Shuriken fifteen times to take down an enemy. I want something with one-shot potential."

Bill laughed, the sound harsh and merciless. "Slow down, murder machine. We'll learn some nasty, hard-hitting spells down the road, but we ain't there yet. If you'd picked Biblioblade or Bibliognost, we'd be having a different conversation. But *no~o*. *You* wanted to be a Libriohexer. The bigger spells that a Libriohexer can cast require the use of an Interspatial

Library because they are material-intensive. Spells like that require multiple tomes all working in tandem to cast."

Ignoring Sam's disappointment, Bill pushed on. "So, for the time being, we're going to learn some practical, no-frills utility spells, things that are going to help us generate the material resources we need to make a Librioheer class work in the long run. Before you complain, this is on *you*. Though, I suppose I can throw you a bone and give you *one* cool spell. No damage output, but it's a showstopper in its own way."

Sam felt that he should've expected this. "What spells were you thinking?"

"The Librioheer basics: *Auto Writing*, *Transcription Twining*, and *Paper Homing Pigeon*. Plus, one specialty spell that I built just because it's cool—but I don't want to ruin the surprise. Now, I've used every single one of these, and some of them have been extremely *handy*, especially since becoming bookified. Not having hands is a major drawback when your primary spell casting ability revolves around writing spells and folding paper. Auto Writing is the only reason I can even make spells. Back before the College locked me up for sedition—in the days when I still had a stomach—I used Paper Homing Pigeon to make all of my fast-food orders. Very convenient, though I suppose it probably has some other uses. Anyway, you get the idea."

Thinking they were done, Sam opened his mouth to ask a question, only for Bill to bullrush forward again. "I wish I had a book to give you, but these spells haven't ever been written down anywhere. They're all stashed away in the ol' noggin. Which means teaching them to you is going to be a tricky, and probably painful, process. But don't worry, I'll be there the whole way to guide you through it. Although, to reiterate, it is absolutely going to hit you like a sledgehammer. Probably best if you take a seat and get comfy so you don't fall over when I blow your mind with all my awesomeness."

Sam rolled his eyes but did as he was instructed, plopping down on the floor and crossing his legs just like he did during his morning meditations. "Good. I want you to breathe deeply and focus on your mana pool. Cycle your power along your channels, but try to keep your mind clear. I'm gonna walk you through a basic guided meditation."

Focusing on the rise and fall of his chest, Sam listened to the sound of his own heartbeat and blocked out every other noise. Immediately, he felt gentle warmth spread through his limbs as mana flowed from his center, first in a trickle, then in a surging river. This particular technique was one that would burn out most novice magic users, but if he'd learned one helpful thing from the Mage's College, it was how to safely handle large amounts of mana. Sam banished the thought from his head and let himself be drawn back into his breathing. The process was almost second nature, and in a matter of moments, tension drained from his muscles.

<Alright, here goes everything!> Bill cackled out a few extra words that almost broke Sam from his trance. <Hope this doesn't actually blow your head open!>

CHAPTER THIRTEEN

A tsunami of unbridled energy came roaring out from Bill, screaming along Sam's mana channels before tearing into his brain. It felt like magma was coursing through his veins while slivers of powdered glass had been injected directly into his skull. Sam tried to focus on his breath, but his lungs didn't want to work properly. His eyes shot open as an involuntary scream was ripped from somewhere deep within his lungs. The glass shards inside his head morphed, the sharp pinpricks of pain transforming into a deep throb, threatening to explode his skull from the inside out.

In one last sudden burst, knowledge bloomed inside Sam's mind. The pain vanished, and a flood of new notifications flashed across his vision.

You have unlocked the following Spells:

Skill Gained: Auto Writing (Novice I): Hand cramps are no fun at all. Save yourself from a serious case of future carpal tunnel with the Auto Writing Spell! Use an Auto Writing rune to twin one Quill to another, allowing you to have a small army of enhanced quills carefully copying your every movement as you carefully write spell scrolls! After enchanting the Twinned Quills, speak the Command Word, Copy-Paste, *to activate and deactivate the spell script. At Novice I, the spell caster may have up to two enchanted Quills deployed at a given time. Accuracy decreased by 5% for each enchanted quill utilized, increasing the risk of catastrophic spell failure.*

Skill Gained: Transcription Twinning (Novice I): Create a sympathetic bond between two sheets of paper, parchment, or vellum. Whatever is inscribed onto the first sheet will automatically appear on the second, thanks to the transcription twinning effect. This allows the caster to mass produce scrolls at an accelerated volume, though a mistake on one copy can lead to a mass ripple effect that can have devastating consequences. Additionally, all spell costs remain the same, so it is also possible to cause a mana chain that will instantly deplete the user's core. Transcribe with care.

Production Cost: The material costs for all transcribed materials remains the same!

Casting Cost: The mana cost for all spells remains the same, multiplied by the number of concurrent spells being cast!

Skill Gained: Paper Homing Pigeon (Novice I): Write a short message (no more than 140 characters!) onto a regular piece of paper. When the spell caster whispers the Command Word, Tweet, *along with the name of the intended recipient, the paper instantly folds itself into a paper pigeon and takes wing, seeking out its intended target at the airspeed velocity of an unladen swallow. Upon arrival at its intended recipient, the enchantment fades and the paper homing pigeon reverts, becoming a normal sheet of parchment once more.*

Production Cost: 5 mana per second until the incantation is completed or the attempt is failed. 1 sheet of paper, parchment, or vellum.

Casting Cost: 2n mana where n=skill level (Paper-aligned magic). Cooldown: 1.5 seconds.

Skill Gained: Quill Wings (Novice I): Craft a specialty cloak of layered quills, which is magically bound to the caster. When the Command Word is invoked, the cloak instantly forms into a set of magical wings capable of bearing the caster aloft. The spell lasts for one hour or until the wings sustain irreparable damage, breaking the enchantment. During the spell duration, the caster can fly at the rate of their running speed, though the action costs stamina to stay airborne. This ability gives the spell caster greater advantage by elevating them above the battlefield, but it can also make them a target to ranged attacks. When the spell lapses, the quills return to the bound cloak.

Production Cost: 1,000 mana Imbued Quills, 10 mana per second until the incantation is completed or attempt is failed.

Casting Cost: 10n mana where n=skill level (Paper-aligned magic). Cooldown: 8 hours.

Sam read over the descriptions of each spell carefully. His eyes lingered on the last one.

"Quill Wings?" His words were half question, half statement, and all amazement.

"Yeah," Bill winked at him. "I figured with all the quills we're gonna have, thanks to the chicken farm, that one would be a good addition. I built that back when I still had a body. I hated always getting stuck at the back of the party, trying to lay down suppressive spell coverage with a bunch of tanks standing in my line of fire. So, I whipped that bad boy up. Floats you up above the fray. It's got drawbacks, especially if you're engaging ranged fighters, but it's worth the risk. The other spells aren't quite as flashy, but they are going to make our lives a thousand times easier. Auto-Writing and Transcription Twinning are basically a production hack designed to be used together.

"You enchant a bunch of Quills using Auto-Writing, then when you write a spell, that same spell is written on two other sheets of parchment in the same instance. Instead of one fireball spell, you now have three. That wouldn't normally be possible but, because you have the Coreless Spell Infusion ability, you can totally make it work. Also, because I'm lazy and I like to cheat, I further developed the Transcription Twinning spell to make the process go even faster." Bill laughed in delight as he imagined turning Sam into a one-man production line.

"You twin two sheets of paper, and whatever you write on the first ends up on the second. But you can also twin that second sheet to a third sheet, and the third sheet to a fourth. *Never* go past that, though. The spell draws too much power and unbalances the whole chain. But, that still means instead of inscribing one fireball scroll at a time, you can inscribe twelve spell scrolls simultaneously… *if* you have the mana and skill to make it happen."

"Divines above," Sam whispered as he thought over the possibilities. "That's incredible. It'll save me so much time."

"You better believe it. Once we unlock your Libriohexer spells, you'll finally realize why you absolutely *need* these spells. Those bad boys are awesome, but they're *expensive*. You'll be able to summon Papier-Mache Guardians, and each one can cost up to a *thousand* sheets of parchment or vellum. A Book Golem? You don't even want to know the price tag on that sucker. Worth it, though. But we have to get our Interspatial Library up and running first, and that…"

Clearing his throat with a papery rustle, Bill faltered. "We'll have to figure that one out. I was researching it back before the College apprehended me and sentenced me to bookification, but I never did iron out all the kinks. It's definitely going to take some time."

"I have no doubt we'll figure it out." Sam felt a burst of exhilaration in his chest. "In the meantime, I was hoping you could do a little research for me."

He stood and stretched his legs, then moved into one of the stalls at the far end of the Pen. He was excited to try out his new assortment of spells, but the last thing he wanted was to accidentally blow up his fancy new chicken egg because of a slip of the pen or a moment of lapsed concentration.

Bill had access to the information of every book he'd ever gotten his metaphorical hands on, but storing that amount of information came with strings: he couldn't recall it all at will, even though it was buried somewhere inside his head. "Specifically, I need you to scour your mental resources and see if you can recall anything about Chicken Farming. While you do that, I'm going to try my hand at some of my new spells and restock our spell inventory."

Sam opened his Unending Flask and carefully pulled each item out of the spatial compartment, arranging them in orderly columns and rows so it would be easier to catalog. First came the paper, great stacks of finely pressed papyrus, high-grade parchment, and even more expensive vellum. All of those supplies didn't come cheap, and though he was affording his habit by jotting off quick and dirty spell scrolls that he happily sold to the highest bidder, he was only making enough to break even at best. Moving that many spell scrolls was just too dangerous, even with Sphinx's connections to the Upright Men—Ardania's Thieves' Guild equivalent.

Hopefully, that would all be changing soon.

Next, Sam added the book-binder tool kit to the growing pile of items: a wood-handled awl with a razor-sharp tip, a wolf-bone fold creaser, spools of waxed thread in various colors, several long, curved needles, and a glue brush with an accompanying glass bottle of epoxy. He also pulled free his ever-growing assortment of Quills. He'd gathered quite the collection of assorted sizes, types, and colors. Some were made of osprey feathers with fine metal nibs, while others had been meticulously crafted from hawk feathers sporting bone tips. The feather variations were many—peacock, eagle, falcon, vulture—and the nib types were just as diverse—iron, gold, silver, bronze, jade, bone… diamond.

Although the differences might seem largely cosmetic to the uninitiated, the variety allowed Sam to write a wider range of spells and make them more powerful at the same time. A decaying spell would be amplified by an onyx vulture quill with a specialized basilisk-bone nib. An air spell? Hawk feather with a crystal tip. A phoenix feather with a bronze nub did wonders for both fire and restorative spells, while kelpie feathers with silver tips did the same for water.

Concentrating, Sam opened his mana channels and carefully invoked the spell to enchant two of his most trusty Quills with the Auto-Writing Spell.

"Copy-Paste," he whispered under his breath as energy poured out from his core, bringing the two quills to life. He watched with wonder as they floated in the air. He moved his quill, and they responded in perfect sync. It might not have been big 'kablooie' magic, but it was very impressive in its own right. He lined up several sheets of parchment and performed the Transcription Twinning spell, binding one to another to another to another. In a matter of seconds, all of the pages were twinned and laid out in a neat grid before him.

Sam took a deep breath, steeling his nerves, and carefully put nib to parchment, writing out the simple instructions to create a Shuriken, then enhancing it with a fireball spell inscription. The motions were second nature—he'd written this spell a thousand times, at the very least—but the process was far more taxing on his core, since all twelve sheets were quickly covered in the same spell form. Overall, though, the results were nearly miraculous. He could normally produce a sheet a minute, and he'd just somehow managed to produce *twelve* in the same span. This was going to change everything, especially as he got more comfortable with the process.

Popping his neck and cracking his knuckles, Sam straightened his back, cleared his mind from distractions, and set to work in earnest. His hands moved with a will of their own, guided by muscle memory as he flew through spell preparation. First, he focused on his Papier-Mache Mage, effortlessly tracing out the sacred geometry, inking the simple Spell Form onto the page, then sewing the loose sheaves together using a modified longstitch bookbinding technique. Refilling that tome normally took him close to an hour, but this time around, he'd managed the task in ten minutes.

Grinning from ear to ear, Sam moved from project to project, working on autopilot while he thought. The time raced by, seconds stretching into minutes, minutes stretching into hours, while he fully replenished his dwindling stores. He took a short break after three hours of steady work to stretch sore muscles and grab a quick bite to eat. Nothing fancy, just a little dried jerky and day-old bread, but it filled the void in his belly. While he munched, Bill shared his findings, which, interestingly enough, also had to do with food.

"Fine," Bill admitted as Sam snacked, "I'll concede that

maybe, *maybe*, there's more merit to this crazy idea of yours than I originally thought."

Apparently, Chicken Farming had some deep, deep roots stretching all the way back to the founding of Ardania. Turned out, as humble a profession as it may have seemed on the surface, Chicken Farming was actually big business. Sam's hunch had been *right;* it was possible to produce animals with magical properties, and the big secret lay in their diet. What the animals ate mattered. A lot. If they were fed with rare ingredients or mana-fortified foods, they could breed genetic hybrids that mimicked those same abilities. The process worked on cows and pigs—on any animal, really—but big farm stock took a long time to raise and a lot of space to do it.

Not chickens… which made them one of the most valuable resources in the human Kingdom.

According to some old economic surveys Bill had pulled up, poultry and eggs made up over sixty percent of the protein the citizens of Ardania consumed. Even more staggering, a whopping eighty percent of mana-infused meats consisted of chicken and chicken byproducts. Bill had to concede that, based on the figures alone—even if the surveys were years out of date—Sam might have stumbled onto a very lucrative venture. It would be work, but they might just be able to get the resources they needed for the Interspatial Library and turn a very tidy profit while they were at it.

His initial objections finally quelled, Bill dove back into his research while Sam settled in for another few hours of crafting. He'd refilled all of his tomes—save for his Rorschach Test, which still only had a single charge—when Velkan slipped into the room on soundless feet with a much louder Finn in tow.

"Divine above, but this place is bloody brilliant!" Finn marveled, gazing around the Husbandry Pen. He spun in a slow circle, mouth agape. "I can't believe this all belongs to us."

"Not yet, it doesn't." Sam stood and dusted his palms on his pants. "So far, we only have the Barracks and this area unlocked, but it's a lot better than our old yurt. Especially the baths."

"Praise be that we won't have to use that old wooden tub anymore," Finn agreed with a shudder. "Of all the things I miss about home, the indoor bathing and the gourmet food tops the list."

"No luck with the food yet, but that's only a matter of time. According to my Dungeon Compendium, the Irondowns do have a kitchen, and if it's half as nice as the barracks, we should be able to find a chef in no time. But enough about this place;" Sam waved away Finn's curiosity, "how was the trip into the city? Where's Sphinx? Any problems?"

"Good, overall," the hawkish boy replied. "Our dearest Sphinx has run off to those Totem Training Grounds to report into Dizzy, but I thought I'd linger around here for a bit. As for trouble, not so much as a whiff. The Mage's College is still on high alert, but it seems as though some of the heat has died off with Octavius gone. That struck me as odd, to say the least, so Sphinx and I did a little poking around. Apparently, the College very much does *not* want to advertise the fact that they lost one of their most promising students to a rogue Warlock. Especially not a Warlock who raided their Library, stole a tome of incredible power-"

"Oh, go on, you," Bill coquettishly purred.

"-and thumbed their nose at the whole of the College. It's a bad look for them, and you know how Nobles are about maintaining appearances. So, they are looking, but quietly; they're even suppressing the news where they can. Even better, from what Sphinx and I were able to gather, you and I aren't the only Warlocks on the College's radar. They just started a city-wide manhunt for someone named Joe. Guy's making serious waves, and much of their focus has shifted to him, especially since it seems that he's still hiding out somewhere in Ardania. A wonderful break for us, I must say. With some of the pressure off, Sphinx and I were able to slip into many of my former haunts and reach out to a few of Sphinx's contacts within the Upright Men."

Sam had many questions, but decided to start with what he needed. "Did you find out anything about the LAW?" .

"*So* glad that you asked, because the answer is a resounding *yes*." Finn reached into his robes and fished out a small leather diary, worn from hard use. "*Ta-da!* This belonged to Octavius. Part of the reason we were having such a difficult time understanding his blueprints is because they are *encrypted*."

"Huh, makes total sense." Bill peered eagerly at the book being waved about. "Mages are constantly trying to poach ideas or advancements from each other. It's a dog-eat-dog world inside the halls of Academia, and that whole bunch would stab their own mothers in the back if it meant making a discovery that might help them climb the hierarchical ladder and get a shot at a tenured position. Even back in my day, we'd code our work to ensure no one else could get their greasy little fingers on breakthroughs that didn't belong to them."

"Precisely." Finn nodded in vigorous agreement. "Many of the core principles detailed on the blueprints are coded, but this is Octavius's personal journal. One of Sphinx's thiefly contacts managed to smuggle it out of his room at the College. It seems the key to deciphering the blueprints is located in a book called *Magical Theory of Sympathetic Magic: Mastering the Arcane Forces of Spell Twinning*."

Sam instantly recalled the thick volume. During his time at the College, he'd spent what felt like endless nights holding a flickering candle for Octavius while the older student had pored over the book's dusty pages.

"Since you destroyed Octavius' Grimoire during our fight with him, we'll need a copy of that particular tome to understand the spell forms necessary to link the towers once we have them built. But we'll also need a copy to unlock the blueprints themselves. Smuggling one out of the Infinity Athenaeum seems like an unlikely option, especially since the book may have been destroyed along with Octavius' Grimoire, but through my contact network, I've found that another copy of the work exists."

"One of the public libraries run by the Scholars?" Bill wondered loudly.

"Right on the head, good Sir Book." Finn glanced at the floating book with a hint of respect in his gaze. "Getting to the volume won't be *easy*, but with a little help, I think it should be possible. Don't suppose you'd care to join me on a little jaunt into the city?"

Sam see-sawed his head from one side to the other. It was still early in the day, and Dizzy and the others would likely be gone for several more hours at least. He quickly checked the countdown timer on his Prime Brood Egg and realized that he had a little more than fifteen hours remaining until it hatched. If Finn's suspicions were right, they would need a copy of this book, and Sam's spells were mostly restocked, so now was as good a time as any to head back into the human capital. Besides, he wanted to pick up some gourmet ingredients for his chicken, and Ardania was the best place to do so.

"What have we got to lose?" Sam finally replied with a lopsided shrug. "Let me just tell Dizzy and the others what we're up to."

With a magician's flourish, Sam pulled a single sheet of parchment from his Flask. He dashed off a quick note:

Dizz, off to the city with Finn. Will be back tomorrow. Also, got a new spell, in case you were wondering.

He leaned over and whispered the activation word into the sheet. Finn watched, confusion dancing across his face for a moment. That confusion morphed into wonder as the sheet of parchment in Sam's hands lifted into the air and promptly folded itself into a delicate paper bird that took wing and darted from the room in a flash.

"A few new upgrades," Sam informed him with a playful wink.

CHAPTER FOURTEEN

The eastern city gates rose up like towering sentinels, standing guard over the shining jewel of humanity, Ardania. The gates were enormous things, easily large enough to accommodate a swarm of T-Rexes, and the connecting walls loomed forty-feet tall with wide ramparts. Conical-helmeted guards, carrying hooked halberds and oversized long bows, patrolled the upper walks. It was an intimidating display and a reminder of *exactly* how much work the Wolfmen had to do if they were going to win the war against humanity.

Sam was glad he'd abandoned the Mage's College and joined with The People instead, but there was no question they were the weaker force. Sometimes, Sam begrudgingly admitted to himself that he missed the splendor and convenience of the city. No walls to scale. No threats from the wild constantly breathing down his neck. Regular indoor plumbing.

The city guards manning the gates watched the ebb and flow of traffic as players trickled back into the city after a long day of grinding and adventuring. It was an hour to nightfall, the sun already falling low against the horizon, so the majority of the traffic was headed in, not out. For most players—other than those aligned with the Wolfmen—a night spent outside the walls was the next closest thing to a death sentence. Sam and Finn didn't talk as they watched the lead sentry, a heavy-set man with thinning hair and bags under his eyes, wave people inside with a flick of his wrist. He didn't bother to ask any questions or even look too closely at who was passing through.

Still, Sam held his breath, hoping the sweat running down his forehead wouldn't give him away.

<Can you please stop trying to look so guilty?> Bill hissed in his head. The book was hanging from his side, motionless. Books were a rarity around these parts, and a magical, floating, talking book would've been a dead giveaway. <Your face might as well be screaming 'I did something wrong; arrest me now'. Just play it cool.>

Turned out that Bill was correct. The guard's sleepy eyes rested a moment longer on Sam and Finn than they had on some of the others, but then he sniffed, yawned, and motioned them through anyway.

"See, I told you," Finn whispered as they passed beneath the portcullis, "the heat has cooled down significantly. It's still best if we mind our Ps and Qs—don't want to attract any undue suspicion if we can avoid it—but as long as we keep our noses clean, we should be golden."

Sam felt an invisible weight lift from his shoulders as they effortlessly slipped into the crowd, quickly lost in a sea of faces. They stuck to the warren of side streets and back alleyways, where guards were less likely to patrol and where Mages from the College would never be caught dead. Not that it was the bad part of town. The cobblestones underfoot were worn from the passing of countless feet, true, but the quaint wooden shops were well-maintained, their wooden shutters thrown wide in welcome, and the peaked roofs were covered with thick thatch or wood-slatted tiles.

The whole place was alive with the hustle and bustle of folk moving about their daily routines, picking up bolts of cloth from the tailor or visiting the local butcher or blacksmith. The air was fragrant with the smell of humanity, and the air buzzed with the noise of business. A hammer fell on metal in the distance, while street hawkers lingered in open alleyways, crying their wares at passersby.

"Refurbished weapons for sale! Guaranteed to keep you safe against even the deadliest opponents." That seemed like a rather dubious claim, since he was missing one eye and more than one limb. The grizzled vet had a few remaining wisps of silver hair wafting above skin like old shoe leather, and the poor fellow looked like he'd lost a fight with a woodchipper. "Limited warranties available with a purchase of five items or more!"

Sam smiled politely at the vendor but kept right on moving.

"Get yer meat skewer, here. Genuine Bunny meat—no rat at all," bellowed another industrious seller, this one a whip-thin man wearing a tunic heavily stained with grease and dirt.

"That vendor doth protest too much, methinks," Finn muttered, giving the dubious little merchant a wide berth.

<Yep,> Bill agreed with a snort, <there is definitely rat meat in those skewers. Abyss, if I was a betting book, I'd say it's *mostly* rat meat.>

Sam had to agree, but the encounter reminded him of the ulterior motive behind his quest. He needed to pick up ingredients for his soon-to-be hatched Chicken Matriarch. Long term, she was going to be his proverbial golden goose, but he needed alchemic ingredients first. That could be a *wee* bit of a problem, since his operational funds were running thin around the edges. He'd started off the game with fifty thousand dollars sitting in the bank, but thanks to the ridiculous price gouging at the College, he'd burned through nearly all of that by the time he'd finally cut ties with the greedy Mages.

His Coreless Spell Infusion ability allowed him to mass produce spell scrolls, which could be sold for a pretty penny, but even that was an iffy proposition. The College tightly regulated magic, and selling scrolls as a Warlock was an easy way to get flagged by the College. So, they'd had to dole the spells out a little bit at a time in order to stay under the radar. As a result,

Sam had just under five hundred gold to his name, the real-world equivalent of five thousand dollars. He figured he'd have to spend most of that to get the ingredients he needed, but if his dad had taught him anything, it was that in business, you had to spend money in a *profitable way* to make more of it.

"Speaking of food," Sam pulled the group's attention back onto himself as he stole a sidelong glance at Finn, "before we head over to the library, I was hoping we could swing by an alchemist. Know anyone who has reasonable prices on bulk items and will deal with us?"

Finn stroked his chin for a moment. "Most of the alchemists worth their salt are sanctioned and licensed by the College—especially the ones who deal with bulk item orders. Given our status, we likely only have two options. One-" He thrust a finger into the air, "we can go with an unlicensed alchemist. But if we do that, the chances of getting fleeced are incredibly high, as there's no guarantee you'll even get what you pay for. There's a reason unlicensed Alchemists are *unlicensed*. Option number two is the better bet. Deal with the Upright Men. You'll get what you want, but the tradeoff is that it'll cost you double what it would to purchase from a legitimate supplier."

Sam frowned. He didn't like the sound of either of those options. Finn noticed the expression. "If you don't mind me asking, what exactly are you hoping to concoct, hmm? If it's some sort of potion, there might be off-brand bulk ingredients we could substitute. The Wolfmen may not be quite as sophisticated in some of their alchemic sciences, but they have some wonderful naturalistic alternatives."

"No, nothing like that." Sam edged around a portly woman wearing an enormous puffy skirt. He winced as he explained, waiting for Finn to mock him just like everyone else had. "I want enhanced ingredients to feed my new chickens."

"Feedstock, is it? Well, that simplifies things considerably! But ingredients aren't the way to go." Finn visibly brightened, then frowned and shook his head. "Oh, no. Aside from being absurdly hard to get, pure ingredients will cost so much more, because they can be used in a thousand different ways. If this is about diet, we should just focus on magically infused foods."

"Wait, what?" Sam stopped abruptly. "Magically infused foods? I've never heard of such a thing. I don't understand. Are they like potions or something?"

"Sort of like potions," Finn nodded vigorously, "and also, no, not at all like potions. Frankly, I'm not surprised you haven't heard of them. They are easier to acquire than bushels of pure alchemic ingredients, but they aren't cheap. *Cheaper*, maybe, but it's a sliding scale. Besides, the types of establishments that serve the kind of food that you're looking for only cater to the very upper crust of human society."

"Oh! You'll see. I know just the place." He grabbed Sam by the sleeve and pulled him into a connecting side street, guiding them like a bloodhound with a scent in his nose toward North Waterside, one of the wealthiest districts in Ardania.

They quickly left behind the less desirable part of the cityscape, trading simple two- and three-story shops of wood and plaster for hulking buildings of stone and granite and marble. The rough cobblestone, likewise, gave way to wide boulevards of fine stone slabs and gas-lit lampposts dotting the sidewalks. There were no hawkers here, no dirt-smudged faces or common folk in rough tunics or linen pants. The masculine inhabitants wore stylish doublets, spell enchanted armor, or velvety robes. The ladies were equally well-dressed in their petticoats, parasols clutched over one shoulder.

Bill whistled softly. "Swanky. This is the kind of place I think I could get used to. I don't even have a nose, and I can still smell that the air is cleaner here. Tell me again why we opted to live in a hole in the ground?"

"Freedom," Sam muttered under his breath. "I'd rather be free with the Wolfmen than living beholden to a system that puts a golden collar around my neck."

"I couldn't agree more. This is the pretty face of the nobility: the fine parties and clean streets. But scratch the paint, and you'll see rot all the way through," " Finn added darkly, then smiled at a passing Noblewoman, who sniffed dismissively and crossed the street without a word. "See that? It's all a façade. Posturing and peacocking. Maneuvering for some minor advantage over peers while the rest of humanity barely ekes by. The Mage's College, which is thoroughly corrupt, props up the whole ugly system."

"I'm not saying you're entirely wrong," Bill replied wistfully. "I've been around a long time, and I've witnessed that ugliness firsthand, but *man,* do I miss the parties and the splendor. Might be fake, but boy, is it fun."

"I'll give you that," Finn agreed, spreading his hands in concession. "Ah, here we are."

Finn nodded toward a three-story building with wide arches and colorful awnings, tables sprawled out on the terrace beneath. Magical torches, shedding warmth but no flames, adorned the outdoor patio to heat the guests from the brisk bite in the early evening air. A sign dangled above the entryway, the *Peacock Parlor.* Sam had eaten at enough snobbish gourmet restaurants in real life to recognize one when he saw it. The clatter of silverware on porcelain plates and the heady aroma drifting out of the archways helped, too. Finn donned the confidence of a Noble, marched up to the hostess, and put on his most winning smile.

He might have been from a poor Noble house, but a Noble was a Noble, and this was his world. "Good evening. My friend and I would like to look at a menu."

The hostesses eyed them for a long bit, her lips pursed into a thin line of disapproval as she surveyed the less-than-immaculate state of Finn's robes. "I'm sorry, sir, but this establishment only caters to those of a certain... *caliber.* I'm sure you understand."

It was one of the most insulting and patronizing things Sam had ever heard. Finn drew himself up, puffing out his chest, his face red and indignant. "How *dare* you? I am the heir of House Laustsen, and my esteemed colleague here is a sorcerer in good standing with the Mage's College!"

Her face paled with each additional word. "We have spent the day hunting wild game, decided to sup at your *humble* establishment, yet you would deny us? Just who exactly are you, anyway, to speak to us so?"

"I... well... I certainly didn't mean to cause offense, m'Lord."

"Yet offense you *have* caused." Finn folded his arms and started tapping his foot. "If I don't have a menu in my hands in less than *three* seconds, I shall be forced to escalate this matter to someone of greater standing."

"Of course," she squawked, frantically scrambling away as her eyes flared wide with a glint of hope.

"That was a total lie." Sam elbowed his friend with a chuckle.

"*Phft*," Finn replied, rolling his eyes. "Obviously. You're a Mage in good standing in the same way I'm the heir to House Laustsen, but she's not going to question that. This whole city breeds absolute deference to Mages and Nobles. Besides, no one would claim such an outlandish thing unless it was true. Lying about things like that is a good way to end up on a wanted list. Fortunately for us, we are already as wanted as you can get."

The hostess scampered back into view a second later with a pair of menus clasped to her chest as though they were life preservers. She bowed deeply and handed them over, muttering apologies and thanks. Honestly, the whole thing made Sam feel a little sick to his stomach. Finn was right; this place might've had a veneer of glamour and sophistication, but really, it was no different than his superficial life in California: this was the very same entitlement and elitism he'd come to this game to escape from.

Sam accepted the menu with a grimace as she backed away, nearly doubled over in contrition. He tried to put the hostess from his mind and turned to the menu itself.

Hors d'oeuvre

Shucked Black Pholiota

Red Wine Goldhorn Vinaigrette, Tarragon Sweet Marula, Pan-Sear Black Pholiota. – 8 gold
Benefits: 42 hour hunger dissipation.

Sautéed Mammoth Trout

Harmony Herb Butter, Roc Whip Lemon, Seasonal Mammoth Trout – 7 gold
Benefits: increase intelligence and wisdom by 5
Lasts 12 hours.

Soup of the Day

Cup 5 gold / bowl 8 gold

Avgolemono with Flame-Infused Chicken

Benefits: 20% Increased heat resistance. Adds 10 fire damage to any physical attack. Lasts 2 hours.

Entrées

Lake Otter Au Poivre

Herb Crust, Bindweed Puree, Sweet and Sour Pearl Figs, Coarse Cracked Peppercorn, Jus – 13 Gold
Benefits: Water breathing. Free movement within water.
Lasts 6 hours.

45 Day Dry-Aged Bear Steak

16 oz. Shaved Shiarrot, Almond Herb Sauce, Pink Cavern Salt – 17 Gold
Benefits: Increase strength and constitution by 10.
Lasts 48 hours.

Dessert

Peacock's Delight

Decadent Cacao Mousse, White Walnut Fudge, Crème de Mint Liqueur, Topped with Vanilla Ice Cream – 8 Gold
Benefits: Increase charisma by 15.
Lasts 3 hours.

Sam's eyebrows climbed as he read over the items. The

meals themselves sounded delicious, and the buffs they offered were impressive, but he could only shake his head at the prices. Maybe Finn was right, and this place really was cheaper than going to an alchemist, but it was still *outrageously* expensive. The cheapest thing on the menu was a small bowl of soup, and even that cost five gold—or fifty dollars. The most expensive entrée was over one hundred and fifty dollars a plate. A full meal here would probably run close to three hundred dollars per person. Sure, he could *hypothetically* afford to eat here, but it would burn through his money in days instead of months, and he would never get enough to feed an entire brood of chickens.

Finn, seeming to catch Sam's mood, leaned over and slung an arm around his shoulders.

"Don't worry, old boy. Remember, I'm a poor Noble; I know exactly how much of a sticker shock it is. Just follow my lead. I *agree*, it is *outrageous*. I too think I've lost my appetite." He beckoned the rude hostess from behind her counter and pushed the menus toward her. "We've decided not to patronize your establishment tonight. Perhaps we will try the Painted Stranger instead. I'm sure they will accommodate us according to our *station*."

He *humphed*, turned on a heel, and stalked off, dragging Sam along with him. Sam had to resist the urge to steal a look backward. "What was that all about? Why check out the menu at all, if we weren't going to order?"

"So that you could see what the food does, obviously," Finn replied, rolling his eyes. "Figuring out the buffs can be tricky, but ordering there will break the bank as surely as paying a visit to the local alchemist. Luckily, unlike the alchemist, there's another way to get what you need."

They took a right, walked up a block, and hung another right, doubling back until the restaurant was in view. This time, however, Finn didn't lead Sam to the entrance, but rather guided him to a narrow alley that ran behind the building proper. Tucked just out of view was a large wooden waste bin, heaped up with spoiling food and old leftovers.

Finn smiled like a loon and waved a hand at the bin as though it were the grandest loot box of all time.

"Behold!" he crowed loudly enough that Sam nearly pounced on him. "You see, unlike pure alchemic ingredients that are good more or less indefinitely, mana and elementally infused food has a half-life, which is why it's so expensive. Here's the catch: they can't serve food that has started to degrade. It would ruin their reputation as surely as a rodent outbreak, so they wind up disposing of pounds and *pounds* of perfectly good food."

"But if it's perfectly good... why don't they just sell it at a discount?" Sam shook his head in disbelief.

"Are you kidding me? Places like these are as much about exclusivity as they are about the food. If plebs like you and I could get ahold of this stuff, the snooty, rich Nobles wouldn't want to eat it anymore," Bill filled in before Finn could open his mouth.

"Wait, so you're saying they would literally rather throw it away than give it to people who would benefit from it?" Sam massaged at his head and tried not to lose his temper.

"Of course," Finn announced with a shrug, as though that should have been the most self-evident thing in the whole world. "But that's good news for us."

He reached over and pulled out a huge hunk of meat that looked delicious despite being dumpster fare. "Your chickens won't care where we got it, and this isn't the only restaurant that serves magically infused food. So long as you're willing to get your hands dirty, we can get more than enough to feed your brood... and it won't cost you a dime."

CHAPTER FIFTEEN

For the next two hours, Finn gave Sam and Bill a guided tour of the dumpsters of Ardania. They hit up ten different waste bins scattered around North Waterside—the Painted Stranger, the Thundering Crow, Papaya Bear, the Willow Harbor, and half a dozen more. The food was as varied as the names; some focused-on seafood that provided water-oriented buffs and debuffs, while others offered extremely spicy takes on Thai that did *wonders* for fire resistance and cultivating flame essence. In no time, Sam had thousands—possibly even tens of thousands—of gold's worth of slightly expired food, all safely stowed away inside his spatial flask.

More than enough to raise a brood of chickens… and if not? Well, there was always more where that came from. Best of all, it had cost Sam nothing more than a little sweat and stench. Naturally, Bill was highly disgruntled about the whole process—said it was beneath them, rummaging through garbage—but Finn actually seemed to delight in the work. The Noble gladly pushed up his sleeves and dove in with great gusto, smiling the entire time he picked through delicious smelling entrees.

"My parents would implode from shame if they saw me."

He snatched up a whole lobster slathered in garlic butter. "Divines above, but I wish they were here."

With his primary mission accomplished, Sam, Bill, and Finn finally grabbed a bit of non-expired food at one of their favorite Inns: the Square Dog. The place was nearly packed to the rafters with dirt-crusted adventurers back from a long day of grinding experience by killing the local fauna with extreme prejudice. The Square Dog couldn't have been more different than the snooty Peacock Parlor. The food was delicious and affordable—even if it didn't offer high-quality buffs—seating was open, patrons were laughing, and music was blasting full-tilt.

A long-haired bard wearing a wine-stained doublet worked a hammered dulcimer, plucking at the strings while he drunkenly slurred out the lyrics to a local favorite called Easy Chances. The atmosphere was festive, and no one cared that everyone was dirty and smelled like old BO, or that the entertainment was about one drink shy of passing out face down in the corner. They were living their best lives and enjoying the wonders of Eternium Online. This had been the same tavern where Sam had first met Dizzy and the others. How different things would've been if the Mages had just let him enjoy a night out on the town.

But it hadn't gone that way. Sometimes, it was the small things that resulted in big changes.

Bellies full and hands washed, Sam, Bill, and Finn reluctantly left behind the merriment of the Square Dog. Honestly, Sam wanted nothing more than to eat and drink and enjoy the music late into the night, but there was business to handle. The Wolfmen were at war, he reminded himself, and if they had any chance of coming out on top, the Pack would need an edge. An edge that Octavius' LAW might just be able to provide. That meant books and libraries, instead of music and parties.

Finn paid their tab and the three of them slipped into the night, bound for Ardania's Library.

The building wasn't far from Ardania's city square—the location where human Players respawned after death or dropped into the game when logging in for a session. Day or night, it was always busy, and the heightened guard patrols roaming the area made Sam a little antsy. But with their heads down and cowls up, no one paid them any mind. Everyone else was too absorbed in running their own quests or getting off the streets for the night. Quickly, they found themselves loitering outside a tall, but rather plain looking building.

"Eh, I've seen better," Bill appraised the library from Sam's side. "This place wouldn't even make it into my top five libraries."

Sam had to agree, especially once they headed into the foyer. The interior was rather demure, the floors marble but unadorned, brass candelabras casting soft firelight throughout the building. Each of the several levels contained numerous towering mahogany bookcases filled with literary works. The place *should've* been impressive, but after spending so much time exploring the stacks of the College's exalted library, the Infinity Athenaeum, it was utterly underwhelming.

But then, how could any library compare to the dizzying labyrinth of interconnected spelled bookcases which composed the Infinity Athenaeum? Sam remembered the place as vividly as the first time he'd entered—summoned by Octavius, no less. The lofty bookcases, filled with the rarest and most powerful books in all of Ardania. Ghostly candles and impossible oil lamps floating in the air, perpetually burning with pale purple witchlight that cast no heat. Coolest of all were the walkways that hung in the air overhead, completely unsuspended—a testament to the College's understanding of spatial magics.

"You're sure we need a book from this dump?" Bill's pages fluttered softly as he spoke.

"It's not a dump," Sam hissed at the book.

"Eh, agree to disagree here." Bill eyed the building as if they were about to walk into an *unsavory* place. "I mean, *technically,* it's better than the actual dumpsters we've been crawling through all night like hobo degenerates, but only a little better."

"Play nice, Bill," Finn whispered through gritted teeth.

"This is a perfectly fine library, and it also happens to be the only location outside of the Mage's College that has the book we need. Unfortunately, that book is located in the restricted section, so I'm going to need a bit of a distraction."

"Good evening," an older gentleman groused from behind a wooden desk which was heavily laden with tomes, quills, and stacks of parchment. Seeing it gave Sam a warm and fuzzy feeling inside his chest. "A bit late to be out exploring the Library, isn't it? Perhaps you two would be better served at one of the nearby taverns?"

"Not at all." Finn casually peeled off his embroidered leather gloves, stowing them in his belt as he swaggered forward without letting an ounce of worry show through. That was one of the things Sam respected about the Noble—no matter what the situation, he seemed to bleed confidence. "I am Lord Beckham Farrowgem."

The librarian arched a brow over half-moon spectacles and folded thin arms across his sunken chest. "I've never heard of Beckham Farrowgem."

"Yes, well, not entirely surprised. I'm ninth in line to the Duchy, so my father doesn't exactly parade me around." Finn pressed on with a snort of derision.

"I suppose that explains it. Still," the man nodded and jabbed a gnarled finger at Sam, "that one there is no lord. As a general rule, I don't let travelers peruse my stacks this late in the evening. Adventurer types tend to be sorely lacking in respect, especially where the tomes are concerned."

"You have a sharp eye," Finn agreed in mock approval. He slipped up to the desk and leaned casually against it. "But this is no regular traveler."

He took a long glance at Sam that seemed to order him to say *something*. Channeling his inner Octavius, Sam stepped forward and raised his nose. "I'm a Journeyman with the Mage's College in the Library Sciences field. I've been studying under Mage Solis."

Instantly, the man's demeanor changed, but instead of a

smile, Sam was met with a scowl. Studying Wolfman body language had taught him a thing or two about human body language as well, and he could read outright hostility etched into every line of the man's posture.

"With the *Mage's College*," the man sneered at him. "Then I suppose you've come to raid my stacks, haven't you? I don't have any unauthorized books of magic, so why don't you turn around and scurry back to your *masters*? Tell them the Scholars aren't encroaching on their territory."

Clearly, Sam had badly misunderstood the situation. He'd assumed fellow book nerds would stick together, but it seemed there was a deep rift between the Scholar faction and the Mages of the College.

<Bad choice,> Bill rasped in his head. <The Scholars and the Mages are in an ages-old feud. The Mages hoard knowledge about magic, so any book that even remotely touches on the topic gets carted off to the College. The Mages look down their noses at the Scholars just like they look down their noses at everyone else. This guy probably does have books of magic lying around, but you better believe he has them stashed away deep in the restricted sections. Tell him you're a bookbinder—that'll get him to change his tune.>

"Sorry, Mister?" Sam realized that the old man had continued talking, but he hadn't even noticed till now.

"I am Senior Scholar and Librarian Boris," the man replied stiffly.

"Well Senior Librarian Boris, I'm afraid you've misunderstood. My fault, really. I'm not here to seize books; I'm here to help render any necessary repairs. I'm a Bookbinder by profession, and I need to repair manuscripts in order to advance in my profession."

"You would have me believe you're a *Bookbinder*?" Librarian Boris's eyebrows tried to climb off his face as Sam talked. "That's a very unconventional field, especially for a Mage of the College. Tell me, *alleged* bookbinder, what is a raised band?"

Sam snorted and rolled his eyes. "The notches along the spine, which comes from the sewing support."

"Hmm… and I suppose you could tell me the difference between the recto and verso?" Boris tested further.

"The recto side of a leaf folio corresponds to the right or front side of a page, while the verso is the left or back side of a printed leaf." Sam leaned against the counter and fixed his eyes on the man. "I feel like you're not even trying—these are softball questions, and I can do this all night. I can just as easily break down the differences between Coptic Binding and Saddle Stitch, or walk you through the basic use of my bookbinder tool kit."

Sam slipped out his leather-bound kit, unrolling it with a flourish to reveal spools of waxed thread, his wood-handled awl, and his wolf-bone fold creaser. Boris stood and gestured for Sam to follow. "Impressive set, but such knowledge can be faked. Still, I suppose I could test you more loosely myself. I have a few manuscripts down on this level that need some tender care. Follow me—what did you say your name was again?"

"I didn't," Sam chuckled as they started to move. "But you can call me Octavius."

"Well, Octavius, you can come with me. As for you, young Lord *Farrowgem*," Librarian Boris turned an icy stare on Finn, "you can wait here, if it pleases you. I think this goes without saying, but don't touch anything."

"I would *never.*" Finn sounded utterly scandalized. "It would be a blemish on the name of my Father, Lord Farrowgem. I will wait right here."

"Very good. See to it that you do." Boris grunted and reluctantly turned and whisked away past his desk and into the stacks, waiting for Sam to follow. He moved briskly, clearly a man who knew this place like the back of his hand. He absently trailed his fingers along the spines of books in passing. Sam glanced at the titles, all mundane and boring as sin. *Unseen Shrubs, Exhaustive Fundamentals on Royal Tax Auditing, The Seamstresses' Anatomical Guide to Inseams*. It was a wonder the library wasn't more popping, what with the friendly staff and the host of interesting books like *Elementary Glass-Making for the Novice.*

"Here we are. This one right here should be an adequate test of your claimed skills." Boris promptly pulled out a tattered volume that read *The Wonders of the Lowland Oryctolagus Cuniculus.* The back cover was missing, the pages were badly worn around the edges, and the spine was cracked.

<That is an absolute tragedy,> Bill bemoaned inside Sam's head. <Who would ever think of doing that to a book?>

<We literally make books explode like bombs.> Sam had to hold in a laugh at his own retort.

<That's totally different,"> Bill insisted. <You're comparing apples and flamingos here. Not even remotely in the same category. Now, let's show this pompous naysayer what we can do, huh?>

Sam accepted the book with a smile and headed over to a nearby reading desk tucked away in a small alcove. He pulled out his tools and set to work, though he made sure to take it slowly. The point here was to buy Finn the time he needed to raid the restricted section and get the book they needed. Thankfully, *The Wonders of the Lowland Oryctolagus Cuniculus* was trashed, so it wouldn't be hard to pad the process. First, Sam removed a small knife with a razor-sharp blade from his tool set and carefully cut the front and back covers an eighth of an inch from the spine, allowing him to easily remove the badly damaged outer binding.

The stitch work beneath the spine cover was in fine shape, so he merely needed to trim some of the frayed cloth with his blade. He added binding fabric, quickly cut into shape, then proceeded to use a horsehair brush to slather glue into place. Reattaching the front and back cover plates took more glue and a liberal amount of cutting, but he'd done so a thousand times, and the motions were as familiar as brushing his teeth. Normally, binding glue took quite a while to dry properly, but thanks to a special reagent called Brier Boxwood Powder, the glue set in seconds instead of hours.

In less than five minutes, the book was the picture of health—the pages realigned, the covers straight and cleaned, the spine new and completely repaired. Sam handed the book over as a thin smile stretched across Librarian Boris's pinched face.

"Marvelous," the scholar whispered, turning it over in his hands. "Who would've thought someone from the College would have such talent. Perhaps I was mistaken about you travelers-"

The words were cut short as a clatter from elsewhere in the library echoed off the vaulted ceiling. Boris' expression turned sour at once.

"What was that?" He glanced over a shoulder, though there was nothing to see. Unsatisfied, he swiveled, glaring at Sam. "I thought I told that Noble friend of yours to stay put. Was this all some sort of ruse?" His fingers dug down into the newly refurbished book in his hands. "A distraction so your friend could raid my stores?"

"No, not at all," Sam protested innocently, though that was exactly the truth.

"Well, we will just see, shan't we? Come with me *now,* or I will summon the city guards and have you arrested!" The librarian turned on his heel and stormed off toward the front counter. There was nothing for Sam to do but follow.

<This is bad,> Bill muttered distractedly. <We can't afford to have this guy bring in the city guards. Our story will fall to pieces if they so much as look at it funny.>

<You don't think I *know* that?> Sam fired back. <But what should we do? I'm not about to attack this guy. He's just some old librarian who hates the College as much as I do. I might be with the Wolfmen, but I'm not a monster.>

<Who said anything about attacking? Man, that got dark quick. We just need to make *another* distraction. Come on; this is elementary-level Breaking and Entering, Legs. I thought you had the basics down pat.>

Bill had a point. It was always good to have a backup plan. Still following Boris, Sam slowed and traced his fingers along the books, just as the Librarian had done on the way in. He focused his mana, letting energy swell and erupt from his core as he triggered Book Maker's Book Bomb. He infused a title called the *Handbook of Cave Crystals* and muttered a trigger word under his breath. He let out a sigh as the magic took, all without the angry Librarian being any the wiser.

They rounded the corner a moment later and emerged into the foyer, where Finn was leaning against the desk.

"What was that noise?" Boris barked without preamble. "I thought I told you to touch nothing."

"Yes, well. My deepest apologies." Finn bowed nearly in half. "I may have accidentally bumped into one of your floor lamps." He straightened and gestured toward a large brass lamp, near the wall. "Knocked it over, I'm afraid. A terrible klutz—which is probably why my parents never loved me. 'You're all left thumbs, Beckham Farrowgem'. That's what my father is always telling me. Thankfully, there doesn't appear to be any damage. If there is, please feel free to notify my estate. My dearest father would never want an outstanding debt to ruin the good family name."

Boris sniffed and eyed the scuff mark on the floor, a clear indication that the lamp had indeed fallen over; probably because Finn really was notoriously clumsy.

"Noted," he coldly announced. "But I think it's high past time you and your friend left. I've decided I don't need any help from the College after all. Please see yourselves out at once."

"Of course," Sam appeased the old man. "We were only trying to help, but we certainly wouldn't want to overstay our welcome. Come on, Lord Farrowgem—best we get back to the College before curfew expires."

"If help isn't wanted, why would we stay?" Finn bobbed his head as if he were disappointed in the library. Together, they turned and headed for the exit. Sam felt relief wash over him. They were actually going to get away with this…!

Which is precisely when an alarm sounded.

Bells clanged overhead the moment they crossed the threshold, and Boris's eyes went wide in shock.

"Thief! You've stolen a book!" His face turned beet red, and his hands curled into fists. "Do you think I would leave you alone without some safeguards in place? The Guards will throw you into the Royal Prison for this!"

"Only if they can catch us." Sam raised his voice and belted out his trigger phrase. "*Le~e~eroy*… Jenkins!"

The floor rattled as the book-turned-bomb exploded, fire and smoke billowing up from deep in the stacks. Sam loved books, and he felt genuinely awful about setting the library on fire, but they were at war with humanity. Sometimes you did what had to be done. The color drained from Boris' face, and his mouth turned into a shocked 'O' as he wheeled around and surveyed the tongues of flame.

"My beloved books!" he squawked in horror. Sam grabbed Finn by the shoulder, and the pair of them hightailed it through the door, the blare of alarms chasing them into the night. As they ran, Finn fished a thick tome from beneath his robes. *Magical Theory of Sympathetic Magic: Mastering the Arcane Forces of Spell Twinning.* They'd done it. A pair of prompts followed a moment later:

Quest updated: Humanity's Sabotage (Ongoing). As a racial traitor, you are required to sabotage human institutions on behalf of the Wolfman Faction! By burning a portion of the Scholar's Library of Ardania, you have successfully contributed to the slow but inevitable (hopefully!) downfall of humanity! Congratulations, you unstable maniac. Better yet, you managed to actively sabotage a human institution while also pilfering a valuable item needed to help turn the tide of war—effectively taking out two birds with one stone! You are not only a maniac, but a very efficient one. Well done… I guess!

CHAPTER SIXTEEN

By the time Sam and Finn had put enough distance between themselves and the Library, they were halfway across the city and wheezing from the run. Neither of them had heavily invested in constitution, so tearing around city streets and back alleyways at a full-on sprint wasn't inside their typical wheelhouse. Full dark had come long before, and the city gates were closed and locked against the night. If they had pushed, it was possible they could have convinced the guards to open up for them. It wasn't illegal to exit the city after nightfall, but no one ever did, because it was a virtual suicide mission. Asking to leave would raise some rather odd questions among the guards, and navigating the wilderness in the dark was dangerous even for members of the Wolfpack. The Wolfmen wouldn't kill them, but there were plenty of other threats lurking around every stone and behind every bush.

So instead, they headed back to the Square Dog Inn, opted for a warm meal, and got a room for the night. Sam's egg would hatch in fourteen hours and forty-eight minutes, and he wanted to be there when it did. So, he and Finn called it an early night, woke up at the crack of dawn, and were among the first wave of adventurers waiting to slip out of the gates the moment that morning's first light hit.

Navigating back to the Forest of Chlorophyll Chaos took a couple of hours, made even longer by a *massive* pack of feral wolves that decided to waylay them. Thirteen of the shaggy-furred creatures rushed them within sight of the forest, fangs flashing, claws tearing up the earth as they closed around Sam and Finn in a ring of death. The wolves just didn't realize it would be *their* death. Mages were rare in the game, and there were two good reasons for that: *one*, the Mage's College had a stranglehold on all things magic, and *two*, magic was incredibly powerful.

"An unlucky number of enemies." Sam summoned a barrage of floating tomes and unleashed a flurry of paper death, while Finn spammed ice orbs and devastating frozen spears, which easily stabbed through fur and muscle. They siphoned up the three hundred and thirty-two experience gladly, then begrudgingly took the time to skin and harvest the pelts.

"Unlucky for them." Finn scoffed as they finished up. A lot of the human-aligned adventurers had recently taken to the practice of slaughtering bunnies, foxes, and wolves and just… leaving the meat and pelts to spoil on the ground. The Wolfmen had *very* strong feelings about such wastefulness and swore up and down that there would be serious repercussions for the laziness and waste, that 'Nature would have vengeance'!

Sam couldn't quite envision how it would all work, but he wanted no part in the vengeance of nature, so he mopped up his kills. Once they made it to the edge of the Forest, things were easy going. Under normal circumstances, navigating the Forest was a nightmare, since stepping in would dump you at a random location.

Luckily for Sam and crew, the Wolfmen had really come through with their handy-dandy location-directing totem necklaces. They arrived outside the Irondown Burrows within just a few minutes' walk. Velkan was milling around by the Dungeon entrance, crouched on his haunches, ears twitching as he surveyed the forest with golden eyes. He straightened as they approached, and a thin twitch of the lips was the Wolfman's equivalent of a broad and friendly smile. "Welcome, friends. It is good to see you returned alive and well. I was starting to worry that the human Mages had captured you."

Bill floated around on his chain animatedly. "Not on *my* watch! I'll blow up the world before I let those jerks get their hands on me again."

"Things got a little tense at the Library," Sam admitted with a shrug, "but nothing we couldn't handle."

"So, your mission was successful, then?" Velkan demanded with a deep stare into Sam's eyes.

"*Oh*, yeah." Sam reached into his spatial flask to fish out the thick tome they'd pilfered from the library. "We got the book. With this, we should be able to finally decipher Octavius' blueprints. We're going to be able to build the LAW, Velkan."

Velkan grunted and flicked his ear. "Good tidings, indeed. In unrelated news, the others have returned from their time at the Totem Training Grounds—if you have no need for me, I will depart for New Narvik. The O'Baba must know of this new development."

"You're good." Sam turned toward his new home. "I'm not going anywhere for a while, anyway. My first chicken egg is about to hatch, and I need to get inside."

"You were able to procure sustenance, then?" The Wolfman appeared genuinely interested. Unlike the others, Velkan took Sam's plan seriously. Soon enough, Sam was sure the others would come around as well.

"More than we know what to do with," he admitted freely, "thanks to Finn and a little dumpster diving."

Sam stashed the book and pulled out a bag nearly overflowing with discarded food. Even knowing where it came from, Sam had to admit the mix of aromas was tantalizing. Savory mingled with sweet, salty waltzed with sour, all of it creating a potpourri of smells that left his mouth watering. His soon-to-be-hatched chicken was going to eat better than the rest of the Wolfpack combined. But it would all be worth it, if his hunch played out.

Velkan closed his eyes and inhaled deeply, tongue lolling out as he seemed to savor the odor. Sam had never seen a body posture quite like it, and he wasn't sure what to make of it. The Wolfmen were a reserved people by nature, but his demeanor was almost euphoric.

"Truly a bounty." Velkan paused as though he had something more to say. "There is much that is not known about our people, but if we have one great weakness, it is this: food. Our people love to eat. It is in our blood. Chicken meat... we love above all things. If you can truly find a way to infuse mana and magic into the meat, you will find a very willing market in the Wolfmen. Speak to me again once you have accomplished this task, and I will introduce you to the Wolfman Marketplace."

Quest alert! Chicken-preneur. Thanks to your blossoming relationship with Velkan of the Redmane Tribe, you have learned that the Wolfmen have a penchant for high quality meat—especially chicken! I told you being a weird egg might just pay off in the end. Thanks to your unique standing as a Wolfman Noble and a Chicken Keeper, you are in a rare position to become the premier Chicken-preneur in all of Ardania! Or at least for the Wolfmen. Once you have managed to create magically infused chicken meat, speak to Velkan again!

"Best I be off." The Wolfman composed himself. "Luck to the work of your hands."

He turned on his haunches and headed off into the trees, quickly disappearing into the thick foliage. Bill blurted out, "Fine, it's official. You were right. I hate to say it, but it seems like this whole Chicken thing really is a good idea. Though, in my defense, it did sound *very* stupid."

"It's only stupid if it doesn't work," Sam shot back. "But I don't think we should count our chickens before they're hatched."

"Terrible. That was just awful," Bill groaned, "and I *like* word play."

They headed into the Irondown Burrows, sticking to the well-trodden pathways they'd previously cleared and carefully avoiding the sections of the dungeon still brimming with traps and bloodthirsty automatons. When they reached the first major juncture, Finn and Sam decided to split up. Finn took the path back to the Barracks—opting to fill Dizzy and the others in on what had happened, then turn his eye on the *Magical Theory of Sympathetic Magic*—while Sam took the other branch, making for the Kitchen, Library, and Husbandry Pen.

Sam's thoughts wandered while he walked, mulling over all the things that needed to be done. He now had enough food to keep his new Prime Brood Matriarch fed for a week or more, but he still needed to prepare the Husbandry Pen itself for all the new chicks he was expecting to produce. Right now, it was a mess of stone stalls, more suited for goats or pigs than chickens; he would need wood and tools to fashion a proper coop. That, in turn, got his mind thinking about all the building materials he would require to make the jump from Bibliomancer to his next specialization: Libriohexer.

He trudged up the gentle rise and pushed his way past the gate which stood guard over the Pen. He froze in shock.

"*Surprise*!"

Kai, Dizzy, Sphinx, and Arrow stood with enormous grins plastered across their collective faces. The nest that Sam had painstakingly built had been left alone, but everything else about the Pen was different. They'd cleaned up the room, brought in fresh hay to cover the floors, and had taken the liberty of converting the myriad of stalls into roosting perches and stacked nesting boxes that looked like oversized cubby holes. Wooden ramps zigzagged across the stalls, allowing the future chicken residents to reach the roosting boxes far from the floor.

"What is all this?" Sam stammered, feeling shock bleed through him.

"We felt bad," Dizzy admitted with a grimace. "We

shouldn't have laughed at you about your whole Chicken Farming idea."

"It's true." Arrow decided not to make Dizzy do all the apologizing. "We wouldn't be here at all if it wasn't for you and Finn. We should've supported you, even if the idea did sound wild, and we failed you as a packmate. When we filled Sphinx in about everything, she sort of showed us the error of our ways."

"Yeah," Kai rubbed at his shoulder, "but she probably didn't need to use the edge of a knife to do it."

"I sure enough did," the Rogue flatly stated. "Sam's ideas may be a little unconventional, but we're supposed to be a team. That means supporting each other."

"She's right," Dizzy shot him a chagrined smile. "We got to talking after we each did a round at the Totem training grounds and decided that, instead of just apologizing, we would put our money where our mouths are."

She waved a hand at the newly renovated pen, and after taking it in one more time, Sam muttered, "I don't even know what to say."

"Usually 'thank you' is a good place to start." Bill bounced the edge of his spine against Sam to get him back in the moment.

The Mage started and smiled at his friends. "Yeah, of course. *Thank* you. This is incredible! But how did you even manage to do it? Where did you get the supplies?"

"Ah, that part was, like, totally easy." Kai waved away Sam's concerns. "I spent some time living on a communal farm just north of San Fran, and, like, I had to tend chickens for a month or two. We told Velkan, and the fur-brother practically tripped over his own tail to help. Say what you will about the Wolfmen, but they know their way around a set of woodworking tools."

"It set us back a little bit," Dizzy tapped a leather pouch at her hip, "but we know it's going to be worth the investment, because your ideas are awesome."

Sam felt lightheaded. This was more than he ever could

have hoped for. It wasn't just that they'd gone out of their way to make this happen; it was the fact that he had friends that cared enough to do it. His parents were well-off, and they had always sent him to the best private schools that money could buy. His education had been top-notch, no doubt about that. But those types of schools were a breeding ground for entitled trust-fund kids and scions of generational wealth who would never need to work a day in their lives, if they didn't want to. Most *didn't* want to.

Not Sam. He'd always wanted more than parties and designer clothes. He'd been an outsider. Socially isolated. He'd never had friends like this. "Thank you all. This means more to me than I could ever tell you."

"We're happy to do it. Now, if you *don't* mind," Dizzy clapped her hands to pull all eyes to her, "we're going to leave this place in your more than capable hands. We worked through the night to get everything done, so I'm going to go grab a bath and maybe a few hours of shuteye."

Sam thanked them all again as they headed out. After they had gone, Sam noticed that Bill was unusually quiet. "You okay? Seems like there's something bothering you."

"Naw." Bill looked away. "This is just… eh, it's a really good group you got here. I've spent the past three hundred years keeping my own company. I forgot how nice it is to have people who care about you around."

"Are you getting sentimental on me, Bill?" Sam ribbed his companion.

"No. Never. *Obviously*. Don't ruin the moment. I'm just saying it's a good crew. Now, if you're done being all weepy-eyed and introspective, I think the fireworks are about to start." He ruffled his pages toward the golden egg nestled in the makeshift nest. It was moving, and cracks spread across the golden shell as something inside struggled to break its way free. Sam checked his incubation countdown clock for the hundredth time. Less than a minute to go. Showtime.

He hustled over to the side of the nest and dropped into a

crouch. He didn't want to miss a single moment. A golden beak punched through the shell, the cracks turned into fissures, and a moment later, the top of the shell popped off with a **crack* to* reveal a downy, fuzz-covered head. Big golden eyes stared at Sam for a long beat; then the chick chirped and shook its body, shedding pieces of golden shell as it stood and tested out its legs for the first time. It was far larger than a regular chick would be —already the size of a full-grown adult hen—but its puffball appearance confirmed that it was indeed a baby. Its feathers were not the yellow of a baby chick either, but rather were a patchwork quilt of metallic gold and silver.

It was a beautiful little thing, and it stared at Sam with strangely intelligent eyes, weighing him as it stepped from the shell and hopped across the floor on feet that were capped with wicked-looking talons.

"It's okay, little guy," Sam crooned, extending one hand. He reached into the spatial flask and retrieved a handful of savory food: Pearl Figs covered with Bindweed Puree. It smelled like heaven. The chick eyed the meal approvingly and hopped forward another couple of steps, hesitant, but clearly hungry.

"Come on and eat already, you little ball of floof!" Bill barked at the chicken. "Do you have any idea what we had to do to get that for you, huh? How many dumpsters we had to crawl through? By we, I mean Legs, because *I* would never stoop so low."

The bird stopped abruptly, and Sam held his breath, afraid that Bill had just ruined everything. Instead, the little bird fixed its eyes on the book that remained floating nearby. Naturally, Bill was scowling down at the chick, because of course he was. But her eyes seemed to grow to the size of teacups in awe. She chirped again, infatuated, and rushed toward Sam's outstretched hand, burying her beak in the food and gobbling it all up in seconds. Hungry indeed. Sam hurriedly scooped out another palmful. She blazed through it with gusto. He offered a third and fourth portion. By the fifth, the little chick finally seemed satiated.

She shook her head, then padded over to Bill and bumped the grumpy floating book with the top of her head.

She was in love.

Congratulations! The Prime Brood Matriarch has imprinted on Sam_Knight and Sir William the Bravi—more informally known as Bill the Book. Though, to be honest, she is really into the book guy. They might be new BFFs. Hey, that's good for you, because she is unwaveringly loyal and will follow you to the ends of the earth and fight beak and claw to keep the pair of you safe. Should the Prime Brood Matriarch perish, she will respawn four hours after death. Would you like to fix her respawn location as the Irondown Burrow Husbandry Pen? Yes/No

Sam selected 'yes'.

Nice! Would you like to name the Prime Brood Matriarch? There is no obvious benefit to naming the Prime Brood Hen—there's no secret reward or anything—but Prime Brood Matriarch sure is a mouthful. Sometimes, I suppose, convenience is its own reward! Be careful, though; once you name her, there's no going back!

"Who's a good little fluffball?" Bill crooned at the bird as she continued to bump her little head against his spine. "You are, that's who!"

Sam didn't have to think long, eyeing the way the little chick looked at Bill. "Floof."

Just confirming here; you want to name the *Prime Brood Matriarch: Floof? Yes / No.*

Sam selected 'yes'.

The chick trilled in happiness and waddled over, already looking for more food. It appeared they could finally start counting those chickens, after all.

CHAPTER SEVENTEEN

Two days later, Sam and company decided to try their hand against the toughest Guardian Junction the Irondown Burrows had to offer. The previous afternoon, with Finn and Sphinx back in the fold, they'd taken a run at the Training Hall, presided over by a mechanical, faceless training dummy clad in heavy steel armor. The training automaton had fought with a blunted sword in one hand and a flanged mace in the other, but he hadn't stood a chance against the Wolf Pack's combined might and magic. They'd handily mopped the floor with the creature, claiming his monster Core and a total of nine hundred and eight experience before activating the room's junction.

After all of the trials they'd gone through so far, taking out the faceless trainer had felt like a badly needed win, and was one that had put a spring into everyone's step. The victory was a reminder that, although they were powerful alone, they were nearly unbeatable when they worked together. As Sam's father had often said when on a construction site, 'teamwork makes the dream work'.

The rewards for their gamble had been excellent. Now they had an archery range, a sparring ring, and an agility room perfect for leveling up dexterity-related abilities. Sam probably wouldn't be spending too much time trying to hone his tumbling skills, but he was excited to have a space to work on his blade work with Bill.

The whole team was floating on cloud nine from their string of victories. Not only had they managed to capture three of the nine Junctions, but Sam had managed to get his chicken farm up and running, and they were on the verge of a breakthrough with the LAW. It seemed like they couldn't lose, which is exactly when Kai offhandedly suggested that they take a shot at the worst the Dungeon had to offer. Chances were high that they would die, but they would never know what they were really up against until they rolled the dice. Besides, what if they *didn't* lose?

As Dizzy reminded them often, they were in a war, and currently on the weaker side. If they wanted to survive when the tensions between the Wolfmen and the Humans escalated to open conflict, they would need to take some risks.

The worst this place had to offer was the *Flame Forge Armory*. According to the Compendium, that was where the master of the Irondowns dwelled. The place was to be avoided at all costs, 'if you value your life'. Sam was a little worried, but he also had some awesome new spells that he hadn't really had a chance to try out… and what better opportunity than against the Dungeon Boss of the Irondowns? Arrow had seemed the most reluctant of the bunch, but Dizzy had helpfully pointed out that Dungeon Boss meant both experience and also epic loot. So far, they hadn't found much in the way of loot.

If the Dwarven folk who had once called this place home had left anything behind, it was bound to be stashed away in the Armory.

So, well-rested, bright-eyed, and fully equipped, Sam and the others made their way to the second level of the Irondown Burrows, past the wild assortment of deadly traps, and to the north-western-most corner of the dungeon: the final room and the home to the Keeper of the Forge. At the end of a long hallway waited a set of steel double doors, ten feet tall and studded with bronze rivets. Even with the doors shut to the world, Sam could feel the heat rolling out from the room on the other side, as well as hear the faint clang of metal on metal.

"Are we sure this is the right choice?" Bill nervously questioned as they crept steadily closer. "I mean, it's no skin off my teeth either way, since I don't exactly have skin or teeth, but I'm getting some serious party wipe vibes off this place."

"This is a risk, which is why Finn and Velkan are under *strict* orders to run if we're going down," Dizzy allowed uneasily, "but everything in life is a risk. My mom used to tell me that the best thing I could do was to get the hardest task out of the way first thing in the morning, and then everything else would be easier from there."

"That's great advice for doing the dishes or hitting the gym," Arrow admitted gently, "but I'm not sure that same logic holds to dungeon bosses."

"But think about how far *ahead* this will put us." Dizzy stole a sidelong glance at the reluctant Ranger. "We take this thing out, and we're *golden*. I mean that in more ways than one. There is probably a literal ton of gold stashed away in there. Think about all of the things we could do with our own Forge. I already picked up Blacksmithing as my secondary profession. With access to my own Dwarven forge, I'll be able to make us some killer gear. Or, at the very least, repair the stuff we have."

"I'm with Dizzy on this one, bro," Kai sided with the leader with a shrug. "The worst thing that happens is we die and lose half a day. The best thing that happens is we take out the Irondown big baddies and make off like kings. Let's do this."

They lined up outside the massive doors while Sphinx took point, carefully investigating for any hidden traps, switches, or mechanisms. The rest of the team used the opportunity to prepare for whatever they might find on the other side. Velkan checked and doubled-checked his simple leather armor. Arrow inspected his quiver—he had at least three different types of shafts, though by far the most numerous were the arrows tipped with the glass acid vials, to be effective against metal. Kai chanted softly under his breath, eyes closed, with one fist pressed against the other. A soft white light enveloped him. That was his Zen Trance ability, which increased his chance to land a critical hit by fifteen percent for ten minutes.

Sam used the opportunity to activate Papier-Mache Mage, plastering himself in conquistador-style armor, then double checked his newest item: the cloak hanging around his shoulders and trailing down to the back of his knees. Crafting it had been a nightmare, even with his formidable skills as a bookbinder, but he was extremely pleased with the outcome. The interior of the cloak itself was carefully stitched together from fifty sheets of the highest quality mana-infused vellum, all stained with a deep black dye. A thousand mana-infused feathers had carefully been affixed to the outside of the leather, in a painstaking process that had taken most of the night.

Hopefully, all the time and effort would be worth it.

"Huh, who woulda guessed it? I can't find a gosh darn thing." Sphinx straightened and shook her head, sounding more than a little bit perplexed. "You'd think whoever designed this place would put at least a few traps on the final Boss Room."

"Unless the Keeper of the Forge is all the defense the room needs," Bill offered, not super helpfully.

"I guess we'll find out." Dizzy's fingers flexed around the heft of her war maul. "Once again, Velkan and Finn, you two can't respawn, so *no heroics*." Her words were sharp, but her gaze lingered for an extra beat on Finn. The Noble had a serious crush on her, and he didn't bother to hide it. She'd never really acknowledged it, but the way she looked at him spoke volumes to Sam. Studying body language really had paid some serious dividends. She cleared her throat and tucked a strand of hair behind her ear.

"I'm serious," she continued slightly more breathlessly. "You two play it safe. Linger toward the back, and make sure you get the abyss out of dodge if things start to go sideways."

"You can count on me," Finn winked and flashed a cheeky

grin. Velkan just nodded his understanding, his golden eyes never leaving the oversized doors. His posture spoke of wariness and reluctance, but he would do his part.

"Everyone, follow my lead." Dizzy took a deep breath, squared her shoulders, then slammed a foot against the doors, flinging them open with a **clang* that reverberated throughout the room. The ringing of steel on steel abruptly cut off, the abrupt silence rather ominous. She stalked forward, Kai on her right, Sphinx on her left, already scanning for any traps that might await them on the other side of the door. Sam, Finn, and Arrow came up the center, with Velkan playing rear guard—making sure nothing nasty got the drop on the spellcasters, like an assassin with the ability to slip undetected through the shadows.

A sense of awe washed over Sam as he got his first good look at the Irondown Forge. He'd been expecting a simple blacksmith workshop—a few workbenches, some tool racks, a smelter and forge, barrels for quenching—but he couldn't have been more wrong. The room was a natural cavern, the ceiling and walls carved of rough natural stone. Ahead, a stone bridge connected to a circular stone platform, fifty feet in diameter. Below ran a moat of churning magma, which lit the room with a harsh orange glow. Another bridge arched away from the platform, connecting to a wide gate protected by an iron portcullis. Even from a distance, it was easy to see the weapons and armor piled up inside the protected vault.

That, and the gold. A fortune in gold.

Getting to it wasn't going to be easy. Waiting for them in the center of the circular platform was the Keeper of the Forge and the Guardian of the Irondown Burrows, twelve feet tall and eight feet across at the shoulders: a steel golem. A hulking contraption of iron and steel and spikes, its entire surface appeared to be engraved with elaborate runes and sigils of power that glowed with fiery golden light. A great helmet with curved horns sat atop its frame. Peeking out from between the joints and from behind the helmet's faceplate was nothing but brilliant magma.

"Not a steel golem at all," Sam voiced after a second, "but a greater fire elemental contained in steel armor?"

The creature carried a glowing golden hammer six feet long with a hammer face as large as a hubcap. Bill agreed with the assessment, "*Yup*. I'm going to go on record and say that this is a *terrible* idea. That thing is at *least* level thirty. We should turn around and call it a day. If you all really have a death wish, Sam and I can give you a thousand paper cuts, which will still probably hurt less than whatever that thing is going to do to us."

"Lo! I bid you welcome, travelers," the creature boomed, its voice deep and inhuman but surprisingly jovial.

That caught everyone completely off guard. So far, the automatons of the Irondowns were powerful and clearly intelligent in their own way, but none had spoken.

The elemental continued, "It has been an age since I've had a proper visitor to the Forge. It truly warms my heart, which is no easy thing, since my heart burns at twenty-two hundred degrees Fahrenheit! Sadly, I must earnestly encourage you to listen to your compatriot there. The floating book fellow. Much as I hate to inform you of this—because I would love a little company—if you lot cross that bridge, I'll have to kill you all in a horrible fashion. Missing limbs. Disembowelment. Roasted alive. Very unpleasant. So best just keep your distance, I'm thinking."

Everyone turned to Dizzy, but she looked just as flabbergasted by this strange turn of events as anyone else. Sam straightened and cleared his throat. "Why do you have to kill us if we cross the bridge? I mean, you clearly don't want to, so why not just let us in?"

"Wish that I could," the elemental replied with true sorrow in its voice. "I'm not much for killing or maiming. Even rending doesn't sit quite right with me, not on the gut level, if you get my meaning. I'm a creature of creation and inspiration by nature. Everyone thinks fire is destructive, but I like to think of it as transformative. I'm an agent of change, applying heat and pressure and force to transform things into the best versions of themselves. Never was built for war. Problem is this."

He reached up and tapped a thick metal finger against a sigil burning on his chest. "This is a command rune. A set of magical instructions that compel me to do certain things. In this case, defend the Forge and the Armory from intruders—which you are. Unless, of course, the masters clear you. I don't suppose the masters *did* clear you? What an enormous relief that would be."

"I've got some bad news," Bill blurted out, "but your masters are *long* gone. The Dwarves that called this place home once upon a time have moved on."

The creature tapped thoughtfully at its chin. "You know, that makes so much sense. The smith who created me, Kizmark Grumblebeard, said he was just stepping out for a cup of coffee—but that was five hundred years ago. Five hundred years does seem like a bit on the long side for a coffee run."

"Would it change anything if we told you we were trying to become the new masters of the Irondowns?" Dizzy offered hopefully. "We've laid a claim to the territory and have already managed to capture three other junctions."

"Does that change anything?" the elemental boomed. "Well, of course it does! That's great news. It would be so nice to have someone around here to tell me what to do. I've just been forging and creating and forging and creating." He hooked a thumb toward the armory. "I've made enough weapons and armor to equip a small army. Just kept building it, because no one told me to stop."

"Wait, so you're just gonna let us pass?" Kai cheered and gave a double thumbs-up.

"What? No, not at all. If anything, I'm going to try to murder you far more intensely." He tapped another rune. "My masters were wise and left me with a set of instructions in case something should happen to them. My job is to protect the armory and test any would-be contenders who would lay claim to the Irondowns. Make sure they're worthy of my master's legacy. That sort of thing."

"You sound surprisingly chipper about killing us for a guy who doesn't like violence or killing." Sam hesitantly looked to the others.

"Why wouldn't I be chipper? Destruction for the sake of destruction is just a shame," the elemental stated simply. "But as I said, my purpose is *transformation.* If you would be the new Masters of Irondown, I aim to transform you into the best version of yourselves to make sure you're worthy. Nothing transforms like the forge's fire. The flames purify, and the hammer shapes with each blow. Admittedly, sometimes a piece of iron breaks in the forging, but that only demonstrates there's a flaw in the metal. My job is to make sure you aren't flawed... and *fix* you if you are."

Everyone glanced at Dizzy again, waiting for her cue.

"Form up," she growled under her breath, a look of raw determination etched into the lines of her face. "Our biggest problem is going to be getting onto the platform. That thing is as wide as the bridge itself—probably designed that way to form a choke point, so the guardian can hold off a superior force indefinitely. If we can encircle it and come at it from multiple angles, we'll probably have a better chance."

"Leave that to me." Sam was more than ready to use his cloak. "I've got a new trick up my sleeve, and I think I'll be able to draw him off. Just be ready to move as soon as you see an opening."

Steeling his resolve, Sam pushed his way to the front of the group and started slowly padding toward the looming hulk of iron and fire.

"Good for you!" the elemental cheered. "Best of luck. I sincerely hope I don't crush your skull like an overripe tomato!"

<I hope you know what you're doing,> Bill sent with a worried chuckle.

<Me too!> Sam replied as he called forth his tomes from Bill's Soul Space.

CHAPTER EIGHTEEN

Sam broke into a sprint, his boots clacking on the stone pavers of the bridge as he closed the distance with the elemental golem. He was going to be at a significant disadvantage in this battle—his Shuriken dealt slashing damage, ineffective against heavy plate mail, and his Papier-Mache Armor suffered an additional point-seven-five damage from the elemental effects of fire and water. But his job wasn't to solo this guy; it was just to distract him and draw him away from the bridge so the rest of his team could gain the platform. *That,* he could do.

With a thought, Sam rotated his Ink Lance and Ice Orb Shuriken tomes to his front two positions and began firing with reckless abandon. Fistfuls of goopy black ink splattered across the creature's armor with wet splats, while faintly glowing paper stars slammed into metal, shattering on impact. Tendrils of frost crept across the armored body, but the frost quickly disappeared, evaporating under the immense heat generated by the fire elemental. The ink blobs fared no better. The creature's armor glowed red-hot, burning the inky splatters away before they could even think of pitting the metal with acid damage.

With a shout, Sam thrust his hand out and conjured his

Quill Blade in a flash of silver magic. He was close now, far closer to the elemental than he had any desire to be, but this was all part of his plan. He darted in low and lashed out with his blade, scoring a direct hit along the creature's belly.

"You're a feisty little fellow, aren't you!" the elemental boomed. "I like that. I think you're overestimating your skills just a *tad*. Between the two of us, I think you could use a bit of practice on your footwork."

"That's what *I'm* always telling him," Bill yelled in delight and fear.

The guardian raised its glowing hammer and swung for the fences. It was a powerhouse, but its attacks were rather slow and cumbersome. Sam ducked beneath the lumbering swing, feeling the monstrous heat of the weapon as it passed overhead. Then he did something no one was expecting.

He turned and leapt off the edge of the bridge.

Shocked cries echoed through the room from his teammates, but Sam put them all out of mind as he watched the magma rush up to meet him. He sure hoped this actually worked. If it didn't, he was going to look like a complete moron when he respawned in eight hours or so. He thrust out his arms, muttered a silent prayer under his breath, then triggered his newest ability. mana rushed out from his core, activating the powerful constructs built into the cloak fluttering from his back. The leather grew rigid, quills fluttered, and a timer appeared in the corner of Sam's vision.

24:59... 24:58...

With a roar of triumph, Sam stretched out his newly formed wings and caught a hot draft of air. The cloak-turned-wings felt like an extension of himself, a new pair of limbs grafted into his back. He banked left, cruising just above the surface of the burbling magma, then pumped his wings on instinct and shot up into the air like a rocket. As he zipped past the lip of the platform, he kept right on going until he hung twenty feet above the elemental—well out of reach of its deadly hammer.

"Huh, haven't seen that trick before." The elemental sounded impressed.

"I'm glad you like surprises, because I've got a few more to show you." Sam rotated the Fire Shuriken tome to the twelve o'clock position and unleashed a barrage of paper stars. The first few went wide—aiming while in the air was trickier than it looked—but the third landed squarely against the elemental's chest, exploding with a burst of gold and orange light. Sam immediately triggered bookmark, then unleashed a barrage of conjured stars that plowed into the guardian with unrelenting fury. A health bar appeared above the elemental, but each hit hardly seemed to even budge the needle.

The slashing damage just couldn't penetrate the thick plate armor. Since the creature was made of living flame, the fire damage was about as effective as shooting a swimming pool with a squirt gun. The explosions themselves at least delivered a minute amount of additional blunt damage—though that wouldn't be enough to kill the keeper. Not unless Sam managed to land ten thousand Shuriken concurrently. But a plume of smoke billowed up after each blow, making it nearly impossible for the elemental to see.

"Well, that is *very* annoying!" the creature grumbled from below. It lifted one hand into the air, fingers splayed back. "But I have a few tricks of my own. Let's see just how good you are with those fancy wings of yours."

With a chuckle, it unleashed a column of flame as thick as a telephone pole. Sam's eyes widened in shock, and he immediately dove to the right, narrowly avoiding the javelin of flame. Sam shouted while furiously pumping his wings, "Bill! Try to keep the pressure on it with the Fire Shuriken!"

"On it, Wings," Bill affirmed. "You just keep us from getting charbroiled alive. Flame doesn't exactly agree with my sensitive skin."

Sam swooped and dove, avoiding the slashing beams of fire while Bill continued their Shuriken onslaught. It was a losing battle in the long run—all it would take was one wrong move on

Sam's part, and they were done for. This cloak was a powerful artifact, but it wasn't fireproof. If the elemental managed to land so much as a glancing blow from that flame lance, the leather and quills would go up in a puff of smoke and Sam would tumble right into the churning magma below. Thankfully, it was a battle he wouldn't have to fight much longer.

The elemental golem was so absorbed in swatting Sam from the air that it had moved solidly into the center of the platform and hadn't even noticed that the rest of the Wolf Pack had managed to encircle it.

"Now!" Dizzy bellowed as she raised her maul and slammed it into the side of the elemental's knee. The rest of the Wolf Pack attacked as one. Finn, still on the bridge, lifted his hands skyward and threw his head back. Icy fingers of blue magic launched into the air. A churning white cloud formed about the Keeper of the Forge, and hailstones as big as Sam's head started pouring down on the guardian, smashing into its head and shoulders. The ice sizzled and melted as soon as it made contact, wisps of white steam wafting upward, but the blunt damage from hailstones themselves slowly chipped away at the creature's health.

Dizzy and Kai fought the creature head-on. Despite being weaponless, Kai's lightning-fast fists and feet dealt a wicked amount of damage, leaving dents in the armor with every strike. Unfortunately, his health bar *also* dipped every time he landed a blow—burn damage from making contact with the scorching hot metal surface. It was probably like trying to fight a hot stove. Dizzy dealt less overall damage than the hard-hitting monk, but it didn't cost her precious health with every hit.

Arrow, Sphinx, and Velkan kept their distance, spreading out around the platform in a semicircle. Arrow and Sphinx launched ranged attacks—acid-tipped arrows from the Ranger, and shadowy daggers from the Infiltrator. Meanwhile, Velkan darted in and used his razor-sharp claws to score deep furrows into the surface of the metal armor before ducking back out. The Wolfman fought smart, never overcommitting and always retreating to a safe distance before the elemental could ever focus its efforts on him.

With so many assailants coming at the guardian from every direction, the creature finally relented its attack on Sam. The torrent of flame died away as Dizzy taunted the creature and drew its attention. While Bill continued to launch Fire Shuriken, Sam opted for a different kind of attack. He reached into Bill's Soul Space and fished out a number of thick book bombs, all brimming with wildly unstable magical energy. He folded in his wings and dove toward the Keeper of the Forge, the hot air stinging his face as he fell like a shooting star. At the last possible moment, he stretched his wings out, catching the air currents and swooped directly over the elemental.

He slammed the books onto the pointed tips of the Guardian's curved horns.

The second he was clear, he screamed his trigger word, activating the pair of makeshift bombs. The elemental staggered and reeled from the dual explosions, its health bar dropping by a fifth. Sam swooped and turned mid-air; a wide grin stretched across his face. "Maybe we really can do this after all!"

Sure, this guy was tough, but they'd grown a lot as a team over the past couple of days.

"Not bad, not bad," the elemental calmly stated, "but I'm afraid you all overcommitted. You see, I *wanted* you on the platform."

It lifted one leg and slammed its foot against the stone, shaking the room. All around the platform, flames erupted from the floor. A circular wall of fire, three feet thick and seven feet high, blistered the air with its heat. Sam threw up a hand, shielding his face from the fury of the blaze, but Arrow wasn't so lucky. He'd been standing too near to the edge of the platform, and the flames consumed him in an instant. The Ranger's screams briefly rang through the cavern before cutting off as his health bar hit zero; his charred corpse toppled off the platform and plummeted into the magma moat below.

The elemental had played them all like a fiddle. He'd

purposely let Sam draw him away from the bridge in order to lure the rest of the crew onto the platform so he could spring his trap. Since Finn was the only one who remained on the bridge, he was the only one not hemmed in by the ring of deadly flame, the only one who had a clear path of escape.

For everyone else, it was kill or be killed, and the elemental wasn't done yet.

The Keeper raised his hammer high into the air and let out a ferocious bellow. Streaks of yellow lighting flashed out, and five geysers of magma erupted up from the moat. Glowing red-orange blobs of magma landed on the platform with a meaty **splat**, but they were more than they seemed. The blobs quivered, and limbs of molten fire popped free. The creatures weren't human in shape, but rather looked like squat toads made of liquid metal and living flame: Lesser Fire Elementals.

The fire toads wasted no time turning on the Wolf Pack. They weren't nearly as large or formidable as the Keeper of the Forge, and they didn't have its protective armor, but what they lacked in size, they made up for with speed and numbers.

Two of the toads immediately tag-teamed Sphinx, flanking her from either side. She launched into a flawless handspring, then flipped into the air, hurling black-forged throwing blades from outstretched fingers. The daggers sank hilt-deep into the nearest toad—not that the toad seemed to care even in the slightest. It opened its elongated frog-like mouth and vomited a wave of magma, which splashed over both her legs. She tumbled from the air with a shriek, while the rest of her throwing daggers clattered to the ground beside her. The second fire frog was already waiting to pounce.

It sprang into the air, its jaws extending as it latched onto her face, muffling her screams. Sphinx thrashed and bucked, but it was a losing battle, and her futile resistance ceased a few seconds later as her health bottomed out and she was unceremoniously sent for respawn. They were already down by two teammates, and although Dizzy and Kai had made a little progress on the Keeper, knocking him down to two-thirds health, Sam couldn't see any way for them to win this battle.

Two more of the toads were closing in on Velkan. Unlike Sphinx and Arrow, if he died… there would be no respawn. Finn was doing his best to help the Wolfman, launching waves of Ice Orbs at the encroaching flame toads. His attacks were surprisingly effective, taking decent bites out of their health while simultaneously cooling their magma and hardening the surface of their skin to ashy black rock.

Unfortunately, Velkan had nowhere to go. His back was already up against the flame wall, and his leather armor wouldn't offer much more protection against their attacks than Sam's own Papier-Mache Armor would.

"*Bill*," Sam bellowed, "we need to help Velkan. Switch over to Ice Orb Shuriken and target the toads. I'm going to try to get him clear of the flame ring!"

"On it!" Bill growled as the tomes circling around Sam shifted. Shuriken slammed into the two Flame Toads closing in on the Wolfman.

Damage dealt: 95. Target slowed 15%!

Without bulky metal plate armor to protect the flame toads, the paper stars cut deeply before shattering. Tendrils of blue ice rippled out after each hit, crawling along the surface of the magma as they slowly transformed patches of fiery orange skin into blackened rock. This was Sam's best chance to save the Wolfman. He wheeled in a circle overhead, conjured his Quill Blade, then threw himself into a sharp dive, pulling his wings in close as he hurtled toward Velkan like a cannonball. One of the Fire Toads spun and leapt toward him, but Sam was ready.

With a shout, he drove his blade through the creature's throat, scoring a critical hit and knocking the creature away. He let go of the blade, leaving it planted in the toad, and reached out for Velkan, hooking his hands beneath the Wolfman's armpits. With a grunt and a heave, Sam pumped his wings, lifting the Wolfman into the air. Sweat rolled down Sam's face, and his muscles strained from the effort of holding the Wolfman aloft. He was a Mage, not a Monk or a fighter, and most of his characteristic points were rightfully sunk into intelligence and wisdom, not into strength or constitution.

His stamina bar was dropping fast from the exertion, but he didn't give up. His arms quivered under Velkan's weight, and his wings felt like they were liable to tear away from his shoulders at any moment. Finally, he cleared the ring of flames - and not a moment too soon. His hands slipped, unable to hold onto Velkan for another second.

Sam felt the breath catch in his throat as Velkan dropped like a stone. Unfortunately, Sam hadn't *quite* managed to make it over the bridge. The Wolfman's chest slammed into the stone walkway while his legs swung over the edge. Wide-eyed, Velkan clawed at the stonework, scrambling to find purchase but unable to do so. He was slipping over the edge and there was nothing Sam could do about it.

Luckily, Finn was already on the move. The scrawny mage dove onto his belly, catching the Wolfman by one wrist, then pulled with every ounce of strength he could muster. That wasn't much, since Finn was even weaker than Sam, but it was *just* enough to stop Velkan's slow slide over the edge. Velkan grunted, lips pulling back in a snarl as he reared back with his free hand and drove his claws into a crack between two stones.

Finn braced himself and pulled while the Wolfman wriggled his legs up and onto the bridge. Sam felt a wave of relief wash over him. They were alive.

"Sam! Watch out!" Bill hollered, jarring Sam back into the moment.

He spun midair, eyes widening in shock and horror as a stream of burning magma flew toward him—hurled by one of the summoned Flame Toads. He frantically flapped his wings, but it was too late. Liquid fire splashed over one of his wings, eating through the leather and quills keeping him aloft.

"Celestial *feces*," Bill spat as the glue and thread holding the cloak together literally came apart at the seams. Sam's stomach lurched up into his throat as he tumbled backward, head over heels. He caught a brief glimpse of Velkan and Finn making a break for the exit, and then the only thing he saw was burbling magma rushing up to greet him like an old friend. A tsunami of heat and pain hit him full on as he belly-flopped against the lava, and then the world went black.

You have died! It was really only a matter of time. Honestly, I'm surprised it took you this long to perish in the Irondown Burrows. You fought hard, but trying to skip straight to the Dungeon Boss probably wasn't the wisest move. You miss a hundred percent of the shots you don't take; I suppose. Still, a little patience will go a long way. You have lost 20,000 Experience. Time until respawn: 8 hours. You will spawn at your current bind point, the Irondown Burrow Barracks. Maybe use the time to think about making better life choices!

CHAPTER NINETEEN

Dying, although painful, had a great upside—Sam had a little free time without Bill to touch base with his parents, check his emails, and surf the web. That took all of an hour, and then he spent the rest of his time pouring over Eternium wikis and forums, although a lot of information was still clearly being suppressed. A number of players and streamers had even complained about somehow getting their content removed almost as soon as it went up, though no one could figure out how.

Sam was hoping to get an inside scoop on Interspatial Libraries, but that turned out to be a complete bust. It seemed the folks running the show over at Eternium didn't want any spoilers leaking to those who weren't already on the servers. Or anyone currently on the servers gaming the system. If Sam wanted to unlock his class specialization, he was going to have to do it the old-fashioned way—which meant no cheats, tips, or walkthroughs. Just mountains of elbow grease and a thimble full of luck.

Since he couldn't turn up anything useful on Eternium, he decided to spend his remaining hours of forced relaxation researching chickens and chicken farming. That, and come up with a game plan for what the Wolf Pack should do next.

The others had spent their own respawns doing much of the same thing. After respawn, they spent the rest of the next week making better life choices.

Kai wanted to take another run at the Dungeon Boss, but was quickly outvoted. As a team, they decided the best course of action involved grinding. Tirelessly. They needed to capture the Irondowns, but their tussle with the Keeper of the Forge had been a humbling experience for everyone involved. Sam looked sadly at his character sheet; having been slapped all the way down to level eight *hurt* on a primal level. While he hadn't lost anything besides experience, his specialization quest had turned grey.

Bill explained that it meant he could still work at it, but he couldn't *finish* the quest before getting his levels back.

Name: Sam_K 'Experimental Forger'
Class: Bibliomancer
Profession 1: Bookbinder
Profession 2: Chicken Keeper (locked until level 10)
Level: 8 Exp: 39,304 Exp to next level: 5,696
Hit Points: 140/140
Mana: 511/545
Mana Regen: 15.73/sec
Stamina: 154/154

Characteristic: Raw score (Modifier)
Strength: 20
Dexterity: 34
Constitution: 19
Intelligence: 49
Wisdom: 48
Charisma: 21
Perception: 20
Luck: 14

Karmic Luck: +1

Clearly, the fire golem was leaps and bounds outside their current skill level. So instead of trying to take any more shortcuts to the top, they focused on consistency over time. They trained relentlessly at the Totem Grounds and hunted monsters in the wild areas outside of the Forest of Chlorophyll Chaos—the others were hoping to unlock their own specializations—and focused on clearing and reclaiming the less challenging Irondown Junctions.

Though the days seemed to crawl by at a glacial pace, their efforts paid major dividends. By week's end, Sam had managed to return to level ten, and they'd captured six more nodes, bringing their total up to seven of eight. He hated that all the bonus experience went to getting him back to where he had been, but the others were just as bad-off.

All that remained was the dreaded Keeper of the Forge, and the truth was that they *still* weren't ready to square off against him again. Their victories over the other Junctions had been bitterly fought and narrowly won. The *Compendium on Protected and Dangerous Locations* had been an invaluable tool, but its tips and clues were generic at best, and the Junction Guardians were deadly.

The Librarian had ended up being a monstrous spider crafted from paper and steel that had hunted by sound and vibration, lashing out from the shadows at even the slightest whisper. Bill's big, fat mouth had brought down the spider's papery wrath before Sam had taken ten steps into the Library, and the creature had slit Sam's throat from ear to ear. He'd *almost* died so quickly it had been embarrassing, only managing to stay alive thanks to his demolished armor being reapplied by Bill in almost the same instant it had been destroyed.

The Mad Mechanical Alchemist had released a toxic acid cloud that had sent both Kai and Arrow for respawn. They'd narrowly managed to clear the Control Room by taking out an armored Centurion, but not before the hooved creature caved in Dizzy's skull with a devastating donkey kick.

That had *still* been a huge win.

With the Control Room conquered, they were able to bring all the Former Junction Guardians back online—this time in their service—and configure the traps in previously seized areas. Now they could safely tread through *most* of the hallways of the Irondowns without having to worry about getting impaled by floor spears, sliced in half by oversized doom pendulums, or charbroiled alive by hidden flame vents. Any enemy trying to enter the Irondowns wouldn't be so fortunate. The Dwarven mechs were actually *delightful* contraptions, once they weren't bent on murder.

The Maintenance Mechs cleaned and repaired—Mop even did laundry—the steely-eyed Robo-Chicken helped tend to the coops, and the Melee Trainer was always good for a few rounds of deadly sparring. The Library unfortunately turned out to be utterly disappointing. Like most of the other rooms in the Irondowns, the Dwarves who had once called this place home had packed up their stuff before moving on, and that had included every single book, leaving behind an entire room of empty bookcases. The Librarian itself was fantastically useful, and Sam had big plans for it, once he got his own Interspatial Library up and running.

The best mech ended up being the Kitchen Chef. Ironic, since it had also been the most nightmarish of all the Guardians to subdue so far.

Octo-Chef, as the Wolf Pack had taken to calling it, was equal parts automaton and octopus. The thing scuttled around on segmented arachnoid legs and had six arms protruding from its iron-forged torso, each wielding a different kitchen utensil. An industrial cheese grater in one robotic hand, a tenderizing mallet in another, a brutal meat cleaver in a third, a rolling pin in the fourth, and a razor-edged spatula. The Octo-Chef had carried an impromptu shield in the last hand—a frying pan, of course—and blasted out gouts of boiling water from its mouth.

It would've been funny if the thing wasn't such an absolute terror.

Admittedly, seizing the kitchen had been worth every burn. Octo-Chef was something of a wonder-worker behind the stove. Sam and company were eating like royalty. That was thanks in no small part to his blooming chicken farm. While the other members of the Wolfpack spent their days either grinding out experience over at the Totem Training Grounds or fulfilling their quota of sabotage missions, Sam had been furiously working on his chicken operation.

Floof was a growing girl and had already swelled to the size of a Rottweiler. The fluffy look had gone away after a few days, and she now sported a coat of metallic gold feathers, sharper than most good daggers.

Despite her terrifyingly fast growth and her enormous size, she still followed Sam and Bill around like a lost puppy, chirping and clucking appreciatively as they tended to the coop. Feeding her had turned out to be more of a challenge than Sam had anticipated. He'd burned through his entire supply of food in less than three days and had already had to make another dumpster-dive run into Ardania. But that had been worth it, too.

Aside from Floof's rapidly increasing size, she'd also started producing eggs. A *lot* of them. Anywhere between two and three dozen eggs per day, depending on her mood and diet. All were larger than a standard chicken egg, closer in size to ostrich eggs, the shells brown and speckled and strangely warm to the touch.

The eggs wouldn't just hatch on their own. They required significant TLC, but in a very game-logic way, they didn't require a rooster to produce chicks. They did require specific incubation conditions to be met—just as the Prime Brood Egg had. So, Sam had spent hours upon hours carting in fresh hay and creating more of the mana-infused heating stones, which he used in the coop stalls lining the walls. Unlike Floof, a properly incubated basic chicken egg would hatch within four hours.

The feathered minions that emerged were just as cute as Floof had been, but they lacked her size and metallic plumage. Like Floof, they grew fast. They never reached her size, but they were all at least twice as large as any chicken Sam had ever seen in real life. Those new chickens quickly took to laying eggs of their own, though these were of the normal variety and couldn't be incubated, no matter what Sam tried. That was fine, because they made for good eating.

He'd also had his first success in hatching a magically enhanced chicken: the first Lesser Brood Matriarch. She had bright orange and red plumage, radiated as much heat as a furnace, and had the fiery temper to match. Sam had taken to calling her Blaze, though Bill offhandedly decided to nickname her 'Spicy Chick'. Sam was feeding Floof a steady supply of fire-enhanced curry, and he was fairly sure that Blaze was the end result. Unlike the others, her eggs *could* be successfully incubated. Her brood all had the same plumage, and the meat itself was deliciously spicy and offered a twenty-five percent fire resistance bonus for three hours.

Over the course of a single week, Sam ended up with three dozen healthy chickens. And with Floof and Blaze producing so many viable eggs, Sam had taken to the process of culling the flock—with a little help from Velkan.

The feathers were carefully plucked, then meticulously cleaned and sorted into another area where Sam and Bill processed them into quills. Regular, run-of-the-mill chicken feathers weren't exactly in high demand, but assuming this process worked, they wouldn't be regular run-of-the-mill chicken feathers for long. Already, the feathers from the Firebirds held fifteen percent more mana than typical unenchanted quills. When used in preparation of fireball spell scrolls, they caused the spell to be three percent more effective. Not a lot, but not nothing. The rest of the feathers were treated and stored to be used as replacements for the Quill Wings Cloak.

Once the feathers were taken care of, the skin was carefully removed and set aside to be turned into vellum. That was a time and labor-intensive process, and it quickly became apparent to Sam why vellum was so expensive to buy. Aside from the ingredients themselves, manufacturing the material was painful and tedious.

First, the skin had to be gently scrubbed clean with a smooth pumice stone, removing any excess feathers or meat, before being stretched tight over a series of wooden frames built just for that purpose. Once the vellum was in place on the frames, Sam would alternate between wetting and drying the skin while working it over with the keen edge of a curved skinning blade, bringing it to the correct thickness. Finally, Sam finished off the process by applying a type of abrasive, powdery chalk so that the skin would accept and hold ink. Added to that, the need to infuse the vellum with mana meant that each piece took more than ten minutes to prepare.

Not a lot of time in the grand scheme of things, but when there were hundreds or even thousands of sheets to prepare, all of those minutes added up *fast*. The end result was still worth it, because buying vellum was a gold coin per sheet, which meant a few hundred sheets could quickly end up being the price of a used car back in the real world. He didn't have that kind of money to burn, not anymore, and he would need thousands of dollars' worth of materials to kick-start his Interspatial Library. All that scraping and curing also had the added benefit of leveling up his Bookbinders Skill by one, bringing him up to level three.

Bookbinder Profession benefits at Level Three: Increases the speed of reading and writing by 65%. Reduces cost and production time for paper, ink, and book bindings by 30%. Salvage and reclaim 60% of damaged paper, vellum, ink, and bookbinding materials.

As for the rest of the butchered chicken—the meat and organs—all went straight to the kitchen to be processed by Octo-Chef and Velkan; the Wolfman, in particular, seemed very pleased by the arrangement. Most of the high-quality cuts of meat ended up going into a cold pantry to be used for meals later on. It was hard to get food out here, away from human civilization. The Wolf Pack still hadn't managed to find a decent place to buy fresh produce, so most of their vegetables and fruits were harvested in the forest, which was always a risky proposition. Getting fresh meat was a little bit easier, thanks to all the rabbits, wolves, and foxes roaming the countryside, but having the chickens on hand was vastly easier.

And tastier.

Even with the crew eating their fill morning, noon, and night—chicken and waffles, chicken and dumplings, chicken noodle soup, chicken tacos, fried chicken—there was still plenty of meat to go around. Not to mention the offal, which no one in the Wolf Pack wanted to touch with a ten-foot pole. The idea of eating chicken hearts just wasn't overly appetizing, even if they did offer some hefty health regeneration buffs. Thankfully, the Wolfmen loved the organ meat and they couldn't get enough of Sam's chicken.

Which was why, today—for the first time—Sam and Velkan were in New Narvik to offload their surplus. They didn't want the meat to spoil, and having a little extra coin for the guild coffers was never a bad thing. Since Sam had managed to produce magically enhanced chicken, Velkan had finally agreed to take him to the Wolfman Marketplace.

The pair of them threaded their way through the sprawling dirt streets of the makeshift city. A formidable palisade wall surrounded the encampment, and as with most Wolfman villages, the houses were built high up among the tree branches, connected by hanging rope bridges. The shops were tucked away at the bases of the trees, where it was easier to spread out wares or work. Sam and Velkan offered polite greetings to the Wolfmen as they passed, and Sam expected them to stop at any moment. The cagey Wolfman guided him deeper and deeper into the heart of the encampment, past most of the shops and stalls that Sam was most familiar with.

"Where exactly are we going? We just passed by Sukin's stall." Sam started faltering. He hooked a thumb toward a lean grey-furred wolf, selling various odds and ends—everything from strips of leather to stringy-looking carrots. “I was sort of assuming that’s where we would sell it.”

Velkan chuffed, ears twitching, the Wolfman equivalent of laughing hysterically.

“No. I told you I would take you to the Wolfman Marketplace. That,” he gestured toward the old vendor, “is not the Wolfman Marketplace. That is the place for young cubs to procure things for the Pack. But you will not make the money you need selling at such a stall. Now that you have a product with real value to the Pack that is worth moving in bulk, it is time you become a true merchant. It is just a little further now.”

He guided Sam past a wooden longhouse set back among a circular grove of trees with a small clearing in the middle. They pushed through the treeline, and Sam froze when he saw two massive wooden poles, topped with a simple wooden beam running across the top. It was just like the Totems from the training ground, though these beams were carved to resemble a crafty-looking fox with a pinched face and sly eyes.

<I’m sensing major energy pouring off this place,> Bill sent into Sam’s head instantly. <Like… *big* time spatial magic. For being uncivilized monsters, these wolf folk sure have a few tricks up their sleeves.>

“This is just like the Totem Grounds,” Sam stated breathlessly, feeling a thrum of excitement run down his arms. Velkan grunted in acknowledgement. “But I don’t understand. The Totems train specific attributes. Does this place do the same thing?”

Velkan offered a bare flash of his teeth. Sam couldn’t quite discern the meaning. Amusement? Excitement? “This is not for training, Sam of the Wolfpack. Fighting and training is of utmost importance to our people, but we are also a people of commerce. As in life, commerce is war. You need a proper battlefield to host such negotiations. This is one entrance to the Wolfman Market, but there are many like it. Each Outpost has a Totem such as this, and they all lead to the one true Wolfman Marketplace. This is a place where our kind go to barter with our kinsman from all over the wild. Its existence is even more closely guarded than the Totem Training Ground. Humanity must never know about what we have built."

"But I'm a human," Sam protested weakly, hoping he wouldn't be kicked out for reminding the Wolfman.

"Only in your flesh. In your heart, you are a wolf. A wolf with a Noble title, no less. Now that you are also a merchant, you are within pack rights to know of this place. Come." He turned on lupine feet and headed between the pillars, vanishing in the blink of an eye.

CHAPTER TWENTY

Sam followed Velkan through the pillars, bracing for the worst. Unlike the most memorable time he'd stepped through a Totem portal, he didn't find himself in the heart of a blizzard with a couple of monsters waiting to mob him. Instead, he emerged into an enormous underground cavern, the ceiling two hundred feet overhead and studded with crystalline stalactites that glimmered from the light of a hundred campfires. All around him sprawled a city of tents and wood-framed shops, manned by more Wolfmen than Sam had ever seen in one place. There were hundreds of them.

Maybe thousands.

Master blacksmiths worked at forges, hammering away at red-hot steel, while leatherworkers patched armor and seamstresses measured and cut bolts of cloth. Alchemists brewed potions, and there even seemed to be a Wolfman barber trimming fur with a straight razor—though they left behind some nasty cuts in the process. That hardly seemed sanitary, but none of the customers complained. More Wolfmen circulated amongst the shops, haggling, buying, bartering for a thousand different items. This was easily on par with anything Ardania had to offer, and all right here under Sam's nose. He'd never suspected a thing.

Quest update! Chicken-preneur. Thanks to your blossoming relationship with Velkan of the Redmane Tribe and your unique position as a Wolfman Noble and a Chicken Keeper, you have been granted access to the Totem Trading Ground, known as the Wolfman Marketplace. You can trade and barter freely, but until the Wolfman Merchant Council fully trusts you, you won't be able to vouch for any other humans.

Perform 10,000 gold worth of mercantile transactions within the Wolfman Marketplace to upgrade your reputation with the Wolfman Merchant Council from 'Reluctantly Friendly' to 'Friendly.' Once you unlock 'Friend of the Merchant Council,' you will be able to vouch for other humans and bring them to the Marketplace.

Ding-ding-ding! World's First! Congrats, you're the first human to ever step foot in the Wolfman Marketplace. Don't get me wrong; there have definitely been human feet here before, but this is the first time those feet have been attached to a living, breathing person and not served up as a snack food. Between us, I'd recommend that you stay on your very best behavior if you want to stay alive. For being the very first *player to access the Wolfman Marketplace, you gain a permanent +2 Intelligence, +2 Perception, +2 Wisdom, and +50 personal fame with Ardania! Title unlocked: Merchant Ambassador.*

Merchant Ambassador: When this title is actively displayed, buying and selling prices are improved by 10%, and you have an +8% advantage on persuasion checks.

Warning! You have surpassed the maximum number of total titles. Please note that all title effects are active at the same time, but the title you have equipped will be the only one that others can see without analysis abilities.

The maximum number of titles you can have at any given time is ten. You must select one title to remove.

1) Stick it to the Man!

2) High Five, I Tried!

3) Budding Anthropologist

4) Bunny Reaper

5) Soul-Bound Level 2 (Upgradeable)

6) Experimental Forger
7) Night Prowler
~~*8) Warlock IV (Mandatory)*~~
~~*9) Racial Traitor (Secret, Mandatory)*~~
10) Chicken Whisper Level 1 (Upgradable)
Option) Merchant Ambassador.

Sam had known this was coming for a while and knew which title to sacrifice: Bunny Reaper. It offered an eleven percent damage bonus against rabbits, but the sheer fact that it was only useful in very specific circumstances meant that it was nearly useless. He chose to delete it and quickly made Merchant Ambassador his new active title.

Name: Sam_K 'Merchant Ambassador'
Class: Bibliomancer
Profession 1: Bookbinder
Profession 2: Chicken Keeper
Level: 10 Exp: 61,482 Exp to next level: 4,518
Hit Points: 150/150
Mana: 645/645
Mana regen: 18.41/sec
Stamina: 165.5/165.5

Characteristic: Raw score
Strength: 21
Dexterity: 37
Constitution: 20
Intelligence: 58
Wisdom: 56
Charisma: 23
Perception: 22
Luck: 14
Karmic Luck: +1

"Sam! Quick sidebar." Bill dragged Sam away from his thoughts as he accepted the new title. Bill sounded like he was in absolute awe, which was very unusual for him. The book wasn't in awe about anything. Ever. ...Other than himself. He *was* a very self-assured book. "I feel like such a moron, but I finally get it now. I know what this is. How this works."

"How *what* works?" Sam inquired under his breath, still looking around wide-eyed.

"The *Totems*. It's been gnawing at me since we took our trip into the training grounds. It's definitely potent spatial magic; I was right about that much. I'm familiar with spatial and temporal pockets—the College used them when designing their campus—but I couldn't figure out how the Wolfmen were able to move the pillars around. Like I said before, spatial magic is usually built around fixed temporal points. I was assuming that the Totem poles themselves were the spatial anchors, but now I'm starting to think that's where I was wrong... and I'm rarely wrong. This place—all of these places—are enormous spatial libraries."

"Wait." Sam stopped abruptly and gestured at the cavern. "But how can this be a spatial library? It's huge. Also, not really a library either."

"The last bit is semantics. We call them 'libraries' because we're Bibliomancers, and we pull our power from books and paper and ink. The space which an Interspatial Library occupies could be filled with anything. Begrudgingly, I'll admit I didn't think something like this was even possible, but it's the only thing that makes sense. That's why they can move them around—because they aren't bound to a location, they're bound to a person. The Totem poles are just doorway access points, just like I'm the access point that allows you to summon orbital casting tomes. But I'm almost positive that this space itself is inside someone's Soul Chamber."

Sam went stiff as though thunderstruck. They were walking around inside someone's Soul Space?

"Is everything alright?" Velkan's gravelly voice held a hint of concern.

"Yeah, fine." Sam cleared his throat. He shot Bill a look:

don't say any more. Velkan had been awfully touchy about the Totems and how they worked. Now wasn't the time or place to ask more about this. "Totally fine. Bill and I were just chatting about how amazing this place is. Please… show us the way."

Velkan's ears twitched, and the hair along his arms rose for a moment—sure signs of distrust. Obviously, bringing an outsider into this space was a big deal, and he had more than a little apprehension about it. The Wolfman quickly schooled his features, the signs of distress disappearing almost as quickly as they'd come. He merely grunted again and waved them on as he headed deeper into the warren of makeshift stalls. Sam hurried to catch up, though it was hard not to ogle at the stalls as he passed.

There was everything from weapons and armor to high-quality glass and top-notch alchemical ingredients. There was even one vendor selling old books, all penned by Wolfman historians and Shamans. Bill buzzed with excitement at those, insisting they stop and take a little peek. The idea of books on magic and history that the College had never even seen before was almost too much for Bill to bear. Velkan growled at them, "Move along. Look at these later. We are here for a purpose."

Eventually, they would be trusted enough to peruse at their leisure. But not yet. This first trip was a business venture. They needed to move with speed and purpose, striking with precision, or else they might be seen as weak targets, easily cheated. Velkan explained that the Wolfmen had some very curious notions about trade. "As with everything else, trade is war. A battle for domination and supremacy between two clashing forces with two differing agendas. A fight between predator and prey. The goal is always to bleed the other dry."

In physical combat, the Wolfmen had strict ideas about honor, but not so much when it came to merchant-craft. There was no such thing as cheating where buying and selling were concerned. If a buyer was unaware enough to purchase a faulty product or pay too much, they deserved to be swindled.

Sam would need to strike a hard bargain, but not so hard

that he looked like a fool for overestimating his merchandise. According to Velkan, he also wanted to avoid making his opponent lose face, which could make him a blood enemy, something the Wolf Pack most certainly didn't need. They were too new to survive a nemesis out for revenge. But Sam also couldn't concede so much ground that he lost face himself; that would dishonor his name, and then no one would ever take him seriously again. It was a fine balance to walk.

Eventually, Velkan stopped in front of a stall covered by a canvas canopy the color of fresh blood. Out front hung a wooden sign suspended from a bronze chain. There were no words on the sign, but rather an ornate crimson marking that was all hard lines and jagged edges. Sam didn't recognize the symbol, but one look at what was arranged on the tables under the canopy told him all he needed to know: this place sold meat. Rabbit, fox, deer, boar, even bear. There were cuts of every variety—chuck and shanks and racks of ribs, red meat glistening on white bone.

Behind one of the tables was a wolf with jet black fur, his shoulders as big as the slab of beef he was working on. He wore a leather apron and held a meat cleaver the size of a dictionary.

"We are here for business," Velkan declared, sweeping beneath the canopy. The butcher took one look at Sam and sniffed, ears laying back flat against his skull.

"I want no part in this business with humans." The butcher waved a cleaver at Sam. "I am not responsible for feeding human whelps unable to fend for themselves."

"We are not here to *buy*," Velkan snarled in the Wolfman tongue, his fur standing stiff, "we are here to sell, and your master will not think kindly of you haggling with a vendor and a Noble on her behalf."

The butcher growled, teeth bared, his golden eyes darting between Velkan and Sam in confusion. Sam had to admit he was more than a little confused as well. Was Velkan implying that the butcher wasn't the stall owner? That question was answered a moment later when a flap at the rear of the tent opened to admit a tawny-furred female wolf clad in sky-blue robes. She wore golden rings on each finger, and her neck was encircled by a thick gold necklace supporting an oversized medallion that bore the symbol of a scale.

Sam knew from his time in Narvik that it was the symbol of a master merchant. The newcomer quickly appraised Velkan and Sam before sniffing and flicking an ear at the butcher. She spoke in the human tongue, voice low and rather bored. "Gachev, leave us. There are more cuts in the back. Tend to the stock while I deal with these two."

"These three, actually." Bill ruffled his pages to get her attention. "The kid and I are like a dynamic duo, but everyone seems to overlook me, on account of the fact that I'm a book."

The female wolf's posture changed subtly as she regarded Bill, floating from the silver chain connecting to Sam's hip. Magical artifacts weren't unknown in this world, but they were rare, and a talking book was something on an entirely different level. The implication was clear: regardless of what Sam looked like, he was a mage, one with real power.

"I stand corrected. I will deal with these *three*," she conceded. The butcher growled, hand flexing around the handle of his cleaver. Finally, he sank the blade into a wooden chopping block on the table and disappeared through the same flap which the newcomer had entered through a few moments before. "I am Ankova of the Shadowlands Tribe. I have never seen a human walk these ways before. It is a thing not done. Yet here you stand. How?"

The question was blunt and forceful. It was a challenge meant to put him off balance, and Sam knew it. Velkan had gotten him this far, but Sam instinctively understood the rest was up to him. The Wolfmen respected strength and honor; allowing another to negotiate on your behalf could only ever make you look weak. Sam reached into his shirt and pulled out a golden medallion, studded with a tiger's eye stone in the center. Etched into the face of the stone was a single runic mark that roughly translated as 'Wolf-Hearted'. A symbol of his standing with The People, it had been given to him for killing Octavius and saving Narvik from his deadly magic.

"I am here by the will of The O'Baba and by the blood I've shed on behalf of The People. I have every right to walk here. Unless you disagree with The O'Baba's decrees?" Sam's tone was cool, and his chin dropped, a sign that he was challenging her standing in the pack. Her lips pulled away from her teeth, but she held her tongue and raised her chin just a hair. Showing such vulnerability was a tacit admission that she acknowledged The O'Baba's authority. "As for why I am here, that is simple enough. This human has wares, if you have coin."

"You think to come here and sell me rabbit meat and venison?" She scowled, showing just what she thought of such a proposition.

"Certainly not." Sam spat to the side; a gesture that would get him tossed out if it were performed in a human-owned shop. "I can see that you already have fine cuts of meat. It would be an insult against your honor and mine to try to sell you inferior quality items, hastily scavenged while my party was out adventuring."

Her shoulders dropped a hair—Sam had thrown her off her guard—but a new wariness seemed to slip into her posture. "What is it that you think we have need of?"

"The finest quality poultry you have ever seen." Without asking for permission, Sam headed over to an empty table and opened his spatial flask. He laid out eggs and the best cuts of regular chicken meat—tenders, breasts, wings, thighs, and piles of organs. Ankova watched him work, her face neutral and impassive. She was desperately trying not to give anything away. But the very fact that she was not openly sneering was a tell in its own way. When he laid out the first spicy chicken breasts, harvested from Blaze's brood, Ankova's eyes widened and her nostrils flared.

It was a small thing, there and gone in less than a blink, but Sam had caught it. So had Bill. The book cackled in his head.

<We got her hook, line, and sinker. She might as well be fawning!>

Ankova schooled her face into a mask of perfect indifference before stalking forward to inspect the cuts. She poked one with an extended claw, then carefully tasted the tip. A good way to get salmonella, although that was probably encouraged among the Wolfmen. She picked up several eggs, testing the weight in her palm. When she got to the spicy chicken breasts, she leaned over and inhaled deeply, the fur momentarily rising along the nape of her neck. She stood and cleared her throat. "Where did one such as *you* come by such meat?"

"That information is not part of the sale, Wolfy." Bill snapped his cover closed as though the secrets were written inside him. Her eyes flicked back and forth between Sam and Bill.

"He's right," Sam echoed the book wryly. "Our supplier isn't any of your concern. All that you need to know is that I can acquire this quality of goods every week. More, if things go well."

She seemed to mull it over for a moment. "If you are consistent, I suppose I could sell these on your behalf. On consignment only. I won't eat losses, and the best I can do is three silvers per pound of meat, one silver per dozen eggs."

That was an *insultingly* low quote, and offering it on *consignment*? That was the equivalent of thirty cents per pound, and ten cents for a dozen eggs. Those prices were low even back on Earth, and *this*? This wasn't Earth. What Sam had to offer was top-notch and hard to come by. Likely, she would sell out in hours and charge ten times that rate or more, especially considering how much Wolfmen enjoyed chicken. Unfortunately, Sam couldn't just call her out without impugning her honor. Sam needed her. He couldn't simply slap her in the face, but he knew she needed him. This was a prime opportunity to get a leg up on other vendors, and she would regret running him off.

As Velkan had warned, this was a dance as much as it was a battle.

"These are premium wares, and that meat there," Sam gestured toward his spicy chicken, "offers active fire resistance. In the human capital, they are selling enhanced chicken breast with similar qualities for nearly nine *gold* a pound. These chickens are fed only the finest quality enhanced ingredients, and there isn't another farmer around that can make that promise."

Sam paused and leaned in, a confiding position. "You're not going to find better anywhere; that much, I can guarantee you. I suspect *I* can find another vendor to peddle my wares if we can't come to a suitable arrangement."

He let the subtle threat hang in the air. Not outright aggression, but a firm reminder that he could, and would, walk away unless she started treating him with respect. After a moment of tense silence, he pushed onward. "The regular meat is worth a gold per pound, and the enhanced chicken is worth two. I could part with the eggs for… five silvers per dozen. Even though it will hurt me inside to do so."

"Even at that price, you're getting a deal," Bill added harshly, "since you're going to turn around and sell them for double. Don't insult us by pretending you're not. Fifty percent profit margins are a great deal, any way you look at it."

"I *suppose* that is a fair offer," Ankova admitted with a dip of her chin while raising her hands, palms up. A concession and an admission that she'd been greedy and had gotten caught with a hand in the proverbial cookie jar.

"We also aren't going to sell on *consignment*," Sam snarled lightly. "If you can't sell what I'm offering you, then you aren't the vendor I want to work with."

That was as close as he dared come to an insult, but it was necessary. He needed to draw a line in the sand and show that he wasn't going to be pushed around. Her eyes narrowed, and Sam glimpsed anger stirring in those golden depths. But she didn't snarl, and her fur stayed flat. She knew Sam was the one holding all the trump cards. She snuffed hard. "Very well. We have an accord. I will pay a single gold mark per pound of regular chicken, and two gold for enhanced meat. Five silver for eggs is also acceptable."

"*Egg*-ceptable," Bill snorted softly, trying to hide his pleasure.

"There is a *caveat.*" Ankova stared them down. "I want *assurances* of delivery. Guarantee me one hundred pounds of poultry per week, and at least fifty pounds of enchanted poultry. Plus no less than five hundred eggs. I want bulk, and I want exclusivity. No other vendors."

Sam did some quick math in his head. His chickens were much larger than anything he'd ever seen before, each one weighing in at close to thirty pounds. Of that, bone, cartilage, skin, and feathers accounted for about thirty percent of the weight, leaving almost twenty pounds of edible meat and organs. He would only have to harvest ten regular chickens per week, and three enchanted chickens, to hit that quota. His coop was already producing those kinds of numbers, and he only expected that number to swell over the weeks and months ahead.

Delivering on the quantity wouldn't be an issue, but there were a few other considerations. At that volume, he would bring in just over three hundred and two gold from eggs—roughly equivalent to three thousand and twenty dollars per week. Not a bad rate. Not a fortune, but that would change once he started to produce other types of enhanced meat and started harvesting monster Cores. He rubbed at his chin while he thought. He was fine with offering Ankova exclusivity, so long as she was a consistent buyer, but there was a catch. She couldn't sell to human markets, and he could.

"Two minor points of contention," he countered, finally deciding he had a good plan in mind. "I'll agree to make you my official distributor for the *Wolfmen*... but I reserve the right to sell to human traders, so long as I meet my weekly supply obligation to you. Also, when other types of enhanced meat become available, I further reserve the right to renegotiate the wholesale price, based on rarity and demand."

"A shrewd pact," Ankova agreed with a sniff, "but one I will accept."

She extended a hand in the manner of humans, which was a rarity. A peace offering of sorts, maybe? Sam took it and gave it a pump. She nearly pulverized the bones in his hand before releasing. Ah, that was more in keeping with the Wolfmen traditions. "You are not at all what I was expecting. I have heard you are different, that you have the heart of a Wolf. Now… now, I think I believe. I look forward to a mutually profitable partnership."

"So do we." Sam finished unpacking their wares—over a hundred pounds of meat in total and just under five hundred eggs. They walked away with a cool one hundred and twenty gold.

An eggcellent start indeed for their fowl empire.

CHAPTER TWENTY-ONE

Sam stepped out of the entrance from the Marketplace and back into New Narvik, breathing in the crisp air.

"We should be getting back." Velkan's words were clear, but Sam lingered. His business was done with the merchants of the Wolfman Marketplace, but his gaze fell on the longhouse, nestled in a ring of trees not far off. The O'Baba's unofficial residence.

His mind leapt back to what Bill had told him when they had first entered the Marketplace. "This place—*all* of these places—they're enormous spatial libraries. That's why they can move around. They aren't bound to a location, but to a *person*, and the Totem poles are just doorway access points."

Sam still wasn't sure if he believed Bill's hunch, but the book knew more about magic than anyone else Sam had ever met. Abyss, he probably knew more about magic and spatial theory than just about anyone else alive. If Bill's theory was correct, then the Wolfmen might have the key necessary for him to unlock his specialization. However, based on Velkan's reactions and stony silence whenever Sam brought up the Totems, it was clear that their resident Wolfman wouldn't be much help in getting to the truth behind either the Training Grounds or the Marketplace. Clearly, it was deep magic and well above his pay grade.

Yurij Brightblood, their Shaman handler, might know the truth, but he barely tolerated Sam and company as it was. There was no way he was going to disclose the most vital secrets of the Wolfmen to some uppity outsider. The O'Baba? She would definitely have the answers that Sam needed, although meeting her eye to eye was about as intimidating as staring down a T. Rex. She *did* have a soft spot for Sam… well, for Bill, at least. The Wolfmen respected the wisdom of age and valued the power of magic. Bill was both old and powerful, and he had chosen to bond with Sam; that kind of endorsement went a long way with the furry-faced folk.

Plus, Sam had saved Velkan from captivity, which had dramatically increased his personal reputation with The O'Baba. Having a high personal reputation with someone here counted for a lot. Still… going to her unannounced was a gamble. She might flay him alive for the act, but all of life was a gamble. He cared about specializing more than he cared about the threat of possible death.

"Why don't you go on ahead without me," Sam decided after a heartbeat of time had passed. "Bill and I have a little bit of business left to take care of."

"Not with the Wolfman Marketplace, I trust," Velkan grunted in reply. "It would not be wise for you to venture there unattended. Not yet."

"No, nothing like that." Sam glanced back toward the long house. "What I'm thinking of doing is *way* riskier."

"You live dangerously, Sam King," Velkan muttered darkly as his eyes followed Sam's gaze, "even by Wolfman standards. May your hunt be fruitful, and your probable death painless."

"I feel like maybe I missed something," Bill cheerfully stated as they watched the Wolfman leave. "Which is probably on me, if I'm being honest. I stopped paying attention a while ago. I tend to do that when you start talking and don't mention my name for a while. So what fresh craziness are you brewing up for us this time?"

"I think it's time we get to the bottom of this whole Totem thing," Sam replied as he made his way down the narrow footpath that led within the ring of trees to the front door of the longhouse. "I gotta ask The O'Baba about it, if I really want an answer."

"You sure this is the smart choice?" Bill nervously chuckled. "I mean, I think it's great. I'm dying to know how in the world they're pulling off their spatial hoodoo, but you're the only one who will actually die if things go south in there."

Sam raised his fist but paused before knocking. "Are you sure that these Totem Grounds are really some form of spatial libraries?"

Bill fell silent and *really* thought about it. "Ninety percent sure. I mean, I can't be one hundred percent sure until I actually have the answer, but I can't see any other plausible explanation. I've studied magic for a long, long time, and the facts fit the theory like a glove. Plus, even though I don't exactly have a stomach, I have a gut feeling that I'm right about this."

"That's good enough for me." Sam let his fist fall three times, rapping sharply on the wood. "You trusted my hunch about chicken farming, so I'm going to trust yours about this. We're a team, and that means we go out on a limb for each other."

"A sweet sentiment," came a grave, matronly tone as the door cracked open, "but a smart one? No."

The O'Baba's golden eyes were narrowed to slits, and she carried a meat cleaver in one hand. Her fur was a metallic silver speckled with white, and she wore a simple silk shawl draped across her back and shoulders, while a long leather apron covered her front. She was rather small as Wolfmen went, her back bent with age, which made it something of a challenge to bow lower than her. It had to be done, since it was customary for a lesser wolf to keep their head and body lower than that of the higher ranked pack member.

"Not even Lords and Ladies of The People call on me uninvited," The O'Baba growled. "You have *five* minutes to convince me of your need, or I will kill you twice for your insolence."

She turned with a huff and disappeared, quickly swallowed by the shadows of the longhouse. Bill whispered, "Not to say I told you so, but… no, wait. Exactly that."

"Thanks for the help and confidence," Sam replied as he steeled his resolve and headed in after the wizened she-wolf, knowing there was a good chance he was walking toward his death like a lamb to the slaughter. This was the right call. Now he just needed to convince the Matron of The People.

The floor of The O'Baba's dwelling wasn't wood or tile, but rather a carpet of lush and flawless green grass, accented in places by the colorful blooms of wildflowers. A number of low wooden tables were spread throughout the hall, perfect for hosting large communal meals, though there were no chairs present. Sam knew from experience that the Wolfmen took their meals on the floor. The idea of a comfortable chair was anathema to their way of life.

It was dark in the hall, but Sam's Darkvision helped him navigate the space with ease. He glanced at the colorful tapestries that adorned the walls. They were beautiful works of art, each woven from gossamer silk and decorated using hard-edged geometric patterns. He pushed his way through a door at the back of the hall, which connected to a large kitchen area, the same place that he'd met with The O'Baba the first time around. Then, just like now, he'd been unsure whether he was going to walk away with his head intact.

The matronly wolf was already standing behind a granite countertop. A wooden cutting board lay in front of her, and she was busy slicing a huge array of vegetables. Behind her, hanging over a massive fireplace, was an enormous potbellied cauldron that burbled with something that smelled divine. She scooped up a handful of chopped radishes and tossed them into the cook pot with a flick of her wrist, then went right back to work, never even bothering to glance in Sam's direction.

"You can spend your entire five minutes sniffing at my stew like a young hungry pup," she broke the silence with a threat, "but I'm not adding more time. If you don't convince me of your need, you're liable to end up in the pot as an ingredient."

"The Totem Grounds," Sam blurted out. There wasn't a tactful way to ask, and he was running out of time. "I need to know how they work."

The **schwick*, *schwick*, *schwick** of her cleaver abruptly stopped, and her lips pulled back in a snarl. She stared daggers at him, her eyes boring deep into his soul like a drill.

It appeared that was the wrong thing to say. But he couldn't back down now or divert his gaze—to do so would be to invite attack. He gulped, suppressed a tremor in his hand, and met her eyes. He needed to project confidence and swagger. He couldn't be openly defiant, but he needed her to know that he *belonged* here by right, just as he'd done with Ankova in the Marketplace. He was a Lord of The People, and her first human ally. He was the first Bibliomancer in three hundred years. He was *not* going to be cowed, not even by The O'Baba.

After a long, tense moment, The O'Baba snorted, and her snarl vanished. "How is it that you have learned of the Totem Training Grounds, hmm?"

"Velkan of the Redmane Tribe." Sam kept the tremble of fear from his words. "He introduced our Pack a week or so back."

She **tisked**. There was now real bite in her words, "I am starting to regret asking you to bring that pup home. What training have you done, then?"

"Bill and I ventured through the Owl Totem—we even met with Great Auntie Owl. Had tea with her. She helped me break the Wisdom threshold."

She flinched just a hair at his words, and some of the tension seemed to drain out of her shoulders. She mused aloud, almost as much for her sake as Sam's. "That is a great rarity. You are sure it was her? Speak the truth, Sir Bill. You would not lie to a young woman such as me."

"Naw," Bill was happy to explain. "It was definitely her. Huge owl lady, crazy curling horns. She gave us tea and even managed to put *me* to sleep. I haven't slept in over three hundred years. She was the real deal. No doubt in my mind."

"Your adventures know no bounds, it seems," The O'Baba replied neutrally with a thin smile. "Why is it that you would need to know about our deep magics?"

"Well, we were trying to figure out how the spatial magics work," Sam started, "but it only really started to click into place when Velkan took us to the Wolfman Marketplace-"

The O'Baba let out a strangled yelp.

"Not only have you gone to the Training Grounds, but you have visited our hub of commerce? In his desire to honor the life debt he owes to you two, I fear Velkan has *overreached.* Even as a Lord of The People, it is not right for outsiders to venture into that place without proper reason."

"We had reason," Sam interjected firmly once more. "He didn't just take us there to do some window shopping. I'm a merchant now. I just struck a bargain with Ankova of the Shadowlands Tribe."

The shock on O'Baba's face was almost comical. "I think, *perhaps*, my ears have deceived me in my old age. You now qualify as a merchant and have just come to an accord with Ankova of the Shadowlands Tribe? She is the most formidable and highly regarded meat-trader in all the tribes. What could you have even *offered* one such as her?"

Try as she might, The O'Baba couldn't keep the incredulity out of her voice. Sam merely shrugged and told her about his blossoming chicken business. By the time he was done, she was shaking her head. "A worthy addition to the Tribe, indeed. Your five minutes is up, but you have piqued my curiosity. I may still kill and skin you just once for your impudence, but I would hear more about why you seek the knowledge of the Totems."

"How's about you let me cover this one." Bill stepped in on Sam's behalf. "You're only going to explain it wrong anyway. So… the kid and I were trying to figure out how those Totem portals worked. On the surface, it definitely seemed like spatial magic, but I couldn't figure out how you were moving those Totems around. I was leaning toward the idea that they were actually dungeon instances, but then we visited the Marketplace, and *boom*. Hit me like a mace to the temple."

"More portal Totems, but this time, instead of going into some wild landscape filled with monsters, we popped out in an interdimensional marketplace. That was strike one against the dungeon instance theory. According to Velkan, the Marketplace has multiple access points scattered all over the continent. Those were strikes two and three. But there is *one* kind of magic that I know of that can account for that: an Interspatial Library. Admittedly, I've never heard of a library that big, but in theory, one could grow that large—given enough time and power. Plus, the entrances to an Interspatial Library are portable."

"Let us say there is some small amount of merit to your line of thinking." The O'Baba slowly began chopping more vegetables. "Why would you need to know about such things? Surely you are not risking your life for a mere intellectual curiosity? A being with your many years must have more *wisdom* than that."

Bill shot back in an instant, "I would *absolutely* risk everything for mere intellectual curiosity. If age and wisdom has taught me anything, it's that curiosity is the mother of innovation and the father of greatness. You don't become a Master Mage without having an unquenchable curiosity and desire to learn. With that said, there is a more practical reason. The kid here has decided that he wants to become an Archivist Summoner. The first step to doing that is to specialize as a Libriohexer. To do *that*, we need to start building out an Interspatial Library. Problem is..."

He faltered and took a deep breath. "Okay, look as much as it pains me to admit it, the problem is I don't know how to do that. If the kid had picked one of the other possible specializations, I could've guided him along every step of the path. But I don't know how to build an Interspatial Library. I know they *exist*. There are myths and legends about them that I believe are more than *just* myths and legends. I also have some theories, but they are just that. I tried to start one myself and managed to create a Soul Space in the process, but something went wrong. I don't know *what*, and I don't know *how* to get from point A to point B. But I think you and your elders do. Back in my College days, I had the pleasure of meeting one of your fur-faced Shamans. Bright kid, and he was looking into Interspatial Libraries too. Now I think I understand why."

The O'Baba was pensive for a long moment, staring off into the distance. "You have lofty goals and ambitions great enough even for a Wolfman to envy. It is admirable. As is your curiosity. But this information you seek, it was one of the coveted secrets of The People. I will speak plainly, since you are an outsider and are still learning our ways. My position among the Tribes... it is not absolute. My standing can change in an eyeblink. There are equally ambitious Shamans among the tribes who think I am too weak to govern during a time such as this, that a stronger hand is needed at the helm during a war. They will not speak such words in the open, but even in my old age, my ears are sharp, and I hear such whispers."

"These whelps would gladly see me fall and another to rise as The O'Baba in my stead. They are waiting for a single slip-up to act. Should I fall, your own standing within the tribe may well be in jeopardy, depending on who ascends. Kosoruk the Savage of White Wyther is chief among my rivals and has no love for humans. Under his paw, you might well find yourself without a People to call your own; an enemy to humanity, and an outcast among the Wolfmen. I have put more trust in you than you can know, but to dole out such a secret of The People would cause my downfall. Yours as well."

"There *has* to be a way-" Sam balled his hands into fists.

She cut him off with a stern look. "Do not lose hope yet, young one. If you would seek the sacred knowledge of the Totems, you must do something to solidify your place among The People. A blow so vicious against humanity that not even Kosoruk could question your loyalty to our kind."

She looked uncertain for the first time Sam could ever remember. "I have news that might serve the two of you well. You and The People both. If you have the courage and boldness to seize the opportunity, that is. There is a Rogue Mage troubling the College and, for once, it is not you, Sam King. He is called 'Joe'. This Rogue Mage has created a big problem for the current College administration. He has stumbled upon a restricted class and has been operating beneath their very noses, openly flaunting their rules. He parades his defiance by refusing to sign their Accords. The spies say, he has even gone so far as to kidnap one of their Journeymen."

She drummed her claws against the countertop. "As you might imagine, it is a bad look for the College. As bad as me helping you and your fledgling pack. The College, you see, maintains their power over the mages through their ironclad Accords. They maintain their influence over everyone else through the total dominance of all would-be magic users. My sources inside the walls of the human capital confirm that they have finally apprehended this 'Joe'. Now they need to prove to all of Ardania that they are still in complete control and they will do so by making an example of him."

"They will punish him *severely* and force him to sign the Accords for his disobedience. My eyes and ears tell me that every Mage in a five-hundred-mile radius is supposed to attend the trial, to witness the Arch-Mage's justice. This trial, it will take place in one day's time." She thrust a bony finger into the air. "It is not my place to tell you what to do with this knowledge. But perhaps there is some kernel here that will allow you to prove yourself a loyal Pack member… even to one such Kosoruk."

Hidden Quest Alert!

Exalted of the Pack: The O'Baba has confided in you that her position within the Pack will be in jeopardy if she reveals the ancient secrets of the Wolfmen Totem Grounds. But if you can prove your loyalty and devotion beyond a shadow of a doubt—even to the most ardent haters of humanity

—she will reveal the secrets you require to unlock the Librioheker Specialization. To gain that kind of trust is no simple thing.

Currently, your reputation with The People is 'Friendly,' but she will not disclose the information until you have obtained the 'Extended Family' rank status. To achieve this, you must strike a fatal blow to a powerful human institution. She has also informed you that the Mage's College is holding a trial for the Rogue Mage named Joe in one day's time. According to her informants, every Mage in Ardania will be in attendance. What you do with this information is entirely up to you, but opportunities like this only come along once in a lifetime!

There is no penalty for failing to accomplish this task! Accomplishing this task will elevate your overall reputation with The People. Reward: +3,000 Reputation with The People. Exp: 10,000. Title: Right Hand of The People. Accept / Decline

Sam gladly accepted, his mind already buzzing with options. "Thank you. I won't let you down."

"I should hope not." Her eyes twinkled. "I know you want *power*."

The cryptic reply made Sam shake his head in confusion. He bowed and backed out of the room. He needed to get back to the Irondowns and talk to the others.

They had the crime of the century to plan.

CHAPTER TWENTY-TWO

Sam returned to find no one in the Barracks, and the Training Arena was equally lifeless. Sam was starting to get worried that something had happened when the smell of fried chicken hit his nose like a sucker punch. His mouth watered, and his stomach grumbled in angry protest. "Just how long has it been since our last meal?"

"Longer for me than you." Bill pretended to be hurt by the question. Sam ignored the book and realized he had been so busy getting ready for his trip to the Marketplace that he'd totally skipped breakfast. Thanks to his impromptu chat with The O'Baba, he'd missed lunch as well. He was famished, and the thought of a warm meal drove every other thought from his mind. He beelined for the kitchen, following his nose more than anything else.

Sam and Bill found the rest of the Wolf Pack crowded around the rough-hewn table where they took most of their meals, mere moments away from digging into the massive spread laid out before them. Silver platters of deep-fried chicken dotted the table, along with sweet coleslaw, a huge bowl of baked beans, and a tray of crispy yellow cornbread. Arrow and Kai were making the rounds with pitchers of honey mead in hand, pouring drinks for the rest of the Pack seated at the table. In the other room, Sam spotted Octo-Chef busily washing dishes in an oversized sink while simultaneously working on something that looked suspiciously like cake.

"Hear, hear!" Finn called while in the middle of spooning a generous helping of beans onto his plate. "If it isn't the man of the hour! Our dearest Sam has returned to us alive and well."

"See, Velkan," Arrow gave the Wolfmen a pointed look, "I told you she wasn't going to eviscerate him. The O'Baba's *nice*."

"I wouldn't say that where she can hear you," the Wolfman warned in a conspiratorial tone. "The O'Baba is notorious for her quick-fire temper. Still, the bet is the bet."

He reached down to untie a small pouch full of coins from his belt and tossed it to the Ranger, who snagged it from the air with nimble grace. Sam choked out, "You were betting on me being *eviscerated*?"

"Hey," Arrow protested defensively, "I was in your corner."

"So what happened, huh?" Dizzy seemed like she was ready to shake him for information. "How did it go?"

"Yeah, are we in business or what?" Arrow questioned around a mouthful of food. "I mean, I love chicken—don't get me wrong—but we're drowning in the stuff here. There's more than we could eat in three months. If we don't start selling it off soon, it's going to go bad. Unless maybe Finn there manages to put it all on ice."

"*Boo*!" Kai called, lightly tossing a roll at the Ranger's head. "That was terrible. Was that an attempt at a joke?"

"All humor aside," Arrow lightly snatched the roll from the air, "what's the deal?"

"What's the deal?" Sam reached into his flask and pulled free the two hefty leather pouches of gold. He dropped them both on the table with a clinking **thunk** that drew every eye in the room. "We got the deal, that's what. Minimum two hundred pounds of poultry per week, fifty pounds of enhanced poultry, and five hundred eggs."

Arrow nearly choked. "Per week?"

"Yep. Should bring us north of three thousand dollars a week—nearly twelve grand a month. It's not a fortune, but it's a start. I think those rates are only going to go up as we start producing rarer types of chicken breeds."

The Pack cheered and hefted their mugs, sloshing with honey mead. Kai slapped the table to get the room's attention. "Okay, enough business talk. I totally gotta know about the Wolfman Marketplace. What was it like, dude? Was it as cool as I'm imagining?"

"Cooler." Sam dropped into his customary seat near Finn. "It's got *everything*. Hands down, it's better than anything Ardania has to offer by leaps and bounds. Plus, there are Wolfmen from all over the continent. It's massive. Bigger than New Narvik, if you can believe it."

"Wait, what?" Dizzy frowned as she realized what that meant. "How does that work? I thought the Wolfmen purposely spread their camps out to prevent human infiltration. Having one mega marketplace sort of seems to defeat the purpose of that."

"That's because it's not a camp." Sam pulled over a plate and started to load it down with food. Chicken thighs and slaw, a heap of beans and several pieces of warm bread. The Octo-Chef was a divine gift from above. "It's a hub with multiple entryways, sort of like the Totem Training Grounds. We think it's actually some sort of Interspatial Library."

"Correction!" Bill exclaimed loudly. "*I* think it might be an Interspatial Library, which is how *you* know it actually is an Interspatial Library."

"But I thought that sort of magic was incredibly rare?" Finn stole a sidelong glance at them.

"Oh, it is." Bill floated down to smell the fried chicken at close range. "At least, among Mages. I've read books on the theory, and I even met a colleague once upon a time who'd managed to build one—though that was a couple hundred years ago. He never did tell me the secret. Mages are like that.

They covet knowledge and like to hide things. Gives 'em an edge when they're trying to get tenure. But the Wolfmen? Yeah, I think the Shamans know the ins and outs of the process. All we need to do now is get them to spill the beans."

"Which leads me to the next thing we need to talk about." Sam decided that now was a good time to break the news. "Bill and I went and talked with The O'Baba. We wanted to know the secret behind the Totem Grounds. She didn't explicitly confirm that they are Interspatial Libraries, but she certainly hinted at it. But she also flat-out refused to tell us how they work. She says there are still factions within the Wolfmen who don't trust us. If we want to get the secret, we need to raise our reputation with The People, and not just a little. We need to obtain the Extended Family rank status."

Velkan's shoulders slumped under the weight of the revelation. "It is impossible. No outsider has *ever* been given such honor. Many *Wolfmen* don't even have such a reputation amongst our people. This status is reserved only for The O'Baba and the most respected clan leaders."

"Maybe not." Sam's rebuttal shattered the sudden tension. "The O'Baba offered me a quest. She said that the only way to do it is to strike a fatal blow against a powerful human institution. A blow so devastating that no one can deny our loyalty to The People. If we can do that, she'll give me the Title 'Right Hand of The People'."

Velkan's breath caught, and his eyes widened comically. "But that is the rank of a High General. Why would she promise such a thing?"

"Because," Bill explained patiently, "she also let us know in no uncertain terms that there is a political faction that is just waiting to see her drop the ball so they can replace her as O'Baba. The sense I got was that she risked a lot by extending us membership in the Pack in the first place. She took that risk, and she needs it to pay off in a big way. She needs allies and we're it."

"Which is also why she dropped a major hint about how we

might accomplish such an enormous undertaking." Sam had everyone's undivided attention to a degree that rarely happened. "Turns out, there is going to be a trial tomorrow at the Mage's College, a big one, for a Rogue Mage named Joe. The Arch-Mage has issued an edict recalling every mage in good standing to the College. They're all going to be gathered together to witness the Arch-Mage's justice."

This time it was Finn who sputtered, eyes bulging. He ran a hand through his lank hair. "Bloody abyss, but this Joe must've really kicked the hornet's nest to get that kind of response. The last time the Arch-Mage issued an Arcana Edict like that, I was still in diapers."

"What happened?" Dizzy demanded.

"Oh, the usual." Finn's head seemed to have gained a dozen pounds by the way he slowly swung it to face her. "Insurrection. That's about the only thing that warrants that kind of response. The Arch-Mage rules with an iron grip, and he doesn't take contenders lightly. About twenty years ago, there was a Senior Mage by the name Talek Berk who went Rogue. An ugly bit of business. He started circulating rumors that the Arch-Mage was using forbidden magics to enthrall members of the College."

"The Senior Mage's consortium denied the allegations, but ol' Talek still managed to recruit a small cohort of upstart Mages to join his cause. Nine of them in total. They infiltrated the College under cover of darkness and blew up part of the western wing. The Arch-Mage himself took down Talek, and the rebellion fizzled without his leadership. The whole lot of them were eventually rounded up for treason against the Crown and College, and every Mage in the Kingdom was ordered to attend the execution. Their cores were fed to the Accords."

Kai whistled through his teeth. "Dude, that's intense. Should we try to help this Joe guy? He's got to be a traveler. Could be a good recruit."

"I'd be onboard with a prison break," Arrow agreed as he leaned back in his chair and dabbed at his chin with a cloth napkin.

"Not a snowball's chance in the Inferno," Bill harshly negated that line of thinking. "They'll be keeping him in the Sanctuary of Solitude."

"Sounds sort of nice," Kai quipped. "Like some kind of monastery."

"It is anything but," Finn replied with a shiver. "The Sanctuary of Solitude is a prison, and not a particularly humane one. It's located in the bowels of the College, not far from the sewers."

His eyes glazed over, hazy and distant. "It's a lonely place. The cells are dark, dank, and cold—plus the whole place reeks like the inside of a chamber pot. That's where they kept me after Sam managed to escape with Bill. I spent many a night down there, chilled to the bone, praying that I would survive to see the morning."

"But if it's close to the sewers, maybe we could break in just like we did the last time," Sphinx offered excitedly. "It would be tough, but we pulled it off once."

"I doubt very much that trick is going to work twice," Finn stated matter-of-factly. "They've probably beefed up the sewer security system tenfold since that stunt. Besides, even if we got in through the sewers, we'd never be able to get him out of his cell. The Sanctuary of Solitude is warded to the gills and heavily guarded. From there, he'll be escorted by the Silencers —the College's anti-mage strike force—to the Accord Chamber. The Silencers are a force of nature. We couldn't beat them in a fight without a small army at our back. Maybe not even then."

"Yeah, we'll never get him out of there," Bill agreed sadly. "I hate leaving a good mage to rot, but I don't see any way to help the poor guy."

"What about the Accord Chamber itself?" Dizzy wondered quietly as the group had a moment of silence for the random gamer, Joe. "Is there some way we can take it out?"

"That was our first thought, too," Bill agreed before shooting the idea down. "But the logistics just aren't feasible. Getting into the Accords Chamber might be doable, but launching an attack would be suicide. The Arch-Mage is going to be present, and he's got enough magical muscle to lock us down with the twitch of his pinky finger. But the kid and I *did* have another thought. Talked it over on the way back, and we think it might be our best chance to cripple the College. Maybe not forever, but at least for a little while."

"Another library run?" Finn quirked an eyebrow.

"No." Sam shook his head and explained, "They'll see that coming a hundred miles off. Like you said, the Arch-Mage isn't dumb. He might be preoccupied with Joe, but there's no way he's forgotten about us. I'd bet all the gold I have that he's expecting us to take a stab at the Infinity Athenaeum. With all the Mages and guards present for the trial, there really is no better chance."

"It would be just like him." Bill chuckled darkly. "He's a monster, but a shrewd one. He'll know this is too big of an opportunity for us to pass up. The problem is, the College is too massive to protect every entry, so he'll focus the few resources he can spare on the areas where he thinks we'll strike."

"Like the Library," Dizzy acknowledged.

"Bingo." Sam gave her a thumbs-up. "Which is why we're going to avoid the Library like the plague. Instead, Bill and I think we should hit the Trustees Arcana."

Finn's jaw dropped and he slapped a hand against his forehead. "Of *course*."

"What in the abyss is the Trustees Arcana?" Kai chuckled at the name as if it were a dirty joke. "Some kinda trust fund for wizards?"

"Not what," Sam leaned forward, "but *who*."

"The Trustees Arcana are powerful mages that serve at the pleasure and discretion of the Arch-Mage," Finn explained to the group. "They're all incredibly high level and powerful, and the Repository of Trustees is the one place that will still be staffed during the Trial."

"Wait." Kai rubbed the bridge of his nose. "I'm, like, more confused than ever. So there's going to be this huge trial, and all the mages are going to be in the Accords Chamber, which means the rest of the College is going to be more or less a ghost town… right?"

"Right," Sam agreed.

"But you guys want to go to the *one place* that still has mages in it?"

"Also yes." Bill smirked at the direction this conversation was going.

"Okay. So yeah. I think you just broke my brain," the Monk groaned. "Maybe break it down for me Barney-style. Why in the world would we want to go to the one place in the College that still has people in it?"

"Because normally, the Repository of Trustees is *impossible* to get too. This might be a once in a lifetime chance to take those old geezers out!" Bill crowed excitedly. "*Man,* would I love to do that. More than a couple of them are responsible for bookifying me! See, the Trustees are all incredibly high-leveled, but they're as harmless as kittens. Sure, any of them can harness and channel more mana than the next five mages combined, but their class precludes them from learning offensive spells."

"So what are they, exactly?" Dizzy was taking notes at this point.

"They're the magical bureaucrats that keep the College running." Bill was still chuckling like an evil overlord. "They do all the important but *enormously* tedious work that no one else wants to do. Basically, the Trustees maintain the infrastructure of the school. They monitor the sewers, care for the grounds, reinforce and strengthen the spatial tethers that hold the College together. Several of them are Contractualists who monitor the ebb and flow of mana to and from the Accords themselves. The College can't run without 'em, but they couldn't fight their way out of a wet paper bag if you gave 'em a map and a sword."

"They're going to be totally vulnerable," Finn agreed with a wicked grin.

"Kinda dark. Still… we do what we have to do." Dizzy

nodded slowly, finally starting to get it. "It'll be like shooting fish in a barrel."

"Precisely." Finn clapped his hands together in excitement. "If we can take out enough of the Trustees, it'll hobble the College. Plus, it's the ultimate chance to power level."

"Hit it on the head," Sam agreed earnestly. "One of the greatest benefits to being on Team Wolfman is that *we* get experience points from killing humans. The system that runs Eternium isn't going to care that we're killing a bunch of defenseless Mages. All it's going to see is that we, a bunch of level tens and elevens, are wiping out characters that have two or three times as many levels as we do. This is going to be an all-you-can-eat buffet of experience. The only catch is that we have less than twelve hours to orchestrate the greatest assault on the College in history."

"Well, what the abyss are we sitting around here for?" Dizzy stood abruptly. "We have *work* to do. Bill, I'll need maps of the College. Sphinx, we're going to need guard uniforms and Novice robes. Arrow, you're on potions."

"Let's *move* people, and I mean now!"

CHAPTER TWENTY-THREE

Sam cleared his mind, squared his shoulders, and casually strode beneath the portcullis and into the courtyard situated outside the eastern entrance to the Mage's College. Today was the day they were going to break the College… or die horribly in a blaze of glory.

The College was a rather unimpressive structure that looked like an enormous soup can sticking up into the air. The courtyard was just as unremarkable as the tower itself—a few neatly manicured trees and a handful of benches for the contemplative soul. There was no art to be seen, no epic statues of wizards in battle or dragons taking flight. It looked less like a place of arcane magic and mystery, and more like a dark-ages IRS building—an establishment dedicated to upholding stuffy laws and the endless minutiae of a grand bureaucracy—which, when he thought about it, Sam realized that was *exactly* what it was.

But despite being as boring and uninspired as drying paint, it was also a place filled with danger. The IRS might not have seemed as scary as the CIA, but from Sam's limited experience in pre-law, they were the far more common and vicious foe.

He reached up and absently adjusted the clear mask

covering his face, a specialty item that had come deep from the vaults of the Upright Men. It featured the grinning portrait of 'the Gray Fawkes,' the infamous Thieves' Guild Leader who had first organized the Upright Men during the early reign of King Henry some two hundred years ago. Once upon a time, the thieves of Ardania had been little more than squabbling street gangs, fighting over table scraps amongst themselves while trying to avoid the cruel arm of the King's justice. Then the Gray Fawkes had come along, forging those gangs into a single organization, powerful enough even to put the Monarch on his heels.

For someone like Sam, such a mask was worth its weight in gold. With a thought and a whisper of mana, Sam activated the item's potent effects.

Mask of the Plucky Rebel. Leading an insurgency? Grand plans to take on a tyrant? Just want to crash into your friend Aaron without getting found out? Well, never fear; the Mask of the Plucky Rebel has you covered —quite literally! With this bad boy, you can be someone else, at least for a little while. But great power comes at a great price. I hope you like facial hair and an air of smirking smugness, because you'll have that in spades.

By activating the effect, the wearer receives a randomly generated username, and any negative status tags are replaced with neutral status tags for the duration of the effect. Moreover, any bounties you may receive while wearing the mask with the effect activated will disappear when the mask's effect lapses. +2 Charisma while worn, +1 Wisdom, +1 Luck; Active Effect 'Social Chameleon' can be activated once every twelve hours with a duration of one hour. Side effect: Regardless of gender, while wearing the mask, you assume the distinguished facial hair of the Gray Fawkes himself.

The mask shifted and changed, blending seamlessly against Sam's face, though leaving behind a telltale set of rosy cheeks, a rakish mustache, and a razor-thin soul patch.

For the next hour, he was a different man with a different name and a sparkling clean slate. Any guard that looked at him would see what Sam wanted them to see: a Mage of the College in good standing. Sam reached up, adjusted the deep cowl covering his luscious locks—there was no getting rid of those—

then straightened the sleeves of his elaborate caster's robes. The garments were crafted from crushed velvet in a deep shade of purple and studded with gems. He should've stuck out like a sore thumb, but nearly a third of the Mages milling about in the Courtyard sported similar garb: members from the School of Silence.

Sam paused and glanced back over one shoulder as the rest of his crew spread out in a loose circle around him. They looked as different as Sam felt. Finn wore his finest robes, though his were burgundy and accented in gold, common attire for a Mage from the Society of Flame. Finn had his cowl pulled up as well, casting his face in deep shadow. Sphinx and Kai both wore cheap brown initiate's robes, cinched about the waist with lengths of coarse rope.

Dizzy and Arrow sported a pair of counterfeit guard outfits, which they had used the *last* time they'd broken into the College. Dizzy had swapped her trademark War Maul for a rather plain iron mace, and Arrow had a quiver of arrows riding one hip and an unadorned wooden bow slung across his back. Neither one stood out in the press of bodies, especially with all the other guards casually circulating through the crowd.

The last time they'd infiltrated the College, they'd come by way of the sewers, but this time, they were going to waltz right in through the front doors. Assuming everything worked according to plan, they would waltz right back out the same way. The notion was so ludicrous and daring that Bill was sure the Arch-Mage would never even consider the possibility. The man was powerful, but he didn't have an ounce of imagination. After all, no one would be stupid enough to simply *walk* into the most powerful and illustrious organization in all Ardania—especially not with every licensed Mage in a five-hundred-mile radius in attendance.

"Alright, old chap," Finn murmured softly beside him. "Are we sure we want to do this? This is our last chance to turn back."

"You know we're not going to do that." Sam shook his head

in annoyance. "You sure *you're* not ready to turn back? You're the only one who won't respawn if everything falls apart. I won't judge you if you decide to call it quits."

"No, no. I'm not going to abandon you." Finn's lips pressed into a thin line, then he reached over and clapped Sam on the shoulder. "Besides, the plan will only work with me. None of the others know how to navigate the College. It'll all be fine. And if not? Well at least it's been one hell of an adventure." He straightened and tugged on the lapel of his robes. "See you in the Repository."

"Let's hope so." Sam returned his friend's smile with one filled with concern. Finn peeled off to the left, and the rest of the Wolf Pack trailed after him, leaving Sam and Bill alone in a sea of snooty faces and arcane enemies.

The others were bound for a spatial corridor that would eventually dump them into the College Dining Hall. They would hit the kitchen first, where Sphinx would add something particularly nasty to today's soup: Blackfyde Tonic. It was an insidious poison, totally benign until it was broken down by the digestive acids in the stomach. The moment that happened, the toxin would seep through the mucous membrane lining the intestine and enter directly into the bloodstream. The toxin wasn't typically lethal, but it would cause hysteria, paranoia, and a terrible case of irritable bowel syndrome. And those were only the *secondary* side-effects.

With a bellyful of Blackfyde Tonic, it was nearly impossible to channel mana. It would temporarily cripple the spellcasting abilities of any Mage unlucky enough to get a full meal. That, and sending them running to the toilet for the better part of the next two days, would render them practically helpless.

From there, Finn would usher the Wolfpack through the annex, down the spatial spiral, and into the deep bunker where the Repository was located. Then they'd hunker down and wait for Sam. Getting into the Repository of Trustees wouldn't be much trouble—not with Joe's trial in full swing—but getting back out would be another story, especially after they started massacring the Mages responsible for holding the College infrastructure together.

That's where Sam came in.

<Get your game face on,> Bill ordered him sternly. <You're a *Mage*. You belong here. Everyone is beneath you. Basically, they're bugs not worth noticing. Just keep telling yourself that, and you'll fit in fine.>

Sam lifted his chin and tried to plaster the most condescending look he could muster all over his face. Back in real life, he'd had a school acquaintance named Barron Calloway. Barron had been the star quarterback, the son of a US Senator, and the biggest bully Sam had ever met. He was the kind of guy who would've fit in perfectly here—probably would've been besties with Octavius. So, Sam channeled the essence of Barron as he strode toward the main entrance. "Just bugs beneath my notice."

There were a pair of guards standing sentry at the entryway, but with so many mages trickling in and out through the doors, they didn't even spare a glance at Sam as he swept into the corridors of the College proper. The building itself was a maze, the endless hallways all virtually identical to one another, and thanks to the power of spatial magic, none of those corridors connected in a way that would make any discernible sense to an outsider. Thankfully, Sam had Bill. Bill had been around longer than anyone else in the College—save the Arch-Mage himself—and had actually been buddies with the first Rituarchitect, Sage Cognitionis, who'd designed the bulk of the College.

<So far, so good.> Bill sent the red flag into the air, and Sam knocked on some nearby wood to stave off bad luck. <Hang a left and head for the archway with the radial spokes.>

Sam didn't hesitate. Confidence was the key to victory, and even a moment of uncertainty would be a warning to any mage or guard in the vicinity. Robes swishing around his legs, he strutted for the archway as though he owned the world and everything in it, College included. He carefully noted the runes carved into the archway stones. Those markings were the real key to navigating this place. They acted as a set of complex instructions for those initiates with a discerning eye. There were hundreds upon hundreds of different symbols. Although he only knew a handful of them from his time at the College, Bill had every single runic combination memorized.

Sam stepped through the archway, and the world tilted on edge, a corridor abruptly appearing on his right. He took that hallway, which was marked by an inverted crescent, walked fifteen paces, then doubled back, and headed through the archway he'd just come through a moment before. Instead of walking into a corridor, he stepped through space-time and into an octagonal chamber with eight more hallways jutting off like the spokes of a bike wheel. Bill directed him to take one of the paths on the left, marked by a triangle with two dots.

Four more left turns, and they emerged at their first stop: the Beginner's Quarters.

The corridor should have been empty. No guards would ever dare to venture into the Mages' private quarters, and the residents should've been gone—presumably, they were all headed to the Accord Chamber—leaving their rooms open and ripe for the plundering. Unfortunately, nothing ever went according to plan. A novice in brown robes loitered near a stairwell, his thumbs tucked into the rough rope belt around his hips.

<Don't panic,> Bill whispered inside his head. <Just follow my lead and say what I tell you to say. Remember, you belong here. He doesn't.>

"You there," Sam parroted the words Bill was feeding him, pinning the poor novice in place with a frosty glare. "What *exactly* do you think you're doing?"

The young man jumped, his face turning an ashy shade of white. "Well, I was just… the thing is, the trial doesn't start for-"

"Enough," Sam barked, cutting the young man off mid-word. "The whole College is bursting at the seams with visiting Mages of great import… and here *you* are, hiding out and clearly trying to avoid work! *Outrageous.* It's a good thing that

Mage Axium sent me to make sure there were no lollygaggers skirting their chores. Since you have nothing better to do than twiddle your thumbs, perhaps you can give Mage *Greentouched* a hand with the grounds. I'm sure he can find something for you to do before the Trial begins… perhaps the Rosebushes could use a trim."

The Rosebushes were Mage Greentouched's pride and joy—they were also carnivorous and responsible for more than a few missing fingers. The poor student's shoulders slumped, fear and regret flashing across his face in equal turns. Ducking his head in apology, the Novice muttered, "Yes, of course."

"Well, move sharply now," Sam coolly demanded. "I'll be in touch with Mage Greentouched, so I wouldn't dawdle if I were you."

Without a backward glance, Sam broke into motion as the student scampered down the spiral staircase. Bill cackled inside Sam's head. <That's the way you do it! I think you might finally be getting a hang of this intrigue stuff. Now let's get a move on—this place isn't going to blow itself up.>

Sam stole a look back over one shoulder, ensuring that the delinquent student really had left. The coast was clear. He ducked into the first room on the right and quickly pulled the door shut behind him with a soft **click.** The rooms on this level weren't warded, as beginners weren't trusted with privacy of any sort. Though, to be honest, locks weren't necessary, since thievery within the College was effectively nonexistent. The penalty for stealing so much as a sheet of paper could range from a whipping to a week spent in the Sanctuary of Solitude. No Mage in good standing would dare run the risk.

Good thing Sam wasn't a Mage in good standing.

The Beginner's Quarters were nicer than those granted to the Novices, but they were still rather sparse and sterile. A simple bed, a wardrobe, a desk and straight-backed chair for study. A nightstand with a porcelain washbasin stood against the far wall, and at the foot of the bed was a large trunk, meant for personal items or study materials. Sam dropped to a knee, flipped the lid, and went to town. There were a handful of books, most of them mundane in nature, but he did find a single magical volume called *Fundamentals of Meteorological Magic*. That one, he slipped into his Unending Flask.

Not a bad find at all. But robbing the College blind was only his secondary purpose. Sam fished out a mundane text called *A Brief History of Arcane Innovation*, pressed his hand against the front cover, and let energy seep out from his core, infusing the volume with enough unstable mana to blow a hole through the roof. But Sam didn't stop there. He fished out a pair of spell scrolls—Fireball and Weak Acid Spray. He inserted one spell scroll into the front of the book and another into the back. A third sheet of completely blank paper went into the middle of the thick volume. Sam tucked the book back into the trunk alongside everything else and snapped the lid shut.

Work done, he peeked his head out to make sure the hallway was still clear.

Not a soul in sight.

Sam and Bill moved quickly through the corridor, stopping at every third door to repeat the process. He quickly raided the rooms for anything of obvious value, then stashed a mundane book rigged to explode and packed with various spells. He used different spell combinations in each room. Weak Acid Spray and Ice Orb in one, Fireball and Paralysis in another. Of course, he made sure to insert a blank page directly into the center of each book. They cleared the Beginner's Quarters in a matter of minutes, then Bill ushered Sam through an elaborate series of turns and switchback, up ramps, and down staircases, eventually landing him in the Journeyman Mage Quarters.

Compared to the Novice and Beginner's Quarters, the Journeymen lived lavishly. They had sprawling king-sized beds, gilt-edged furniture, huge magically-fueled fireplaces, and their own private bathrooms. It was a *hundred* times nicer than Sam's bunk in the Irondown Barracks, and a *thousand* times cushier than any Inn room he'd crashed in since coming to Eternium. But, just like the Beginner's Quarters, these rooms didn't have locks. The

College might give you a nicer leash as you moved through the ranks, but it was still a leash.

As a Mage, you were College property. Period. End of story.

Like the rooms themselves, the gear was also significantly better. Sam and Bill made out like bandits. He picked up ten different monster Cores of various grades, several health and mana regen potions, a Phial of Swiftness that increased Dexterity by five points for thirty minutes, and gold and silver coins by the bagful. Then there were the books. Sweet, sweet books. *The Handbook of Counter-Curses. Principles of Exotic Summoning. Practical Guide of Uncommon Wonders. Field Book of Interplanar Monsters.* Once again, his main goal was planting more book bombs.

There was some small part of Sam that wanted to venture higher into the Expert, Master, or Grandmaster Quarters, just to see how they lived, but the risk was too great. According to Bill, everything would be guarded by powerful magical wards, and their risk of discovery would increase tenfold. They were already running the ultimate risk; no need to get greedy. Once they finished rigging the Journeymen Quarters, they popped in and out of several of the classrooms, paid a visit to the training arena, and stopped by at least ten different storerooms where all the pragmatic odds and ends were kept tucked away for the janitorial and maintenance staff. Brooms, mops, ladders, plaster.

Book Bombs went into every nook and cranny. There was no way they were going to take down the College as a whole, but they *were* going to inflict as much property and collateral damage as humanly possible. Hopefully, once the alarms started ringing, there would be so much chaos unfolding that the guards wouldn't know where to look.

<Alright,> Bill finally cut him off after Sam had finished stashing a final bomb in a linen supply closet filled with brown Novice robes and scratchy sheets. <They're starting the trial. I can feel power building in the air. If we're going to do this thing, it's now or never. It should take us four minutes to get to

the Repository of Trustees, but we're going to have to move fast. Better let the others know we're good to go.>

Sam slipped out a sheet of paper and a quill, then hastily jotted off a note.

The packages have been delivered. En route, four minutes. Clear the way. – S.

He leaned over and whispered Dizzy's name along with the Command Word: *Tweet.* He watched, enchanted by the process, as the sheet of parchment folded in on itself, sharp creases forming, one right after another, until a perfect origami bird perched in his hand. The creature turned its paper head and regarded Sam for a heartbeat, then leapt from his finger and took to the air, zipping down a nearby corridor and disappearing in a flash of spatial magic.

Without looking back, Sam and Bill took off at a run, following the little paper pigeon deeper into the bowels of the College.

CHAPTER TWENTY-FOUR

Sam bolted down a spiral staircase that cut through the annex, his legs pumping furiously as he tried to make up a little extra time. He'd just rounded the last turn when a wave of vertigo slammed into him like a shield bash. The whole world wobbled, and his knees threatened to give out on him completely for the briefest moment. He grabbed hold of the wrought iron handrail to steady himself against the sudden push and pull of gravitational distortion. Most of the spatial magic connecting the College like an inscrutable labyrinth was flawless—the transitions from one plane to another completely seamless.

The Annex… not so much.

It was one of the oldest parts of the College, created back when Sage Cognitionis had first been cobbling things together. Spatial magic done poorly could have all kinds of complicated side effects; everything from time pockets and gravity wells, to spatial anomalies and axis inversions. As a result, the College Annex, like most annexes, was where they stuck the people the College loathed; those Mages who had gotten on the wrong side of the Arch-Mage, or the handful of non-magical professors who taught more mundane subjects like dungeoneering or monster anatomy.

Sam wasn't bound for the Annex—no, the Repository of Trustees was buried even more deeply than that. The nauseous feeling finally passed, and Sam resumed his downward trek, spinning round and round and round like a corkscrew drilling into the earth. Finally, the staircase dumped him into an ancient hallway of gray stone, dimly lit by an iron candelabra protruding from the wall. The air down here was damp and cool, but also so thick with mana, it was almost palpable.

<Can you feel that?> Bill inhaled deeply, like someone smelling an apple pie fresh from the oven. <I just want to stand here and soak it up. We gotta be getting close now. Stay sharp. There's no telling what we might run into this deep.>

<What is that supposed to mean?> Sam was taken aback at the concern that ran through Bill's thoughts.

<Nothing. Just, you know... there *could* be some weird stuff down here, is all. When mana pools like this, it can have all kinds of odd side effects. Remember the jellies down in the sewer?>

<How could I ever forget? Those were some of the first creature's I ever fought in Eternium.> He shuddered at the memory of the gooey blobs of elemental magic which could only be killed by Mages, thanks to their magical nature.

<Those were the result of congealing residual mana,> Bill continued. <This much power just hanging around in the air could have equally unpredictable consequences. So, head on a swivel is all I'm saying.>

<You're such a comforting presence, you know that?> Sam picked up his pace while simultaneously trying to look in every direction at once. Admittedly, it *was* creepy down here, though he wasn't sure if that was because it was dark and dank, or because Bill had just opened his big fat mouth.

Sam padded along on silent feet but slowed when he heard a rustle of movement up ahead, just around the next bend. If there was someone or something down here, there was no way he'd be able to talk his way out of a fight. The trial was already in full swing up above, and no one came down here by accident.

Sam licked his lips and summoned his Orbital Tomes. They sprang free from Bill's Soul Space, spinning slowly around Sam in a lazy circle. He quickly cast Papier Mache Mage, then rotated Fire and Ice Orb Shuriken to his front two positions. Spells at the ready, Sam inched forward. He rounded the corner and came face to face with the business end of a sword.

Then let out a sigh of relief.

"Oh, thank celestial, it's only you." Arrow dropped his blade.

"Did you guys have any problems?" Sam quizzed as he joined up with the group.

"No problems getting here," Dizzy quickly brought him up to speed, "but there were a few *tiny* issues waiting for us..."

She stepped aside to reveal two dead guards next to an ancient-looking wooden door. "No one mentioned there would be sentries. But we managed to get the jump on them before they could sound an alarm. How about you? Any issues?"

"Nothing I couldn't handle." Sam cracked his knuckles ominously.

"Hey, hate to break up this fun little reunion," Bill spat at them, "but our window of opportunity is closing fast. At best, we have *minutes* left until the old Arch-Mage gets done bumping his gums and punishes that kid. As soon as he finishes, every Mage in the Kingdom is going to pour into the halls. We want to be scooting along *way~y* before that happens, so how's about we get this show on the road?"

"No better time than the present." Dizzy held up a ring of keys and gave them a little jingle. She slipped a huge brass key into the lock and turned the tumblers with a click.

"On three," she whispered, readying her heavy mace. "One... Two... *Three!*"

She reared back and kicked the door open, then rushed in with a war cry. Kai, Sphinx, and Arrow followed hard on her heels, leaving Finn, Sam, and Bill to bring up the rear.

Sam was half expecting an arcane dungeon, complete with shackles, torture equipment, and chandeliers crafted from human remains. Instead, it looked like the medieval version of a cubicle farm. There were neatly ordered desks, situated in neatly ordered rows and columns. Each workspace was covered with stacks of parchments, scrolls, and dossiers. A red-faced Mage with thinning hair, basset hound jowls, and a prodigious gut straining against his fine sapphire robes sprang to his feet.

"What is the *meaning* of this!" he bellowed, hands balling into tight fists. "You lot know full well, no one but the Trustees are allowed to set foot in here! Why, I'll have your credentials pulled for this insolence!"

"That ship has already sailed," Sam replied, pushing his way to the front. He dropped his cowl, pulled his foppish hat out, and placed it on his head. With Bill floating by his side and six magical books orbiting around him like planets, there was no mistaking exactly who he was.

"Impossible," the red-faced Mage sputtered. "It can't be. You're... you're that warlock. The Bibliomancer. But... but how?"

"That's not the question you should be asking." Sam's books were in position. "The real question you should be asking... is how you're going to get out of here alive."

"*Wilhelm*," the man bellowed at a mousy Mage with a shock of silver hair and thick bifocals. "Sound the alarm!"

The mousy Mage broke from his desk and dashed to a nearby section of wall covered with runic script. He didn't make it three steps. Arrow peppered his torso with feathered shafts, dropping him on the spot.

Experience gained: 1,620 (College Trustee, Sage Ildor the Meticulous, Lv. 25)

Some small part of Sam felt bad about this, but then he reminded himself that this was all part of the game. Not to mention the fact that they were at war—one he intended to win. The sudden influx of experience was also nothing to scoff at. Sixteen-hundred points for a single kill? That was *insanity*, and it had taken Arrow all of three seconds to put ol' Wilhelm on the floor. Sam strode further into the room with a smile and began slinging spells. Shuriken screamed through the air, but the red-faced Mage wasn't ready to go down without a fight.

He thrust his hands forward and conjured a hexagonal shield of brilliant crimson light.

"You've made a grave mistake," the Trustee snarled, "and now you shall pay for it in blood!"

He unleashed a blob of burning red mana that smashed into Sam's pauldron, eating through a portion of his armor and health. "Archibald! Wynnefreede! Battle Stations! Letterford, free the mana Kraken! The rest of you, retreat into the Vault. Quickly, now!"

"Mana Kraken?" Sam mumbled. "That probably isn't good."

"Bill, I thought you said they were as harmless as kittens," he hollered as chaos erupted all around them when the Trustees broke into action. "'They couldn't fight their way out of a wet paper bag if you gave 'em a map and a sword.' That's a direct quote!"

"Clearly, I made some tactical miscalculations. But *you* listened to me, and you have no one to blame for that but yourself. Now, if we are done pointing fingers in all directions—because I think it's safe to say we all share some of the blame here—let's figure out how to kill all these geezers!"

A willowy Mage thrust both hands forward and started hurling javelins of silvery energy, but Finn responded in an instant. He chanted, hands flashing through a series of complex motions as he conjured icy orbs that intercepted each bolt.

Meanwhile, Dizzy charged in, slamming into the red-faced Mage with her shoulder. His shimmering crimson shield saved him from suffering any damage, but it didn't stop physics. Force equals mass times acceleration. Dizzy was huge, heavy, and moving like a freight train. The man flew backward through the air, slamming into a desk and slumping to the ground. Without focused concentration, his force shield guttered and died. Sam took the opportunity to Bookmark the mage before unloading a barrage of Shuriken. His paper stars landed with deadly power, slicing through fine robes and exploding in flashes of orange and gold.

The man was dead in seconds, and even more experience flooded into Sam like a torrent.

Exp: 2,577 (College Trustee, Sage Etrix the Auditor, Lv. 29)

Dizzy didn't waste a breath, already moving onto her next target, her mace swinging for the fences. On Sam's left, Arrow flipped a desk onto its side for cover, then began picking off the fleeing Mages who were making for a heavy circular steel door located at the back of the room. Apparently, most of the Mages *were* harmless—and they were all trying to get out of Dodge before the reaper came calling. Kai bounded across the floor to intercept them. One of the Trustees, a gaunt man with sunken eyes and razor-sharp cheekbones, upended another desk and hurled it at Kai with a flick of his wrist.

The Monk leapt into the air, glowing like a golden star before slamming a foot into the oncoming desk. The desk exploded in a hail of shrapnel, splinters of wood and bits of paper flying off in every direction. Kai touched down, then bounded into the air again, landing a spinning roundhouse against the man's temple. The gaunt Mage's knees folded and he went limp, dropping to the ground in a heap of limbs. One swift knife-hand strike to the throat finished him on the spot. More experience still.

*Exp: 1,215 (College Trustee, Master Lucius Tanicius Excingus, Lv. 22; 405 * 3 difficulty)*

Sam grunted in pleasure as a golden light streamed through him, the signal that he had reached level eleven. He almost lost his concentration, but the retreating Mages were getting close to the vault door and safety. Kai was a thousand times quicker; he hurdled over another desk, leapt into the air, pushed off a wall, and landed in a crouch before the hulking metal door. In a flash, a group of nine Mages were suddenly pinned between a deadly Monk and a steadily advancing party of Mage killers.

The Mages wheeled around, wide eyed and terrified, looking for some way out. Any way out.

There were still a few standing their ground, but they were fading fast.

A willowy female spellcaster had an arrow protruding from one shoulder and a pair of ice lances sticking out from her stomach. She wasn't long for this world. A broad-shouldered Trustee clad in glowing mage armor was attempting to go toe to toe with Dizzy, but that was a losing proposition. True, he was *technically* bigger than she was, and he seemed to know how to handle his summoned shillelagh, but he was losing ground to her superior strength and constitution. Once she carved through his mage armor, one good knock to the head would send him off to the afterlife.

In the back, Kai advanced on the party of hapless Mages like a deadly wraith. He looked for all the world like a wolf who'd just stumbled upon an unprotected flock of sheep. Unfortunately for the sheep, wolves tended to travel in packs. With a primal howl, Sam and Bill opened up with a bevy of spells. Fireball Shuriken exploded while gobs of viscous ink splattered over robes, quickly gumming up legs so the Trustees couldn't run. Sensing an opportunity, Arrow shifted his focus and unleashed a hail of arrows, while Kai danced through the throng of cowering Mages.

Bodies fell like hail… and experience poured in like flood waters.

Exp: 1,152 (College Trustee, Master Lovelace the Studious, Lv. 21)

Exp: 2,448 (College Trustee, Sage Wynnefreede the Blunt, Lv. 28)

Exp: 1,857 (College Trustee, Sage Amalia the Ponderous, Lv. 26)

All around the room, more and more of his teammates rose into the air, sheathed in golden light. Finn had finally killed the offensive spellcaster, and Dizzy had dispatched the tanky Mage, the last semblance of resistance. There were still six Mages left standing—quite possibly enough points to drive Sam up another level. Maybe this thing was actually going to go off without a hitch after all.

<Earth to Sam,> Bill squawked in his head. <We've got movement at our three o'clock!>

Sam turned his head and noticed a faint distortion beelining away from the hulking vault door. "Nope, not today."

He took aim and let loose with more Shuriken. The blur fizzled and faded, revealing a pudgy man in his middle years with flowing silver hair. One of Sam's Shuriken grazed his bicep, leaving a deep slash in his opulent robes. "There's no escaping this, pal."

"Who says I'm trying to escape?" The man gave him a cold smile that never quite reached his eyes. He turned on a heel and dove, his hand slapping against a plain section of wall near what looked like a tea-station. The man fell to the ground with a thud, but the bright red handprint on the stone wall began to glow and pulse. The Mage slipped onto his hands and knees and quickly scampered toward an overturned desk. "You never should've come here. Now you're about to find out *why*."

The floor rumbled, and a huge fissure formed down the face of the wall. Sam watched, horrified, as an ethereal blue tentacle, as thick as a tree trunk and studded with suction cups, emerged from the crack. A second tentacle joined, then a third... a fourth, and a fifth. Those ghastly limbs pulled, and a bulbous head covered with glowing red eyes emerged from the wall. It looked like a giant squid, but one made entirely out of mana.

"What the abyss is that?" Sam's whisper was the first to break the sudden, horrified silence.

<I'm guessing the mana kraken!> Bill shouted into his head. <Also, trouble! Don't just stand there looking at it, run *away*!>

It was already too late. A tentacle flashed across the room like a lightning strike, wrapping around Kai, who was busy dispatching the last of the Trustees. The mana limb snaked around his torso in three quick loops, and the Monk barely even had a chance to cry out in protest. With a mewling roar, the creature flexed the tentacle and crushed its prey like a soda can.

Sam watched in sickened horror as Kai's top half toppled forward, completely disconnected from the bottom half. He was dead before he hit the ground, which was probably a small mercy.

"Fall *back*!" Sam yelled over the din of battle. "I'll hold it at bay."

He planted his feet and let loose with everything he had in his arsenal. Fireball Shuriken plowed into the ethereal monster but didn't seem to do more than superficial damage. His Ice Orb Shuriken were slightly more effective, but only *slightly*. Ink Lance did absolutely nothing.

<Anything physical isn't going to have any effect,> Bill sent as the others fought for the exit. <Remember how I said pooling mana could have weird effects? This is what I was talking about. That thing has no true physical essence. It's wild mana with a crude mind. Any physical attack component won't even touch it. Only pure *magic*.>

That certainly explained why his attacks were so ineffective. Sure, each Shuriken had a spell component, but most of the damage was physical slashing damage. Still, it was better than what anyone else could do, with the exception of Finn. Sam kept spamming his spells as quickly as he could cast them. *Anything* to buy his friends a little more time.

He aimed at the creature's myriad of eyes, hoping to blind or disorient the kraken. But that didn't seem to work either. Arrow jumped a desk, only feet away from the exit, when a mana tendril lashed out like a striking cobra. It wrapped around his leg and the squid reeled him in with a screech.

Sphinx, who'd actually made it through the door, bolted back in. She sprang onto a desk and vaulted into the air, executing a flawless aerial flip while simultaneously hurling a flurry of daggers. The black-steel blades were about as effective as shooting a duck with a super soaker. The mana kraken simply absorbed them before plucking the Rogue from the air like a pop fly.

Arrow screeched in fury, but only for a moment. Sphinx

didn't even have time to do that. In the blink of an eye, the creature pulled both of them into its gooey mana center. Rogue and Ranger instantly *dissolved,* their bodies liquifying in the space of a second.

<Do your job and move your *legs*, Legs!> Bill thundered at him. <I don't want to find out how long it takes that thing to dissolve magical books.>

As much as he hated himself for it, Sam turned and bolted for the exit while the mana kraken was busy eating his friends. They were beyond help, and he still had friends that had a chance to survive this mission.

Just before he dove through the doorway, he sent a half-dozen fireballs at the smug, relieved Mages that had managed to survive to that point. Only Bill saw as their laughter turned to snarls of fury and fear in that instant.

CHAPTER TWENTY-FIVE

<Celestial *feces* but that was close!> Bill swore in Sam's head as he skidded through the door, panting from the effort.

Sam's retort was cut off as golden light enveloped him in a halo, briefly lifting him from the ground. The experience from the final kills had only been shared by a fraction of the original party, which meant he had gained enough to hit level twelve. That came with a host of benefits: he automatically received two Intelligence, Wisdom, and one Dexterity, not to mention four characteristic points he'd get to spend at his leisure. Now certainly wasn't the time or place for that, but the sudden added bonuses left him feeling like a million bucks even after losing most of his team.

The second his feet touched the ground, he shot away from the door at his highest possible speed. Dizzy had already made it into the hallway and slammed the doors shut the second Sam was past the threshold. Sam took a quick look around, frantically searching for Finn.

Kai, Arrow, and Sphinx were all goners, but he felt weight lift off his chest when he saw that Finn had made it out in one piece. After seeing what had happened to Kai, being in one piece was an enormous victory. Dizzy looked deeply shaken but simultaneously relieved… at least until the doors started rattling as though something was trying to pull them open from the other side.

Eyes wide, Dizzy spun and grabbed hold of an iron door ring. The doors shook more ferociously, but she held the ring fast in a white knuckled grip. "This thing wants out, and I'm not going to be able to hold these doors for long. Sam, I think it's time we trigger the escape plan."

"Right. Right," he repeated, shaking his head to get himself back into gear. The escape plan. Just because they'd made it out of the chamber of certain death didn't mean they were in the clear. They still had a whole College to navigate. He reached into his flask and pulled out a single sheet of paper. It was a rather plain, unremarkable thing, but in Sam's hands, with his unique abilities, that single sheet of paper was a Weapon of Magical Destruction. That single sheet was twinned to a sheet of paper tucked away in the Book Bomb he'd planted in the janitor's closet near the junior faculty lounge. Whatever he wrote on this sheet would appear on that one.

That sheet, in turn, was twinned to the sheet located in a book bomb in an annex classroom… which was twinned to the bomb located in a supply closet housing novice gear. On and on and on it went, one enormous daisy chain of books, fifty strong, all twinned together. All tied to the sheet of paper in Sam's hand. Anything he wrote on it would appear simultaneously in every volume strategically scattered throughout the College. Creating such a long chain of spelled papers was *incredibly* dangerous and wildly irresponsible—transcription errors increased fivefold with every duplication. Any spell he wrote was not only guaranteed to fail, but certain to explode.

Terrible under any circumstances other than this one. There was no way he could set off all those planted book bombs at once, not using command phrases and not over such a vast distance. But with Transcription Twinning, he could do the impossible… or kill himself. He had a relatively massive mana pool, and even if Bill assured him that he could survive this spell, Sam had the gut feeling that any little thing could drain his core into oblivion and then eat through his health like a ravenous wolf.

Sometimes you just had to throw the dice.

The doors rattled again, this time more forcefully, and the wood groaned from the strain. Dizzy had sweat rolling down her face. "Come *on*, Sam!"

Sam licked his lips, drew a quill, and then copied the most basic spell he could—an easy spell he'd practiced a thousand times: Ice Orb. He drew the first loop, imbuing the lines with mana, and his hand flowed through the motion. Right before he got to the end, he whispered a silent prayer and pulled a line short, raising his quill and breaking the spell form. The effect was instantaneous. The scroll erupted with a flash of blue, slamming Sam against the wall as hoarfrost spread across the ground and climbed over his robes. The cold was terrible, but the damage was minimal. Bill had picked the spell, knowing that of all Sam's spells, it was the one he was most likely to survive.

But that wasn't the only effect. Even in the bowels of the College, Sam could feel the rumble of explosions rippling through the grounds. Every single twinned paper had likewise blown, triggering not only the Book Bombs themselves, but activating the myriad of spell scrolls tucked away in the pages. Even half freezing to death, Sam couldn't help but smile. It had worked. Unfortunately, his joy was short-lived.

The pain that hit him next was a thousand times worse than the exploded Ice Orb spell scroll. A roaring filled his chest cavity as his core emptied in a rush—rudely ripped out to fuel the small army of failed Ice Orb spells. He couldn't stop the scream that tore its way from his throat. This was worse than anything he'd experienced before. He clutched his chest as though trying to physically prevent his core from being ripped from his body. In a matter of seconds, his mana was gone, and stars swam across his vision.

Next, his health started to drop like a stone.

So much for Bill's math. Several notifications flashed across his eyes.

Skill Increased: Book Maker's Book Bomb (Beginner IV).

Skill Increased: Spell Alchemy (Novice III).

Transcription Twinning (Beginner V).

Transcription Twinning had increased to Beginner Level Five? That seemed excessive, but the thought felt like it belonged to someone else. Sam was sure that was important, but he couldn't quite seem to remember why. To his right, the doors to the Reliquary of Trustees rattled ferociously. Dizzy shouted, but the words were all jumbled together. For some reason, Finn was by his side, but black was creeping in around the edges of his vision. Sam was sure that this was the end. But then, miracle of miracles, the pain abruptly ceased, and his rapidly dwindling health stabilized.

He was low. Fifteen of one-hundred and fifty.

"Drink this, old boy," Finn was saying from a great distance. His friend thrust an odd vial full of red liquid into Sam's shaky hand. But Sam's head was so fuzzy that he simply stared at it. Everything felt so far away. Detached.

<Snap *out* of it, Legs!> Bill bellowed in his head. <You gotta drink the potion.>

"Potion? Why?" he mumbled half-heartedly.

<Because you just got your brain sucked out through a bendy straw. Listen, it'll make all the bad feelings go bye-bye. That's all you need to know.>

"Okay." Sam managed to take the vial from Finn and throw it down in a single long gulp. The potion hit like a haymaker. His health bar rocketed up to seventy-five percent, and the haze clouding his thoughts cleared somewhat. He blinked and quickly gained his feet. He'd done it. He'd survived.

"You need to go *now*!" Dizzy yelled at them over one shoulder, her face beet red from the strain of holding the doors.

"What about you?" Sam demanded even as he realized that she meant to sacrifice herself.

She grunted and shook her head. "If I let go for a second,

these doors are gone, and that thing is going to kill us all. I can buy you another two minutes. Just… just make sure it's worth it. Make sure Finn gets out of here alive. That thing will tear me apart, but I'll be back in twelve hours, tops. He won't. It's up to you, Sam."

"I promise," he solemnly swore. "I'll get us clear."

Sam took one last look at Dizzy, now wholly consumed with holding the doors shut, then turned and took off at a run. The health potion had taken care of the damage, but his mana reserve was recovering at a snail's pace. Thanks to the *generosity* of the College, Sam had a ready supply of mana potions, all lifted from the Journeyman quarters. He popped a cork on a glass vial and downed it as they moved, feeling power and energy surge back into his center. His thoughts came together as his mental energy was refreshed, and his body and mind worked more naturally.

The vial didn't top him off, but it brought him back up to two-hundred mana and left him feeling human again. He slipped the empty vial back into his flask—waste not, want not—then ushered his sole surviving teammate up the corkscrew staircase and back into the upper College. Sam made it about three paces into the connecting annex hallway when the entire world erupted with noise and power and motion. Stones groaned, the floor rattled the teeth in Sam's head, and a wash of mana flooded through the hallway. Sam dropped to a knee, staring around and trying to discover the source of the explosion. He'd already set off all his Book Bombs, so it couldn't be that, and even all of them going off at once couldn't possibly release so much mana.

"What in the abyss was that?" Finn managed to ask as the rumbling finally subsided.

"Was that… was that us?" Sam wondered right as Finn spoke.

"Phft. Not on your life," Bill replied with more than a little awe filling his voice. "I honestly have no idea what that was; and I know what almost *everything* is. It was big, that much I can tell you. Bigger than anything I can even begin to imagine… whatever the abyss it was is going to change the fate of Ardania. Nothing will ever be the same. Honestly, I don't feel like sticking around to find out how the world just shifted."

The annex was still abandoned, but that all changed by the time they rushed through an archway and into one of the central hubs that connected several of the main corridors. Sam just had to stop and gape at the madness sweeping through the halls like a plague. There were guards everywhere, but they seemed just as frazzled and confused as Sam felt. Some were running around, screaming about fires and magic out of control all around the College. That bit had to be Sam's handiwork, but just as many were just… standing there, looking completely lost.

Watching the Mages was even more bewildering.

About a third of them were openly weeping and sobbing uncontrollably. Another rough third looked like they'd just seen death in the flesh; those were mostly muttering about the destruction of the College, and grumbling that nothing would ever be the same again, almost verbatim what Bill had said.

"How will we survive this?" a long graybeard whispered to a Mage in opulent red robes. "The Accords are *everything*. They are the foundation and cornerstone of our people!"

"It will be lawlessness and anarchy," the other replied. "At least for a time."

"But anarchy creates a void," a third spoke firmly, "and that void will be filled by those willing to do what must be done."

CHAPTER TWENTY-SIX

Sam lost the thread of the conversation as he pushed and shoved his way through the press of bodies with Finn in tow, trying to get to the next archway. Clearly, something had happened to the Accords, though what, he didn't know. Was it possible that killing so many of the Trustees had somehow weakened the Accords? Bill had mentioned the Trustees were responsible for maintaining the College's magical infrastructure. Still, that seemed unlikely. This level of destruction was well beyond what Sam's Book Bombs could account for, which meant some other external catastrophic event had occurred. Maybe something to do with the trial?

Sam just wasn't sure. But if it *was* some sort of catastrophic event, that didn't explain the *last* third of the Mages. They weren't weeping or grumbling. They were *celebrating.* There were hugs and more tears, but those were clearly from joy. The only other thing he could tell about them was that they were *powerful.* Experts and Masters at the minimum.

"This is bloody madness," Finn whispered in his ear. "Just what in the world happened while we were down in the Repository?"

"They can't hide something this big for long." Bill tried to get them to focus. "We'll find out soon enough, but now ain't the time for it. We need to stay focused. If we play our cards right, I think we might just be able to get out of here in one piece after all. But not if we keep standing around here until we finally do bump into someone we know. Take that archway on the right—the one with the inverted triangle and the three squiggly lines."

Moving as quickly as the congested hallways would allow, they wove through the corridors, keeping their heads down and doing their best to look like they were moving with a purpose, not escaping, but important Mages who had places to be. But it was hardly necessary; the weeping and rejoicing were in full swing, and no one seemed to have any care for two random attendees wandering through a college packed to the gills with Mages of every shape, size, and rank. The guards were the only ones that seemed to be keeping it together, and *they* were busy putting out the numerous fires Sam had started.

Either that, or investigating whatever had happened during the trial.

They were nearly in the clear when Sam rounded a corner and slammed face-first into a wall of a man wearing the colors of a guard sergeant. Sam bounced off as though he had run into a literal wall and found himself sprawled out on the ground. He shook his head and looked up… right at the worst possible person in the entire College. A burly man decked out in silver-edged plate mail named Geffery the Red. Not two paces behind ol' Geffery was the second-worst person he could've run into—besides the Archmage himself—Geffery's partner, Karren the Blade. She was lean as a hungry wolf and carried a finger-slim rapier at her hip.

"Good heavens, so sorry about that, Senior Mage," Geffery stammered, the color draining from his face. "What with all the chaos, and the crowding… well, I should've been more careful."

Apologetic was the right tone to take with an unhappy senior Mage. Knocking one flat on their back in the middle of a crowded hallway was a good way to end up on sewer detail for the next year. Which was precisely where Sam and Finn had first met Geffery and Karren. They'd been the guards who'd accompanied the cohort of young Mages down into the sewers to clear out the jellies that tended to build up over time. They were also the same two guards that Sam had ambushed the last time he'd infiltrated the college; knocking them unconscious, stealing their tabards, and leaving them bound and gagged down in the muck below the College. If there was anyone who could ID Sam and Finn, it was these two, and they had a grudge to settle.

"It's no bother." Sam kept his head down. "Mistakes happen, especially with so much confusion."

"Let me help you up," Geffery extended a rough-calloused hand.

"No. I don't touch people," Sam ordered, keeping his face cloaked by the heavy cowl.

"I insist, Senior Mage," Geffery grabbed Sam by the arm and hauled him to his feet with ease. The guard was huge and deceptively strong. Sam's cowl fell away from his face. In that instant, he knew their luck had run out. Recognition flashed through Geffery's eyes, and a scowl pulled down the corners of his lips. "*You*! Of course you're here. I bet you're behind this, aren't you? Intruders! To arms, to arms!"

Sam heard the rasp of metal against leather—the sound of weapons leaving their scabbards. Geffery bellowed, even louder than before, "We have Rogue Mages! Seize them!"

Geffery lunged, but Sam was already dancing away. He wheeled around, gave Finn a push in the opposite direction, and took off at a dead sprint. Geffery and Karren were trailing behind them, and a few other guards were glancing around in confusion. Normally, Sam and Finn never would have stood a chance in a foot race against the pair of guards, but these weren't typical conditions. The congestion in the hallways made it much harder for the two bulkier armored guards to slip through the crowd—not to mention, they couldn't just bowl over the Mages in their way.

Knocking the wrong Mage over, even if it was in the pursuit of Rogue Mages, could have serious repercussions. Docked pay. Loss of rank. Even time in the Sanctuary of Solitude for a grave enough offense. Sam and Finn had nothing to lose, so they gladly shouldered aside their stuffy, robe-wearing counterparts—leaving squawks of anger and indignation in their wake. Bill guided them through a series of complicated and simultaneously convoluted twists, turns, and switchbacks, hoping to shake the pair of guards in the labyrinth of spatial corridors, but Geffery and Karren weren't giving up without a fight.

They weren't gaining ground, but neither could Sam, Finn, and Bill seem to lose the pair. Worse, a few more College guards had joined the pursuit.

<Do you want the good news or the bad news?> Bill questioned as they rounded another turn.

<Good news,> Sam replied mentally.

<Well, we're almost out of the College.>

<That's great. What's the bad news?>

<I'm out of turns, and we still have to make it through the courtyard. No way to lose them. Our only hope is that they won't follow us out into the city.> Bill delivered the information in a deadpan tone, clearly not trusting their luck at all.

"Let's just hope they haven't closed the portcullis," Sam muttered under his breath.

They tore around a final corner and shouldered their way through a set of massive double doors that led out onto the western courtyard. There were more Mages milling around on the cobblestones, most of them clumped together in small groups and talking in muted whispers. The great steel portcullis was up, but standing directly in front of the archway that led beneath the outer wall of the College was a platoon of Guards—not College Guards, but elite Royal Guards that worked for the crown.

"Stick a fork in us." Finn nearly came to a halt as he saw

what awaited them. "Our goose is bloody-well cooked, old boy."

"Stop them!" Geffery boomed, charging into the courtyard, Karren the Blade only a handful of paces behind him. "Guards. Stop those two mages! Rogues! They are Rogue Mages."

A stony-faced guard in chain mail responded at once. He pulled free a hand-and-a-half sword from a scabbard at his hip and barked a series of orders. His platoon fanned out in a half-arc, blocking off the exit completely, before interlocking their square tower shields and lowering wicked looking spears. A moment later, there was a resounding **clank** as huge gears lurched to life and the portcullis dropped, effectively sealing Sam and Finn in the courtyard—trapped between the onrushing Geffery and the royal guards.

<It was nice knowing you, boys,> Bill sighed dramatically. <I'm sure they'll lock me up for another hundred years.>

Sam ignored the book. There had to be a way out of this. There *had* to be. They hadn't made it this far to die in this courtyard, just a hundred feet from freedom. He had two Rorschach spells ready to deploy. Maybe he could use both and then attempt to fly over the walls with his Quill Wings Cloak while carrying Finn. Except that wouldn't work. He might be able to carry Finn, but Rorschach only worked on anyone who had a lower intelligence level than Sam. It would probably distract the guards, but there were fifty Mages in the courtyard, at least a few of whom wouldn't be affected by the spell.

Trying to fly away would make them an easy target, and all it would take was one fireball to kill them both. Sam felt his stomach sink as he realized there really was no clever way out of this one. They'd taken an enormous gamble and lost. Now the bill was coming due, and Finn would be the one to pay the ultimate price.

"Hold!" The city guard commander bellowed. "What in the pit is going on here exactly, eh?"

"Take them into custody," Geffery ordered Karren over one shoulder. He turned to the city guard commander. "There's been an incident at the College. Some sort of explosion. Or a series of explosions. Possibly even an assassination attempt against the Archmage, if some of the rumors floating around are to be believed. It's hard to say exactly. The College Guard is still trying to sort all the details. But *these* two are definitely involved somehow. Rogue Mages, the both of them."

"Rogue Mages?" The city guard commander said, a question in his voice. He squinted, a frown forming on his face. "You're not making any sense, man. I'm looking right at the pair of them. I don't see a Rogue Mage tag."

"*What?*" Geffery spit. "But of course they are. I would know those two anywhere. They *are* Rogue Mages. Traitors to the College and to the Crown, and likely behind whatever is happening inside these halls!"

"You're barking mad," the guard commander shot back. He was no longer looking at Sam and Finn, but rather staring daggers at Geffery. "They can't be actual traitors. They don't have tags!"

"I think I can clear this up." Finn sauntered forward with a smug look plastered across his face. "Obviously, the stress of this situation has impaired good Sir Geffery's judgement. Or perhaps he thinks we are someone other than ourselves—mistaken identity does happen. We tried to explain the situation, but he attacked us. My compatriot and I tried to flee instead of engaging him, because we didn't want to hurt a loyal College guard just trying to execute his duties. But I can quite assure you, we are no traitors. Surely if we were Rogue Mages, you could see that, yes? It is my understanding that it is *impossible* to fool the Deep Scan ability of the city guards, isn't that right, Commander?"

Sam had no idea what was going on, but he was smart enough not to look this gift horse in the mouth. He kept his trap shut and silently prayed that Finn knew what in the heck he was doing.

"Exactly correct," the commander replied with a grim nod. "There are certain countermeasures and classes that can fool many guards, but Deep Scan never lies. It sees the world how it really is and tells us the truth of the matter. The fact is, these two do *not* have Rogue Mage tags, though this one *does* have a heavy Warlock penalty on him. I wouldn't trust him to hold my valuables, but as far as I can tell… there is no bounty on their heads. The pair of you are simply mistaken."

"Just as I tried to tell them." Finn sounded apologetic. "As for our standing in the College, I can vouch for myself and my compatriot here. I am Lord Finneas Laustsen of House Laustsen, and this fine fellow is a powerful natural-born Mage in his own right. Now, instead of wasting time with us, why don't you go investigate what the actual problem is? If you would be so kind, please take Sir Geffery and his partner there with you. I have tried to be a good sport about the whole affair, considering the circumstances, but my patience is wearing thin. If we are not allowed to continue on our way, I may become irritated and speak to your company commander about needlessly harassing a Noble."

"Of course, m'Lord," the guard commander sighed, clearly used to dealing with Nobles. "Of course. Break ranks. Hitchens, get that sally gate open immediately. These two men need to be about Kingdom business."

In a matter of seconds, the city guards had formed up and were marching toward the College, whisking Geffery and Karren away with them. Geffery looked positively thunderstruck as he was hauled away. "This isn't over! I *know* it was you! I don't know how you pulled this off, but I know! I'll find you two yet!"

"Apologies for him, m'Lords." The guard commander quickly ushered Sam and Finn through a smaller wooden sally gate. "Some men crack under the pressure. We'll get to the bottom of this, you have my word."

The commander gave them one final tight smile and a small wave before heading back into the courtyard. The sally door slammed shut behind them, leaving them outside of the College and in the city, and not a guard in sight. They were free! Bill spoke softly as they quickly hoofed it toward Cheapside, "Does someone want to explain what black magic voodoo just happened?"

"Check your notifications," Finn chuckled softly.

<Yeah, yeah, just give me a sec,> Bill sent, silent for a moment. His pages rustled in astonishment, and he spoke aloud once more. "No way. They're *gone*. The Accords, they've been… *dissolved*? That… it shouldn't be possible, but there it is, clear as day. The three of us were Rogue Mages under The Accords, but no Accords means no charges. We just got a *massive* get out of jail free card. I'm sure it's a loophole that someone will eventually fix, but until they do… we have total amnesty, boys."

"How long do you think that'll last?" Sam instantly tried to plan what they could get away with.

"Long enough for us to get clear of the city, and that's all that really matters." Bill laughed and laughed. Sam still wasn't sure what exactly had unfolded, but at the moment, he honestly didn't care.

It felt like Christmas morning.

CHAPTER TWENTY-SEVEN

It took nine hours for Sam, Finn, and Bill to make it back to their Dungeon-turned-Den. There was an announcement about the dissolution of the Accords, but there were no specifics on how it happened; so assumptions started getting thrown around like candy at a parade. Though the remaining Mages tried to stamp down the rumor mill, those ugly whispers spread like wildfire through the streets of Ardania. For every fearful tale that died, three more popped up in a city-wide version of Whack-a-Mole.

"The College was broken," some whispered.

"The Archmage is dead," said others. Most of those rumors placed the blame squarely at the feet of Joe—the now notorious Rogue Mage who'd been standing trial. In one tavern, Sam heard that Joe had summoned a Celestial Whale into the chamber where the Archmage was squished as the beast flopped around looking for water. In a back-alley market, a conspiratorial merchant said that Joe had made an alliance with a dark power, that he'd broken the Accords through a sheer effort of will. A portly blacksmith offhandedly mentioned that Joe had thrown away his humanity, siding with the Wolfmen.

That one, Sam knew was false. The rest? No one knew the truth, not for certain. Many of those same rumors said the College was beyond salvation, and that a new order would rise in its place. Sam doubted that. Even with the Accords gone, he knew the College was far from finished. They were powerful, well-financed, and connected to every royal house in Ardania, not to mention the King himself. The College was a powerful tool designed to keep the masses in check, and King Henry would never let such a useful tool be discarded so easily. Sam was sure the College would be back, under new management maybe, but back all the same. As Sam's father often said, the more things change, the more they stay the same.

Still, reasserting that dominance would take time.

In the interim, the dissolution of the College was a perfect excuse for people to act out in the worst possible ways. Rioters terrorized the streets, drinking and yelling and fighting with reckless abandon; looters worked their way through North Waterside, stealing anything that wasn't bolted to the floor. Sometimes more than a few things that *were* bolted to the floor.

The city was in turmoil, and Sam couldn't have been happier about it. He even used the chaos as a cloak to pilfer goods from a variety of high-end restaurants, stocking up on valuable food supplies for his brood. The downside was that the Royal Guards were also out in force, bringing order with an iron fist. They even had contingents of state-sponsored Mages with them—an overwhelming display of force that explained in no uncertain terms that the College was still to be feared, no matter what anyone may have heard.

Sam and Finn had to avoid those like the plague, lest they get shanghaied into one of the guard patrols. Worse, the city gates were also locked down for the better part of five hours. Sam and Finn finally managed to slip through just before dark, when the guards opened up to let any stranded adventurers back into the city before nightfall. They padded out, earning a few odd glances in passing, but no one said anything. The guards had bigger things to worry about at the moment than a couple of newbie adventurers seeking their own death.

Dizzy and the others had already respawned by the time they made it back to the Irondowns. Sam was more than a little surprised about that; in his experience, the game's AI often punished stupid or reckless deaths. According to Dizzy, everyone in the party had received a paltry five-hour respawn time. Apparently, the AI was mightily impressed with the sheer gumption of their raid, and it seemed that being dissolved by a mana kraken was punishment enough for any recklessness they may have engaged in.

Sam wanted nothing more than to head to the Barracks, get a long soak in the communal tub, then sleep for the next ten or twelve hours, but Dizzy wouldn't hear of it. She crossed her arms and shook her head. They had somewhere else they needed to be, she told him—her tone indicating in no uncertain terms that there would be no debate about the issue. Sam simply sighed in resignation and followed her away from the Irondowns, through the tangles of the forest, and to the edge of New Narvik.

They scaled the walls, just as they'd done a thousand times before.

Sam crested the out wall but froze at the top.

Arrayed before him was a throng of Wolfmen gathered in a great circle, their luminous eyes staring up at him. At the far end of the gathering, a wooden dais had been erected. The O'Baba waited on the platform, staring at him just like the others. Sam felt a lump of fear and uncertainty form in his throat, but he didn't speak. The moment felt enchanted somehow, and he didn't want to be the one to break it. Finally, The O'Baba threw her head back and let loose a long, piercing howl. One by one, the other Wolfmen joined, each offering their own voices to the night. The sounding was a haunting melody that raised the hairs along the nape of Sam's neck.

The Wolfmen cut off their howls all at once, their eyes fixed on him in expectation. Bill sent in a conspiratorial tone, <I think you're supposed to answer back.>

Sam glanced at Dizzy and Finn. Both just shrugged. Not knowing what else to do, Sam threw his head back and offered up a howl of his own. Below, the Wolfmen dropped their heads in a sign of respect and parted ranks, forming a narrow pathway for him that snaked its way to the dais. The O'Baba was still on stage, but a few other familiar faces had joined her. Kai, Sphinx, Arrow, and Velkan. The O'Baba snorted and motioned for them to join her. When they finally made it to the stage, The O'Baba raised a hand high.

"Hear me, Redmane Tribe," the ancient she-wolf said. Her voice was soft, yet the quiet of the night carried her words like a trumpet. "We gather to rejoice and celebrate in the kill of the pack. For many years, we have fought a war of attrition against the humans of Ardania. Yet tonight, these new wolf pups have done what we have only dreamt of. This night, with great daring and boldness, they landed a *terrible* blow against the Mage's College. This very night, one of our oldest, most formidable enemies has fallen. Though they will recoup their strength in time—as all worthy enemies do—it is cause for celebration!"

Another round of huffs and howls filled the night, but The O'Baba wasn't done yet. She raised her hand once more, cutting off the merriment. "There are those among our number who have doubted the sincerity and value of these humans with the hearts of wolves. They have questioned my judgment in admitting them to our ranks and granting them the honors of Nobility. But no longer. Let the actions of this night still every wagging tongue, and wag every still tail! These seven have demonstrated beyond a shadow of a doubt their commitment and loyalty to our cause. They have proven this not merely in words, but through spilled blood. So tonight, we will honor them. For their actions, I name *each* of them a Lord or Lady of The People, and promote Sam_K to the auspicious rank of

Blood Baron! I also name them *Extended Family*! They are blood and bone and fur, just as we are-"

"Wait." Sam forced himself to the front. "I apologize, O'Baba, for interrupting. I cannot say how thankful I am for your kind words, but I cannot accept such honors under false pretenses. The truth is-"

<What in the abyss are you doing?> Bill hissed at him. < Don't be a moron. You're ruining everything. We're almost in.>

<The right thing,> Sam sent back with a mental sigh. "The truth is, we *aren't* responsible for the destruction of the Accords. From what I've managed to piece together, it seems that a Rogue Mage named 'Joe' is responsible for bringing down the Archmage. Our raid was a success. We managed to assassinate a number of powerful Trustees and plant some explosives throughout the College, but we can't take credit for everything that transpired. The Wolfmen are a people of honor, and I couldn't live with myself, knowing I had gained favor through lies and deception."

The Wolfmen milling in the audience broke out into muted whispers. The O'Baba offered them a wolfish grin, one of her ears twitching in amusement. "I told you, Kosoruk of White Wyther."

She had spoken softly, staring in victory at a lanky wolf with white fur standing nearby. He was swathed in a heavy cloak, and a series of scars crisscrossed his muzzle. "You doubted, but I *told* you he would have the heart not to take credit for a kill that belongs to another."

Then, more loudly for the rest of the assembled wolves, she spoke again. "This is already *known*, Sam the Blood Baron. Our eyes and ears have told us such things. But your willingness to speak truth is only more reason to elevate you and your pack mates. As for the College, though you may not have caused its fall, it is fallen. You contributed. Perhaps you even did more than you know. We have a saying in the old tongue: *Kruzhji ro kraz Gufetchitse*. A little blood from all, kills the enemy. Wolves are creatures of the pack."

Sam could only gape in shock as The O'Baba continued, "Only one wolf can land the killing blow during the hunt, but hamstringing an enemy is no small thing. All actions are cumulative, and all actions contribute to the kill, regardless of who lands the final blow. Perhaps removing Octavius created an opportunity for their downfall. Perhaps killing the Trustees weakened the Archmage in ways we cannot foresee. In our eyes, it matters *not*. We honor the kill, and we honor your integrity."

Nearby, Kosoruk pulled back his lips, revealing yellowed fangs, then dipped his head and laid his ears back flat against his skull, an acknowledgement of the truth in The O'Baba's words. The assembled Wolfmen erupted in cheers. More howls echoed throughout New Narvik as torches rippled through the crowd and great bonfires flared to life, followed by the clamor of pipes and the raucous hammering of bass drums. Wolfman mead flowed like water, and battle-scarred warriors engaged in an odd sort of staged combat, equal parts dance and sparring match. Bodies and weapons twirled in time with the music, drawing bright splashes of blood and good-natured chuffs of mirth.

Every time blood was shed, a new dancer rotated in, trying their hand against the reigning champion. The display was beautiful, strange, and a firm reminder that there was still a lot about the Wolfmen that Sam didn't know. Sam paused when he saw Yurij BrightBlood standing apart from the rest of the revelers. Their handler had his arms folded across his chest, ears laid back against his skull, and his eyes narrowed in suspicion. Somehow, they had managed to win over Kosoruk of White Wyther—hater of humankind—but not grumpy ol' Yurij BrightBlood.

Go figure.

The Shaman sniffed dismissively, then turned and disappeared, forgoing the festivities entirely. The O'Baba followed Sam's gaze. "Do not worry about Yurij. He is a grumpy old wolf, even less easily impressed than I. You will win him over in time, I have no doubt. Now go. Enjoy the celebration. It is for you. You will be welcome at any fire, and this night, you will eat and drink your fill."

The others took off, though Velkan lingered behind. Sam went to follow, but The O'Baba snagged his wrist before he could depart. "Not you, Blood Baron. You have fulfilled your end of the pact; now I shall fulfill mine."

Quest complete! Exalted of the Pack: Hey, hey, hey. How about that! You pulled off the seemingly impossible. Not only did you help to contribute to the downfall—sort of—of the Mage's College, but you've also managed to prove your loyalty and devotion to the Wolfmen beyond a shadow of a doubt, even to the most ardent haters of humanity. Color me impressed. You have earned 12,500 Experience points for completing this quest, and have been personally elevated to the Rank of 'Blood Baron', which is one step lower than a Tribe head. Additionally, reputation with The People has increased by 2,000 points, from 'Friendly' directly to 'Extended Family.' Among the Wolfmen, there is nowhere you aren't welcome.

The O'Baba has also agreed to grant you a special reward for your daring: a meeting with the elusive Totem Shaman. What you gain there cannot be given, only understood.

Golden light engulfed Sam, lifting him into the air as euphoria swept through his body. With the added experience points from completing the quest, he'd just leveled up for the third time that day, hitting level thirteen.

Name: Sam_K 'Merchant Ambassador'
Class: Bibliomancer
Profession 1: Bookbinder
Profession 2: Chicken Keeper
Level: 13 Exp: 98,112 Exp to next level: 6,888
Hit Points: 150/150
Mana: 667/667
Mana regen: 19.07/sec
Stamina: 165.5/165.5

Characteristic: Raw score
Strength: 20

Dexterity: 34
Constitution: 19
Intelligence: 60
Wisdom: 58
Charisma: 23
Perception: 24
Luck: 14
Karmic Luck: +1

Sam had four Characteristic points to distribute from hitting level twelve, but once again, he knew that now wasn't the time or the place to take care of that. The O'Baba was waiting for him, and he was finally about to get some long overdue answers about how to unlock his next specialization. Having a few extra points might even come in handy, depending on what he learned.

"It is time for you to meet the Totem Shaman," she solemnly informed him as he closed out of his menu. "Velkan, take our newly minted Baron to the Bakkuo. You are expected."

CHAPTER TWENTY-EIGHT

Velkan guided Sam and Bill away from the warmth of the firelight and the festivities of the night. Sam wasn't at all surprised when the taciturn Wolfman brought them past The O'Baba's longhouse and to the carved fox totems that connected to the Wolfman Marketplace.

"Ha! I knew it," Bill crowed smugly. "*Told* you this place was some kind of Interspatial Library. I mean, I couldn't put my finger on it exactly—mostly because I don't have fingers—but how could it not be? Amiright or what? I continue to impress myself."

"Both of you should feel *greatly honored*." Velkan's tone was more a warning than anything else, as he glanced over one shoulder. "To be entrusted with a secret such as this is no small thing. Shamans are revered among The People, and only the greatest among the Shamans are entrusted with the secret workings of the Totems."

"But why *this T*otem?" Sam quizzed as they stepped through the arched poles and were instantly whisked away to the Wolfman Marketplace. "I mean... why not take us to see Auntie Owl, Father Bison, or Cousin Crow? Is there something special about this one?"

Velkan hesitated before reluctantly answering. "I am not a Shaman, so many of these things are above me, but I will answer as best as I am able. Let us walk while we talk—it is quite a distance to the Bakkuo's yurt."

Velkan moved at a quick pace into a warren of tents and stalls, all of which were dark and closed for the night. The Marketplace was eerie without the cry of hawkers or the hustle and bustle of bodies moving and shopping and selling. Sam had been stuck at a mall after hours once, and it had felt the same: a place that was meant for life, but was dead and vacant.

Their guide led them on a merry adventure through the bizarre, ushering them past stands with weapons and armor, beyond empty blacksmiths and banked bakeries, the massive brick ovens cold for the night. There were a few stalls displaying books of Shamanic power—Sam was tempted to stop and examine those—but Velkan didn't even offer them a second look. He was single-minded in his focus.

"The training totem grounds are old, old magic," Velkan suddenly started explaining as they walked. "They have been a part of our history for hundreds of years. Perhaps even *thousands* of years. Whatever the case, they are older than our eldest elder. Father Bison. Brother Peacock. Sister Rat. Cousin Crow. Great Auntie Owl. Uncle Monkey. They are divine beasts of legend and myth, as old and mysterious as the magic of their totems. They are bound and loyal to The People by an ancient compact, but they cannot be reasoned with. Cannot be bartered with. The fact that you met Auntie Owl face-to-face is truly astounding, but doing so again would be next to impossible."

They headed down the meatpacking district, past stalls lined with hanging slabs of beef and cured meats arrayed on display tables. "Among the Shaman, there are whispers that the Totem beasts used to be… both more and less than they are now. Wolf-men, as I am."

"What?" Bill sounded confused to the point of hostility.

"You're telling me that ol' owl face from the cave was a *Wolfman* once?"

Velkan shrugged and did a poor job disguising his irritation at hearing Auntie Owl spoken of in such a way. "It seems as unlikely to me as it is to you, but that is what the elder Shamans say behind closed doors."

"But the Marketplace is different," Sam offered an educated guess.

"Indeed," Velkan huffed, ears twitching. "Still old, understand, but much younger than the Totems found in the Training Grounds. There was a Shaman of great renown called simply 'The Bakkuo' by those who knew him. About three hundred years ago, this was."

"Wait, three hundred years ago?" Bill suddenly sounded uncertain.

"Indeed. Very odd by our standards. The Bakkuo dedicated his life to understanding the magic of the Totems—even going so far as to journey to the human capital to search the great stacks of the Mage's College. This was before the Archmage rose to prominence. He was determined to figure out how to reproduce the Totems, and apparently he succeeded." Velkan waved around at the Marketplace. "It is said that the Bakkuo stumbled upon the secret of the Ancient Ones, but he has never shared the knowledge with another. Perhaps you will be the first."

He snuffed and dipped his head toward a dimly lit tent nestled all the way in the back-most corner of the Marketplace. The Wolfman sniffed at the air before finally nodding for them to proceed inside. His posture spoke of… not quite fear, but wariness. The tent ceiling was claustrophobically low, and the whole place smelled vaguely of wet dog mixed with a fragrant scent Sam couldn't quite place. Sandalwood maybe? Cedar?

A colorful rug was spread out across the ground, and arrayed around the floor lay a variety of pillows. That was a red flag in Sam's mind. The Wolfmen abhorred creature comforts, even small ones such as pillows—they made the body and mind soft—yet the owner of this tent didn't seem to care about conformity. The tent was gloomy, lit only by a single candle carefully positioned on a low wooden table in the center of the tent. Sam blinked a few times, waiting for his eyes to adjust. While he stood there, temporarily blinded, the skin prickled along the back of his arms.

Something was watching him from the shadows.

<This place has the creepiest vibes,> Bill whispered inside Sam's head, even though he didn't need to. <Not necessarily bad mojo, but powerful. Wild. I don't think I've ever felt anything quite like it before.>

"Welcome," creaked a weathered voice, emanating from a pile of blankets in the corner. As Sam blinked to adjust his eyes, he realized there was a Wolfman buried in that heap of fabric. He was a wizened creature with rheumy eyes, his coppery-red fur mangy and interrupted by leathery bald patches sprinkled across his muzzle, head, and neck.

"Well, don't be strangers," the voice creaked at them. "It has been an age, and an age again, since I've had a proper visitor. So few come to me these days. Sit. Let us talk."

Velkan moved first. He dropped down onto a cushion across from the old creature, shifting uncomfortably. Likely not because the pillow was uncomfortable, but because he was uncomfortable using such luxury. Sam didn't have any such reservations, but he also wasn't sure what the right thing to do here was. Were the pillows a test? A way to see if he was worthy or up to the unspoken Wolfman code? That was more in line with what he knew about the Wolfman, yet his gut was telling him no. Everything about this situation was unconventional, and the old wolf on the other side of the flickering candle was nearly teetering on the overflowing mound of pillows.

Sam decided to listen to his gut. He dropped onto a pillow near Velkan and leaned back on his hands.

"Good, good." The old Wolfman smiled, baring his teeth, though there didn't seem to be any malice in the act. "It is so nice to see a young man not entirely beholden to the ways of

The People. The fact that you are a human is a bit surprising, true, but perhaps that is a good thing."

"Why is that a good thing?" Sam felt oddly free to speak, and wondered if this Wolfman had an incredibly high charisma.

"Humans, they are agents of change. Of all the races, they are the least set in their ways. Some of the other races tend to have fairly monolithic cultures. Not so humans. They are chaos and order, precariously balanced on the edge of a knife. It is both their strength and weakness. There is danger in that, but also glorious freedom. My People, not so. But I am older than any other living Wolfman, and I remember a time before we were this way. So austere. Rigid. Some of my best friends in a far bygone age were human, you know." He frowned, creases running across his forehead.

"This is what two hundred years of war has done to us." He shrugged narrow shoulders. "This utter denial of self and comfort was a philosophy started by a long-dead contemporary of mine. Zhidkov Lukyan, he was called. He was an ascetic who formed the Order of Abstemious. Zhidkov eventually ascended to the role of O'Baba, and it was under his leadership that we became what we are today. But listen to me ramble."

He waved a hand through the air. "You young pups don't care about such ancient history. What has brought you to my tent, hmm?"

"Forgiveness, Grand Bakkuo," Velkan hunched forward until his muzzle was nearly pressed against the floor, "but The O'Baba sent us here."

"Don't beat around the bush," Bill interjected cheerily. "We want to know about the Totem Training Grounds. Before you get any ideas, you should know that I've been around even longer than you, so all the smoke and mirror ain't going to impress me."

The old wolfman's face lit up with something that might be mirth. "It has been *far* too long, Sir William the Bravi. Not in all my years did I ever suspect I would see the likes of you again."

That stopped the book cold. Only a handful of people knew

his true name, and this old, blind Wolfman wasn't one of them. "How do you know that name? You better start talking, because me and the kid can sling some serious spells if we don't like your answers."

The old wolf cackled madly, rocking back and forth. "I am not surprised you don't recognize me. Time has not been kind to these old bones, though you have changed quite a lot yourself. The last time I saw you, you were certainly taller. If memory holds true, you had a few more limbs and a few less pages."

"*Gengi*?" Bill was incredulous. "No. Can't be. Wolfmen live a long time, but not *that* long."

The old wolf guffawed even more loudly. "I've unlocked a few secrets since the last time we spoke. But even with my magics, I have become rather long in the tooth, as they say."

"You two know each other?" Sam remembered Bill reminiscing about Wolfmen he had met long ago, but it was still surprising to think they'd be around. Velkan looked equally thunderstruck at the revelation. The Wolfman glanced between the elder Shaman and Bill as though seeing the floating book for the first time. Velkan had always had a healthy respect for Bill and his abilities—all of the Wolfmen did—but now Velkan looked at the book as though he might be partly divine. Easy to understand, considering that this Bakkuo guy seemed to be the Shaman equivalent of the Pope.

"Eh, it's a long story," Bill grumbled an answer, clearly confused himself, "but the short side of it is that ol' Gengi here was a Shamanic Scholar back when I was still kicking around on a pair of functional legs. Those were the golden days, before the Archmage rose to power and instituted the Accords. Of course, Mage folk and Wolf folk have never been on the greatest of terms, not even then-"

"But we weren't at *war*," the old wolf finished. "There were a handful of us that worked together on a few odd projects. Sort of a student exchange program."

"Yep, the interspatial libraries was one of those projects.

Gengi was trying to figure out how to make one, and so was I. He never told me about the Totems, but we spent more than a few nights together flipping through old tomes looking for an answer."

"I was the one who helped him forge his Soul Space, you know," the wolf bragged with a wink. "A poor excuse for the proper Interspatial Library. We were wrong about so many things... but such is the way of youth. It was at least a small step in the right direction."

"Yeah, but then everything changed," Bill released a sigh. "King Henry won the war, and the Archmage rode his coat tails right into power."

"With the Civil War officially settled," the Wolfman continued, "your human Nobles decided they needed a new enemy to unite the common folk again—certainly couldn't have them turning their eyes on the nobility. My people were easy candidates."

"Eh, you guys always were fairly standoffish," Bill agreed easily. "Look pretty scary as well."

"Yes, but less so than we are now," Gengi offered with a snort. "But listen to us, babbling on while the world teeters on the edge of oblivion. You have not come to chit chat about the old days. You are here to finally learn the secrets that have so long evaded you. Though to be honest, I am a bit shocked. I'd always assumed you'd given up the pursuit of carving a Library."

"Not my choice," Bill flapped his pages in explanation. "Honestly, I was hoping my new partner here would choose the path of the Biblioblade, but *no~o~o~o*. Not this kid. Always has to do things the hard way. Decided he wants to be an Archivist Summoner. I tried to talk him out of it, but when he gets an idea stuck in his head, you just can't shake it. He's like a dog chewing on a bone."

"There is wisdom in this," the wolf chuckled, fixing his rheumy eyes on Sam. "I have heard about you, young pup. Many a tongue waggles about the wolf-hearted human who is raising so many hackles. But I never thought to meet you for myself. Few of my own people ever earn the right to visit my tent. To do so as an outsider? There must be something special in you."

"Hey, hey, hey," Bill interjected. "Credit where credit's due. He's okay, but if we're being honest, I'm the real brains behind the operation."

The wolf wheezed a dry laugh. "You may have changed in appearance, but you are still the Bill I always remembered."

"So, level with me," Bill bulled onward. "Are you going to tell us the secret or what?"

The wolf seesawed his head from side to side for a moment. "Many Shamans have come through those flaps looking to learn the secret, yet I have never let it leave my lips. Not once in two hundred and six years."

"Were they unworthy?" Velkan nodded his understanding. "Was it a weakness of the mind, or one of the flesh?"

The aged Wolfman chuffed. "Not weakness, but strength. I told you, our people are so very *rigid.* So unbending and unyielding. There is a certain strength in that, but also a fatal weakness. Like the oak, they stand strong against the blowing wind… until they don't. They snap under enough pressure because they are unable to bend and change. To learn the secret of the Totems requires suppleness. Flexibility. To learn this skill requires that you give up some of what you are. No Wolfman alive can give up being a Wolfman, but you, Sam… you have already given up a portion of your humanity.

"You have become a creature of two natures. Man and wolf. Three, really, since you have created a Soul Bond with Sir William. In that lies the secret." He reached up and tapped conspiratorially on his nose with one long finger. "Beast Core Cultivation. Becoming something both more and less than you are—that is the first step. I started my journey as a Shamanic Druid, and my base specialization was as a Soul Familiar, a relatively common affinity among Shamans. Those with a Soul Familiar share a strong bond with an animal companion. They can call on them for aid, and even communicate telepathically."

"So, you basically become besties with a pet bear or something?" Bill dryly grumped. "Got it."

The wolf elder chuckled. "Something like that. After studying through reams of ancient Shamanic texts, I knew the secret to creating an Interspatial Nexus was such a bond. More than one text alluded to it, but none detailed the specifics. The *how*. I reached out to the College, hoping the secret might be found there. I didn't uncover the whole answer, but our time together led me to another clue: a technique unknown to my people, called the Path of the Tattered Soul. Most Shamans specialized as Soul Familiars make it a point to find the biggest, most powerful creatures. Binding with large, sentient creatures is difficult, and trying to manage a dragon or a phoenix is a full-time job. Not so… a rat."

The Druid snapped his fingers, and a rat scampered out from the blankets and perched on his gnarled finger. His blankets shifted and moved. There was something roiling beneath those covers. A moment later, he pulled them back to reveal hundreds of rats, all surrounding him like body armor.

"Oftentimes, small, innocuous things are often far more powerful in their way—assuming there are enough of them. Using the Path of the Tattered Soul, I learned to fracture my core into ten thousand pieces. Through time and great patience, I have bonded each sliver of my core with a rat or a crow or a spider. Small, weak things that go without notice. Their power lies not in the damage they can deal, but in the secrets they can steal. After things devolved with the College, I could no longer pursue the College's Library. So I used my spies to infiltrate the highest level of the Library, the Vaunted Sage's Level, where the most powerful secrets are kept." The wolf elder seemed exceedingly pleased with himself, and something he said sparked Sam's memory. He knew that area well—it was where Bill had been locked away. Before he could comment, the Druid continued.

"I found a tome on Spatial Architecture, penned by none

other than the Rituarchitect, Sage Cognitionis, the brilliant mind behind the folding College. I learned that the Spatial Corridors are powered by artifact generators, which fold space. Those generators are created using powerful Beast Cores, attached to fixed spatial anchors. That was when everything clicked. The answer was under my snout the whole while. The Totem Poles weren't the fixed spatial anchors, the Totem *Guardians* were."

"Slow down. You're hurting my brain," Bill demanded with a slight whine to his voice. "How can a *person* become a fixed spatial anchor?"

"Why, by transforming their own core into an artifact generator, of course. They were once Soul Familiars like me, but instead of merely forming a bond with a monstrous companion, they merged their core with their companions. The Totem Guardian became both more, and less, than they were. Part Wolfman, part monster. A living artifact. With such a generator, they could create a spatial pocket capable of holding a building, or a library, or even this." He waved his hand around to indicate more than the tent they were in. "A marketplace. All fixed to themselves as the temporal anchor."

"So, what you're saying is that I need to be a Soul Familiar to be able to do this?" Sam suddenly felt crestfallen. Was it possible that he'd come so far, only to learn that what he wanted wasn't even possible?

"Yes," the Wolfman stated gravely… but then he cracked a thin, wolfy smile. "Good thing you already are one. You have forged a Soul Bond with Sir William. He is an artifact—the College saw to that when they transformed him into a book. When you picture your core, do you not see two cores spinning within you? A larger and a smaller?"

Sam nodded.

"That is what a Soul Familiar looks like; two cores, separate, yet connected. In order to become a Beast Core cultivator, you must merge the two." He raised two fingers then intertwined them as one. "This will give you the power to create a spatial pocket large enough to accommodate your library. It will grow as your common core grows."

"Well, this sounds like all upside." Bill perked up at once. "Sign us up."

"There is a *complication.*" The wolf held up a hand, as though to physically stop them. "You have a Soul Bond, but unfortunately, Bill's core is too weak to accomplish the task before you." He narrowed his eyes, and Sam felt a shiver dance along his spine. "As I thought. When they transformed your corporeal form, they also stripped your core down to its foundation. Although you are a powerful artifact, your core is only rated at 'Rare'."

"Well that is *insultingly* low," Bill huffed his displeasure. "Just one more kick in the shins from the College, I guess."

The Wolfman shrugged narrow shoulders. "It is about raw power. You are still getting yours back. To merge and become a proper Beast Core Cultivator, your core must be rated at Artifact or above. You will get there in time, as you increase in level."

"How high do we need to be in order for this to work?" Sam let out the question to stop Bill from throwing a fit.

"Level twenty-five. Perhaps even as high as thirty?" The Wolfman wiggled his nose in thought. Once again, it felt like the air had just been knocked from Sam's lungs. Level *thirty*? He'd never manage to make it that high before his summer was done —especially not without specializing. "But there is another way."

"I too had the same trouble. Finding an individual rat with an Artifact-level core was no easy thing—by which I mean it was an impossible thing. Instead, I had to bond with ten thousand souls, each one a tiny core, constantly cultivating and feeding me energy. There is no master greater in the Path of the Tattered Soul. With enough core nodes to draw on, you can jump-start the Beast Core Cultivation process and merge your cores. For an old friend, I am willing to share the secret—

though you will have to find a sufficient number of suitable creatures to bond with."

A lightbulb clicked on inside Sam's head. "I'm not too concerned about that. If you're willing to teach us, then I am ready to learn."

"Very well." The ancient Wolfman lifted a hand. "It all starts with the breath. Do as I do."

CHAPTER TWENTY-NINE

Fingers of purple and gold were peeking over the horizon by the time Sam and Bill returned to the Irondown burrows. They swung by the barracks and found the beds full with snoozing bodies, all except for Kai. That guy was a rockstar of self-discipline. Not even a long night of hard partying would keep him from his morning yoga routine.

Sam hadn't slept a wink, and though his body insisted he pass out face-down on his bunk without so much as taking off his boots, his brain was too excited for sleep. He knew that if he tried to take so much as a power nap, his internal monologue would be nattering at him incessantly. And if his *internal* monologue wasn't up to the task, Bill certainly would be.

So, instead of hitting the hay like any sane person, Sam splashed a little water onto his face in the bathing hall, then headed for the kitchen for a bite to eat and a small pot of highly caffeinated tea. Octo-Chef whirled to life the moment he entered, breaking into impressively efficient motion as soon as Sam placed his order. Mechanical arms cracked oversized eggs into a sizzling hot frying pan, others diced precooked chicken into small cubes, and a third whipped up a creamy hollandaise sauce, all while the chef brewed a strong pot of burbling black tea.

Watching the android work never failed to impress. With a breakfast sandwich in one hand and a steaming cup in the other, Sam made his way to the Husbandry-Pen-turned-chicken-coop. He let himself in through the iron gates, only to be hailed by a flurry of happy clucks and flapping chicken wings. Even though most everyone else was asleep, his formidable chicken army was already up and busy.

The mechanical chicken keeper was zipping through the pen, sprinkling fresh hay along the floor and harvesting large brown eggs, which it stored in its belly—ready for eating or selling. Many of the hens loitered in their hatcheries, but a legion of fluffball chicks scampered around the pen, chirping happily under the watchful gaze of the Brood Matriarchs.

Floof had grown significantly even in the span of a few days' time. She now stood as tall as Sam, with wings that looked like they belonged to a California condor and legs as thick as a horse's. Her fiery gaze softened the second Sam and Bill appeared. She dropped whatever she'd been doing and rushed them like a velociraptor ready to eviscerate him with her formidable talons. But at the last minute, she slammed into Sam like an overgrown puppy, nuzzling his chest fiercely and chirping love songs at Bill.

"Yeah, yeah," the book groaned in faux-grumpiness. "It's good to see you too, Floof. Looking better than ever."

She clucked at him and dropped her head. Blaze was slower to approach, naturally deferring to the Prime Matriarch, but still interested in getting a few head pats, although Sam would have to be a little more cautious about patting her in the future. She hadn't gotten any bigger since the last time he'd seen her, but her plumage had changed. Her rear tail feathers were no longer just reddish in color; they tapered at the end, transforming from plumage to actual golden flame. Thin plumes of smoke drifted up, and glittering embers rained down when she moved. Those embers didn't set anything on fire, but they certainly gave Sam pause.

"Celestial Feces," Bill snorted when he saw her, "I think our chicken has a smoking problem. Should we get her into counseling?"

Sam facepalmed, even though he knew it only encouraged Bill. "Not sure counseling's going to help with that."

The bird came up on Sam's right, dipping her head low, then scooping his hand onto her beak. She cooed happily. Tentatively, Sam ran his palm along her silky plumage, pausing only a moment before brushing his fingers through the tongues of flame. They felt warm to the touch, but didn't so much as singe his skin. If anything, they were soothing.

"On a serious note," Bill flew a little closer, but still well away from the flames, "what's happening to her? I'm not really an expert on chickens, but I'm ninety percent certain they aren't normally on fire, unless they're roasting over an open flame."

Sam pursued his lips as he stroked Blaze with one hand and Floof with the other. "Well, they're monsters, right? I mean think about the bunnies out in the wild areas. The longer they survive, the stronger they get. The bigger they get, the more they change. These things aren't any different, and I'm pretty sure they level up passively through eating and egg laying. They've been doing a lot of that. I think they're evolving. It's the only explanation."

"Evolving into *what*? They're *chickens*."

"I guess only time will tell," Sam murmured as he stroked the flame feathers. "Though I'm guessing they're going to evolve a lot faster once we're done with the binding."

"Eh, about that. I'm still not so sure this is what anyone would call a good idea. I mean, the idea of creating an Inter-spatial Library is awesome, but the idea of tying our collective soul to a bunch of chickens—even magical ones—seems, I dunno… demeaning, I guess? I'm a simple book, really; all I want is fame, power, knowledge, money, and the adoration of the masses. Seems like this will make people look down on us."

"They won't be looking down on us for long when Floof gouges their eyes out." Sam offered with a shrug. "Besides, all of the pieces are adding up. Our conversation with Auntie Owl brought us here, and what are the chances that we'd meet with an old friend of yours who knows how to split our core in order to bond with a bunch of lesser monster cores? This is a jigsaw puzzle, and we finally have all the pieces."

"Yeah, but there's no going back from this; you know that, right?" Bill's words were more statement than question. "Are you *sure* I can't persuade you to walk this back a few steps and maybe try for Biblio Blade instead? We'd make a great Paper Samurai. Eventually. Assuming you could master the foot work."

"Sorry, Bill. This is what I want, but..." Sam faltered and glanced at the floating book. "But it's not just about me. This is your core, too. You heard the Bakkuo; we both need to be of one mind to accomplish this. If you *really* hate this idea, I'll reconsider. We're partners. Either we're going to forge this new path together, or we won't do it at all."

Bill was silent before begrudgingly agreeing. "Fine... let's become Soul BFFs with a bunch of cluck heads. This is *probably* a terrible choice, but who knows. Maybe not. Like I always say, there's a fine line between crazy and genius. I'm too egotistical to think anything I do is crazy, which only leaves genius on the table."

Sam nodded and sat cross-legged on the floor. He smiled and patted at his knee, calling the two massive chickens over to his side. With confused clucks, they plopped down beside him, Floof on his left, Blaze on his right. Sam wrapped an arm around each of them and felt their feathers envelope him like a goose-down blanket. Their warmth was a comfort, and he felt oddly at peace about the decision, even knowing what they were about to attempt was insane—and those were the Bakkuo's words. So many things could go wrong, and if even one of them did, it would be the end of his path as a Mage.

"Let's take it nice and easy," Bill muttered as Sam closed his eyes and cycled mana through his core in a rhythmic hum.

Sam breathed deeply—in through the nose and out through the mouth, just the way Kai taught him—and focused on the thump of his heart and the air rushing through his lungs. Fear and doubt warred with each other in the back of his mind, but he knew those emotions were anathema to his purpose. If he doubted or faltered, it could undo everything. According to Bakkuo, the key to success was utter confidence and complete mastery of self. Sam banished his nagging fears.

Everything had guided him here, to this time and place and circumstance. This was meant to be. The dominions had all been carefully arranged, and now, all he needed to do was push over the first one and start the cascade.

Finally centered, Sam envisioned his core.

In an instant, he stepped into the Soul Chamber that contained his power. His core was far smaller than it had been before, refined by the process of advancement. Floating in the air was a dollop of shimmering mercury, no larger than a penny, and swirling around it like a beautiful halo was a gaseous cloud of white, gold, and opal. Tendrils of gas snaked away from his core, disappearing into the yawning tunnels that connected to this central chamber. Those were visible representations of his mana channels. One thin tether also zigzagged away from the circle of quicksilver, connecting to a secondary ball of swirling golden energy.

That was Bill's core, connected to his own by an immutable mana bond.

Stepping out from behind the secondary core was Bill, decked out in his ridiculous frilly outfit—foppish hat perched on his head at a rakish angle, his sword quill at his side.

"If we're going to do this thing, we'd better get busy. Assuming my buddy is right, this could take a while." Bill extended his hand and conjured a three-legged stool and a mahogany desk, heavily laden with ink wells, parchment, and quills. He took a seat with a groan and began working his way through the binding spell the Bakkuo had taught them. Sam conjured a seat and desk of his own and did the same, carefully working through the spell script, which was ridiculously complicated. In theory, Sam could've used Auto-Writing and Transcription Twinning to move the process along more quickly, but he didn't dare.

This was a new spell form, and one that he was unfamiliar with. Making a single mistake inside his Soul Chamber could have devastating consequences, and compounding that mistake ten-fold could break his core irrevocably. Still, it went faster than normal, since they never had to worry about running out of ink or parchment, mostly because none of it was real. This was a place of imagination.

The spell forms they were making didn't actually exist. The scrolls were simply a mental manifestation of his intention; a crutch designed to help Sam channel and manipulate the vast flows of mana that would be required to first shatter his core and then reassemble those shards into something new and whole.

He and Bill worked in silence for the next hour, and then came the utterly tedious work of covering the walls of the cavern with the spell scrolls. He and Bill hung each sheet like wallpaper, canvassing every square inch with carefully overlapping pages until they had a mosaic of parchment. It was a time-consuming endeavor, true, but this was actually the easy part. Once they were finally finished with the task, it was time for phase two: tethering the other two monster Cores to his own, just as he'd done when he'd first bonded with Bill. Thankfully, he wouldn't be doing that part alone.

Bill would forge the bond with Blaze, while Sam would confront Floof.

Sam focused on his left hand, sensing Floof's warmth and the silky texture of her feathers. He tapped into his Core, sending a thread of mana coursing through his channels and down his arm. As he pressed his palm flat against Floof's chest, he felt the thump of her heart and the gentle throb of her beast

Core. He homed in on that and forced the mana flowing along his arm into the creature. The enormous chicken stirred uncertainly—trying to connect with her Core was like trying to walk through a bog filled with knee-high quicksand. Every inch was a battle that sapped his strength, and the only thing that kept him moving forward was sheer force of will.

After a time, the resistance lessened, then dissipated entirely, like a thick fog being burned away under the light of a new day. He blinked his eyes as he found himself in a Soul Chamber very different from his own. He wasn't in a cavern, but a giant nest—the walls built from woven hay, tall grass, and tree limbs. The floor was also made with twigs and debris but was liberally coated with metallic feathers in all hues. Sitting in the center of the nest was Floof's Core. Naturally, it looked like an enormous chicken egg. The egg had a translucent shell, and inside was a swirling universe of blues and blacks, littered with sparkling motes of light.

It was one of the most beautiful things Sam had ever seen. Like peering at the spiral arm of a far-off galaxy. Surprisingly, the egg-core wasn't the only thing in the room.

The floor rattled and rumbled as a creature emerged from one of the many mana channels that connected to the central nest. It was Floof—or, at least, a version of Floof. Perhaps this was how Floof saw herself. She dwarfed Sam, her body long, serpentine, and graceful. Not a chicken so much as a dragon covered in metallic plumage. She stalked forward on powerful hind legs, while her enormous wings were tucked up against her sides. Instead of tail feathers, she had a lashing tail covered in spikes. She canted her oversized head and stared at Sam with the golden eyes of a predator, nestled back in a reptilian face.

In biology, Sam had learned that there was one theory that suggested that dinosaurs hadn't entirely disappeared, but rather had evolved into modern birds. Floof was like that, but in reverse.

In her soul, she was a Dino-Chicken... and she was terrifying.

CHAPTER THIRTY

"Hey girl, it's just me: Sam. We know each other. We're buddies. Feel that?" Sam tried to sound soothing as he crept toward the egg at the center of the nest. He stroked her feathers with his hand back in the real world. "That's just me."

The reptilian mega-chicken clucked suspiciously but made no move to stop him. He stole another few inches closer, extending a hand toward the egg. Now that… *that* she didn't care for. Not one bit. She hunched forward, scaly lips pulling back from wicked fangs. The feathers running along her nape and back stood up on end, and she let out an alarming hiss. 'I don't know what you think you're doing, but touch my Core and you're mincemeat,' that sound said. But Sam couldn't stop. In order for this to work, he had to connect a thread of his mana to the Core, then take a thread of her mana and run it back to his own core.

He licked his lips and took another tentative step. The hiss increased to a guttural **click-click-click*.

In the real world, Floof adored Sam and Bill, but Sam was attempting to mess with her Core. A creature like Floof could die and would respawn in time, but not if her Core was destroyed or absorbed. To let Sam get even *this* close without mauling him was a display of absolute trust. Letting him actually tinker around with the center of her being? That was a huge ask. But that was exactly what Sam needed to do. The Bakkuo had warned that this would be the second most dangerous part of this whole process.

"I'm sorry about this," he murmured soothingly, "but it's really for the best. I know you can't understand that, but trust me. I have no intention of hurting you."

He took another step.

One step too far, apparently.

The massive chicken-turned-dinosaur let out an ear-shattering roar and charged, clawed feet pounding against the nest floor. A scaled leg, capped by talons the size of short daggers, sliced through the air, the blow aimed at Sam's throat. He threw himself to the side, falling back on his Judo skills as he tucked into a tight roll that quickly brought him to his feet. To his dismay, a mouth full of razor-sharp fangs was waiting for him. He danced back and tried to summon his Orbital Tomes; he needed to defend himself, but he didn't want to hurt Floof too badly in the process.

Unfortunately, no books appeared.

Bill wasn't there, as he was likely facing off against Blaze's Soul Chamber Guardian at that very moment. Without Bill, there were no Orbital Tomes of casting. No paper shuriken. No magic at all.

An angry cluck reverberated in the air as Floof's mouth shot forward again, attempting to take Sam's leg off below the kneecap. He backpedaled again, opening up a little distance, but this was a game he couldn't play indefinitely. Dino Floof sidestepped the egg, obviously trying to back him into a corner where he would no longer be able to retreat.

It was working.

She fanned her wings out, the span easily thirty feet from wingtip to wingtip. With another angry hiss, she flapped, conjuring an enormous gust of wind that swept Sam from his feet and slammed him into the far wall of the nest. Before he could even get his bearings, the reptilian avian whipped one wing forward and unleashed a flurry of foot-long metallic feathers. They streaked toward him like arrows, and Sam had a sneaking suspicion they would impale him just like any other projectile. Panicked, he thrust his hand forward and called forth the first thing that came to mind: the writing desk he'd created back in his own Soul Scape.

It appeared with a glimmer directly in front of him. The razor-sharp feathers slammed into the wood, bits of debris flying off in every direction.

Sam laughed. "That's right, this place isn't real."

The damage he suffered here would hurt—could possibly even kill him—but this place existed in the mind more than anywhere else. Maybe he couldn't summon his magic tomes, but the only real boundaries were the limits of his imagination. With a thought, a metal kite shield appeared on his left arm. He never would have been able to wield something like that in the game—he didn't have the strength or stamina for it—but here, it was light as air and stronger than the strongest metal.

He leapt out from behind the feather-riddled desk and advanced on the oversized chicken.

"I'm not here to hurt you, Floof!" he called over the lip of the shield. "This is all for the best; trust me on that."

She responded by sending another wave of feathers flying toward him. He ducked down and braced his shoulder against the shield, hoping it would hold under the onslaught. Metal clanged against metal, and the feathers fell away without so much as denting his shield. Sam loved the class he had, but he had to admit there was a certain appeal in playing a character that wasn't quite so squishy. He lifted the shield and broke right, trying to circle around the gargantuan chicken, but she was a lot quicker and more agile than she appeared at first glance.

She spun, her tail flying toward Sam like a baseball bat. No way would he be absorbing that with the shield. He dismissed the shield, dropped onto his belly, and barrel rolled, letting the appendage **whoosh** over him. A descending foot almost crushed him, but another roll to the right allowed him to narrowly avoid the attack. Sam scrambled to his feet and bolted forward, slapping a hand against the side of the translucent egg. He could feel the steady thrum of potent power buzzing just beneath his fingertips. Working fast, he channeled mana into a needle-fine point, then drove it down into the shell. It felt like trying to drill a screw into a two-by-four using nothing but his fingertips.

Sweat broke out across his brow, but he kept the pressure on, pushing the mana deeper and deeper into the egg. Finally, a tiny hole appeared, and a hair-fine wisp of mana floated out like steam rising from a coffee cup. Bingo. Sam fed more and more of his own mana into the hole, creating the first stage of a soul tether.

Just in time.

He sensed more than saw a fresh round of feathers screaming toward him. Instead of conjuring his shield, he blinked and found himself clad in a suit of heavy plate mail. The feathers slammed against his back, knocking the wind out of him even through the armor, but the metal itself held firm and rebuffed the feathery barrage.

More importantly, the armor bought him the handful of seconds he'd needed to complete the first part of his task. A shiver raced down his spine as his mana took hold, slowly intermingling with the latent energy inside the egg. He cut off his own flow of energy and hunched forward, pressing his lips against the tiny hole, then deeply exhaling. The Bakkuo had walked them through this part several times. To Sam, the process sounded a bit like siphoning gas from a full tank. His mana tether acted as the siphon itself, and blowing into the core puncture primed the pump, allowing mana to flow out.

After a second, he pulled his mouth away and watched as a thin stream of brilliant silver liquid poured from the hole, pooling in front of him. Ever so gently, Sam wrapped the mana thread leaking from the egg around his left hand. Prize literally in hand, he spun and darted back the way he'd entered—but Floof was blocking the ethereal passageway that connected to his own Soul Chamber.

She was hunched low, golden eyes narrowed in anger as she looked at the wispy thread of energy twined around Sam's fist, her visage practically shouting 'That belongs to *me*, human.'

There was only one way out, and Floof was guarding it. Sam dismissed the clunky metal armor, knowing he wouldn't be able to move fast enough to do what needed doing. He hunched forward and charged her, keeping his head low. She let out a confused **cluck**. Clearly, she wasn't expecting him to just bum rush her. He was small and squishy, while she was huge and powerful, but by the time she reacted, it was already too late. Sam dove straight toward her, tucking into a ball and rolling right between her oversized legs. She wheeled about in a flurry, flapping her wings and opening her jaws wide.

Opalescent light built in the back of her throat, and Sam knew in that second that if he didn't do something, he was as good as dead.

"Sorry about this, Floof," he yelled, summoning a replica of his Quill Blade to his right hand. With a roar, he leapt straight up, jamming the blade into the underside of her scaly jaw. The tip of the blade sliced through skin, feather, and muscle, and continued right through her top jaw—effectively pinning her mouth shut. Silver blood gushed out, and she reared back, lashing out with a kick that caught Sam in the chest, one sharp talon slicing through his armor and leaving a deep furrow across his skin. The pain was intense, but the adrenaline pumping through his veins dulled the worst of it.

Floof was frantically trying to dislodge the sword lodged in her jaw, which was fine by him. So long as she was busy with that, she wasn't trying to eviscerate him.

"Sorry again, Floof! It'll totally be worth it," he called over one shoulder as he turned on a heel and took off at a sprint, leaving the giant chicken in the rearview mirror. He slid to a stop once he got back to his own Soul Chamber.

Sam was panting, sweating, and bleeding profusely from the slash running across his chest. He doubled over, planting one hand on his knee while he took in great wheezing breaths. The Bakkuo had warned them that convincing a Monster to share their Core was no easy process, but he had conveniently neglected to mention that it would involve fighting Godzilla-Chicken. But then, the Bakkuo had formed his bonds with rats, spiders, foxes, and any number of lesser creatures. It was distinctly possible that he hadn't had to go through the trial Sam had just endured.

"Went that good, huh?" came Bill's voice from across the chamber.

Sam glanced up and straightened his back. The Bibliomancer was leaning against the wall with a molten gold thread of mana wrapped around one fist. He looked terrible, even worse than Sam felt, like someone had run him through an industrial-sized paper shredder. His clothes were in tatters, he was covered in nicks and claw wounds, and his facial hair had been singed off. He had no eyebrows at all, which was a hard look to pull off; to be honest, he *didn't* pull it off, not even a little. Sam lifted a hand to his mouth and tried to stifle the snicker building in his throat. His attempts weren't entirely successful.

"Yeah, har har har," Bill grumbled as blood seeped from the corner of his mouth. "Laugh it up, funny guy—doesn't look like you did so great yourself."

"You're not wrong," Sam admitted with a shrug, "but at least I came back with all my hair."

"It's all laughs, but you didn't see what I was up against in there!" the Bibliomancer protested. "I thought I was going up against a spicy chicken sandwich with legs, not an honest-to-celestial *Phoenix*! That thing was literally made of flames. On an unrelated note, I retract my previous statement about people looking down on us for bonding with chickens. Once Blaze turns into whatever the heck *that* thing is, she'll just immolate anyone who laughs at us."

Bill sighed and glanced down at the fiery mana thread clutched in his fist. "So, we gonna do this thing, or what?"

"I'm certainly not putting my thread back. Not after what I went through to get it." Wearily, Sam pressed the thread against the silver dewdrop that was his Core—so very different than Floof's enormous egg-shaped power source. Because he'd already formed a mana tether, Floof's mana took almost at once. A wispy tendril of opalescent power braided the two strands together until they became one. Sam gasped as new power flooded into him, and an unnatural awareness of the enormous chicken blossomed inside his head.

It wasn't quite the same as the bond he shared with Bill. But it was close.

He couldn't hear her thoughts, but he could sense her feelings about things: a burbling concoction of fear and anxiety mixed with curiosity and even a hint of excitement. Sam stole a sidelong look at Bill as the Bibliomancer did the same thing with Blaze's mana tether. A shiver rippled through Bill as he fed the wispy thread of power into his own Core, effectively binding the spicy chicken as his animal familiar. Step two, done. Only one step left to go and, according to The Bakkuo, that was the most dangerous step of all.

What came next had the potential to destroy Sam's Core entirely… or transform him into something both more and less than human.

CHAPTER THIRTY-ONE

Sam took a position near his Core with straight legs, bringing his hands together. His right hand curled into a fist that rested against his left palm. Bill took a position directly across from him and mirrored the pose. They looked like two martial artists squaring off before a bout. Though Bill was normally flippant and easy-going, he looked serious as a heart attack right now, with worry lines etched into his face.

Bill knew what was at stake here, and he knew what would happen if things went sideways. Sam wouldn't be the only one to suffer the consequences. One misstep, and Bill's Core could shatter beyond repair—and since Bill didn't have a physical body, shattering his Core would mean utter destruction.

The real form of Bill the book breathed in deeply, bowed his head, then began to move. Sam followed suit, dropping into a deep horse stance with his arms waving and his hands dancing through a flurry of complicated motions. Although the gestures looked odd, they felt like second-nature, since he had completed them a thousand times before. These were the same motions he used for Coptic-Binding—his primary technique for binding loose page leaves into a book. This task was bigger, but in many ways, it was the same: he was taking many small things and making them into one unified whole.

Sam let energy build in his core, and the dollop of quicksilver in front of him began to glow. As power built in his chest, Sam uttered the ancient words of the old Wolfman tongue passed down by the Bakkuo.

They meant nothing to Sam.

After all this time, he spoke the modern Wolfman dialect with almost perfect fluency, but their old tongue was still a mystery. But that didn't matter, so long as he recited the words correctly and imbued them with the right intention. Sam overlaid all four Cores in his mind's eye, imagining them swelling and shrinking until they became one. His hands continued to bob and weave as he envisioned using a golden thread of mana to sew the four Cores together.

Sam circled left while Bill circled right, both chanting the odd words in unison. Power continued to build in the air, slowly at first, like a static charge from running feet across a carpeted floor. Soon, the buzz had transformed into a deep and steady thrum; blue-white lightning arced wildly from Sam's core, and his immaculate hair stood on end. Still, Sam didn't stop: he moved faster. Twirling and dipping, jumping and diving, executing sharp pivots and quick kicks, he maneuvered the complicated motions all while maintaining the incessant chant and the familiar hand gestures.

Stitching. Sewing. *Binding.*

Mana swelled with every pass around the Core, and the arcs of lightning increased in both frequency and intensity until Sam's Soul Chamber looked like a fourth of July display in rural America. Starbursts of power exploded overhead, and threads of gold and silver meandered about while the air thickened to the consistency of molasses. Sam took those strands and used them like twine, stitching them back into his Core with a needle of raw will. Every movement became a thousand times more difficult, and before long, Sam's limbs seemed to weigh a thousand pounds apiece.

The Bakkuo had warned them this would happen, but hearing about it and experiencing it in real time were two *very* different things.

Sweat broke out across Sam's chest and shoulders, while more perspiration dotted his brow and dripped down into his eyes. Every breath felt like he was sucking wind through wet cheesecloth, and keeping up the rhythmic chant was the next best thing to impossible. His muscles shook from the strain, but he caught Bill's eye. The Bravi looked to be struggling just as much as Sam, but he wasn't quitting. They had gone way too far to turn back; interrupting a spell this complex would unleash all that pent-up mana without a direction or purpose.

It would explode right in their faces.

Bill couldn't stop chanting any more than Sam could, but he offered Sam a quick nod. "You got this. *We* got this! Almost there; don't give up on me now."

Sam steeled his resolve and pushed through the resistance, fighting to complete another circuit around his Core, which now pulsed frantically in time with his heartbeat. He tried to take another step, and it was like slamming into a brick wall. There wasn't an ounce of give. Still, he pressed against the indomitable wall of energy, throwing not just his physical strength against the barrier but the entirety of his will. After a moment, something shifted. A thin crack of opalescent light snaked along the invisible barrier barring his path. He pushed harder, and the crack spread, growing into a fissure.

Finally, Sam heard an audible **crack**, and then the world exploded in a tsunami of light and heat and pain. The breath left his lungs, and for a time, he was weightless, floating in a sea of nothingness as he tumbled through an endless universe of white walls and floors and ceilings.

Then he hit the ground like a sack of bricks, and his chest erupted in agony. Bill was on the floor writhing in pain right next to him. Above them hung Sam's Core, except it wasn't *just* Sam's Core. It was fragments of four different Cores. Shards of golden and silver eggshell, glittering pieces of Bill's gray-green

Core, and splatters of liquid mercury all hovered like suspended rain droplets.

They were loosely connected by a thousand hair-fine strands of mana. The fragments slowly circled each other, dancing in their own way, just as Bill and Sam had moments before. It would have been stunning, if not for the terrible implications: the spell had worked, and they'd just shattered all four connecting Cores.

Now came the final piece of the spell. Happily—terrifyingly—this part was out of their hands.

They'd already done the leg work, and either they would survive, or they would die within a matter of seconds. Stealing a ragged breath, Sam tore his gaze from the spinning kaleidoscope of Core fragments and turned to observe the pieces of paper lining every inch of the Soul Chamber. The papers started to rustle and shake, a sound like a whirlwind filling the room. This was it. The moment of truth.

The first sheet of parchment ripped itself free from the walls and shot toward the Core fragments like an arrow. More pages tore themselves loose, first in a trickle, then in a flood, then a raging hurricane of paper. The sheets of spelled parchment glommed together into an enormous piñata—all of the Core fragments gathered at the center like the treats waiting to spill out. The ball of paper began to spin, and slowly the pain lessened, then faded.

A handful of thin cracks appeared along the surface of the paper globe. Sam gritted his teeth and pushed himself onto his hands, never taking his eyes off the slowly spinning orb. The white light leaking out grew in intensity until the ball of paper no longer resembled a piñata, but rather some distant sun sharing its brilliance with the universe.

When the light finally dimmed, the paper was gone, and something *new* remained: a Core the size of a basketball that looked like a work of stained-glass art. Not a newly unified Core, as Sam had expected, but a hodgepodge of pieces—glittering green here, opalescent eggshell there, silvery metal in other places—all grafted together by thin lines of glowing golden thread. It also wasn't spherical, but rather resembled a doughnut; circular, with a fist-sized hole directly in the center.

Sam wanted nothing more than to shut his eyes, curl into the fetal position, and sleep for the next fourteen hours, but there was still one final task to complete. With a groan, he gained his feet and stumbled toward his Core on unsteady legs. Bill was passed out on the ground, eyes closed, though his chest was rising and falling in a steady rhythm. Sam wished that the Bravi were conscious enough to walk him through the last step in the process, but it looked like he was on his own.

He curled his hand into a fist and thrust it into the circular hole at the center of his remade Core. He could see clean through the hole, but his fist encountered an invisible pocket of resistance. It wasn't solid like a brick wall, but spongy and somehow damp, almost like a membrane that could be punctured without much effort. After all he'd done to get here, the idea of low effort was wildly appealing. Sam applied gentle pressure, and the membrane popped.

A rush of air enveloped him, swirling around in a vortex that pulled him inward. He screamed, but the vortex stole the sound—not even a peep came out. He had experienced this once before, while in a faulty spot in the annex.

This was a gravity well.

It felt like a giant was crushing him in the palm of an enormous hand, but the pressure passed almost as quickly as it had begun. He blinked, and found he was no longer in his Soul Chamber at all. He was in a featureless cube, not much bigger than a large walk-in closet. Sam spun in a slow circle and found a hole hanging in the center of one of the walls. On the other side was Bill's slumbering form. He'd done it! Sam threw back his head and howled in victory. He'd *done* it!

He'd just created an Interspatial Library.

As though to confirm it, a notification dinged in his ear and a flurry of pop-ups appeared:

Alert! You have embarked on the Path of the Tattered Soul and have fundamentally altered your Core, incorporating not just one Beast Core, but three! By Soul Forging a new Core, you have immediately upgraded the Title Soul-Bound Level 2 to Soul-Bound Level 4! Effect: Receive a one-time character bonus as a result of absorbing the entirety of the Bibliomancer's Sacred Tome's Characteristic Points. +1 Strength, +3 Dexterity, +1 Constitution, +5 Intelligence, +4 Wisdom, +2 Charisma, +2 Perception, -5 Karmic Luck (Artificially Artifact bonus).

Notice! You have unlocked the maximum rank for Soul Bound; the title Soul Bound Level 4 has been changed to Tattered-Soul Level 1 (Upgradable). Bind more Beast Core Fragments to your already tattered Core to gain additional bonuses and upgrade this title to a maximum of Tattered-Soul Level 5, unlocking additional bonuses with each successive level. Until the maximum rank, this title cannot be combined with any other title nor removed for any reason. Warning! Level equalization. By permanently bonding your Core with the Bibliomancer's Sacred Tome's Core, the Prime Brood Matriarch (Floof), and the Lesser Brood Matriarch (Blaze), your levels will be aggregated and readjusted.

Calculating... Inflationary Discrepancy... Calculating... Core Stabilization Discrepancy... Calculating... You have fundamentally changed your entire being. You are now more, and less, than you were. Your characteristics are no longer as they were, and a portion of the characteristics from each bonded individual have been reassigned to another.

New aggregate level assessment: Level 10. Characteristic points have been updated. Current buffs will remain in effect.

Warning! Whenever you upgrade the Title Tattered Soul by bonding additional Beast Core Fragments, your aggregate Core and character level will be readjusted accordingly. Proceed with caution.

Name: Sam_K 'Merchant Ambassador'
Class: Libriohexer
Profession 1: Bookbinder
Profession 2: Chicken Keeper
Level: 10 Exp: 55,000 Exp to next level: 11,000
Hit Points: 130/130
Mana: 667/667
Mana regen: 34.03/sec

Stamina: 176.5/176.5

<u>Characteristic:</u> <u>Raw score</u>
Strength: 22 -> 25
Dexterity: 42 -> 40
Constitution: 21 -> 18
Intelligence: 65 -> 60
Wisdom: 62 -> 69
Charisma: 25 -> 30
Perception: 26 -> 45
Luck: 14 -> 10
Karmic Luck: -4

Profession increase: Bookbinder (10/10). Celestial feces, you somehow managed to bind your Core with not one, but three other Cores, all using a relatively obscure bookbinding technique. That's... not how that skill is supposed to work. You know what? I'm not even mad; that's amazing. In one fell swoop, you've become a Master Bookbinder. You know the deep mysteries of Coptic binding, Ethiopian binding, long-stitch binding, and a thousand other methods besides. You can tell the difference between vellum and parchment at a thousand paces and are as familiar with various paper forms as they are with the backside of their own hand.

No damaged book stands a chance against you. As a Master Bookbinder, you have unlocked skills far surpassing those of even the most sought-after craftsmen, for you now understand how creation itself is bound together. After all, what is reality, if not a series of smaller pieces bound through energy into something greater than the sum of its parts? Understanding this fundamental truth allows you not only to bind the pages of a book, but to bind things of a separate nature together. Use your unconventional skills as a Master Bookbinder to bind a spell to a sword or two small rocks together into a bigger rock.

Profession benefits at Master Level: Increases the speed of reading and writing by 90%. You barely need to flip through a book to know the secrets contained within. Reduce the cost and production time for paper, ink, and book bindings by 75%. Sew spells to objects (enchanting) using mana thread—all creation costs and Core costs remain the same as traditional enchantments. Sew elements of a similar nature together to form something greater than the sum of their parts.

Quest update! A Libriohexer Walks into an Interspatial Library…

Hot dog! You've done it, you crazy son of a gun! Despite the odds stacked against you—and trust me, rea~a~aly stacked against you—you've discovered the secrets of the Wolfmen Totems, managed to turn yourself into a Beast Core Cultivator, and carved out a little extra-dimensional space to call your own. I mean, it's small and bleak, but it is technically a functional Interspatial Library. Honestly, a place that size in New York would probably run you three thousand a month, so I suppose it could be worse.

Reward, Class Change: Libriohexer!

You've also gained 2,000 Experience Points for your trouble. Huzzah!

You have unlocked the following Spells:

Mummify (Beginner I)…

Origami Costume (Beginner I)…

Origami Structure (Beginner I)…

Origami Guardian - Small (Beginner I)…

Alert! You have learned a sub-variant of Orbital Tome of Casting: Summoned Shelf of Casting! Summoned Shelf of Casting can be used in lieu of Orbital Tome of Casting as a spellcasting mechanism and has the same rank as the primary skill, Orbital Tome of Casting.

Summoned Shelf of Casting (Beginner I)…

Sam's eyes glazed over as he glanced at all the notifications. He was so exhausted, the words were all a jumbled mess in his brain, so he skipped reading the final notices beyond just their names.

He had one big take-away, though: he'd done it. He'd managed to successfully turn himself into a Beast Core Cultivator—one who followed the path of the Tattered Soul, no less. It was a huge achievement, and yet it hadn't come cheap or easy. A knot formed in the pit of his stomach when he looked at his character sheet and saw his total experience. A paltry fifty-five thousand. Plus the two thousand from completing the quest. After a little quick mental math, he realized this shift had cost him thirty-six thousand, three hundred and ten experience points, dropping him three hard-earned levels.

Power carried a steep price tag. Sam knew it would be worth it in the long run. Humanity was going to be in for a rude awakening once he figured out how to fully utilize his new abilities. He suppressed an enormous yawn with his fist, and his legs trembled, threatening to rebel against him if he didn't take a load off. The world would get a rude awakening… but it would have to wait for him to catch a solid eight to ten hours of well-deserved shuteye.

CHAPTER THIRTY-TWO

Sam stood in front of the double doors that let into the Irondown Library, arms folded across his chest. He stole a glance at Bill, who was floating at his side, as per usual. "You're sure we can just take them? Aren't they sort of attached to the dungeon?"

"Sure, *technically,* they're a part of the dungeon, but who cares?" the book announced hungrily. "I mean, the dungeon belongs to us... more or less. Besides, where exactly did you think we were going to get all the material for *our* Library, huh?"

Sam shrugged and started to walk forward. "I dunno. I thought we would build it ourselves, I guess."

"What about me makes you think I'm some sort of handyman?" Bill flapped wildly to call attention once again to the fact that he was a *book*. "I've been a sword fighter, a mercenary, and a scholar. Handyman ain't anywhere on that list. I can't *hold* a hammer, for one, and my knowledge of how to build a bookcase ends with the fact that you probably need wood. You're a bookbinder and... chicken keeper. So unless you know something I don't, neither of those skills is gonna help us a whole lot. Which means we're going to *steal* stuff. Lots of stuff. It's not like this place needs all those bookcases anyway. Once we finish capturing the Irondowns, we'll turn it into a rec room or something for the new recruits. Now stop fighting me, and steal those *doors* already."

Sam sighed and reluctantly pulled free his engraving awl. After fighting and subsequently bonding their Cores to both Floof and Blaze, they'd managed to successfully create an Interspatial Node, but now they needed to create a totem access point; a way to pierce the veil and step between dimensions at will so they could actually store stuff within their fancy new Library. That started with these doors.

Thankfully, Bill seemed to have a firm idea of what to do, now that they'd managed to create the Interspatial Node itself. Using his new abilities as a Master Bookbinder, Sam carved a series of location and binding runes into the wooden frame—those would tether the physical material to his Library and allow him to summon and dismiss the doorframe at will. The work was tedious and painstaking—wood wasn't nearly as malleable or forgiving as paper—but the symbols were familiar ones, even if arranged in some odd patterns. Unfortunately, he couldn't use his Coreless Spell Infusion to magically enchant the door, since the spell was so much more powerful than anything he'd built before.

Thankfully, with the abundance of pilfered beast Cores he'd lifted from the College, that wasn't a problem at all. Once Sam was done with the spell construct framework, he inserted ten Cores into ten key locations on the frame and activated the binding spell with a trickle of his own mana. Unlike most of the spells that he built, this one cost him next to no mana. Just the faintest trickle of energy was required to kickstart the process, and after that, the beast Cores took over and did all of the heavy lifting.

They burned bright gold, releasing waves of arcane energy that powered the sigils and runes, which erupted to a blazing life of their own as they settled more deeply into the wood. When the spell finally finished running its course, Sam felt a strange connection form with the Library doors. It wasn't quite like the connection he had with Bill, or even with his Chickens—it felt more like he'd just grafted in another limb.

No, not a limb... like having a third opening bloom on the center of his forehead. He focused on that image and 'closed' the eye. The floor rumbled and the walls shook; dust rained down from overhead as the doors abruptly disappeared from reality. Beyond was a rough hole in the wall that peered into the Irondown Library. Next, Sam 'opened' his new eye, and the doors reappeared in a blink.

"Don't just stand there," Bill urged him excitedly. "Go in already. Let's see what we have to work with!"

Sam licked his lips, suddenly feeling both nervous and giddy, and strutted toward the doors. They opened for him on silent hinges, obeying his will. Inside waited a cube of a room, three hundred square feet, still bigger than his quarters at the Mage's College had been, but only fractionally. The walls were blank and featureless—slabs of black nothingness. Not stone or plaster, just pure void. A shiver sprinted along Sam's spine as he stepped across that threshold.

"It ain't much to look at," Bill whispered in awe, "but we did it. A genuine Interspatial Library. Well, more like an Interspatial broom closet at the moment, but as we level up, it'll grow in size and scope. Honestly, this is way better than my first attempt. I ended up with a Soul Space, but it also broke three ribs and put me in the infirmary for the better part of a month. I couldn't keep down *food*, believe it or not. I'd eat something, and everything would just sort of pop out through the interspatial hole in my stomach. Won an eating contest that way, before they put me in hardback. Listen to me ramble... you've got better things to do. It's time to go on a shopping trip!"

"You mean stealing, yeah?" Sam allowed himself to be persuaded, but he'd definitely let Bill know he was reluctant about it.

"Yes, *obviously*, I mean stealing. To the Library!"

They recruited Finn and Velkan to aid in their larceny,

finding that the two were more than happy to lend a hand. Velkan said he had nothing better to do, and Dizzy was trying to run Finn through a physical training routine to help fortify his strength and constitution. Said routine involved combat sparring and weight training. Since Finn was made entirely of left feet and had the muscle definition of an eleven-year-old boy, that translated to a lot of sore limbs and getting pummeled with blunt sticks. The mage had leapt at the opportunity to get away before she broke anything in her overzealous attempts to 'bring him up to the minimum'.

Together, Velkan and Finn moved several bookshelves from the Irondown Library into Sam's newly minted Interspatial Node, while Sam and Bill set up their workshop in one corner.

They installed a cramped writing desk, a three-legged stool, and a variety of shelves to hold quills, inkwells, unused parchment, and binding materials. A couple of candelabras were bolted to the walls to provide candlelight, though the room didn't actually need an independent light source. The walls, though featureless and black, cast an odd sort of witchlight that perfectly illuminated the space, but the warm orange glow from the candles made it feel far homier.

"Eventually, this place really would be like a second home," Sam mused, thinking about eventually having a private bedroom and office tucked away inside, along with his entire poultry-to-parchment manufacturing operation. "Only a matter of time."

Once the bookcases and furniture were moved in, Velkan headed out to take care of some business in New Narvik—Sam suspected he was going to report in with The O'Baba. Finn offered to accompany the Wolfman, though Sam suspected he was really just trying to avoid more training sessions with Dizzy. Finn loved being around the frazzle-haired tank, but he loved not getting beaten senseless even more.

Bill and Sam spent the rest of the time going through all the various magical and mundane texts they'd acquired over the past several weeks. Most of the books were destined to be fodder for book bombs, but they'd also picked up a few gems that had some excellent utility.

"Not a bad haul, all things considered." Bill seemed satisfied as they surveyed their handiwork: three large bookcases filled nearly top to bottom with books of various shapes and sizes. "I mean, it's not a grand library *yet*, but I know lesser Noble houses that would kill to have even this many magical texts. Abyss, we probably have more genuine magic books than the Scholar's Library. You should be proud. You've put in a lot of hard work, and all that elbow grease is finally starting to pay off. Speaking of paying off, now that you and I are bonafide Librohexers with access to our own Interspatial Library, we can finally learn the *cool* spells. The big spells. You ready to get magical?"

Sam rolled his eyes. "More utility spells? Maybe a spell of floor sweeping, or a Mystic Ritual of Dewey Decimal Sorting?"

"*Please*. Everyone knows rituals are overpriced enchantments and totally bogus," Bill growled matter-of-factly. "I'm talking about magic-goes-boom spells. I'm talking 'fury from *heaven*' spells! I'm talking 'armies of paper' spells! See, that's the thing. Everything that we're going to learn now, we literally couldn't have used as a mere Bibliomancer. The component costs are too high. Even if I could have taught them to you, there would've been no way to cast them."

"Now that we have this bad boy?" Bill was positively giddy as he admired the room. "Well, that's a different story entirely. We're going to bury our enemies in books and drown them in ink. I'm thinking we'll start with a nasty area-of-effect spell that has lots of versatility—like I said, huge cost associated, but that's going to become irrelevant before too long. Go grab that copy of *Fundamentals of Meteorological Magic*, would ya?"

Sam pulled down a thick volume embellished with gilt edging. The book was a complicated one that covered a myriad of different meteorological phenomena, along with certain explanations of ways that mana manipulation could be used to achieve similar results. There were two additional spells that Bill was interested in, and both were located near the back. The first was an incantation for conjured rain. Essentially, it allowed the caster to summon a storm cloud capable of dumping monsoon levels of water over a given point for a short period of time. Powerful, though straightforward and simple.

When Sam pointed out that the spell was designed predominately for agricultural irrigation and not for combat, Bill just cackled like a loon. "In the right hands, *anything* can be used for combat. Remember, some skills and abilities have compatible synergy. That means they work together in such a way that you can combine them together into a single awesome new skill. The College always frowned on Initiates 'creating' unauthorized types of magic, but that was one of my specialties. Now, my question to you is this: do we make a *very* dangerous damage per second spell... or do we make a powerful crowd control spell? The real question is: which would you rather have? Bear in mind, we only have the resources for *one*?"

Sam only had to consider his choices for a second. "Crowd control."

In Eternium, most spells didn't have the capacity to distinguish between friendly and hostile forces. If he cast a spell that did lots of damage for long periods of time, there was a good chance it would cause splash damage to his fellow teammates. If he were playing solo, there was no doubt that was the direction he'd have gone, but since he planned on operating with a team, a crowd control spell was the better option. He needed to make sure he was the best packmate he could be.

With his new bonuses as a Master bookbinder, learning 'Storm Cloud Conjuration' was a piece of cake. As soon as the spell officially appeared on his status sheet, Bill had him combine *that* with both Ink Lance and Weak Paralysis. That was more than a little concerning, since both spells were staples in Sam's current offensive line up, but Bill assured him the payout would be worth it.

Since they were combining three skills, the cost was a staggering two hundred gold. Luckily, he could foot the bill with plenty left to spare, thanks to his chicken earnings. Combining a skill with another took twelve hours, plus an additional twelve hours per skill added, but thanks to his Experimental Forger Title, that time was reduced by fifteen percent.

Extreme skill synergy detected! Storm Cloud Conjuration, Ink Lance, and Weak Paralysis all share similar features and can be combined to form a new skill. By paying two hundred gold, you can combine these three skills into one single unique skill. The level of the new skill will be the average of the original skills, and any remaining skill points (rounded up) will be returned as free skill points! If you do not have the necessary gold on hand, you may combine these skills at a later date or choose to have the money taken from your bank account.

You are about to combine three skills: Storm Cloud Conjuration, Ink Lance, and Weak Paralysis. Are you sure? Yes / No.

He hated to see good spells go, but he trusted Bill's wisdom and hit 'yes'.

Time until skills have combined: 20:24:00.

In a flash, the knowledge regarding all three spells was rudely ripped from his head, gone in a snap of the fingers. Not only could he no longer cast or inscribe any of the spells, but he couldn't even fathom how he had ever been able to do so. It was a disorienting experience that left him feeling momentarily queasy. This wasn't his first rodeo, however, and before long, the sensation passed.

Next, Bill had him learn a second spell from *Fundamentals of Meteorological Magic*, this one a powerful offensive Whirlwind Cantrip. It was a spell that was closely associated with the Aeolus Sorcerer, the very class Sam had once been before joining his Core and fate with Bill as a Bibliomancer. The spell was a powerhouse that called forth a massive whirlwind that would cut and slash anything that got in its path of destruction.

Naturally, Sam couldn't cast it.

Bill took care of that too, by having him merge two more skills—Rorschach Test and Paper Pigeon, an odd combination Sam would have never tried on his own. But Bill guaranteed that this would also have an extreme skill synergy. The book could be an annoying know-it-all, but the fact that he was a skill trainer who *did* pretty much know it all definitely had its perks from time to time.

Sam spent another two hundred gold and received another twenty-hour notice. While they waited for their two new spells to combine, Sam sat down in a meditative pose and went back through his notifications from the day before, reading through the other new spells he'd earned after unlocking his Libriohexer Specialization.

Mummify (Beginner I): Unleash a flurry of flying paper that wraps around a target, binding them in a cocoon of Papier-Mache. Opponents must make a saving throw against Dexterity, or Mummify will incapacitate them for .5n minutes, where 'n' is equal to the skill level. Beginning at the Apprentice Level, Mummify can target more than one opponent at a time, and at the Journeyman Level, Mummify has a 1n% chance of controlling the mummified opponent, causing them to fight on behalf of the caster for the duration of the spell. Production Cost: 20 mana per second until spell script is completed or the attempt has failed. Casting Cost: 50 sheets of paper per cast.

On the surface, it seemed like Mummify was a more powerful version of Weak Paralysis. It probably wouldn't be effective against a Rogue or any other high Dexterity build, like a Ranger or Monk, but it would be a great ace in the hole against beefy Constitution-based tanks or spell-slinging mages. If he could level the skill up to the Journeyman rank, he'd be able to not only target multiple enemies at once, he would be able to conscript them into his army.

Origami Costume (Beginner I): Paper is a versatile material, and when combined with the right inks, it can be folded and formed into intricate costumes capable of hiding not just your clothes, but even your identity. Wrap a marked target in a layer of flexible and versatile Papier-Mache, which can perfectly mimic clothing or armor. Origami Costume does not count as Mage-Armor and offers no additional protections against damage, but it does mask all negative titles while active. Cost: 20 mana per second until spell script is completed or the attempt has failed. Casting Cost: 25 sheets of paper per cast.

Sam nearly salivated after reading through the description

of Origami Costume. His Mask of the Plucky Rebel was an amazing item, but the problem was that they couldn't get another one. Sphinx's Infiltrate ability could also help conceal negative status, but as with the mask, it had severe limitations. Namely, she couldn't use it on more than a handful of people at any given time. But with this spell, the only limitation was the resource component. As the Wolf Pack recruited, their sabotage missions would only get bigger and more elaborate; this would allow them to gain access to all sorts of human establishments and all of the prepared spell books within.

The following two spells were summoning-oriented, and the material costs of each gave Sam actual heart palpitations.

Origami Structure (Beginner I): Create a Papier-Mache Wall that measures 5 feet wide by four feet tall by two feet thick. The wall acts as a semi-permanent barrier and cannot be moved until it is destroyed or reabsorbed by the caster. The created wall can bear up to 500 pounds and acts as a summoned creature with 250 HP.

The wall will absorb damage until its HP is fully depleted and will then disintegrate, consuming all used materials. The caster may reabsorb the wall at any point; material reclamation is equal to the total percentage of remaining Health belonging to the structure. For example, 100% of the material will be reclaimed if the wall is undamaged, while only 90% of the material would be reclaimed for a wall at 225 HP. A damaged/recalled Origami Structure may be recast without supplemental materials but will spawn with the same amount of Health Points it had when recalled.

Origami Structure has an additional .75 resistance against the element effects wind and earth but suffers an additional 0.75 damage against the elemental effects of fire and water. As this skill advances, you will be able to create larger and more intricate structures with progressively higher HP values. Production Cost: 50 mana per second until spell script is complete or attempt has failed. Casting Cost: 150 sheets of paper per cast.

Origami Guardian - Small (Beginner I): Summon a small origami guardian inside of an unoccupied space within a thirty-foot radius of your location. These origami guardians are completely loyal to you and are friendly to your companions. Although lower-level origami creatures are not necessarily the sharpest crayons in the toolshed, they will obey all verbal commands given by the caster and will defend themselves or allies, unprompted, against threats.

Summoned Small Guardians have the following stats: Strength, 7; Dexterity, 6; Constitution, 8; Intelligence, 5; Wisdom, 3; Charisma, 3; Perception, 5; Hit Points, 90. The Small Origami Guardian will absorb damage until its HP is fully depleted and will then disintegrate, consuming all used materials. The caster may reabsorb the summoned guardian at any point; material reclamation is equal to the total percentage of remaining Health belonging to the creature. A damaged/recalled Origami Guardian may be recast without supplemental materials but will spawn with the same number of Health Points it had when recalled.

The caster may have an active number of Small Origami Guardians equal to 1n where n = skill level. List of currently available small creatures to select from when creating an Origami Guardian - Small: Horned Rabbit, Feral Fox, Jelly (non-elemental), Chicken, Maintenance Automaton Keeper. Origami Guardians have an additional .75 resistance against the elemental effects of wind and earth but suffer an additional 0.75 damage against the elemental effects of fire and water. Production Cost: 30 mana per second until spell script is complete or attempt has failed. Casting Cost: 150 sheets of paper per summoned creature.

Summoned Shelf of Casting (Apprentice IV): You have learned a sub-variant of Orbital Tome of Casting, Summoned Shelf of Casting! Summoned Shelf of Casting can be used in lieu of Orbital Tome of Casting as a spellcasting mechanism and has the same rank as the primary skill, Orbital Tome of Casting. Because of the high cost associated with many Libriohexer spells, the Libriohexer summons not a single tome—or even six—but an entire bookshelf's worth of firepower.

The bookshelf itself must first be magically enhanced and permanently bound as a summoned totem. Once prepared, it can be called at will from the Interspatial Library and will be tethered to the caster until it is dispelled back to the Interspatial Library. The enchanted bookshelf levitates above the ground, and its position can be shifted by the Libriohexer with the merest thought. Only one bookshelf may be summoned at a time, and the bookshelf cannot be more than ten feet away from the caster at any given point. The Libriohexer can still utilize Orbital Tome of Casting as a spellcasting mechanic, but Orbital Tome of Casting and Summoned Shelf of Casting cannot be equipped as the Primary Casting Method at the same time.

"What did I tell you?" Bill crowed as Sam finished reading. "*Awesome*, right? You wanted to go with Biblioblade… aren't you glad you listened to me and stayed the course? I mean, sure, the material production costs are through the roof, but thanks to your chicken farm, we've essentially created a book-making mill, so that shouldn't be a problem."

"Still going to have some wicked hand cramps." Sam stared at the production cost for his Origami minions and his Papier-Mache Structure. "Even with Auto-Writing and Transcription Twinning."

"Eh, we'll get that ironed out eventually," Bill whispered in a conspiratorial tone, "but until then, best you get working. You're not just the Legs in this relationship, you're also the hands. Those spells aren't going to write themselves."

Sam sighed and headed over to his work desk. He was sure that Libriohexer was going to be a blast, but he hadn't realized just how much writing it would involve. He glanced at the countdown clock for his new skills. Twenty hours left to go. "Better get a pot of tea. It's going to be a long day."

CHAPTER THIRTY-THREE

Sam worked for the next six hours, magically infusing ink and chicken vellum, inscribing scrolls, prepping quills, and meticulously binding books. Thanks to hitting the Master Rank as a Bookbinder, he was ten-fold faster, but there were just so *many* things to do. He worked until his hands cramped and his fingers bled from countless needle pokes, until his back screamed and his legs were numb from the stool beneath him. Finally, when his stomach was grumbling in protest and his eyes were watering from the strain of working by candlelight, he took a break and headed out to grab a quick bite and to check on the others.

Sam had lost all sense of time while working in his Library—walled off from the rest of the world as he was—and was surprised to find that it was early evening already. He searched the barracks and kitchen looking for company, but both were empty. He popped by the Alchemy lab next, but it was deserted too. The only pack member he could find was Kai, who was busy practicing a complicated routine on the Dexterity course in the Training Hall. Sam lingered in the doorway for a beat, watching the Monk maneuver through an elaborate kata while precariously balanced on the top of a set of wooden poles.

Kai executed a series of leaps, strikes, and powerful kicks, all foreign to Sam, but interspersed throughout were a variety of precise turns and thrusts that he recognized as Judo techniques. It was impossible to miss the crouch and pivot that were surefire signs of Ippon-seoi-nage, a one-armed shoulder throw, or the sweeping motions of Harai Goshi. The Monk finished his kata by turning a perfect handspring on a balance beam less than four inches wide, then executing a flawless backflip to dismount. He landed like a comet, golden sparks erupting around him in a halo. With a flourish, he launched a final strike, arm extended, and a shimmering yellow fist erupted from his palm.

"What in the name of a hobo eating a hotdog was that?" Bill barked in shock. "Was that *magic*? Certainly looked like magic to me. mana projection, if I had to guess."

"Uh, not sure if it's magic or not. Uncle Monkey explained it in terms of Chi, not mana, but I guess it could be a similar mechanic." Kai grinned and stood tall. He tapped at his chest. "I have this ball of power inside me. Sort of this golden energy Core. It's filled with Chi. I've been learning to push and channel it through my body along meridian lines. It allows me to move faster, reinforce my body, stuff like that. Now that I've specialized, I can even project it."

"Yep, mana Manipulation." Bill nodded sagely as the others ignored him.

"Wait. You *specialized*?" Sam's eyes went wide, and he rushed over to slap the man on his back. "Are you kidding me?"

The Monk's grin spread even wider, and he shook his head in mutual wonder. "I know, it's totally wild. Our raid against the College pushed me up to level thirteen, but I still wasn't sure how I wanted to specialize. There were a bunch of bland Monk subclasses, but nothing that really spoke to my soul, ya know? But that next day, I went and visited the Monkey Totem, and you'll never guess who I met."

"Uncle Monkey?" Bill dryly replied.

"Whoa! Great guess!" Kai clapped in excitement. "Zhen Zexian, otherwise known as Uncle Monkey. I must've visited that totem training ground twenty times and never saw him before, but there he was. The dude shot me in the face with a poison dart the second I stepped through, which was pretty uncool of him. But then we had, like… this epic Crouching Tiger, Hidden Dragon-style battle. I lost because, ya know, he shot me in the face with poison. *But* then he gave me the antidote and invited me to become a disciple of the Monkey Fist."

"What did you say?" Sam pushed for a clearer explanation.

"Well, like, *yeah*, obviously. It's totally rad. He walked me through a bunch of new katas to help loosen my Chi and taught me all these new moves. I learned the Endless Fury of the Monkey Fist technique, which allows me to stack multiple blows against a single opponent and deliver them all as a single attack. My new Gorilla Body ability passively restores a little bit of health whenever I land a critical hit. Plus I can use Simian Agility to increase my speed four-fold for twenty seconds. To top it all off, I can also dislocate my joints, which gives me a fifty-percent increased chance to evade. Those are the big ones, but I also got this bad boy! Look."

The rope belt entwined around his waist twitched and moved. It wasn't a belt at all, but a monkey tail.

"You have a tail," Sam stared at the new limb as though he had just been shown something *very* offensive.

"Right? How cool is that!" Kai didn't seem to catch the leery expression he was earning. "Not quite as cool as a talking book, but still not nothing. It acts as a fully functional limb, and I can extend it crazy far."

The tail snaked away from his body like a striking cobra. The most shocking thing of all was that it kept going, and going, and *going*. It extended out a good thirty feet before slamming into a training dummy like a bo-staff. "I may not be a Mage, but I'm really starting to come into my own, I think. I'm glad I stuck with it. But listen to me go on and on. I haven't seen you since the party. What happened? Everyone was having a blast, and you just sort of disappeared on us. Did you learn what you needed to know about the Totem stuff?"

This time, Sam was the one who was showing off. He opened his third eye, and the doors to his Interspatial Library blinked into existence. "Yeah, you could say that."

"Dude! That is amazing. Tell. Me. *Everything*!" The pair of them headed off to the kitchen while they talked. Sam told the Monk about his cryptic meeting with the Wolfman Shaman known as the Bakkuo, his subsequent battle of wills against Floof and Blaze, and all the shiny new abilities he'd unlocked. Once he was done, Kai filled Sam and Bill in on the rest of the crew while the Octo-Chef whipped up a meal of fried chicken, buttermilk waffles, and heaps of gooey syrup.

After Finn had bailed on their training session, Dizzy and Arrow had decided to head off to the Totem grounds for a round of training. Their fearless tank was grumpy that Sphinx and Kai had both unlocked their specializations, while she still hadn't. She was the leader of the Pack, and she believed that meant she should be leading from the front, not trailing behind everyone else. Velkan and Finn still weren't back from their errands in New Narvik, and Sphinx was out on an infiltration mission—sabotaging another one of the Rabid Inquisitors' pledge rushes.

"There's just one thing about your specialization that I have a serious question about. If you're Soul Bonded with two chickens, does that mean you're part chicken now?" Kai nearly choked, so he took a moment to lick his fingers free of grease and syrup once he'd cleared his throat. His face visibly paled as he glanced down at his empty plate. He dropped his voice low. "Is this... like, cannibalism for you now?"

Sam laughed, then paused for a long beat to consider the fried chicken still on his plate. Was he part chicken? No, definitely not. "That was not the question I thought you were going to ask. Frankly... I didn't even consider that?"

"I'm a M*onk*, man." Kai tried to look deep and knowledgeable. "That's my nature: to ask the tough, introspective questions."

"Well, I'm not sure what the answer is," Sam admitted as he thought it over, "but my heart says no, and so do my tastebuds. I prefer to think about them as pet chickens. I mean, I'm bound with Bill too, and I wouldn't consider myself part book."

"If only you were so *lucky* as to be part book." Bill ruffled himself and stretched. "There's a lot of benefits to being a book, you know."

"Yeah, like no hand cramps," Sam glared at Bill in faux anger. "Although that's only because you don't have hands."

"Hey, hey, *hey*. No need to get personal," Bill replied with a sniff.

Sam rubbed at the muscles in his right palm. "All jokes aside, I'm going to need to find a way to automate some of this work. Even if we have unlimited resources, the preparation time is still insane, and that's even with all of Bill's production hacks."

"Dude, I don't envy you." Kai reached out and clasped Sam's shoulder. "I mean, don't get me wrong, your class is awesome, and I'm sure it'll only get better, but spending all that time scribbling away at paper and sewing books together… it would drive me insane. I'd take training on the agility course over that, any day of the week. Too bad you can't find a way to grow an extra limb like me. I bet an extra set of arms or two would come in handy. Huh. *Handy*. See what I did there?"

Sam had stopped listening as soon as 'an extra set of arms' was mentioned. A thought began to form in the back of his head as he glanced at the Octo-Chef. "An extra set of arms… or maybe eight extra arms. You're a *genius*, Kai. Monks really are the embodiment of wisdom."

"Uh, glad I could help?" He arched an eyebrow. "Not sure what I said. Was it the chicken thing? The cannibalism dealio?"

Sam shook his head. "Nope. I have no intention of skipping out on the chicken and waffles. You *did* give me a great idea, though. Not sure if it'll work, but it's worth a try. Gotta run."

He shoved the last bite of savory chicken into his mouth, then turned on a heel and took off for the Irondown library. "Bill. The Library Guardian. It was created to defend the library, but what are the chances that it's also trained in basic book maintenance and repair?"

"I would say that kind of thing is too complicated for some automaton to do," the book replied, "but then, the Octo-Chef never ceases to impress me with his cooking. So… who knows? Even if it can repair books, it still wouldn't be able to ink spells for us or imbue items with mana."

"Yeah, there's no way it'll completely automate the process," Sam agreed with a sparkle in his eye, "but any place we can cut down time will be a huge benefit. Besides, if our chickens keep evolving, eventually we won't have to imbue vellum or quills with mana at all—they'll just naturally come that way. The Library Guardian can probably help us prepare the materials."

Sam slid around a corner and tore through the gaping hole that led into the library. The hole where doors had stood guard not so long ago. There were still tons of empty bookcases filling the room, though no books remained in sight. Anything of true value had already been packed up and carted off to Sam's fancy new Interspatial Node.

After a few seconds of searching, they found the Librarian Automaton perched in a shadowy corner, where it had built a rudimentary lair of webs and debris. It looked like a large spider centaur—its lower body that of a mechanical arachnoid, its upper body that of one of the maintenance automatons.

The guardian regarded them from its lair of webs, alert but unmoving, until it was called upon for service. It had stayed like that since they'd captured the Library, due to the fact that they hadn't had any use for it. Sam reached into the Spatial Flask and pulled free a mundane book with a badly mangled spine—one of the many projects he needed to take care of. He tossed the book on the floor with a loud **thunk**. The spider creature moved almost faster than Sam could see, zipping down a line of spun silk like the member of a tactical swat team fast-roping out of a helicopter, then attacked the book with ferocious intensity.

Silk flowed from its mouth, and its legs weaved in frantic motion. In less than five seconds, the damaged text had been repaired, and the spider was already busy placing it on a shelf off to the left.

"Well, I'll be a monkey's uncle." Bill let out a low whistle.

"I think Kai has probably got the market cornered on that," Sam absently teased. "Let's see what else it can do."

For the next two hours, they moved their chicken vellum refinement operation into the mostly empty library, tasking the mechanical librarian with cleaning and processing the leftover chicken scraps. The spider was surprisingly good at cleaning the hides, and it even secreted some sort of acidic compound to help cure the vellum. Its many legs made stretching the chicken leather a breeze, and it could sew and bind loose pages into spell tomes three times faster than Sam could manage, even as a Master Bookbinder. The thing seemed custom built for this sort of work.

While the Arachnoid Librarian toiled, Sam got back to work himself, reinvigorated to finish inscribing his legion of spell tomes. Time passed in a blur of ink and paper, and at some point, he had nodded off inside his Interspatial Library. He woke up groggy and disoriented, with a terrible crick in his neck. Even so, he ignored all of that when he realized that his two new spells had finished combining.

Ink Mire Storm Cloud (Beginner I): Summon a vengeful storm cloud, centered on a point within line of sight and spreading out in a 75-foot radius. A torrent of inky rain falls from the cloud, splattering all those within the Area of Effect. Each target must make an immediate Constitution-saving throw or suffer from full body paralysis for 1n seconds, where 'n' is equal to the spell skill level. All those caught in the downfall are mired by enchanted Ink, drastically restricting their movement rate. Not to mention, the ink is ridiculously hard to get out of fabrics, so even if they walk away from the fight, you'll still have the last laugh! That dry cleaner's bill is going to be outrageous.

Ink Rain slows the movement rate of affected parties by 12+(n/2)% for 30 seconds. All paper-aligned creatures are immune from the effects of this spell and move freely through the Ink Mire. This spell will affect friendly forces within the AoE. Production Cost: 5 mana per second until the spell script is completed or attempt is failed. Casting Cost: 300 sheets of ink-soaked paper per spell cast. As only the ink is used when this spell is cast, the paper can be re-inked at a later time! Casting Time: 8 seconds!

Murder of Crows (Beginner I): This one's for the birds! Conjure a vicious whirlwind of origami crows that will peck and tear and slice at any enemy inside the Area of Effect. The conjured crows deal magical slashing damage and may be augmented with elemental effects by layering in additional spells, according to their own mana cost. Damage and range for each crow in the murder is derived from the base skills, Magical Origami and Origami Activation. Origami Crows do an additional 0.5 damage against earth-aligned beings but suffer a 0.5 penalty against fire-aligned beings.

A Murder of Crows is a terrifying sight to behold; any enemy caught in the center of the vortex who fails a Wisdom check will additionally suffer 1n psionic damage, where 'n' is equal to the skill level, and will be forced to scream, 'Oh no, the birds are coming! It's the end of the world!' This one is a doozy! Even better, the summoned crows are capable of distinguishing between friend and foe! Production Cost: 50 mana per second until the spell script is completed or attempt is failed. Casting Cost: 350 sheets of paper per spell cast.

A surge of excitement washed over Sam as he read over the newly earned spells.

He was going to be unstoppable. He still had all of his Paper Shuriken and his wide array of Book Bombs, but now, he'd also be able to augment them with fortified structures, paper minions, and powerful AoE spells. All that was left to do was to test all of his wickedly awesome abilities in battle, and he knew exactly who to try them on. As preparations were complete, he moved to gather the Wolf Pack together and take another run at the Keeper of the Forge.

It was time they claimed the Irondowns as their own.

CHAPTER THIRTY-FOUR

"Alright," Dizzy bellowed from the front of the party. "This is it; a chance to redeem ourselves! We ready to *do* this?"

Sam glanced away from the hulking doors that stood guard over the Irondown Forge and double checked his gear for the hundredth time. His Papier Mache Armor was already in place, and his Quill Wing Cloak hung down his back. Only one thing left to do now. He thrust a hand out with his palm extended. He felt the connection to his Interspatial Library buried in the void just outside of real space. Concentrating, he tugged on the invisible tether and summoned a hulking mahogany bookcase, three feet wide and six feet tall, covered in runes that burned with cobalt power.

He'd spent hours carving the delicate spatial summoning sigils and outfitting it with the scant few monster Cores he had left in his possession. It had been a costly and time-consuming project, but looking at it... he knew it had been worth the sacrifice.

The bookcase contained seven shelves, and each shelf was loaded down with books. So many books, in fact, that the case would've been impossible to budge, if not for the fact that it floated half a foot above the ground and trailed along behind Sam like an obedient puppy... except this puppy had *teeth.*

To the casual observer, a floating bookcase might've seemed funny, but Sam knew the truth. That bookcase was an arsenal of destructive magic. Tomes upon tomes contained Paper Shuriken. Enough volumes were available to conjure a small army of paper pets. Plus, he'd stocked plenty of heavy-duty artillery spells if things got out of hand; Sam was sure they would get out of hand.

"We play smarter this time." Dizzy started laying out the strategy, absently adjusting a short leather cloak wrapped around her shoulders. "We know the Keeper of the Forge is going to try to lure us onto the platform so he can cut off our retreat—so we need to make him *work* for it. I'm going to try to draw aggro, get him to focus on me, while our ranged support peppers him from the rear. Sam, you're our aerial support. Everyone knows what we need to do; now we just need to do it. Keep your heads on straight, follow the plan, and we'll get out of here in one piece."

She took a deep breath, faced the doors, and kicked them like they owed her money. The great panels flew inward as unbearable heat rolled out in a tidal wave. They moved in a tight wedge formation, Dizzy at the head, Kai and Velkan at the sides, everyone else bringing up the rear.

Sam's gaze slipped toward the vault on the far side of the room, piled high with weapons and armor and gold. This was the last obstacle that stood between them and victory—once they took down the Keeper of the Forge, the Irondowns would officially belong to the Wolf Pack, along with all of the sweet, sweet loot secreted away in the armory. There was enough there to keep the coffers full for months, and they could use the weapons and armor to equip an entire resistance force.

The only thing standing between them and their goals was the Keeper.

"Do my eyes deceive me," the Guardian boomed in delight, "or have my would-be masters returned? I was afraid our last encounter may have left a bad taste in your mouth. Never was fond of a mouthful of ash, myself."

"Can't scare us away that easily," Dizzy called out, bringing up her maul and letting it rest against her thick iron pauldron. "We were cocky last time—overestimated our own abilities, and underestimated yours. But we aren't going to make that same mistake again. This time, we've come prepared for whatever you have to throw at us."

"It pleases my fiery heart to hear!" the guardian bellowed his happy reply. Despite his cheery disposition, he was exactly as intimidating as Sam remembered. Twelve feet of iron and steel and spikes were all wrapped around a Core of impossibly hot, sentient magma. The fire golem peered at them through the slits of his great horned helm. "As I informed you during our last encounter, I am not a creature of destruction by nature. I yearn to refine, to improve, to forge and purify. Your untimely and gruesome deaths weren't personal, I can assure you.

"However, I must warn you," he continued in a darker tone, "I won't go any easier on you this time around. If anything, this battle should be far more difficult, since I've seen your fighting styles and strategies before."

He lifted his enormous golden hammer and pointed it directly at Sam. "Those fancy wings of yours won't catch me unaware this time. I suspected you would be back for another bout, so I used my time to create some nasty new surprises to *truly* test your mettle. I hope you've brought your best, because you're going to need it. Now, enough talk. *Have at thee*!"

Sam was entirely unprepared when the double doors slammed shut behind them with a resounding **clang**, and the Keeper of the Forge immediately conceded the central platform as he charged across the connecting bridge like an angry rhino. That was both unexpected and *hugely* unfortunate. They'd spent hours talking through this raid, and they'd built their entire battle strategy around their last encounter with the Boss. That strategy involved taking the platform quickly and boxing the creature in while Dizzy kept the Keeper's focus, and the ranged fighters were tasked with taking out the summoned minions.

Bosses didn't usually deviate a whole lot from encounter to encounter in video games. Apparently, Eternium took a very different approach to high-level boss raids. With a few steps, their entire plan crumbled.

Kai was the first to leap into action. He blurred across the bridge at superhuman speed. The Keeper didn't even slow down—he was as wide as the bridge itself, and he clearly intended to steamroll the Monk and drive him into the magma flows below. But thanks to Kai's new Simian Agility, he somehow slipped between the elemental's enormous legs, then leapt straight up and landed on the metallic back.

Kai grunted in obvious pain as the blistering heat radiating off the armor ate into his health. But then he started raining blows down on the Keeper's head, his fists moving in a whirlwind of golden flashes. As a Monk, Kai had already had a Critical Strike bonus, but he also had a powerful Critical Strike ability that drastically increased his chance to land critical hits when attacking without a weapon. Since his new Gorilla Body ability passively restored health with every critical hit, Kai's health regen somehow managed to outstrip the passive burn damage he was receiving from the super-heated armor.

Probably because he was landing ten blows a second.

The relentless onslaught surprised the Keeper just long enough for Sam to cast one of his brand-new skills, Origami Structure. In an eyeblink, one of the books on his shelf sprang to life and vomited a stream of paper into the air. Pages fluttered and flowed, binding together into a wall directly in front of the elemental juggernaut. That wall wouldn't hold him forever, but it did halt his advance just long enough for Dizzy to dash forward and confront the Keeper head-to-head. She jumped onto Sam's conjured wall and used the added height to lay into the guardian's chest with her war maul.

The Keeper stumbled back from the sheer fury of her strikes. With Kai smashing fists into his head, it seemed like he couldn't focus on rebuffing Dizzy. Slowly, he fell back toward the platform, driven by Dizzy's might. Sphinx and Finn bounded forward, taking cover behind Sam's summoned wall, then carefully picked their shots with ranged weapons. Finn launched foot-long spears of glittering ice, while Sphinx hurled shadowy throwing blades.

Unfortunately, the narrow bridge didn't allow the Wolf Pack to adequately spread out, but Sam could fix that. He turned and jumped from the edge of the bridge, activating his Quill Wings. Sam caught a scorching hot updraft and glanced back, a grin spreading across his face. His bookshelf was still trailing behind, levitating in the air despite the fact that there was no floor beneath it. "Abyss yeah. I'm gonna exploit the feces out of that mechanic."

"Velkan, Arrow!" he shouted over the din of the battle. "Hop on!"

He'd read the description for Summoned Shelf of Casting at least a dozen times, and there was no indication that the amount of physical weight on the shelf impacted its levitation ability or movement rate. The Wolfman and the Rogue didn't even hesitate; Velkan sprang straight up and latched on with his claws, scrambling up the shelves like they were ladder steps until he was perched on top. Arrow, by contrast, bounded into the air like a trained acrobat with Cirque du Soleil, landing in a crouch with his bow drawn and an arrow ready.

Sam banked hard right, giving the elemental a wide berth, and coasted over the platform. Despite being locked in a heated battle with both Dizzy and Kai, the Guardian seemed to immediately sense Sam's plan. He thrust one oversized arm straight out and started launching a hail of flaming fireballs, each as large as Sam's skull. Sam dove and barrel-rolled, narrowly avoiding each blast, the whole while hoping the Keeper didn't start taking potshots at Velkan and Arrow, who were basically sitting ducks.

One fireball tore past Sam on the left, missing his wing by a matter of inches, but then he was above the central platform, and his passengers were leaping through the air to safety. The Wolfman landed just a few feet behind the Keeper and immediately went on the offensive, throwing himself at the golem of fire and steel. Everywhere his claws touched, the metal sizzled and corroded. Since Velkan primarily did piercing and slashing damage, he was at a significant disadvantage against a heavily armored enemy like the Keeper. Still, they'd come prepared.

Sphinx had unlocked her secondary profession a week back: Noxious Brewer. That subset of Alchemist turned out to specialize in creating poisons instead of health potions. It was a natural fit for her, given her role as thief, killer, and infiltrator, and with the Irondown Alchemy Lab at her disposal, she'd managed to whip up some pretty inventive creations.

In this case, she'd concocted a potent acid that had no effect on organics but was rust on steroids against anything metal, and Velkan's claws had been painted with the stuff.

Meanwhile, Arrow darted across the platform and onto the thin bridge that connected to the vault on the far side of the room. The bulky iron portcullis prevented him from going into the treasure vault itself, but the bridge would be much easier to defend and would offer him the range he needed to work his bow effectively.

The Keeper wasn't having any of that.

"Jolly good show!" he thundered before he began to spin like a top. In a heartbeat, he was a whirling dervish. The spin didn't last long, just enough to put Dizzy on her heels, while simultaneously tossing Kai into the air like an angry rodeo bull. The Monk flipped through the air with wide eyes as his monkey tail shot out and latched onto Velkan. The Wolfman responded by planting his feet and helping guide the falling Monk onto the central platform. The Keeper used the second of breathing room to raise his golden hammer high and conjure his magma minions. Yellow lightning flashed overhead, and geysers of bubbling lava lanced skyward, landing on the platform with wet splats.

The lava quickly condensed and formed into squat toads

made of liquid metal and living flame: five Lesser Fire Elementals. At least *that* was the same as last time.

Dizzy was already launching a fresh assault on the Keeper—supported by Sphinx and Finn—but Velkan and Kai suddenly had other things to handle. Three of the squat monsters advanced on the melee fighters, while two more broke off and dashed toward Arrow, trapped between a rock and a portcullis on the far bridge.

"Showtime." Sam conjured a second Origami wall, positioning this one right in the center of the far bridge. It wouldn't last indefinitely, but the frogs wouldn't be able to just bum rush Arrow and toss him into the flames below.

For his part, Arrow ignored the conjured fire elements completely and concentrated his fire power on the Keeper. His arrow tips weren't made of metal but a rare obsidian glass and, like Velkan's claws, they were liberally coated in Sphinx's new poison. They punched through the Keeper's armor like a knife through a pad of hot butter, taking off a little slice of health with every hit.

Sam needed to help free up the others. Despite having twenty books on his fancy new shelf, he could still only cast two spells at once through the power of Dual Casting.

<Bill!> he sent at the speed of thought, <Spam Ice Orb Shuriken while I bring out our new friends!>

<On it!> the book replied gleefully. An endless stream of glowing cobalt folding stars sliced through the air and slammed into the platform below. Bill didn't seem to be targeting any single minion, but rather was attempting to draw their attention away from the rest of the Wolf Pack. Another book sprang from the second shelf down, this one at Sam's command. With a small flare of mana, he activated the spell within.

A river of paper erupted from between the covers like a geyser, coalescing into the shape of a fox. Sam triggered another book, and another, and another still. In short order, he had constructed ten origami minions on the central platform below: five foxes and five gangly Papier Mache Automatons. The automatons each wielded a mop, mallet, or buzzsaw.

"Mount up and attack!" Sam barked his orders at them. "Harry the minions, and protect the members of the Wolf Pack at all costs!"

Each of the conjured creatures quickly scampered onto the back of one of the foxes. Mounted and weapons ready, they attacked with remarkable speed and agility. His minions were operating at a significant disadvantage, since they were made out of paper, and the elemental toads were literally living flame, but they were willing to fight to the last cinder.

The toads promptly ignored Kai and Velkan, choosing to focus on the creatures whacking them over the heads with mops and mallets. Opening their enormous mouths, they hurled great gooey globs of magma, hoping to burn the opposition to ash. Yet Sam's minions were too fast. The foxes easily dodged the ranged attacks, pulling in close enough to lash out with snapping teeth before retreating to a safe distance. It was still a lopsided battle in favor of the fire toads, but at least Sam had helped to level the playing field a bit.

Another book leapt into his waiting palm. This was a more complicated spell, one that required not only significant resources, but also had an eight second casting time. Thankfully, the Keeper was still utterly focused on his battle with Dizzy, and the fire toads had their froggy hands full with Sam's paper henchmen.

Bill continued to lay down suppressive fire as Sam began to chant, reading the words carefully inscribed onto the first page of the book. Power built in the air around him, and an errant breeze tugged at his hair. The pages of the book flipped frantically as he spoke, while fat droplets of ink rose from the paper, forming into an orb of churning black power.

He spoke the final word of power, and the inky orb blasted off like a rocket.

CHAPTER THIRTY-FIVE

The orb of magic stopped above the central platform and immediately ballooned outward, turning into a jet-black cloud that filled most of the cavernous room. Ink began to fall, first in a spurt, then in a great torrent, drenching everything below. The magma toads shrieked as the inky rain sizzled against their fiery hides; even the Keeper seemed momentarily caught off-guard. Two of the five frogs seized up on the spot and toppled over to one side, temporarily paralyzed. The ink pooled into small puddles, and black tendrils wrapped around stubby legs, drastically slowing the lesser elementals down.

Not just them. The Keeper of the Forge had resisted the paralyzing spell, but the tongues of black ink were crawling along his limbs, gumming up the works and exposing him to more of Dizzy's frenzied attacks.

By contrast, Sam's teammates were completely unaffected by the falling ink rain. The droplets splashed against an invisible bubble that moved with each member of the team. Even though they danced and battled through pools of black, the ink actively shied away from them. Bill cackled triumphantly. "See, I *told* you it would work!"

Even though Sam hadn't outright said the idea wouldn't work, he'd certainly had his doubts. He'd used his new Master Binder abilities to enchanted each of the simple vellum cloaks with an Ink repulsion spell, which hadn't been nearly as complicated as it had sounded. The glass vials that they'd previously created to contain ink basically had the same properties. Applying those principles to the cloaks which his team was now wearing had been a cake walk, especially with his Coreless Spell Infusion to power the items. The craftsmanship itself still left a lot to be desired, but function over form would just have to be his driving motto for a while.

"I didn't say it *wouldn't* work," Sam protested as he lined up his next spell. "I just said trying it in the middle of a boss fight without testing it first was a big gamble."

"Phft. Waste that much ink? Hard pass." Bill's line of thinking had been exhaustively explained when they had been planning, so Sam didn't bother to react.

Below, the advantage had shifted. Kai and Velkan suddenly had the upper hand against the fiery elementals. Sam's minions didn't wear those cloaks, but they were naturally immune from the effects of the spell, and they exploited the sudden opportunity to their utmost advantage. They blitzed the temporarily paralyzed toads, conjured foxes lashing out with their fangs while their riders relentlessly stabbed and bludgeoned the incapacitated lesser elementals to death. When a killing blow was finally struck, the blobs of lava simply evaporated, leaving behind blackened scorch marks on the platform, but no corpses.

Without missing a beat, Sam's origami army turned on the remaining fire toads. The summoned elementals were now wildly outmatched. Bill continued to spam Ice-Orb Shuriken at the creatures, taking out sizable chunks of their health, but Sam wanted to contribute in a more concrete way. He pulled several books from the topmost shelf of his bookcase, then dove toward the action. He dropped each book once he was above one of the toads. He triggered the pair of Book Bombs with a shout, "Book 1 goes boom! Book 2 goes boom!"

He'd augmented each with Ice Orb spells, so they erupted in showers of frosty blue magic. As he swooped around, he pulled another pair of books free from the top shelf and dove again. Thanks to his Quill Wings and his Floating Bookshelf, he could basically play the part of an aerial bomber. "Book 3 goes boom! Book 4 goes boom!"

More eruptions of magic and mayhem. His large-scale ink spell was finally dissipating, but it was too late for the summoned fire elementals. Between Velkan, Kai, the origami minions, and Sam's offensive spellcasting, they didn't have a leg to stand on. The last one died in a flurry of kung-fu fists and icy explosions, courtesy of Bill's barrage of Shuriken.

As for the flaming Keeper of the Forge, he wasn't doing so hot either.

Dizzy wasn't letting up for even a second. The tank threw herself against the Keeper like an angry honey badger, her war maul blazing through the air as each blow landed with a resounding ring and a flash of sparks. She wasn't personally doing that much damage overall—her skillset was definitely focused on absorbing punishment—but she was keeping him utterly distracted. That allowed Finn, Sphinx, and Arrow to rack up some clean hits. They'd already managed to drop the Keeper just below fifty percent health. Without the Keeper's summoned minions to get in the way, the entire Wolf Pack could focus their efforts on the Dungeon Boss.

With a war cry, Dizzy triggered her Meteor Charge ability. Red light bled from her skin as she rushed the Keeper, dropping her head low and ramming one of her metal pauldrons into his gut. The blow wasn't meant to injure, rather knocking the Keeper backward by a solid seven feet, right into the center of the platform, which had been their game plan from the get-go. Kai abruptly broke left, while Velkan circled right, so they could come at him on all sides, simultaneously giving the ranged fighters an unobstructed field of fire.

The Keeper was back up to full speed now—the remnants of Sam's ink rain had all been burned away by his scorching armor—but Sam could fix that. True, Sam had only prepared one Ink Mire Storm Cloud spell tome, and he'd burned through that, but he still had a few other surprises tucked up his sleeve. Bill focused his offensive spell power on the Keeper while Sam called up another of his new spells: Mummify. With a flick of his wrist and a trickle of mana, more pages took to the air, carried forward by currents of magically conjured air. The pages glommed onto the Keeper, wrapping around his arms and legs and clinging to his faceplate like a facehugger.

The pages almost immediately began to smolder and char on the edges, ruining the overall mummify effect, but they still made it impossible for the hulking Guardian to see a thing.

"Blasted *pages*!" The Keeper bellowed at the top of his lungs, blundering around blindly and clumsily swiping at the papers clinging to his armor. "I can't see a thing. Very effective and terribly frustrating. Well done, indeed!"

The Wolf Pack tightened around him and intensified their attacks. Velkan's claws left deep furrows in the steel, Kai's fists dented his armor, and Dizzy's war maul rang out like a gong with every hit. Sam's own paper army was dishing out their fair share of damage as well, attacking the Keeper's feet with reckless abandon.

It was time for Sam to try his last big spell. A thick tome bound in jet-black leather rocketed to his hand.

"*Swarm*," Sam hissed, flicking the book out like a frisbee. The cover snapped open, and the book floated midair. Suddenly, the roar of a hurricane filled the cavern, drowning out every other sound as a cyclone of paper erupted upward in a funnel. The pages folded themselves as they sprang from the book, miniature wings and beaks forming as the paper crows came to rudimentary life. They almost looked like paper cranes —if one didn't know any better.

Sam hadn't seen this attack in action yet, so he'd half expected to see the whirlwind form on the target. Instead, it arched up into the air, then descended on the Keeper of the Forge in a cone, narrow at the top and wide at the base. He'd also spent a lot of extra time and mana to augment each sheet with a simple Ice-Orb enchantment so that the crows would deal frost damage against whoever he unleashed them on.

The flock of conjured corvids moved with one mind, swooping and diving as they circled. Their razor-sharp beaks jabbed inward like a thousand knife stabs, while blade-edged wings left icy slashes in their wake, and the guardian's health plummeted down, down, *down* with each pass of the murderous birds. Amazingly, the crows were intelligent enough to avoid the other members of the wolf pack entirely, swooping within inches but never hitting them.

The grace and precision on display was uncanny.

Below, Kai bounded up into the air, golden light coalescing around him, then came down with a conjured fist the size of a wrecking ball. "Endless Fury of the Monkey Fist!"

A sharp crack like a gunshot rang out, reverberating off the high ceiling. The Keeper's health had finally dropped below twenty-five percent. An angry orange fissure formed in his horned helm, then quickly spread down the rest of his armor in a spiderweb of cracks and fractures. A second later, the Keeper exploded, fire billowing out in every direction, accompanied by a wave of metal shrapnel.

The explosion incinerated Sam's paper minions on the spot, turned the whirlwind of crows into a cloud of drifting ash, and hurled the rest of his team members back. Dizzy landed on the bridge, sprawled out on her back. Only sheer luck kept her from toppling over the edge and into the lava below. Kai and Velkan —both far lighter than the armored tank—weren't so lucky. The blast wave hurled both from the central platform. Kai's tail shot out, but there was nothing for him to latch onto. Sam watched in horror, knowing there was no way he could get to both of them in time. Abyss, he wasn't even sure he could get to one of them in time.

He was fast in the air, but not that fast. Still, there was *one* thing that might work.

"Sorry, Kai!" he called, turning his attention to the

tumbling Wolfman. Getting burned alive by magma wouldn't be fun, but Kai would respawn. Velkan, not so much.

Sam focused on the falling Wolfman and opened his third eye, summoning the doors to his Interspatial Library. For now, he could only summon them within line of sight, but there was no rule that said they must be summoned on solid ground, or even with a normal orientation. The portal appeared horizontally above the magma like a giant life raft and snapped open with a thought. Velkan plunged into the interspatial compartment and disappeared a few feet before landing in molten death.

The doors snapped closed and vanished as Sam closed his third eye, and then the mana feedback from forcing the doors open and closed so rapidly hit him in the head like a freight train. Barely able to see through the terrible migraine, he moaned and watched the remainder of the fight progress.

Down on the platform, the light from the explosion had faded, and the Keeper stood in the center. He no longer wore armor at all, but rather was a humanoid blob of white-hot light, a creature of pure fire.

"Good show," he cheered and clapped for them. "I can't ever remember a party managing to destroy my armor casing. It just doesn't *happen.* I'm below twenty-five percent. Unbelievable, honestly. Maybe you really do have a chance at defeating me."

"Probably not, though. My armor protected me, but it also protected others from my true nature." He faltered and shrugged, then raised his hand and aimed a gout of magma as thick as a telephone pole at the prone form of Dizzy.

"No!" Finn shouted, thrusting both hands forward. A glimmering blue dome of ice formed in front of the unconscious tank. Fire met frost, and a curtain of white steam rose into the air, temporarily concealing Dizzy, Sphinx, and Finn from the deadly elemental. To buy them time, Sam activated his Tome of Fire Shuriken and let loose with a barrage of folded stars while Bill spammed Ice Orb.

"I've had just about enough of you." The Keeper turned

away from the wall of steam and focused his deadly gaze on Sam and Bill. "You've been an absolute nuisance! Again, well done, but I'm afraid the show stops here for you."

He raised both hands and let loose with a hail of fireballs. Bill caught his breath and bellowed, "Evasive action, Wings! We've got incoming!"

Sam barrel-rolled right and pitched forward into a tight dive, narrowly avoiding a trio of fireballs. But there were more coming. So many more. Bill unleashed more Ice-Orb Shuriken, not trying to hit the Keeper, but focusing instead on the incoming orbs of flaming death. He managed to intercept nearly half of the fireballs. The paper stars exploded on contact, and the Ice-Orb effects blunted the explosive power of each fireball. That still left a lot of fireballs to dodge. Sam spun and rolled, but his Stamina was taking a beating. Staying aloft was relatively easy, but this type of evasive aerial action was the equivalent of running wind sprints over and over again.

Below, Sam's teammates had taken up the fight, slowly and steadily chipping away at the Keeper's health, but the fire elemental simply ignored them. He knew that Sam couldn't evade forever, and unfortunately… he was right. The Mage was built for firepower, not fancy flying.

Sam maneuvered over the center of the platform - just in time. A stray fireball clipped his right wing, and tongues of flames rapidly spread across his Quills. Sam let out a yelp as the spell holding him aloft fizzled, and he dropped toward the ground. Off balance, he hit with a grunt and felt something **pop** in his ankle. A lance of pain raced through his body. He'd twisted his ankle more than a couple of times in Judo, and this felt far worse than that. Probably a minor fracture. He still had a few health potions that he'd lifted from the College, but those were stowed away in his Spatial Flask. He didn't exactly have thirty seconds to stand there and rifle through his bag to find and chug one.

The Keeper stomped toward him; murder etched into the lines of his molten body. Worse, there was no one to stop him.

Dizzy was still passed out. Finn and Arrow were launching ranged attacks, and Sphinx had broken onto the platform to try and draw his attention, but the Keeper continued to ignore her blades. Sure, the elemental was losing health fast without his armor—down to almost ten percent now—but he still had more than enough life to take Sam out. After that, the others would quickly follow.

If they were going to win, Sam had to end this fight, and he needed to do it now. He still had Shuriken galore, and enough Book Bombs to choke a horse, but he'd burned through the rest of his new offensive spells.

No more minions to summon. No Ink Storms, no Crow Whirlwinds.

But he wasn't dead yet. He'd come prepared with one last emergency backup plan. He'd been hoping it wouldn't come to that… but they were all out of options. With a grimace, Sam gained his feet, which sent a renewed wave of agony running up his leg. He conjured his Quill Blade, canted his shoulders, and raised his sword into the guard position, just as Bill had taught him.

"Good for you, not giving up." The Keeper offered Sam a begrudging nod of respect. "I really do admire your tenacity. But if you rely on blade work, this battle is already over for you. Being good with the blade is all about footwork, and you're in no shape-"

"That's what *I* always tell him." Bill's agreement seemed to be a source of great amusement to the Boss.

"Oh, under different circumstances…" The Keeper laughed as he appraised Bill. "There's always next time."

The white-hot elemental advanced, raising his hammer high for a killing blow. Sam tipped his hat and winked at the flaming behemoth. "Footwork is overrated. Look up."

Sam forced open his third eye with a scream of pain, and the doors to his Interspatial appeared overhead, once more horizontally aligned. The doors sprang open directly above the Keeper… and a series of angry squawks poured out from the

Spatial Library, along with a host of feathered bodies. This time, instead of raining ink, the air was filled with something far more fowl.

Floof and Blaze landed on the Keeper, followed by thirty angry hens and a very confused-looking Velkan. The Wolfman was covered in feathers and shallow scratches, but he was alive, all the same. Sam let out a ragged sigh of relief. He'd been fairly certain his brood wouldn't attack the Wolfman, but they hadn't exactly been thrilled about being crammed into what amounted to a glorified walk-in closet.

All that time pent up in the Library had made them *disgruntled*, and they now had a perfect target to take their feathery aggression out on. Floof let out a blood-curdling cluck of outrage and attacked. Blaze was right behind, her beak punching into the Keeper's molten body. The rest of the brood followed the examples of their fearless, feathered leaders. In moments, the fire elemental was swallowed beneath a pile of beaks and talons and flapping wings. Sam wanted to join, but by the time he hobbled over with his broken ankle, the elemental was already dead.

Experience gained: 5,000 (Keeper of the Forge)

Sam ignored the notification, even though he appreciated the increase. There would be time to read prompts and loot corpses once the job was done. But the job wasn't done. Not yet. Killing the Keeper was only one half the battle. He fished a health potion from his Spatial Flask, chugged it in one long pull, then headed across the far bridge and toward the closed-off armory. On the wall next to the portcullis waited a golden handprint inscribed within the stone: the final activation rune. He pressed his palm against the marker and released a burst of mana that left him cold, shaky, and exhausted to the bone.

Now the job was done.

He dropped to the ground and leaned back against the wall, groaning in mental pain as a flurry of notifications appeared.

Congratulations! You have claimed Junction 8 of 8. Reward, Exp: 500.

Quest update! A Den to Call your Own III. I am shook. *Honestly, I can't even believe it. You monkeys somehow managed to capture all eight nodes of the Irondown Burrows, a lost dungeon located in the dark heart of the Forest of Chlorophyll Chaos. You beat the Keeper of the Forge with a bunch of chickens? I couldn't make this up even if I wanted to. As a Wolfman-aligned Guild, you have officially claimed the Irondown Burrows and have successfully managed to convert it into your Guild Den. All of its resources and minions now belong to you and can be utilized as you see fit.*

Additionally, you've finally earned the respect of the Wolfman Shaman Yurij Brightblood, which is no small thing, believe you me. That guy hates everyone.

+1,000 Reputation points with The People. +4 free Characteristic Points. +7,000 Experience.

The extra Experience points have been awarded for not only completing the mission, but being greatly entertaining. Your Guild has also been officially included on the Grey Player's Leaderboard. If the other players weren't aware of you before, they sure will be now. That should make your recruitment efforts... easier.

Golden light surrounded Sam, lifting him from the floor in a halo of ecstasy, then gently setting him back on his feet. Between taking down the Keeper and clearing the mission, he'd just hit eleven for the third time, and he had four new points to distribute, thanks to the generosity of Eterium's AI. Although his first instinct was to drop them into wisdom and intelligence, he decided against it. He needed mana to create his spells, but once his spells were cast, they took almost no mana to activate.

What he really needed now was to boost his Stamina, especially if he planned to continue his escapades as an aerial support caster. Plus, these were essentially free points, so he decided to add three of them to strength, raising his stamina, and the remaining point into constitution, so he would be slightly less squishy.

Name: Sam_K 'Merchant Ambassador'
Class: Libriohexer
Profession 1: Bookbinder

Profession 2: Chicken Keeper
Level: 11 Exp: 69,500 Exp to next level: 8,500
Hit Points: 103/140
Mana: 311/667
Mana regen: 34.03/sec
Stamina: 198.5/198.5

Characteristic: Raw score
Strength: 28
Dexterity: 40
Constitution: 19
Intelligence: 60
Wisdom: 69
Charisma: 30
Perception: 45
Luck: 10
Karmic Luck: -4

"Not too bad at all," Sam thought as he reviewed his character screen—especially for a Bookbinder and humble Chicken Farmer.

CHAPTER THIRTY-SIX

"Can you believe all this stuff?" Dizzy held up a metal breastplate with silver filigree. The Keeper of the Forge hadn't dropped any loot to speak of, other than a hefty Core, but the Armory was near to bursting with goodies.

"Nope. I literally can't believe it." Arrow was sprawled out on a nearby pile of coins. He flapped his arms and legs, making snow angels in the clinking mound of loot. "I always wanted to be Scrooge McDuck and backstroke through a pile of gold."

"I don't think we're quite there yet," Sam laughed as he leaned in to examine a gemstone more closely.

"Maybe not." The Ranger grabbed a handful of coins and let them rain from his fingers. "But it's more than I'll probably see in five years. Working as an intern for a tech company doesn't exactly pay a premium wage. This is a lot."

"It's hard to say for certain how much there is without a proper count," Finn muttered as he tried to run actual calculations, "but we of the House of Laustsen are perpetually broke, and as a result, we are keenly aware of coinage and prices. The other houses joke that a Laustsen can spot a copper at a thousand paces. Sadly, they aren't wrong. I'd say we have at least three thousand in gold there, and probably twice that in silver marks. It's a tidy sum, to be sure. Not enough to put us on equal footing with even the most minor Noble House, but I'd wager it's far more than almost any human guild has at this point, unless they are funded by the Crown itself."

"That's not factoring in all this gear." Dizzy swept a hand toward the weapon rack lining one wall. A matching armor rack neatly filled the opposite side. "The craftsmanship is out of this world. I can't believe the Keeper of the Forge made all this stuff."

"You sure can say that again," Sphinx agreed as she turned over a finely polished dagger with a fat ruby set into the hilt. "This stuff would fetch a gosh-darn fortune on the black market. We won't get premium rates from the Upright Men, but I have to imagine all of this gear would add another ten thousand gold to the total. Some of this stuff is even enchanted."

She flipped the dagger into the air and caught it with a flourish. "This little sucker right here adds plus-three to dexterity, grants a stealth bonus, and secretes a neurotoxin that can be used to poison a target once per day."

"No," Dizzy retorted sharply and suddenly. "We're not selling any of it. Not a single thing."

That earned her a confused look from Arrow.

"We don't need *money*." She waved at the pile. "If we ration this wisely, it'll last for a month or more, and with Sam's chicken business in full swing, we're going to be making money faster than we can spend it. Besides, I refuse to supply the human-aligned players with gear like this. We're at *war*. Even if we sell this stuff to the Upright Men, it's eventually going to make its way back into circulation, where it will be used against us."

"Not to mention," Bill joined in, "we're going to need supplies to equip our new recruits. The fact is, the players that are already doing well with the humans aren't gonna want to leave a sweet gig to join up with the Wolfmen. That means we're gonna get the losers. The washouts. The people at the bottom of the barrel who are struggling to move up the ranks inside the guilds. People like that aren't going to be coming with full purses or the best gear. We're going to have to equip them. This stuff will help, but so will the fact that Legs and I can now place some limited enchantments on items."

"Spoken like true Wolfmen," barked a gruff voice. Sam turned to see Velkan padding into the armory, along with another Wolfman. Not just any Wolfman, though... their handler: Yurij Brightblood. The austere Shaman entered with his hands folded behind his back. That was a shock. A pose like that—open and exposed—was a sign of ease, only used between equals.

"It is good to see you again, Wolf Pups. Though Pups you are no longer, I suppose." He paused, glancing around the vault. "What you did at the College, it was impressive. A big win for The People; yet, it was still not enough to convince me of your worth. Unlike most of The People, unfamiliar with the ways of magic, I know exactly who the Trustees are."

"To the uninitiated, killing a room full of high-level Mages *sounds* impressive," he continued scathingly, "but we all know that you targeted them precisely because they were weak and easy to dispatch. It was a victory… but not a sign of strength. Not to me. Killing a bear cub is not the same as killing a full-grown bear matriarch, even if the experience points are the same. But this…"

His nostrils flared as he took in the armory. "This is a different thing entirely. The Irondowns are a brutal testing ground. There is a reason these ruins have stood untouched for five hundred years or more. This place is a clockwork machine, built to murder… yet you have subdued it."

He nodded in grim appreciation and stalked forward to trace his claws over the surface of a steel breastplate. "Now *that*… that is strength. You have won the trust of The O'Baba. You have earned the trust of the clan leaders. You have even earned the trust of our most elevated Shaman. But this day, you have finally earned *my* trust. The truth is, I am more than I seem. I am known as the Wolfbane Tribune. The O'Baba knows who I am and what I do. It is a job without pomp. A thankless task, performed from the shadows. It is my role to watch and evaluate, to root out traitors, and see all secret threats lying in wait for The People."

"You're The O'Baba's spymaster," Bill announced for the rest of the group as he made the connection.

"No," Yurij Brightblood replied sternly. "I work with her, but my authority is my own, given to me to be a check and balance against all our kind, *even* her. I warned her against you. Told her that bringing you into our fold was dangerous, and that should you fail, there would be… consequences. Yet, I have watched you. Time and time again, you have risen to every challenge. Faced every obstacle. Accomplished the seemingly impossible."

He nodded at the armory. "This is the pinnacle of your achievements. You have earned my respect."

Quest Updated III! A Den to Call our Own. You have claimed the Irondown Burrows as your Guild Den, and by doing so, you have earned the begrudging respect of your Wolfman handler, Yurij Brightblood. Which is good news for you, since Yurij's none other than the Wolfbane Tribune—an independent agent who can act as Judge, Jury, and Executioner among The People. He also happens to be the one who holds your fate in his hands, so good job winning him over. Reward: His approval, which is more than enough reward.

"Because you have earned my respect," Yurij continued speaking, ignoring the vacant eyes that indicated someone reading a notification, "I have decided to grant you the right to act as emissaries for The People. You may now recruit human allies on our behalf. I trust in your judgement and believe you have the best of intentions for our kind, so any human you accept will become one of our blood. You also can form treaties and alliances as any other Clan Leader would, and such compacts will be honored by all of our People."

He waited a long moment, but no one tried to speak over him. "It is a great honor, and one that I never thought to bestow on a human. I am glad to be proven wrong… but don't make me regret it. Now, go. Recruit. Build. We have a war to win… and the battle will be upon us much sooner than any of them knows."

ABOUT JAMES HUNTER

Hey all, my name is James Hunter and I'm a writer, among other things. So just a little about me: I'm a former Marine Corps Sergeant, combat veteran, and pirate hunter (seriously). I'm also a member of The Royal Order of the Shellback--'cause that's a real thing. I've also been a missionary and international aid worker in Bangkok, Thailand. And, a space-ship captain, can't forget that.

Okay ... the last one is only in my imagination.

Currently, I'm a stay at home Dad--taking care of my two kids--while also writing full time, making up absurd stories that I hope people will continue to buy. When I'm not working, writing, or spending time with family, I occasionally eat and sleep.

Connect with James:
AuthorJamesAHunter.com
Facebook.com/WriterJamesAHunter
Patreon.com/JamesAHunter
Twitter.com/WriterJAHunter

ABOUT DAKOTA KROUT

Author of the best-selling Divine Dungeon, Completionist Chronicles, and Full Murderhobo series, Dakota Krout was chosen as Audible's top 5 fantasy pick of 2017, has been a top 5 bestseller on Amazon, and a top 6 bestseller on Audible.

He draws on his experience in the military to create vast terrains and intricate systems, and his history in programming and information technology helps him bring a logical aspect to both his writing and his company while giving him a unique perspective for future challenges.

"Publishing my stories has been an incredible blessing thus far, and I hope to keep you entertained for years to come!" -Dakota

Connect with Dakota:
MountaindalePress.com
Patreon.com/DakotaKrout
Facebook.com/TheDivineDungeon
Twitter.com/DakotaKrout
Discord.gg/mdp

ABOUT MOUNTAINDALE PRESS

Dakota and Danielle Krout, a husband and wife team, strive to create as well as publish excellent fantasy and science fiction novels. Self-publishing *The Divine Dungeon: Dungeon Born* in 2016 transformed their careers from Dakota's military and programming background and Danielle's Ph.D. in pharmacology to President and CEO, respectively, of a small press. Their goal is to share their success with other authors and provide captivating fiction to readers with the purpose of solidifying Mountaindale Press as the place 'Where Fantasy Transforms Reality.'

Connect with Mountaindale Press:
MountaindalePress.com
Facebook.com/MountaindalePress
Twitter.com/_Mountaindale
Instagram.com/MountaindalePress

MOUNTAINDALE PRESS TITLES

GameLit and LitRPG

The Completionist Chronicles,
The Divine Dungeon, and
Full Murderhobo by Dakota Krout

Arcana Unlocked by Gregory Blackburn

A Touch of Power by Jay Boyce

Red Mage and
Farming Livia by Xander Boyce

Space Seasons by Dawn Chapman

Ether Collapse and
Ether Flows by Ryan DeBruyn

Bloodgames by Christian J. Gilliland

Threads of Fate by Michael Head

Lion's Lineage by Rohan Hublikar and Dakota Krout

Wolfman Warlock by James Hunter and Dakota Krout

Axe Druid,
Mephisto's Magic Online, and
High Table Hijinks by Christopher Johns

Skeleton in Space by Andries Louws

Chronicles of Ethan by John L. Monk

Pixel Dust and
Necrotic Apocalypse by David Petrie

Henchman by Carl Stubblefield

Artorian's Archives by Dennis Vanderkerken and Dakota Krout

Made in the USA
Las Vegas, NV
28 July 2024